Demon
in the
Machine

Lise MacTague

BELLA
BOOKS

2018

Bella Books, Inc.
P.O. Box 10543
Tallahassee, FL 32302

Printed in the United States of America on acid-free paper.

First Bella Books Edition 2018

Editor: Medora MacDougall
Cover Designer: Sandy Knowles

ISBN: 978-1-59493-567-1

Other Bella Books by Lise MacTague

Five Moons Rising

On Deceptions Edge Trilogy

Depths of Blue
Heights of Green
Vortex of Crimson

Acknowledgments

Thanks as ever to my army of alpha and beta readers: Lynn, Christina, Nita, Amy, Eden, Brooklyn, Fern, Shari, and of course Penny. You are amazing, and I couldn't do this without your critical eye and encouraging words. Every book I've written is better for your contributions, and this one is no different.

Many thanks to my amazing editor, Medora MacDougall, for helping me make this book all it can be and more. We've polished this one until it gleams, and I'm hoping there will be many more. Thanks to the entire crew at Bella for giving lesbians their own voice in publishing, and for including mine in that multitude. Our stories deserve to be told and I'm glad I get to be a part of that.

Thank you to Sandy Knowles for being willing to work with me on the cover. It's fantastic, but I know it took us a few tries to get there! Thank you for your patience and your creativity.

Finally, to my readers: I can't thank you enough for continuing to stand by my work, even when I keep jumping from one genre to another. Knowing that you'll be reading and (hopefully) enjoying my stories keeps me writing them.

About the Author

Lise writes speculative lesbian fiction of all flavors. She is the author of the science fiction trilogy *On Deception's Edge*, the paranormal adventure *Five Moons Rising*, and this steam punk novel. She grew up in Canada, but left Winnipeg for warmer climes. She flitted around the US before settling in North Carolina where the winters suit her quite well, thank you very much. Lise crams writing in around her wife and kids, work, and building video game props in the garage, with the occasional D&D break. Find some free short stories and more about what she's up to at lisemactague.com.

Dedication

For Lynn. I can't put in words how glad I am that you came into my life. Every day is brighter because you're in it, and every night I sleep sounder by your side. I am honored beyond measure that you agreed to be my wife. I love you, sweetness, and I can't wait to see what the rest of our life has in store for us.

CHAPTER ONE

"Here it is, Miss Riley. Have you ever seen anything so beautiful in all your life?" Charles Yorke, Eighth Earl of Hardwicke, gestured expansively at the horseless carriage that gleamed under the coach house's electric lights.

From her vantage point by the door, Briar had to agree: it was certainly impressive. She cast her eyes over its curving lines. As with the other horseless carriages currently on the market, it differed very little in design from a conventional carriage. The driver's seat was forward and up from the passenger compartment, which was larger than that in the earl's other horseless carriage. The motor housing seemed much smaller than that of his older model, and there was no seat at the back for the fireman who had been needed to keep the boiler stoked on it. That was some progress. The lone horse still in residence in the coach house looked lazily over its shoulder, then blew out a long breath as if in disapproval before bending its head back to its evening basket of oats.

"It's certainly shiny."

"More than that," Hardwicke said. "It improves upon many of the deficiencies of previous models. The engine isn't steam fed, for example. Instead of stoking it with coal, the boiler takes a cylinder."

He nodded. "So much cleaner than coal, and it lasts much longer as well."

Briar had no particular desire to know so much about the mechanics of this nor any other horseless carriage, but her employer was excited. It behooved her to at least pretend to be interested. She stepped into the coach house and stopped in her tracks.

The carriage crouched in the gloomy corner, drinking in the bright lights from above and seeping shadows across the floor. It looked as though it stared at her and awaited her approach. Its intentions were not good, and she knew it.

You're mad, Briar said to herself. The smile with which she favored the earl was brittle. She tried to cover her unease by settling the edges of her skirts just so. *It's a horseless, the earl's newest toy. It certainly doesn't want to hurt you. How could it? It's a carriage!* When she put it in such terms, her trepidation sounded foolish. Taking strength in the absurdity of the situation, she took a couple of steps closer to the carriage. *It won't hurt you. It's an inanimate object.* The mantra helped, and eventually she stood next to one of the tall wheels at the back. She reached a hand out to touch it, simply to prove to herself that she could. With some consternation, she realized her hand was trembling. Whatever was amiss, it seemed to be getting worse.

"Are you well, Miss Riley?" The earl's voice was solicitous, though somewhat anxious. He had plans for Briar that evening, hence her evening gown and reticule. Those plans required an entrance. He was eager to show off his latest technological acquisition to the others of his set, but since he couldn't stomach yet another ball, she was going in his place.

"I am merely overcome by this…handsome contraption." She wouldn't say "damnable," not in his company.

The earl was willing to accept her explanation and didn't press her further on it. One simply didn't press a lady. Fortunately, his gentlemanly sensibilities were too deeply ingrained to dig more deeply into her discomfort. By the same token, Briar was loath to reject his offer of the new carriage as conveyance to the ball. It was exceedingly generous, and her fear was irrational and uncalled for. She knew it. However that knowledge did not diminish it in any way.

The chauffeur stood next to the carriage's open door. Resplendent in the earl's household colors of black and green, he held his hand out toward her. One eyebrow crooked up a fraction of an inch, the only expression of concern he would allow himself.

Briar gave him a slow nod. A smile would not come, not this close to the hated contraption. It wanted her. The feeling crawled up her spine until she felt the hairs on the back of her neck lift and her scalp prickled with the need to be watchful. She breathed as deeply as she could with the corset binding her ribs.

Another step toward the horseless sent dread rolling through her. She concentrated on Johnson, on his black eyes and high cheekbones, on the dark skin that contrasted so pleasingly with the white shirt cuffs sticking out of the sleeves of his jacket. He was an exceedingly handsome man. It was too bad there was such a taboo on relations with those of a lower social status. She wouldn't dream of going against those strictures, but it wouldn't have mattered had she been among her mother's people. There wasn't a taboo that side of the family wouldn't gleefully break. That she was even contemplating the way Johnson's shoulders filled out his coat while her brain screamed at her to run told her how much her mother's daughter she was.

But she was also her father's daughter. That side believed in rationality and decorum, and it would be damned if it didn't get into that carriage and go to that ball.

She took another breath then accepted Johnson's hand, grateful just this once for some help into the carriage. She twitched her skirts into the passenger compartment before something underneath could hook them and drag her… *Where? Where is it going to drag you, Briar?* Her inner voice was scornful. And frightened.

She settled on the seat, fussing with her skirts as she tried to focus on the evening's plans. Her body *knew* she was in for a world of pain and was only willing to be overridden by logic for so long. Briar's heartbeat vibrated behind her sternum, forcing her breath out in short gasps. There could be no doubt that the wrongness she'd sensed when she entered the coach house was centered on the horseless. She sat, poised on the edge of action against a power she could neither see nor hear. It didn't exist, and yet she felt as though she stood scant inches from a roaring bonfire, one she had to traverse to get to her destination. Briar closed her eyes, and tried to center herself. She opened eyes screwed shut against the terrors she had no doubt awaited her. *This isn't the first time you've seen terrible things*, she reminded herself.

With a start, she realized they were underway. The carriage's wheels rattled over London's cobbled streets. It made for quite the racket. Country roads with their hard-packed dirt were much quieter, though their sudden ruts threatened to throw one from the seat if the driver was not careful. For the most part, she preferred cobbles. This night, however, the noise along with her more metaphysical discomforts promised for an interminable ride.

The earl simply had to have the newest gadgets. Most of the time, it was a harmless amusement. Briar enjoyed seeing Hardwicke reduced to a little boy over his latest toy, but not when it put her in such an uncomfortable position. His delight made for an odd dichotomy when she considered his other interests. That was, after all, the reason she was stuck in the carriage on her way to an event that promised to be stultifying in its boredom. The earl collected old manuscripts, but only those of a most specific sort. Through the papers of magicians, users of infernal energy, he believed he could track the ebb and flow of human magic-users. He was active in the House of Lords, but that was merely a front, a convenient excuse. Most of his fellow politicians would have been shocked to discover that Charles Yorke, the Eighth Earl of Hardwicke, chaired the Committee on Demoniac Interference (Super Secret).

He hadn't told her in the beginning, of course. One did not simply announce one's membership in a secretive group within the upper echelons of Her Majesty's government. Briar prided herself in being able to winkle out connections, whether it be between people and their possessions, people and other people, or between different objects. She was good at it, or the earl wouldn't have hired her. For months, Briar had known all of it, except the official name of his organization. He hadn't been surprised to find out she'd already sussed out the truth when he told her, though he'd been impressed by her discretion.

She released a pent-up sigh of irritation. All of it meant she had no other option than to suffer through the ride to yet another social gathering. There was nothing to do except prepare herself for the tiresome debutante ball to which she was headed while trying to ignore the constant dread gnawing at her bones.

The Baron Selborne was elderly and had a reputation as a gentleman scholar. The earl was practically salivating at the idea of getting his hands on Selborne's papers and library. Fortunately for the earl, the baron had a granddaughter who was in her first season. Unfortunately for Briar, that meant she had to make an appearance at the ball and charm her way into an offer to see his library.

The carriage door opened and Briar blinked in surprise at the chauffeur.

"Are we here already, Johnson?" It seemed impossible; she hadn't felt the carriage come to a stop.

"Yes, miss." He smiled at her, one corner of his mouth lifting higher than the other and flashing a hint of white teeth at her. "Were you out for a nap?"

"Hardly." Briar sniffed at the idea but couldn't help the smile that crept onto her face. The chauffeur never missed an opportunity to needle her or flirt, as long as they were alone, of course. "I'm sure we have naught but your skill to credit for the smoothness of the ride."

"Of course." He stepped out of the way and offered his hand in assistance to alight. "This new carriage surely is a marvel."

This time, Briar ignored the hand held out to her. "The earl does enjoy his toys."

Johnson gave her a half bow and closed the door behind her. "I'll be waitin', miss."

"Thank you, Johnson."

He climbed onto the front of the carriage and maneuvered it away from the front of the palatial house that rose before them. Theirs was not the only new horseless carriage. Indeed it seemed a full quarter of the carriages now disgorging their occupants and parked along the wide avenue were of the new type; the other horselesses were of an older manufacture. A few horse-drawn carriages counted among the vehicles, though those were far in the minority. Likely, those were the carriages of minor rural nobles who couldn't afford the newest conveyances. Briar paid them little heed. None of them were likely to have materials of interest to her employer.

For a moment longer she stood, eying the carriages as they came and went. The older models worked well enough, though they shuddered occasionally as their steam boilers needed to be vented. Those carriages required both a driver and a fireman to stoke the coals and keep them running. The new carriages required only the driver, the ramifications of which Briar hadn't considered until that moment. Supposedly the new engines were also steam-powered, but if that were the case, did those cylinders both feed the engine and vent it so it didn't explode? She would have to ask Johnson later. A small shudder, more the memory of her disquiet than a true reaction, shook her. Soon. She would find out soon.

"Miss?" A footman stood discreetly at her elbow.

"Oh. Yes." Knowing her response was rather inane, Briar swept past the servant toward the front of the house. Light glowed from every window, it seemed, turning the darkness of night into artificial dusk confined to the front lawn. She joined the back of a group of giggling young women who were being chaperoned by a much older woman. She looked tired. Briar sympathized. Keeping up with the flitting lovelies would be a monumental task for the night, especially given the glances they were sharing with a group of young men loitering just inside the entryway. The girls' interest was clearly reciprocated. No looks were spared for her, of course. At her apparent age in her mid-twenties, she was quite on the shelf. Beyond that, her breeding was unknown, which made her an even less attractive prospect for marriage. She didn't mind. The boys who came to these affairs were pretty enough to look at on occasion, but by and large, she preferred to watch the women.

Despite her best efforts, a few brave souls did manage to get their names on Briar's dance card. They whirled her around the dance floor before escorting her back to her spot along the wall. At least none of them stepped upon her toes. She was a good enough dancer, her reflexes saw to that, though her heart was rarely in it. She found it difficult to move in sync with a man. Their insistence on being the ones to direct the dance was tiresome, but convention dictated it must be so and she wasn't there to draw attention to herself.

Deciding that enough time had passed, Briar made her way from the dance floor and to the other end of the hall. Tables were set up there and young men and women refreshed themselves after the exertion of dancing. Older men and women dotted the tables as well, chaperones to the younger set or there upon their own recognizance. Many of the older set talked among themselves, those there to keep an eye on younger female relatives glancing over occasionally to make sure their young charges hadn't disappeared into a corner on the arm of some young man. Within sight of the dance floor sat the Baron and Baroness Selborne, who were alone at a table with a couple of empty seats. They chatted amiably with each other.

A glint of glass peeking out from under the edge of the long tablecloth caught Briar's attention. She wrinkled her nose at the whiff of brimstone that followed along soon after. The scent of burning rock was not one she'd anticipated smelling in a place like this. Curious, she picked up the object. A fine crystalline lens winked at her, reflecting hundreds of points of light from the room's glittering chandelier. Etched into the bronze ring holding it in place were runes of infernal power and the source of the smell. She turned the curious device of crystal and brass over in her hand and traced her fingertip over the characters. A broken hinge was attached to one side. It had clearly come off something else, but what?

The lens held in her left hand, Briar continued on toward the baron and his wife. She plastered a gracious smile upon her face.

"May I join you?" she asked.

"Of course." The baron stood hurriedly, his generous paunch barely clearing the table. The baroness smiled back at Briar with equal graciousness. He pulled the nearest chair out for her and Briar perched gracefully upon the edge, the bustle of her dress allowing her to do no more.

"Thank you, my lord," Briar said. "Are you enjoying the evening?" Small talk was as tiresome as the rest of the evening, but a necessary evil. She paid less than half a mind to the inane platitudes she spouted. No, her attention was on the odd lens she'd found on the floor. What was a thing like that doing here? It would have been strange enough on its own, but add in the scrawlings of infernal magic and it was an enigma. Briar had no patience for unknowns. She worked her left glove off her hand while exchanging comments with the baroness about the weather and drew her fingertip along the top of the brass lens holder.

Briar looked down as the door swung open slowly, propelled by a black-gloved hand. She blinked or tried to. Lenses didn't blink, so neither could she. Whatever she'd been expecting when she tried to read the lens, this was not it. Objects carried with them a strange point of view, one she was quite used to. Their utter lack of curiosity over their circumstances was refreshing. They experienced no emotions at all, unlike the people she had to deal with every day whose every feeling intruded on her unless she was meticulously careful. This was unusual, however. It was rare for her to be pulled completely into the experiences of an object. She wondered what this one had in store for her.

The only source of light in the large room beyond was the smoldering coals in the banked fireplace. There wasn't much to make out; shadows cloaked this room as deeply as they had the hall from which they'd entered. The lack of light didn't seem to be a problem. Whoever carried the lens crossed the room with perfect confidence. If Briar hadn't known better, she would have said the owner of the lens lived here, but then why the skullduggery? Books filled shelves from floor to ceiling. The gloved hands caressed the thick leather spines, lingering here and there as they traced gilt lettering. The hand stopped on a particularly weighty volume and grasped the top, then pulled back.

The book didn't come off the shelf, rather it tilted backward before the hand returned the leather-bound volume to its resting place on the shelf. It was some sort of latch. Briar had heard of such things, but she had never witnessed one herself. The earl thought they were pointless fripperies, more useful for those who wished to claim the cachet of having a hidden compartment. Inevitably, those with such compartments couldn't resist showing them off, at which point they lost their singular advantage. A stout safe with the most advanced locking mechanisms was what Hardwicke relied upon. Of course, that also included some nasty traps of a magical variety. There seemed to be none of those here.

Without missing a beat, the hands busily plucked books off the shelf beside the trick volume. They stacked the books in neat piles on the floor. Instead of the plaster wall behind the built-in bookshelves, a dark hole was revealed. The shelf was far deeper than it should have been.

The owner of the hands knew as much. He pulled out long boxes, emptying them somewhere before replacing them. Briar watched as he pulled a larger box. The lock upon it was assaulted by the hands, wielding delicate tools, and the box swiftly revealed its secrets. Gold sovereigns winked sullenly, reflecting the scant light from the coals in the fireplace.

The coins disappeared also, swept out of sight by those questing hands before he reached for more boxes, pouches, and bags. Nimble hands opened the nearest bag and extricated a string of brilliantly glowing diamonds. The jewels gleamed with an internal fire that practically licked the edge of each gem. Their glitter wasn't natural. Even the finest diamonds didn't gleam so on their own. One box held a selection of bejeweled rings. Some rings lacked the glow of the others, and those were ignored. They went back into the safe with the now much emptier box. The hands continued their deft sorting. Any jewels that didn't glow, he left behind. A thick stack of banknotes disappeared into the same place as the glowing jewels.

The whole process of looting the safe took less than five minutes. When there were no more bags or boxes to interest the owner of the lens, he replaced the row of books quickly and precisely. The books were replaced on the shelf in the reverse order from which they'd been taken. He fussed over them for a moment, tweaking one a little further out, pushing another one back into place. It was quick work, and before long the shelf looked exactly as it had when they'd entered. What had happened here wasn't obvious at all. Depending on how frequently the owner of the safe checked his valuables, the theft might pass unremarked for quite some time.

Briar expected they would leave the way they had come. Instead, she was carried over to the drapes. A hand reached out and parted the heavy curtains. Large windows went up almost eight feet. The dim

London night beckoned beyond the leaded glass panes. The owner of the lens glanced back across the room. Briar suffered a moment of vertigo as shelves with their books flashed past her. They focused on the door for a second, then turned back. The hands had lost their smooth deliberation. Instead, they flew with decisive haste. With a quick twist, they unlatched the nearest window and pulled open the window barely far enough for a human body to slip through. A moment later he was up on the sill, turning back to face into the room. His hand twitched the drapes back into place behind them.

The hands slipped a hooked length of wire over the latch and pulled the window shut. With a small twist, the wire pulled the latch into place, then was pulled through slight gap between the window and the one next to it. That was neat; there would be no more sign that someone had left that way than perhaps a small scratch.

They dropped away from the window, the side of the building flashing past them, then they slowed until they seemed to be floating a few feet off the ground. The last few feet came up suddenly, then they bounced up, some ten feet in the air before falling in an arc, London's dark streets whizzing by.

"Are you all right, my dear?" The words emanated from the dark around them. That wasn't right.

CHAPTER TWO

"Miss Riley, are you quite well?"

Briar blinked, her eyes taking a moment to adjust to the brightly lit ballroom. Vivid colors swirled out on the dance floor, resolving into gaily dressed women who danced by on the arms of soberly dressed men. Even there, flashes of color peeked out from beneath dark jackets or in the breast pockets of their coats.

She turned and smiled stiffly at the elderly man and woman at the table with her. They wore twin expressions of dismay, perhaps not accustomed to a young woman suddenly dropping into a trance. Briar hoped she hadn't been drooling. That would be most undignified. She covered her discomfiture by pulling her glove back on.

"I am fine, my lord and lady." What were their names again? She'd been sent there specifically to engage them in conversation and to determine what in their collections her employer might find of interest. Instead, she'd found something altogether more fascinating. "I require a breath of fresh air, I think."

The elderly baron nodded gravely. "You do look a trifle pale, Miss Riley."

His wife nodded with more energy, looking for all the world like a small bird bobbing for seeds. "You do, at that." She stood, alighting from her chair in one motion. "Come, let us go onto the terrace."

"Thank you." Briar smiled, trying to mask her irritation. "You're too kind." She *was* too kind. Briar didn't think she'd ever acclimate to the human assumption that women were too weak or indelicate to be out on their own. It certainly wasn't the case where she was from. But then, the entirety of polite society would disintegrate into chaos if even half the things she'd endured growing up came to pass here.

Still, the terrace was a good idea. It was warm in the ballroom. The heat of the gas lamps and the dancing throng combined to a stifling degree. That, coupled with her return from reading the lens, made fresh air a necessity if she was going to regain her concentration and accomplish the evening's task.

She managed not to wobble as she stood up. The corset wrapped around her ribcage made drawing a full breath an impossibility but added some much needed support. The ball was still going strong and it was much too early to make her excuses and leave. After a few moments she'd be right as rain and would finish what she'd been sent there to do and could be on her way home.

At her side, the baroness chattered gaily about something. Briar listened with half an ear, not overly interested in the latest fashions. Her employer always saw to it that she was dressed in the latest of high couture before sending her off to one of these soirees. Though she appreciated the dignity and decorum the locals' clothing brought with it, sometimes the combined layers were quite stultifying when compared to what she'd worn in her younger days. She didn't yearn for the near-nudity of her upbringing, but dressing then had been much simpler and something she could accomplish on her own. However, appearing in a state of extreme undress would have closed the doors of high society to her. And heavens forbid they should see her true form. That would not have done at all, for their sake and hers.

Cool air washed over her as they emerged onto a long terrace. Clumps of young women conversed quietly in the lamp light that poured through the open doors. They made every attempt to embody the reserve befitting a young lady, but their excitement was nonetheless palpable, a shared feeling of energy that helped bring Briar back to herself. The dimly lit lamps smoking on the walls did little to dispel the gloom of a London evening. Tall trees and thick bushes ringed the terrace on all sides, seeming to soak up what little light made it that far. Muffled whispers and other noises from the underbrush reached Briar's sensitive ears. At least a couple somebodies were involved in some unchaperoned amusement.

"Is that better, my dear?" the baroness asked, her voice brimming over with solicitousness.

"Much. Thank you, Baroness." Briar turned the lens over in her hand. It had been the glint of reflected light that had first drawn her eye to it where it peeked out from under a long tablecloth, but the unmistakable feel of infernal energy had compelled her to pick it up. How did such an object come to be in a place like this? The question had prompted her to surrender to her own curiosity and give the item what she'd thought would be a cursory reading. She hadn't counted on being pulled into the lens's point of view. Usually, she received the barest impression from an object. She might be able to determine who it belonged to or how old it was. Rarely, she could experience what the object had been through, but that generally required a strong emotional attachment, either from her or from the item's owner. That such an innocuous thing could hold that kind of emotional resonance was unusual, to say the least.

"Are you overcome by such episodes frequently?" The question was delicately phrased, but the baroness's eyes glittered in the light. It seemed the woman loved to gossip.

"Not at all." Briar's smile was practiced. "It was quite warm in there, but I'm feeling much recovered already." She turned the lens absently between gloved fingers.

"What is that?"

"I'm not sure. I found it on the floor. I thought it was pretty."

"Indeed?" The baroness seemed unconvinced. The lens itself was unprepossessing, a simple piece of crystal. It was the bronze mounting that interested Briar, etched around as it was by the intricate design still glowing faintly with energy. It was doubtful the baroness could make out the glow; she likely didn't have the ancestry to do so. Briar did, much to her constant dismay.

"I have particular tastes, I suppose." Briar placed the lens on the stone terrace railing in front of her. "Much like the baron. I've heard his collection of manuscripts is quite extensive."

"He seems to think so." The baroness tutted and shook her head. "He spends most of his time poring over them, and it's been even worse since his latest acquisition."

"Is that so?" Briar tried to suppress her excitement. This was what she was here to find out. She reached out to stroke the edge of the lens again. "Where did he acquire them?"

"Somewhere on the Continent." With an airy wave, the baroness dismissed the line of questioning. "But enough of dusty tomes. How is the earl?"

And there it was. Not long after the inquiry after the earl's health would come the probing into why she attended so many events in his stead. She turned her smile back on. "He is well, though busy with the workings of Parliament." It was a true enough statement and one that deflected many of the following questions.

"Of course."

"Excuse me." A young woman joined them at the railing. Briar looked down her nose at the pretty young thing in her pale green gown that made a pleasant contrast with bright red hair. Isabella Castel, only daughter of the Viscount of Sherard, was one of her least favorite people. The girl fancied herself a wit and spent much of her time playing to a group of hangers-on who laughed at every one of her jokes and clever put-downs. The Sherard girl had a nickname for everyone or so it seemed. Briar knew what hers was, and she didn't appreciate it. She didn't wonder how she'd been saddled with "The Stick." Many of the young women found her too rigid, even for their tightly held code of morality, simply because Briar strove for decorum in all things.

"Yes?" The cool word hung in the air between the three of them, but Miss Castel seemed not to notice.

"Where did you get that?" Miss Castel reached toward Briar's hand.

"This?" *Surely she doesn't mean the lens?* If this girl had anything to do with the object, Briar would eat her reticule. She twitched it out of the Sherard girl's reach. "I found it on the floor. Surely it isn't yours."

"Of course not." The reply was sharp and color bloomed in the Sherard girl's cheeks, washing away her freckles. Her pale complexion did her no favors when it came to hiding her emotions. "It belongs to my brother. I use it as a…good luck charm. I'd like it back." She stretched out her hand, hazel eyes fairly snapping in anger.

Her brother was the second-storey man then. Briar wondered if he knew his sister had the lens or not. There was no point in holding on to it. If the Sherard girl claimed it, it was undoubtedly hers. She dropped it into Miss Castel's waiting palm. The girl whirled on the heel of her dainty slipper and stormed off. Who knew she had so much fire to her? In her anger, the Sherard girl was a far cry from the insipid little thing Briar saw dancing across the floor or in a tittering knot with her friends. Briar watched after her for a moment before turning back to Baroness Selborne. The baroness shook her head at Miss Castel's retreating form.

"Such rudeness," she said. "Still, it is no surprise given who her mother is."

This kind of gossip was of no use to Briar. It would tell her nothing of Selborne's holdings and beside that, she had little interest in the Sherard family and especially not with Miss Castel.

"I am quite recovered. Shall we return?" She followed the baroness back to the table where the baron was deep in conversation with another gentleman. Both men stood upon their return. To her disappointment, they turned their conversation away from what they'd been discussing. It was something about the new engines, but that was all she'd been able to hear.

"My lord," Briar said to Baron Selborne. "Your wife tells me you've made an exciting acquisition. May I inquire as to its origin?"

"Quite so!" Baron Selborne puffed himself up with excitement. "It is a fascinating treatise on..." he leaned forward and lowered his voice conspiratorially, "...demoniac workings during the early Ottoman Empire."

"That does sound fascinating. I'm sure the Earl of Hardwicke would be very interested in viewing such a unique work. May I have him contact you?"

A complicated expression passed over Selborne's face. He seemed to be at war with himself. On the one hand, Briar could tell he was pleased that the earl might be interested in his manuscript, but on the other he seemed to have other concerns. If Briar had to guess, she would say he wasn't keen to admit such an ungentlemanlike interest. Well-bred men did not deal with magic. It was one thing to admit such a propensity to her, but quite another to do so to a peer, especially one so connected to Parliament.

"I can assure you, he will exercise the utmost discretion," Briar said in what she hoped was a soothing tone.

"For heaven's sake, James," Baroness Selborne patted her husband on the hand. "Earl Hardwicke won't take your collection."

"Of course not." Briar was shocked at the idea. While the earl might be interested in acquiring Selborne's manuscript, he would never stoop to confiscating it.

"Very well." Selborne still seemed a tad anxious, but he nodded to his wife. "You may have him send 'round a card."

"Thank you, my lord." Briar inclined her head graciously. "How is your granddaughter enjoying her season?"

The rest of the evening passed more quickly than she'd anticipated. Time and again, her eyes were drawn to the Sherard girl, often without realizing it. There was no sign of that other Miss Castel full of spirited fire; instead the vapid girl full of giggles and ill-conceived jokes was on full display. The Sherard girl caught her glance once, but Briar shifted her gaze quickly, not wanting to be caught staring. It wasn't until after the Sherard girl had left for the night that Briar sent a footman for Johnson.

The ride home was uneventful, though she was filled with the same malaise as she had been on the way to the party. The back of the carriage was spacious, to be sure, but there was no room to pace, no matter how much she wanted to. The trip took much too long, and yet Johnson was at the door, his hand out to help her down, in no time. As soon as she was out of the vehicle, her claustrophobia dissipated, pricked into nothingness like a soap bubble.

"One moment, Johnson," Briar said as he made to get back into the driver's seat. "I left something inside." Sure enough, when she clambered back in, the impatience and dread returned. That was fascinating. She would have to take a look at what made this machine run. Her mechanical skills were next to nonexistent—her talents tended in the opposite direction—but something was afoot. "Thank you, Johnson." He nodded and winked before pulling away. She stared thoughtfully at the retreating carriage.

A delicately cleared throat got her attention and she made her way through the door being held open for her by a bleary-eyed but patient footman. The night had been much more interesting than she'd anticipated. That should have been a good thing; nothing was worse than boredom. And yet...

* * *

The workshop was completely empty. It was late, so the echoing emptiness of the cavernous set of underground rooms wasn't unusual. Her father must have come to a stopping point on his latest project, something that dealt with the storage of demoniac energy. His current obsession wasn't one she shared; Isabella preferred tinkering with projects of a more mechanical nature.

The existence of the series of underground rooms would be a surprise to many, not least of all their neighbors. The Sackvilles especially would be astounded to discover the rooms dug beneath the basement of their townhouse. Astounded and righteously offended most likely. The Sackvilles were new enough to their riches and position that they took decorum very seriously. To find out the viscount next door and his daughter were tinkering with mechanical devices under their very feet would offend them greatly, of that Isabella was certain.

They'd be even more offended to discover what else the viscount's daughter was up to and what she was wearing while doing so.

Isabella dropped into a deep knee bend, bouncing on the balls of her feet and feeling the stretch of her hamstrings. Dancing was a decent warm-up, but it did little to limber her up, not when she had to wear that blasted corset the entire time. Of course well-born ladies acted with dignity and decorum; they couldn't breathe deeply enough to get up to anything else. She'd long since changed out of the flowing gown and binding corset she'd been forced to don for that night's ball.

The ball… Isabella twisted her torso, willing the bones in her spine to pop. They finally did and she sighed with relief.

The ball had not gone as planned. How could she have been stupid enough to drop the lens? And to have snooty Brionie Riley, of all people, pick it up? The woman had been much too interested in it. Why did she even bother to show up at the various balls and other glittering events that made up the season? She danced very little and spent most of her time socializing with the older set. Those people were deadly dull, but The Stick seemed to flourish with them.

Energy still flowed through Isabella. She needed to do something about it before the end of the night or she would spend too much time staring at the ceiling of her darkened room rather than sleeping. But there was work to be done before she could indulge in her exercises.

Isabella made her way over to a long workbench and placed the lens upon it. The broken hinge needed replacing before she lost the lens altogether. This one was quite important to her. It allowed her to tell which gems were real and which were glass or paste. Without it, she would have to pay someone to appraise each piece and that was money they simply didn't have. Better by far that she fix it now, rather than leave it for later and lose it because she forgot.

She pulled out a pair of spectacles on a ribbon. Neither of her parents required such help to see, and in truth she didn't either. The spectacles were a handy excuse to peer at the jewelry of her peers with that lens. Isabella was proud of the lenses it carried. They were a modification of her own design. The hinges could be twisted off and a lens could be moved from these spectacles to her goggles. The versatility more than made up for the slight weakness in the hinges.

Isabella peered at the hinge through a magnifying glass mounted on a movable arm to the edge of the workbench. As she suspected, there was a crack in the housing where a tiny screw held together the complicated hinge. It allowed the housing to flex the tiniest bit, which had allowed the arm holding the lens to slide free. She would have to replace the entire hinge. Fortunately, the arm wasn't damaged, as it was part of the same piece as the metal rim around the lens itself.

As she worked, Isabella hummed to herself. Her father was likely in bed at this hour, so she didn't have to worry about disturbing him. The evening's final waltz played itself over in her head, looping around and around. She and Millie, her best friend, had taken a turn on the floor at the same time. Millie had been ebullient from a night of dancing, and they'd paid scant attention to the gentlemen who danced with them. Instead, they'd been quite rude and had spoken with each other over their partners' shoulders. The men hadn't minded, both of them having been friends to her and Millie for a long time. She supposed she should have felt some guilt for not paying more attention to poor Simon, but that would only have encouraged his rather misplaced affections.

She continued to hum as she tinkered, paying close attention to the pieces of hinge she reassembled. This wasn't the first time she'd broken a hinge, and it likely wouldn't be the last. There had to be a way to strengthen the attachment. Isabella's mind wandered along those lines as she put the finishing touches on her repair and examined it with utmost care to make sure there were no other areas of weakness. To her relief, the new hinge was as sturdy as she could make it. She clipped it on to her spectacles, then popped it back off again. The action was smooth, but once on, it held fast. A warm glow of accomplishment filled her. It was one of the things she loved about working with her hands. When she made something, she used her own skills and it was hers alone. Beyond the knowledge she'd gained from her father and tutors, there was nothing she owed to anyone. It was too bad she had to keep her skills to herself. Her set simply wouldn't understand her affinity for an activity that was so unladylike.

She could feel her eyebrows drawing down. Isabella smoothed her brow with careful consideration. There was no point in fighting this battle. It was one she couldn't win. As the only daughter of Viscount Sherard, she had responsibilities to the family.

The last thought echoed inside her head in her mother's voice. Isabella rolled her eyes and stood up. It was time to indulge in something where her mother's lectures couldn't intrude. She tidied the workspace, putting her tools away but leaving the spectacles on the bench.

The workshop's far wall was festooned with rings, pipes, and bars at various places along its twenty-foot height. Isabella eyed the top bar. That was tonight's goal. She needed to push herself a bit.

She sprinted across the floor on light feet and leaped, grabbing a thick vertical bar. It was a reasonable approximation of a drainpipe, though attached more securely than those she'd encountered in her various excursions. She'd have to retool that and make it more in line with what she was likely to come up against.

It was the work of a less than a second to brace her feet on the wall and scamper up the pseudo-drainpipe. From there, she reached over to a horizontal bar that jutted out of the wall a mere three inches. She swung her way onto its lip, toes crammed against the wall, giving her a little more grip as she reached for the bar barely within reach of her outstretched fingertips.

What had been with the questions from Brionie Riley about where she'd gotten the lens? It looked enough like a monocle that no one should have known differently. Plenty of people wore them. Certainly, the lens had some demoniac enhancements to it, but most people would be none the wiser. The only reason Isabella knew the runes were there was because she'd asked her father's partner to add them. She herself couldn't see the runes; that wasn't one of her talents. She could break down a steam engine in less than an hour and scale a twenty-foot wall in seconds, but she had no affinity for demoniac manipulation.

Her hands slapped down on the bar that had been her goal and Isabella hung there for a moment, the weight of her body a pleasant pull on her shoulders. Had The Stick bought the excuse that the lens belonged to her brother? The stiff woman had eyed her quite queerly when she'd said that but had dropped the questioning. Not that continuing would have been easy as Isabella had quite rudely left the conversation. Still, she wouldn't have put it past the inquisitive Miss Riley to follow her to ask more questions. She was constantly inquiring as to this or that, or so it seemed whenever Isabella overheard one of her deadly dull conversations.

Something would have to be done about Brionie Riley. She could not be allowed to interfere in Isabella's activities. She needed some… distraction.

Isabella pushed off the wall, arching her back and tucking into a backward flip. She made one complete turn before she straightened up out of the roll and struck the floor. Somehow, she'd come out of the flip somewhat cockeyed. One foot hit before the other. Rather than trying to stick the landing outright, Isabella tucked again into a somersault, then popped up.

"That was sloppier than normal," a woman's voice remarked behind her. "Perhaps you need more practice?"

"Mama!" Isabella turned smartly, her cheeks warm. "I thought you'd be abed."

"I was." Althea Castel walked slowly toward her. Even with hard-bottomed shoes and cane, her movements were almost soundless. Tall and beautiful, even in her middle years, Althea moved like a woman many years her senior. Isabella could still see the beautiful girl her father had first met in her face and hands, but it was hard to see her move so cautiously.

"Was it your leg?"

Her mother grimaced. "The older I get, the more it stiffens up. Make sure you never get shot, daughter of mine. It is mightily inconvenient long beyond the original injury."

"Thank you, Mother." Isabella nodded gravely. "I shall make it my life's work not to get shot."

"I expect nothing less." Althea grinned at Isabella's serious retort. "Speaking of work, how was it tonight?"

Now was not the time to bring up her slip-up with the lens. "It went well. I have two possible targets. After I case the houses, I'll know which one to move on next."

"Very good." Althea paused for a moment, then sighed and continued. "The money from your last foray is almost gone and I must pay the servants. I want you to be as careful as possible, but we are in dire need of more funds."

"Very well." Isabella would have to move more quickly then. If she was very careful, perhaps she could do each job in successive nights. "Millie Ornelas has an exquisite new ruby necklace given to her by her fiancé. He should be my next target."

"I shall invite them to tea. Millie will certainly reciprocate with an invitation for you."

"Mother, I don't wish to steal from her. She's my friend."

Althea shook her head in disappointed reproof. "When we are solvent once again, you'll be able to make such distinctions. Until then, we shall do what we must to survive."

"But, Mother—" Althea's hand cut off the rest of her protest.

"I know this is difficult for you, Isabella. It's hard for all of us, but we must make do. In a few years your brother will be back, and all will return to normal." She withdrew an envelope from where she'd tucked it in her cleavage. "He's sent another letter." Althea laid it down on a nearby bench. "I'll leave you to your exercises. From the look of that last dismount, you need the practice."

"Yes, Mother."

Althea made her way out through the gloom-shrouded workshop. Isabella watched her go, then looked down at the letter. She willed it to burst into flames. This was all Wellington's fault. Without him, they wouldn't be practically destitute, reduced to stealing from their friends. *I'm not reading it.* Of course she would; she wouldn't be able to help herself. It had better not be like the last one, where he'd written to request money without any thought as to what it would mean for the family to provide it, not after what he'd done.

No, not again. Isabella transferred her glare to the bar at the top of the wall. This time her dismount would be perfect.

CHAPTER THREE

The first thing Briar did upon awakening the next morning was to make her way down to the carriage house. That horseless needed some attention. She couldn't allow her fears to rule her, especially not one so ridiculous.

The carriage house was shuttered and dark. It smelled slightly of hay and horse manure. There was one horse still stabled here, though the earl had relied almost exclusively on the horseless for a few years. From time to time, the servants needed some mode of transportation, and the conventional carriage was more than good enough for them. The horse eyed her incuriously over the wall of its stall, then went back to dozing or whatever it did when it wasn't working.

Briar closed the door behind her. The skin on the back of her arms prickled immediately, small hairs rising at attention as they had the previous evening. Briar rubbed them briskly to dismiss the gooseflesh and convince herself that there was nothing in the room that would harm her.

She took a deep breath to settle her nerves and rein in her fancies. She threw the switch by the door and the carriage house was bathed in the light of uncovered bulbs high above. Shadows snapped into place and she jumped, convinced the horseless had moved.

"Don't be silly," Briar told herself out loud, needing to fill the small building with something other than her paranoid fancies. "What could a carriage possibly want to do with you?"

"What do you mean by that?"

The innocent question was delivered in a high voice and curious tone, Briar noted dimly as she leapt into the air. She somehow landed facing the questioner, who stared at her with wide eyes.

"Imogene!" Briar gasped, trying to regain her breath and composure but accomplishing neither. "You shouldn't sneak up on people!"

The girl managed to look amused and bashful at the same time. She ducked under the bar at the back of the horse's stall, then stood before her, picking pieces of detritus from her arms. Her dress was festooned with straw and hay.

"Were you sleeping with the horse again?"

"Of course not." Imogene was all indignant refusal. She held up a small book. "I was reading. My tutor isn't here until after breakfast, so I can do what I want."

"And if no one finds you when the tutor comes, all the better?"

"Maybe." She scuffed the toe of her shoe on the dirt floor. At fourteen, Imogene was getting too old for such tomfoolery.

Briar suspected she knew as much, but there was something about the earl's youngest daughter that reminded Briar a bit of herself. Briar knew what it was like not to fit in with one's family. Imogene's situation was quite different than hers had been, and she thanked all the gods for that, but it didn't change the feelings of disconnectedness one had when those who were closest to you had no idea what to do with you. Her heart went out to Imogene, though her behavior was not in the least bit decorous. There would be time enough for her to conform to the expectations of her father and sister and Briar would not be party to it. Nor should she be.

At least Imogene could be useful. Briar needed to know who manufactured the horseless, but she was neither wearing the appropriate clothes nor was she in the frame of mind to check herself.

"I can forget I saw you in here if you do something for me," Briar said.

Imogene looked up at her, lively interest in her eyes. "What do you need?"

"I need to know who made your father's new carriage, but I'm not dressed to climb around looking for the manufacturer's mark. If you'd do that for me, I will pretend I never saw you this morning."

Imogene disappeared beneath the carriage in a flash but not before putting her book safely to one side. It was an instinct Briar approved of.

"Where should I look?" Imogene asked, her voice somewhat muffled.

"Try beneath the undercarriage." Now that she had someone to do the looking for her, Briar had no need to stand so close to the hated device. She backed up until her shoulder blades touched the outer wall, being careful never to take her eyes off the horseless.

"There's nothing here."

"Keep looking," Briar called. "Maybe the engine?"

Imogene scrabbled deeper beneath the carriage. If she'd felt even a quarter of the malevolence Briar experienced when she went near the horseless, she wouldn't have been so eager to dig around beneath it. A vague sense of guilt tickled annoyingly at the back of Briar's head. Had she sent Imogene into harm's way? Surely the discomfort was only in her own mind, a byproduct of her discomfort with the newest technologies. Except progress didn't bother her; Briar had quite liked the earl's old horseless. She enjoyed traveling by train or dirigible, finding both infinitely preferable to travel by horseback or stagecoach. The invention of the fountain pen was one she quite approved of. She'd found quill pens messy and inefficient. So why did *this* carriage bother her so much?

She was about to call Imogene back out when the girl called out. It was gibberish, from what Briar could hear.

"What was that?"

"Mirabilia Carriageworks," Imogene said again, enunciating each word carefully.

From the Latin mirabile, Briar's mind translated automatically, *meaning wondrous. Someone has a sense of humor.* "Very good," she said aloud. "Now come out of there before someone happens by and we're both in trouble."

Imogene scooted out from under the carriage, her dress covered in dirt. It was a good thing she'd been filthy going in, or Briar would have some explaining to do. Except that she hadn't seen Imogene, not according to their agreement. It was time to go. She had what she'd come for.

"Thank you, Imogene. I never saw you."

Imogene's grin seemed all the brighter for the grimy streak that slashed across her lips. Briar shook her head. Hardwicke was going to have his hands full with her in a year or two.

She closed the door to the carriage house behind her, then realized the electric lights were still on. There was no way she was going back in there. Imogene would take care of it for her.

The rest of Briar's morning was spent tracking down as many copies of the *London Times* as she could find, then skimming through them for mentions of the Mirabilia Carriageworks. Finally, right before she was about to give up and go join the earl and his family for the noon luncheon, she found her first mention.

Mirabilia Carriageworks becomes Mirabilia Manufacturing, the small headline said. The article that followed was short on words and content. All Briar learned was that the company was expanding into other types of manufacturing. She reread the ten lines the newspaper had devoted to the news again and again, hoping to glean something more useful, but there was nothing. No mention of the types of objects they would be making or when they would appear. The newspaper was one of the oldest she'd gathered. What had Mirabilia gotten up to in the past month?

It was time to expand her research. Lunch forgotten, Briar folded the paper in half and retreated to her chamber.

Her room was above stairs; the earl considered her a special kind of employee, one who was too valuable to live with the serving folk. The room was cheerful, especially on this day when sunlight flooded through the double windows on the room's south wall. The woodwork practically glowed from the sun's rays.

That wouldn't do at all, not for what Briar had to do. It was too bad, really. She loved the sun. Perhaps it was the result of a childhood spent in the dark places of another world. Or perhaps it was because so much of her work took place in dark and dusty libraries. The sun was an enemy of paper, right there with mold and silverfish.

She drew the heavy drapes, still in their winter weight. The housekeeper, Mrs. Houghton, thought her strange indeed for insisting upon the heavy velvet, even in the warmest months, but lightweight muslin didn't shroud the room in shadows like she needed it. She snugged the drapes close to the wall with a couple of lead weights. It was time.

The dark room wasn't difficult for her to navigate. To her eyes, it was only as dark as the beginning of the twilight hour. A human would have had a devil of a time moving around without walking into something. She had no such handicap. What she needed was in the closet. She stared reflectively at the door before opening it. How many years had it been since she'd last resorted to this method? The situation required it, but she couldn't be pleased about it. There was something going on and she needed more information.

Briar reached into the closet and shouldered aside her heaviest dresses. She needed the mirror hung behind them, the reflective surface turned toward the wall. The edges were sharp and she handled them with care. It would not do to activate it before she was prepared.

Mirror held in one hand, she locked the door to her room and pushed a chair under the doorknob. Satisfied no one could interrupt her, Briar rolled aside the large circular rug in front of the window. Runes glowed a dim magenta at her. They hadn't been activated in a long time. She carefully composed herself in the middle of the runic circle.

She drew both hands along the sharp edges of the mirror, paying no mind to the stinging pain in her palms. Blood flowed freely and the inscription on the mirror sprang to life. The fire of bright magenta shifted to brilliant crimson as it spread from the edges where she held it. In no time, the back of the mirror burned brightly with runes inscribed to make the walls between planes thinner.

The mirror's surface no longer reflected any light. It was a matte black that sucked in what little daylight there was in the room. It wasn't enough. The earl's home had protections against infernal magic and these often interfered. Briar slapped her left hand down on the runes around her. Magenta chased by crimson crawled across those runes as well. The circle filled completely, and the mirror went through another change. It glowed with sullen color that shifted through the spectrum visible to humans and beyond.

Briar waited. The mirror was doing its work, seeking through the infernal plane for the recipient to which it was tuned.

The mirror shimmered once and suddenly a face looked back at her. Skin of opalescent grey shone at her. Despite knowing better, Briar couldn't help but be drawn in by the perfect contours of the woman's cheekbones, the eyes of smoky embers that stared back at her, one perfect eyebrow arched in question—or maybe amusement. The flawless red eyes crinkled slightly above full lips in a beautiful smile, one that exposed sleek black teeth slightly pointed at the ends. A bright red tongue peeked out from between her lips and casually caressed her bottom lip. It was easy to overlook the onyx horns that curved proudly back from her forehead and the faint rustling that accompanied her movements as leathery wings were settled and resettled against her back with each motion.

Briar closed her eyes for a moment to steady herself before opening them and regarding the woman in the mirror.

"Hello, Mother."

* * *

It wasn't the tallest townhouse Isabella had burgled, not by a long shot, and yet it loomed over her in the scant moonlight. Fog wreathed the full moon almost completely, creating a shining silver patch in the sky that did little to illuminate the streets below. Had the night been a little clearer, she wouldn't have risked it, but Althea had stressed how short their finances had gotten. Too much lower and even Isabella's father would notice. They hadn't gone to such pains to keep him in the dark about the true state of the family's fortunes to have that inconvenient truth exposed now. In two more years, Wellington would be finished with his schooling in Germany and would be back home. Things would return to normal. Then she could stop stealing from her friends.

The back garden was well tended and neat. Plants only now greening up from winter stretched all the way to the high brick wall that ran the perimeter. The gardener had been hard at work. The scent of freshly turned earth filled Isabella's nostrils, and she had to work to keep from leaving footprints in the soft ground. The space was tiny, as was typical in London. Having any sort of garden in the city indicated great wealth, but it left her few options for concealment. Her vantage behind a very square bush didn't have an ideal view of the house out of necessity. If a servant peered out and saw her lurking among the budding flowers, she would lose her chance at the house. Millie's rubies alone would keep Isabella's household going for a few weeks, not to mention what else she might find while she was in there.

So she waited for the last of the lights in the windows to go out. There was a small window of time when she could strike. The servants would finally bed down after their masters, but they would be up before the sun to prepare the house for the day. One window, high up in the servants' quarters, still spilled light out into the night. It was likely an oil lamp. The color was too warm to be gas, which in turn was warmer than that of electricity, though neither were as orange as the light from a fire. That she could identify a type of light source only from its color through a window was not a skill Isabella had ever thought she might have. It was probably the most innocuous of the skills she'd acquired since she started her second-storey work.

Isabella tried not to fret. Sweat trickled down her back and between her breasts, both places she couldn't reach. There was nothing worse than waiting. She risked leaning out to take a closer look at the window. Had someone fallen asleep with the lamp still burning? No, there was movement in the room and Isabella ducked back behind her hedge.

Moments later, the light went out. Isabella sighed with relief. Soon she would be able to go up. The mysterious servant only had to fall asleep now. Thirty minutes should be more than enough in her experience. It had been some time since she'd last been interrupted by the occupants of a house, and she preferred to keep it that way.

When she judged enough time had passed, Isabella stood and advanced stealthily up to the house. The moon's sullen silver glow gave enough light to be collected by her goggles and illuminate the garden. She pulled a small pistol-looking device from the back of her belt and aimed it up at the left-most brick chimney. With the pull of the trigger and a small report, the small hook was away. It buried itself in the brick and proved well-seated when Isabella tugged experimentally at the line. She didn't need it to climb, rather it was a guide to make sure she didn't go winging off into the night or through one of the windows lining the house's rear facade.

She hooked the end of the line into a winch at her belt. The tension tugged at her trousers, hard enough that she could feel it but not enough that she was in any danger of losing her pants while standing in the garden of her best friend's parents.

This was it. There was no more delaying now.

Isabella shook out her arms, the throttle and steering mechanisms for her jump pack settling into her hands with twin clicks. The pack vibrated on her back as she increased the throttle, then pushed off when she released it. A sound like a cresting wave released behind her and she was launched on twin streams of air. The winch at her belt hummed as it guided her upward. She twisted the steering mechanism in her right hand and extended one elbow. Her target, a window on the second storey, swung into view. Immediately, she cut the throttle and turned in midair, allowing the last of her boost to direct her onto the windowsill.

A twist and pull dislodged the small harpoon from above. The winch whirred and the harpoon got hung up on the edge of the rain gutter for a moment before pulling free with a clang. Isabella winced and froze, her ears peeled for any sign that someone had heard the noise. That was sloppy—and right over the window where the last light had gone out. To her relief, no one threw open the windows to look out into the night. She pulled off the hook and stored it in one of the many pouches at her waist, then turned her attention to the window on the second floor that was her goal.

The night wasn't warm enough that the window had been left open. Isabella squinted at the crack between the window and casement. It had been too much to hope for this to be a double window, like those lining the front of the house, giving an impression of alternating glass and brick. The windows on the back were fewer and sparer. It didn't matter the kind of window, however. There was always a latch. This window had two; it was the work of a moment to slide a thin metal pick into the crack where the sill met the window and lift each one.

Isabella had seen the types of latches on the windows in her friend's house. She'd been disappointed. Didn't Millie's father know the upper echelon was being targeted for a series of daring burglaries? Did he think himself beyond such things? It was a fairly common attitude Isabella had found and one that worked to her advantage, but if there had been a few measures in place, Millie's home wouldn't have been worth the risk to burgle. As it was, they were fairly inviting her in.

The window opened without so much as a creak. Isabella dropped quietly from the windowsill to a thick rug richly patterned after the Oriental fashion. A large armoire dominated one wall of the large dressing room. Beside it was a dressing table. Not two days earlier, she'd watched Millie stow the ruby necklace in the top drawer on the left-hand side.

Isabella pushed down the lens that allowed her to winnow out real jewels from fake ones. The drawer didn't budge to her gentle tug at first, but the simple lock yielded readily to her lock picks. Into one pouch went the rubies that almost burned through her lens. Since she was there, she took the time to look through the rest of Millie's jewelry. A surprising amount of it was glass or paste, but those with real gems joined the rubies.

She took a moment to listen at the door to the bedroom, but she heard nothing more than the gentle snores of one fast asleep. She debated whether or not she should take a look inside, then shook her head sadly. Millie didn't deserve to lose the necklace her fiancé had gifted her. At least she knew Nelson could well afford it and would likely replace it with commendable haste. He adored Millie and treated her quite well. Theirs was the kind of match she might aspire to if she'd had any interest in the harsher sex. As it was, Millie's engagement had been an unsurprising blow.

Though Isabella might have dreamed of a day where she could tell Millie how she felt for her, the engagement had made that impossible.

As close as she was with the girl, as much as she enjoyed her company and envisioned what her full lips might taste like, even Millie didn't know the real her. She didn't even know that Isabella liked to tinker with machinery. She saw only the facade of the genteel girl-child that Isabella had crafted to display to polite society. Millie took such joy in the trappings of high society. When they were together, the charade became easier to bear. In less than a year, that would be over. Millie would be safely married, and who knew if she would still have time for her friend.

It was time to move on. Other treasures were surely hidden in other dressing tables. These would keep her own family together, and there was no time to lose.

CHAPTER FOUR

Another tiresome ball, thought Briar. *At least I didn't have to sit through the ride in that horrible carriage*. The earl hadn't understood why she'd been so insistent upon using his older horseless but had eventually conceded to her request. Having her arrive in a carriage that was the height of new technology might be a feather in his cap but not at the price of her peace of mind.

She was supposed to be cultivating a relationship with the daughter of a minor baron, but the opportunity to approach her or her parents had simply not been there. Whenever she finished a dance with one vapid young gentleman, there was another to take his place. It was maddening. She had work to do, but the boys had apparently decided she was too entrancing to avoid. The only explanation was that her shroud wasn't working, though she'd tested it three times already. As usual, it was battened down, not even a hint of her true nature could escape it.

So why then could she not avoid yet another dance with a young bore who would tread upon her feet and try to keep her diverted with banal comments about the weather? Briar permitted the latest one to lead her out onto the floor and allowed her mind to wander, responding to his inane babble with short answers that may or may not have been appropriate.

Her mother had thought her shroud was too effective, but then she always did. The Fourth Minister to the Ruling Council of Lust could never understand why Briar wanted to fit in with the humans of the mortal plane. As a succubus, Carnélie reveled in her unabashed sexuality. Their race was carnality unbridled. Briar controlled that side of her nature with an iron fist, never allowing it to take over her life. Not that she didn't feel attraction. The gentleman who twirled her about now was a fine specimen of humanity. His face was quite symmetrical, and he had nice hard shoulders beneath his coat. Certainly, she found him attractive, but she had little desire to act upon the attraction. Her mother would likely have him in some back room already, which was how Briar had been conceived.

Still, if she was a disappointment to Carnélie, at least her mother had other daughters who were happy to be something more befitting her appetites.

She smiled automatically at something the lordling said to her, then looked away. The smile was almost always a logical response to what brainless young men of substance said to a lady.

Her mother had made her divest herself of the shroud when she had contacted her, and for what? Not much. Briar had known it would happen; it always did. Carnélie always refused to acknowledge her until she looked more attractive and not like the dowdy human woman she pretended to be. And for all that, she'd been useless. Carnélie had no information on what might be going on. There were always plots to interfere in the mortal realm among her infernal half-brethren. Infernal magic couldn't exist without the mortal realm, and the more infernals who occupied a corner of this world, the more magic they could send down to the infernal realm. It seemed there was nothing going on beyond the normal level of scheming, certainly nothing that should have put Briar so on edge.

Even worse, her inquiries had not only exposed her location among the mortals to her mother, but they'd also piqued Carnélie's interest. If Briar couldn't figure out what was going on, Carnélie would likely decide to visit. Disaster almost always followed in her mother's wake. Briar was quite comfortable in the life she'd constructed for herself. Her mother would destroy that in days and she'd have to reinvent herself once again.

"Are you quite well?" her dance partner asked. "You have the most frightful scowl."

It was true. Briar relaxed her brows with some effort and did her best to affect a light smile. "I can never recall the steps to this part of the dance. Forgive me."

He looked down at her, one eyebrow raised in polite doubtfulness. "You're doing quite well if that's the case. I thought perhaps…" He sneaked a quick glance over his shoulder toward one corner of the room.

Briar followed the look. Isabella Castel was ensconced with her usual entourage of fluttering ninnies. She had her head bent and was whispering in the ear of a boy wearing a waistcoat of the most horrid shade of chartreuse. The covert looks being directed Briar's way were easy enough to read. No wonder she'd had no time. Someone was determined to waste it.

Enough of this. Briar walked the young man backward, much to his shock. He was accustomed to leading, but when she took over and guided them adroitly to the edge of the dance floor, he was powerless to do anything but follow along. As soon as they reached the edge of the floor, Briar abandoned him, leaving him gawking as couples weaved and bobbed behind him. If she hadn't been so angry, she might have been amused at his gaping mouth. She'd seen more intelligent looking goldfish.

She'd lost sight of the Sherard girl, too many people stood between them, but Briar knew where she was. Her face set in a deliberately pleasant mask, Briar started forward through the throng. Her steps gained speed as she walked. Glittering ladies and nattily dressed men gave Briar surprised looks before moving out of her way, almost leaping in one case. Apparently her mask was slipping. Briar didn't care. She had work to do and that silly girl was interfering with it.

A hole opened up in the crowd straight to the Sherard girl, who had the grace to look concerned for a moment before an expression of amused condescension settled lightly over her face. She turned back to the young man bent toward her and placed a hand upon his forearm. He melted back into the crowd of lovelies around her.

"Miss Riley." Miss Castel bent her head in graceful welcome. Mischief glittered in her eyes, the slightest crinkles in the corners the only indication of her amusement.

"Miss Castel." Briar made no attempt to warm the frost that rimed her voice. The Sherard girl could get frostbite and lose digits from it as far as she was concerned.

"Miss Riley!" One of the young women Briar usually saw at that girl's side stepped forward. She clapped her hands in excitement. "How wonderful to see you. Are you here to thank Isabella?"

"Thank her?" Surely the brainless simpleton was joking.

"Of course. She saw how lonely and partnerless you usually are at these affairs and determined a most brilliant plan to remedy that. Isn't she wonderful?" The girl bestowed upon Miss Castel a brilliant smile. A delicate shade of red crept up the Sherard girl's cheeks. She snapped open her fan and hid behind it, refusing to meet Briar's eyes.

"There's no need to make such a thing of it, Millie." The Sherard girl fanned herself a tad vigorously. "I'm simply trying to help out a friend."

"So we're friends now?" Briar asked, her voice steady. "Is that right?"

"Of course we are." Millie reached over and delicately drew Briar into the center of the little group with a hand on her forearm. "I must declare that I'm quite excited to learn more about you. The stories are…well, there are always stories, aren't there?"

"I'm sure there are. I'm really quite boring. Surely you have more exciting pursuits than interviewing an avowed bluestocking."

"And yet we still see you at these affairs," Miss Castel said. "Do you not tire of the company of your books?" A chorus of muted giggles followed her arch question.

"One can tire of almost any company, no matter how riveting it thinks it is." Briar smiled thinly. "But that of books never disappoints. They have none of the caprices of humans, after all."

"How sad." Millie sighed lightly. "To have only books as bosom companions. I think I might die."

Briar stared at the girl, trying to figure out if she was trying to be insulting. It was impossible to tell for certain, but Briar thought perhaps she wasn't. Millie fingered the black ribbon at her throat that she was wearing instead of jewelry. If Briar remembered correctly, at the previous ball the girl had worn a splendid necklace that had positively dripped with rubies.

"Not as sad as losing your rubies," Briar said, taking a guess. "Were they stolen?"

Someone made of less stern stuff might have burst into flames at the glare Miss Castel directed at her. Briar blinked, not sure she'd seen the anger on the Sherard girl's face. It was gone as quickly as it had come.

Millie sighed again, bosom trying to escape the constraints of her corset. "They were, along with other items nearly as precious to me." She paused and looked around the group which had suddenly grown quiet. "Spring-Heeled Jack paid us a visit two nights ago."

A collective gasp shuddered through their small crowd. Briar nodded to herself.

"Not your gift from Nelson?" Miss Castel's voice was sharp with shocked condolence. Briar thought perhaps she could have toned back the reaction.

Millie didn't notice. "I'm afraid so. He's quite upset, of course. Father has gone straight to Scotland Yard about it. He says the local constabulary is obviously quite out of its depth, or the ruffian wouldn't still be at large." She stroked the black ribbon at her neck. "I have determined to wear this ribbon until he is brought to justice and my jewels are returned to me."

The others in the group murmured their agreement, with many of the girls pledging to do the same. The Sherard girl was curiously silent.

"Thankfully, the earl has no worries in that regard," Briar said firmly. "He employs the latest theft-deterrent techniques and machinery." She leaned forward to Millie. "May I be assured of your confidence?" At Millie's excited nod, Briar continued. "He has recently acquired the Blenheim Gem."

Millie's lips shaped a perfectly round O of surprise.

"The Blenheim Gem?" Miss Castel's whisper was all reverence. "No one has seen that for almost a century. Where did he find it?"

"He came across a mention of it in one of his manuscripts." Briar shrugged. "It was a simple matter of tracking down the owner from there." It was true enough, the earl's manuscripts did contain at least one mention of the gem. He had no particular interest in it, but Briar had been able to track ownership of the engraved gem using her own particular talents. It was currently hidden in the crypts beneath a ruined abbey in Shropshire. Briar had no interest in such fripperies, but it had been a useful exercise.

"That would be something to see."

"Indeed it is. I have been privileged in my viewing of it. The descriptions do not do it justice."

"Do you not worry about the curse?" Millie asked.

"Of course not. Curses don't exist." Briar was lying through her teeth. Curses very much existed, and the Blenheim Gem might well be the focus of one, but she had a reputation to maintain. Ladies of her standing had no time for the mystical world, never mind that Briar worked infernal magic as well as most of her mother's race.

"I heard the first owner of the Blenheim Gem went mad. He was convinced he'd been turned into a turnip." Millie clearly enjoyed being the center of attention. She looked around at the rapt faces of the little group. And they were rapt. Nothing could liven up a dull ball like the story of someone else's misfortune. "His son inherited it and disappeared without a trace on the moors of Scotland. The gem was sold and the dealer of antiquities who acquired it lost two ships in a freak storm off the Cape of Good Hope."

"The earl isn't concerned, nor am I. I have seen no evidence of curses. As far as I know, he has no root vegetable aspirations, nor has he expressed an interest for long walks on the Scottish moors."

"Nonetheless," Millie said. "You are practically begging for your house to be robbed. Ours was, and none of *our* jewels had an accursed reputation."

The Sherard girl looked like she might start salivating, then shrugged and adopted an air of insouciance. "That's as may be. But come, Miss Riley, Lord Kirkup awaits an opportunity to take a turn around the dance floor."

The young man with the chartreuse waistcoat materialized at Briar's shoulder, his hand held out to her.

Enough is enough, Briar thought. If she wasn't going to get the earl's work done that night, then she had work of her own to do.

"My Lord Kirkup." She smiled painfully. "I am afraid I am suddenly overcome with a splitting headache. Thank you for the request, but I must take my leave."

He looked relieved and raised one shoulder in a half-hearted shrug aimed at the Sherard girl, who for her part seemed quite satisfied. Briar could only surmise she'd gotten what she wanted: a chance to embarrass Briar and be rid of her for the evening.

True to her word, Briar left not long after. She never did get the chance to delicately probe at Lord and Lady Griffith, but there would be other opportunities. If their daughter had been part of Miss Castel's set, then she might have wounded two pigeons with one throw. Hopefully the groundwork had been laid and it was only a matter of time.

It was late when she arrived back at the townhouse, though not as late as it would have been had she not made her excuses early. Briar wasn't tired in the least. She had research to do. She holed up in the library with the stack of papers she'd collected the other day and went through them methodically for any mention of mysterious burglaries. There was always crime in London, but she had a decided hunch that the burglaries perpetrated by Miss Castel's brother would be easy to spot.

When she came across any mention of a burglary, she set the broadsheet aside into its own pile. The stack she'd managed to acquire was less than a month's worth, and yet the issues that contained burglaries outnumbered those that didn't. Her next step was to cut the burglaries out and arrange them chronologically across the top half of her desk. She marked a timeline in chalk along the top edge. The numbers were shockingly bright against the wood's dark varnish.

Next she went back through the papers and removed any mention of Spring-Heeled Jack. Those went down on the desk as well, in a chronological tier along the bottom of the desk. Burglaries mentioning the mysterious figure went between the two rows to create a third tier.

Briar stood back and regarded her handiwork. She chewed meditatively at her lower lip. There was more to it, she knew it. One last piece to the puzzle, and she would have what she needed.

She left the library and crossed the large landing in the middle of the house, past the door to the servants' stair, the garderobe, and linen closet and into her room. She had another desk in there, where most ladies would have had a dressing table. A small mirror served that purpose when she needed it. Briar kept the invitations to each ball she attended, covered with precise notes on who she'd spoken to and who else had been in attendance. She liberated the stack from beneath her diary and returned to the library.

In a final tier, she laid the invitations down in chronological order. The burglaries that coincided with sightings of Spring-Heeled Jack took place three to four evenings after balls Miss Castel had attended. Not all of them, to be certain, but enough to confirm her suspicions. Timing was the important piece now. She knew about when she could expect a visit from Miss Castel's brother.

More preparations still remained, however. Careful not to disturb her work, Briar removed a large notepad from her desk and a fountain pen from the top drawer. She went back through the articles about Spring-Heeled Jack with careful attention, stopping now and then to jot notes down upon the pad.

CHAPTER FIVE

The library was dark. It had been tempting to leave a lamp burning on the table at the center where Briar had laid the ornate wooden box. Apparently, she had been reading too many novels. As dramatic as the scene would have been, the lamp would most assuredly tip her hand to Jack. She didn't need the light, after all. The runes graven in a large circle around the table glowed faintly to her eyes, providing enough light to see by. They'd likely be invisible to Jack, unless he had a fair amount of demon blood running through his veins. It wasn't outside the realm of possibility, but she wasn't overly worried.

The shroud she pulled around herself was different on this night, as it had been on the three previous nights she'd lain in wait for the second-storey man. She'd hardened it, rendered it opaque, and settled into the darkest corner of the room. The only flaw with this hardened shroud was that it was easily broken. She couldn't move more than a twitch without it shattering and revealing her in her true form. Her normal shroud was always a thought away, but the hardened one was more difficult to summon. Still, it would have been nice to have had a book. Perhaps the new Jules Verne novel that sat unopened upon her night stand. When she'd purchased it, she'd assumed it was another adventure story like his *Twenty Thousand Leagues Under the Sea*. Upon closer examination, it seemed this one was a fantastical romance, certainly not something appropriate for someone of her intellectual stature, and yet, it beckoned her.

The lens she'd discovered at the ball ten days ago had come off a pair of compound goggles, of that she was certain. The earl owned a pair, and each lens had a different function. Jack would be foolish not to have one that could distinguish living beings.

Jack had another hour to reveal himself or she was going to have to give up another night as wasted. The clock in the hall had recently rung three. She fumed at the waste to her time. If she had to attend the following evening's ball to drop more bait, that would be an even greater inconvenience. Her own work was suffering, but the mysterious source of terror she'd discovered in the carriage was too important to leave alone. She knew it in her bones, and her mother's interest had only solidified her worries.

Fretting would make no difference. Briar schooled her mind into some semblance of calm. The urge to worry still lingered at the edges of her determined focus.

Wait. What's that? There it was again. A creak so quiet that if she hadn't been listening for that precise sign she would have missed it. *Could it be?*

One of the library's heavy doors swung silently open. It was little more than a crack, barely enough for a dark figure to slip between them. Briar held her breath. It was definitely Jack. She could tell by the dark helmet over his head and his heavy shoulders. He matched the newspapers' fantastical description. Briar had been prepared to discount the more outlandish tidbits, but if anything the newspapers had missed some details.

As she'd supposed, a pair of goggles rested over the front of his helmet, giving him an insect-like appearance that hadn't been mentioned in the local rags.

Slowly, Briar let out the breath she'd been holding. Jack made his way carefully across the room until he hovered over the table, his head swinging this way and that. Briar moved like a striking snake. She pulled the pen knife from her pocket and jabbed it into the flesh of her palm. Blood dripped from her hand onto the flat stone on the floor in front of her. It blazed into brilliant life, magenta tendrils racing from it to touch the dimly glowing circle around the table. Crimson flames lit the center of the room in brightness even Jack would be able to see. Faster than he would be able to blink, they wove into a cage around him and the table.

He stood for a moment, rooted to the ground and stunned by the turn of events. Briar got to her feet, allowing her usual shroud to fall over her features. She walked slowly forward, allowing him to see her by the light of the magic cage she'd constructed around him. She said nothing, allowing the weight of his situation to press in on him. Silence was an effective tool, one she employed with great joy. Her victory was even sweeter for how perfectly it had turned out. Jack had no idea what he was in for, and the longer he had to wait, the more amenable he would be.

She lit an oil lamp on a nearby table, then took her time turning up the gas in the two wall lamps nearest to the crimson cage. As she moved, Jack turned to keep his eyes on her, aside from that he moved not a muscle. Briar smiled to herself.

When she was finished bringing some light to the library, Briar took a seat in a near chair.

"What do we have here, I wonder?"

Jack said nothing in return. The lenses of his goggles reflected an eerie mix of blood-red fire and soft gas light.

"You may as well take off your helmet," Briar said. "You won't be leaving unless I will it, and right now I'd like to see who tried to rob my employer."

Jack still said nothing, defiance in every line of his body until his shoulders drooped. He bent forward and grasped the helm in both hands, pulling it off.

Brilliant red locks tumbled out from under the helmet, ringing around Jack's shoulders. Briar stiffened with shock and leaned forward.

"Miss Castel?"

"Surprised, Miss Riley?"

Briar scrambled to regain her footing. "Of course I am. Who wouldn't be surprised to discover a viscount's daughter creeping into one's home?"

Isabella Castel smiled tightly. "No one will believe you if you tell them. You may as well let me go." She looked at the glowing and shifting bars around her, then up.

"You won't be able to escape that way. I did my research on your capabilities. And I'm prepared to reveal your identity if need be." This part Briar had prepared for. She stood and wheeled a large bellows camera on a tripod next to the table. She opened a bag and pulled out a square tray and placed it on the table with another tray. Following those were a couple of glass bottles. Isabella's eyes followed her movements closely.

Briar surveyed her prep-work with the camera. Satisfied that all was in order, she moved closer to the cage of magic.

"I'm afraid I'm going to have to make you hold still for a few minutes. The light in here is not ideal for photography." She shrugged. "But what can you do?" Briar bent forward and touched her still-bleeding palm to a small set of runes that bumped off the main circle. They'd glowed faintly until the introduction of her blood, then flared to life.

"What are you—" Crimson tendrils extruded from the rapidly shrinking cage and tightened around Miss Castel, holding her in place. One snaked under her chin, holding her mouth closed and she glared twin daggers of murderous anger at Briar.

"It will take but a few minutes, I expect." Briar tucked her head under the hood and lined up the image, making sure to center Miss Castel's face in the glass. There, the girl's face was visible and identifiable, as was enough of the library that anyone who knew it would be able to confirm its identity. Unfortunately, the bands of magic she was trapped in were also visible. That would be difficult to explain should she need to show the photograph to anyone, but Miss Castel didn't know that. Briar removed the glass plate from the back of the camera and poured the contents of one of the bottles into the tray, dipped the plate into it, and finally returned it to the camera.

Miss Castel made a few noises deep in her throat, but without being able to open her mouth, Briar could make out none of the words. The intent was clear however. Miss Castel's face had flushed an angry red, visible even in the crimson light of the magic bands that wrapped her around. That was fine; the girl was a thief after all. What could drive the daughter of a viscount to such behavior, Briar wondered? It seemed like an odd thing if she were simply on a lark.

Briar ducked under the camera's hood to check on the progress of the image. It barely existed, ghostly outlines of magic fire were all she could make out.

"This may take longer than I thought." The Sherard girl didn't appreciate the update.

Briar ducked back and forth for the next thirty minutes until she judged the plate passable. She removed it from the back of the camera and quickly dunked it in the fixing solution waiting on the table. While the image was fixed, she spat upon her palm and rubbed the tips of two fingers in the spittle. She bent forward and drew those two tips where the small circle protruded from the larger inscription, severing the connection. Immediately, the magical bonds retracted, taking on the form of a cage once again. Miss Castel staggered but managed to keep from falling over.

"Now that we understand each other, we can begin." Briar displayed the glass negative to her captive. Isabella was easily recognizable.

"What do you want? You went to a lot of trouble to get me here."

As had been the case the night Miss Castel reclaimed the lens from her, she showed no sign of the flighty debutante. This girl was in full control of her emotions and intelligent. For a moment Briar wished she knew more about this Isabella Castel.

"I am in need of someone with your skills to procure something for me."

"What could you possibly need so badly you'd trap somebody to get it?"

Briar hesitated. "I'm not sure."

Isabella stared at her, eyes wide with disbelief. "You lured me here, trapped me using magic, and you don't even know what it is you need me to get?"

"That's right." The girl's incredulous tone grated on her. "You're in no position to question me."

"Then perhaps you could let me out of here so we can discuss the terms of your…request."

With the gracious nod of her head, Briar rubbed her palm on the focus stone in her pocket. The brilliant red interlocking bars flickered momentarily, then went out. Not even a glowing trace was visible to her eyes, but the smell of brimstone hung heavy in the air. Isabella didn't seem to notice. She lifted the lid of the box that had been her target. A rueful smile spread across her face when she realized it was empty.

Briar alighted upon a chair and gestured for Isabella to take the one across from her. As the girl crossed the floor toward her, Briar took the opportunity to view her costume more closely.

How no one could tell that Isabella was a woman beneath those clothes, Briar didn't know. The pants were tight against distinctly feminine hips. The swell of her breasts were evident now that she knew what to look for, though they were somewhat obscured by the harness that held a contraption to her back. The device was what gave her such heavy and powerful-looking shoulders. Briar was intrigued to see the flexible tubes that ran from Isabella's back down her arms. She had no idea what purpose those might serve. Pockets of all shapes and sizes decorated every spare inch of the costume.

Isabella withstood her scrutiny without a word. A small smile played around one corner of her lips.

Suddenly discomfited by the knowing look, Briar pressed forward. "Mirabilia Carriageworks is doing something untoward. I'm not sure what it is, or how they're doing it, but I need to know more."

"Mirabilia? They've made some astounding advances in horseless technology. What could they possibly be doing that you'd be willing to capture me to check up on them?"

"I don't know!" Some of Briar's frustration bled through in the vehemence of her tone. Isabella leaned back in her chair, and Briar took care to modulate her voice. "I don't know enough about such devices. I am not a mechanist, but I am…sensitive in other ways. There is something wrong with their storage devices. Something evil."

* * *

Something evil. Those two words simmered between them. Isabella stared at Miss Riley. She was composed, by all outward appearances, but something about her poised stillness belied her lack of composure. She didn't know Miss Riley particularly well. The woman lurked around the corners of balls and other gatherings. She was almost too old to be part of the glittering set and seemed to have little interest in being there. An inveterate bluestocking, she never seemed to notice the slights and cutting remarks directed her way. Her unflappability was legend and was one of the reasons Isabella went out of her way to send little barbs at her. Miss Riley was a challenge, a small way to make her evenings pretending to be a shallow-thinking debutante a little more interesting. She'd never shown a crack in her facade, but Isabella could swear she was terrified tonight.

"I haven't had the opportunity to see one up close. My parents haven't purchased one of the new carriages." Something evil seemed overly melodramatic, but if the unflappable Miss Brionie Riley was frightened, there had to be more there. "I'm a fair hand with mechanical devices. Perhaps I can take a look." At Miss Riley's look of doubt, Isabella motioned to take in her burgling suit. "I made this, so I think I can hazard a guess at what's going on."

"I don't have one of the devices on hand. But you could come around on the morrow and take a look at what powers our carriage." The tension bled out of Miss Riley's shoulders. She nodded decisively. "You will come to call tomorrow. If you don't, I shall make sure the proper authorities receive copies of the photograph." Her hesitance overcome, Miss Riley hopped up and started pacing the length of the room. "Then you shall infiltrate the company's headquarters and return with proof of their deeds."

"If I may make a suggestion before you send photographs to Scotland Yard?" Isabella knew she had to play this carefully. She couldn't afford to irritate the woman who held her freedom on a glass plate in her left hand.

Miss Riley glanced over at her.

"I'm certain I have more experience in such clandestine activities than you do," Isabella said. "Infiltration without observation is almost certainly doomed to failure. I watched this home for three nights before entering. I will need to observe their headquarters for at least that length of time before going in."

"Very well. But tomorrow we will look at the carriage so we may have some idea what you'll be looking for."

"Agreed." Isabella stood and carefully wrapped her hair up before settling the helmet over it. She settled the goggles carefully over her eyes. "Tomorrow then," she said by way of good-bye.

Miss Riley might have the upper hand, but Isabella saw no reason to act as if she believed that was the case. She crossed the room to the windows and opened one. It was easy enough to see in the library's gloom now that she had her goggles on again. She hopped up on the windowsill, shook twin levers into her hands, then stepped into open air. The street's cobbles rose up to meet her, but she activated the thrust device on her back before she smacked into them. Isabella landed hard on the cobbles and bent her knees to absorb the shock, the braces on her legs doing most of the work. She set the device off again and launched into a long arc away from the earl's towering townhouse.

It was impossible to resist the urge to look back and see if Miss Riley watched her out the windows. A slight wobble overtook her, but she compensated without thinking by sticking out her right arm and activating a secondary thruster.

Brionie's silhouette was barely visible in the window.

Isabella grinned and continued her arcing way down the avenue, then over hedges and into back alleys. It didn't take long to get home as the crow flies, but it took a little longer as the crow hopped. She couldn't contain the little frisson of excitement that churned at the base of her spine. She had been caught, and while that was concerning, this new venture promised stimulation the like of which she hadn't yet experienced. Even a forced partnership with the frigid Miss Riley couldn't restrain Isabella's excitement.

But how frigid was she, really? The inspection Brionie had given her in the library had been intense and thorough. There was definitely more to the reserved bluestocking than met the eye. The prospect of discovering more about the enigmatic Miss Riley was almost as exhilarating as the idea of breaking into Mirabilia's headquarters.

That line of thought was going to end up with Isabella colliding with the side of a building, so she carefully banished all musings on Brionie Riley from her mind and concentrated on getting home in one piece. A crash would certainly bring questions from her mother, and that was a discussion to be avoided at all costs.

CHAPTER SIX

"Miss Riley?" The earl's inquiring tone broke the morning silence. There was usually little chatter at the breakfast table. The earl and his daughters sat in silence broken only occasionally by the clinking of cutlery against their plates or by a softly murmured request to one of the footmen. Briar was enjoying her morning cup of tea and some lightly buttered toast; she rarely ate much upon first waking. The food sat heavily in her stomach if she ate too much, and she felt sick for much of the rest of the day. She raised her head to acknowledge her employer.

"Yes, my lord?"

"The footman has a letter for you." He squinted at the envelope in his hand.

Who would be sending her a note at this hour of the morning? All she could think was that it was from Isabella. *She had better not be trying to extricate herself from our meeting.* "Thank you. I shall take a look at it."

Hardwicke placed the letter back on the silver tray next to his elbow. The footman picked it up and carried it over to her. Briar smiled her thanks as she picked up the letter. She carefully broke the seal on the envelope. The paper of the letter inside was heavy;

there was no way someone could hold the paper to the light and get some idea of the contents. Briar approved of Isabella's discretion, if in fact she'd thought of it. Perhaps the paper was so heavy because of Isabella's handwriting. She had a heavy, looping stroke that wavered occasionally. Briar left off her analysis of Isabella's handwriting and applied her attention to the contents of the note.

Madam—

Regarding this morning's agreement to meet: I doubt you have the facilities to properly examine the carriage. Therefore, I propose changing the location. I have the requisite equipment and access to expertise in dismantling the power source that concerns you so. If you are amenable, please send word to Sherard House on Cavendish Square. I shall expect you before noon.

—Isabella Castel

So she wasn't trying to get out of it. The proposal made sense. They had a coach house on the premises, but with two horselesses and a conventional carriage, it was cramped and Briar suspected it contained the barest essentials for repair work, which likely wouldn't do for a more robust dissection of the offending machinery. If Isabella thought they'd have a better go of it at a different location, then she could see the wisdom.

The signature on the note was quite informal. What did that mean? Briar had seen her in a somewhat compromising situation, that was for certain. She lifted the paper to her nose and inhaled. Was that…motor oil? There was a dark blot in one corner that Briar had initially taken as an ink spot, but closer examination revealed it as a dark grease spot. When she lowered the letter, Briar met the earl's bemused gaze across the table. His daughters were no less interested in her behavior.

"Is that a letter from a suitor?" young Imogene asked brightly. She had a couple years before her debut yet and was overly interested in the very slow dance between men and women of high society.

"Imogene." Her elder sister hissed a quiet reproof. Lillie didn't always break her fast with them, only when her husband was out of town. The Baron Aveland had considerable business interests upon the Continent and was frequently absent. As an advantageously married woman, she should have had less interest in Briar's personal affairs, yet her eyes were as bright as her sister's.

"What? I want to know. Miss Riley never has gentlemen calling."

"I'm sorry to disappoint." Briar put the envelope down and picked up her cup again. Perhaps if she acted as if nothing were untoward, they wouldn't notice the heat in her cheeks. "I will be going out this morning."

"But you smelled the letter." Imogene wouldn't be deterred. "That only happens if it's from someone you like. The novels all say so."

"Then you are reading quite the wrong type of novels."

"And you're blushing."

"That's quite enough, Imogene." When she opened her mouth to protest, Hardwicke raised an eyebrow at her. That was enough to temper young Imogene's enthusiasm. She subsided into her chair and prodded sulkily at her eggs. "Don't forget we have an appointment to keep this afternoon," he said to Briar. "Selborne is giving us a tour of his collection."

Of course. How could she have forgotten? Usually the prospect of working with a new set of manuscripts was enough to keep her up the night before. Well, she had been up the night before, but not out of excitement. "Of course. I won't be late."

"I know."

Briar was never late for anything. To be less than ten minutes early for an appointment meant she was running late, at least in her own eyes. But if she was going to be on time to her rendezvous with Isabella, she had to get moving. She signaled to the footman, who brought her a piece of paper and pen. She hesitated, pen hovering over the surface of the paper for a moment before writing one word: *Agreed*. She signed it formally and addressed the outside of the envelope. After quiet instructions to the footman to have it delivered immediately, Briar took her leave.

"My lord. My lady. Imogene." She received polite nods of the head from Hardwicke and Lillie. Imogene waited until her father and sister had returned their attention to their breakfasts before sticking her tongue out at Briar. Most days, the impertinent child usually amused her to no end, but today was not one of those days. Briar settled for a dark glare in return, which only prompted a snicker from Imogene.

Dressing took longer than usual, for some reason. She couldn't seem to settle on a dress. The dithering was uncharacteristic, to say the least. Finally, Briar decided to simply put on the first suitable dress and let it be. She doubted Isabella would be interested in what she wore. Briar wasn't interested in her own outfit, usually. All sorts of things were off today, it seemed.

The only flaw in Isabella's plan occurred to Briar as she waited for Johnson to bring the carriage around. If Isabella had come to her, Briar wouldn't be forced to suffer through another interminable ride in that thing. The now-familiar sense of impending doom closed around her as soon as she stepped inside the carriage. She watched out the small window as they made their way slowly through London's cramped streets. Anxiety mounted to irritation the longer the drive took. When an elderly couple crossed the street slowly in front of them, Briar leaned out the window. A cool breeze caressed her face and she realized she was sweating. And about to shout rudely at someone. When the gentleman looked at her inquiringly, Briar smiled instead.

"Good morning," she said with a jerky nod, rather than "Get out of the way, you doddering fools." The urge was still there, but she ground it down.

The sensation was familiar, she realized with a start. This was how she felt when she was on the plane of her birth. Her mother's domain awakened many of these same feelings within her. Quickness to anger, a rush to violent reaction were both hallmarks of the demonic side of her nature. Compared to her half-brethren, she was physically quite weak and thus had become accustomed to reining in impulses that would be very damaging if she tried to act upon them in infernal company.

By the time they rolled up to the front of a tall townhouse, Briar was mopping at her face with a handkerchief. The strain of keeping herself together had her shaking. She had the door open and was flying out of the cab before Johnson barely had the vehicle stopped. The pavement in front of a house was normally not the place to regain her composure, but she still took her time. This was no condition in which to visit with Isabella. To give herself a little extra time, Briar checked her pocket watch. To her astonishment, the entire trip had been only a hair over twenty minutes. Part of her agitation had been the certainty that they would be late. Instead, they were ten minutes early.

Isabella might not even be prepared for her visit. With that thought, Briar strode up the steps to the front door. She rang the doorbell smartly. If Isabella wasn't ready, that was her own problem. It would serve her right for putting Briar through additional discomfort.

She was preparing to ring the bell again when it opened. A footman, much too old for the position, looked up at her. The pronounced curve of his spine rendered him much shorter than he must have been in his youth.

"Miss Brionie Riley here to see the Honorable Isabella Castel."

"Of course, Miss Riley. Miss Castel said you would be by. She awaits you in the workshop."

A workshop? Here? The townhouse wasn't nearly as impressive as the earl's, but the neighborhood did not suffer from a lack of class. Isabella's neighborhood was quite comparable, and Briar found it difficult to believe there was a larger garden here than at the earl's home. Wherever would they keep a workshop?

"Your man can take the carriage around to the coach house. If you'll follow me?"

He turned, a labored affair that had Briar's back aching with sympathy. They made their slow way through the house. It was immaculately clean and suitably less impressive than the earl's.

That was not unexpected. Viscount Sherard's home in the city aspired to no higher rank than his title. There was a subtle air of shabbiness to the house, however. It took Briar a while to put her finger on it. If they hadn't been traversing the stately halls so slowly, it was possible she might have missed it. For one thing, there weren't enough servants for a house this size. The footman should have been enjoying his retirement, a grandchild upon his knee. The cuffs of his jacket were the slightest bit frayed. Here was a bare spot on a carpet, and there the tied-back drapes couldn't quite hide how threadbare the velvet had gotten.

She'd heard no rumors about the family's fortunes. If they were destitute, surely she would have heard something. The only thing the higher set enjoyed discussing more than who was richer was who had fallen from grace. The Sherards never came up. Isabella always had the latest fashions and new gowns when she attended the balls. Certainly, she had mentioned that they hadn't yet gotten one of the new horseless carriages, but there were many who had yet to do so.

They stepped out a side door and into the small back garden. A gazebo dominated much of the small green space. It was here that the footman left her.

"Miss Castel will be with you shortly."

"Thank you."

Briar folded herself onto the gazebo's narrow bench to wait. Hopefully she wouldn't have to wait three days for *this* appointment with Isabella. Of course, the burglar hadn't known they had an appointment the last time. Minutes ticked slowly by with no sign of Isabella. This was not her definition of shortly. To her dismay, Briar found she hadn't yet recovered from her discomfort in the carriage; she fairly vibrated with anxiety. A grinding sound filled her ears, setting her teeth on edge.

No, it wasn't that formless worry. Briar grabbed at the edge of the bench to keep from falling over. Her grip made no difference; she continued to slide down. She wasn't moving, the gazebo was, or more accurately its floor was. There was nothing for it but to wait as the floor laboriously ground downward. She looked up with some discomfiture as the opening receded further away from her. She had to be more than ten feet below ground, then twenty. It was quite dark at the bottom of this hole. Was Isabella returning the favor of being trapped? If she was, she would find that Briar was no shrinking violet.

The floor lightened. She'd arrived at her destination. Isabella could have warned her. Instead, the target of her ire stood at the bottom of the lift, a broad smile upon her face.

Machinery lined the large underground room. It was an incomprehensible wall of dials and gauges, of sparks and steam. The lights around the top of the room were reflected back by dozens of polished metal surfaces, and beneath the smells of metal and oil lurked the scent of brimstone. On the heels of the smell, she caught the glow of infernal runes here and there. Maybe half the machines seemed to include runic embellishment of some sort.

"What do you think?" Isabella extended her arms and turned slowly in place. "Isn't it beautiful?"

"That's one word for it." Briar walked slowly down the shallow steps leading down from the gazebo's displaced floor. "It certainly is bright." She had to hand it to the girl. This was an inspired solution. Going underground would give her a lot of room; still it wasn't without its pitfalls. "Aren't you worried about the river?"

"The Thames?" Isabella shrugged. "We pump excess water up and out. There's no need to worry. Plus, we never have to water the garden."

"I see." Feeling more than a little dazed, Briar followed along behind Isabella as she crossed the long workshop floor.

"Sorry you had to wait so long. I wanted to get your carriage down here first." True to her words, on the other side of the workshop the horseless carriage waited for them. Johnson was nowhere to be found. "Your chauffeur is waiting belowstairs," Isabella said, correctly surmising who she was looking for. "I shall send for him when you're ready to leave."

Briar turned halfway around and tried to reorient herself, with a little success. Some of the feeling of being overwhelmed receded. She knew where she was, if nothing else.

"So what are you going to do now?" she asked.

Isabella's delighted smile widened into a grin. Her eyes fairly sparkled with excitement. "Easy, we're going to take it apart. Father!"

"Take it apart? I must be back to the earl's by early afternoon. You can't take it apart."

"Never fear. We're just going to take have a look at the engine, since that's what you're so worried about. It'll be back together and running in a tick."

A loud bang from nearby had Briar trying to climb three feet into the empty air. She cast about wildly and her eyes fixed upon a cloud of smoke that billowed up from the source of the noise. A moment later, a lanky man in filthy coveralls emerged from the small cloud. He waved a stained handkerchief in front of his face. His face was blackened with soot, except where his goggles had been. A shock of bright red hair stood on end on top of his head. It was easy to see from where Isabella got her coloring. He was lanky and would have towered over his daughter and Briar alike were it not for a slight stoop.

"That didn't work." He coughed once into his hand and stood glaring distractedly at the hulking device that was revealed when the smoke cleared. It looked to Briar like a large coil with more coils affixed to its top. A lonely light blinked slowly on one side of the machine.

"Father." Isabella took the man's elbow and gently turned him around to face them.

"Hmm?" He blinked twice at her, then gave a small start when he noticed Briar standing to one side. "Oh! We have a guest."

"We do. This is Miss Brionie Riley. She had the concern about the power source in the new horseless carriages from Mirabilia Manufacturing. Brionie, this is my father, Joseph Castel, the Viscount Sherard."

Briar started a bit at Isabella's use of her given name. She hadn't realized they were on such intimate terms, but then they both knew much more about the other than even their closest acquaintances did.

"Excellent! It's good to have concerns, young lady." Isabella's father beamed at Briar. "Too many inventions are rushed into production these days. Safety is the most important part of any invention."

"Quite, my lord." He seemed to be the poster child for the importance of safety.

He waved away her formality. "You may call me Joseph when in the workshop, my dear. This is no place to stand on ceremony. Shall we get started?" He rubbed his hands together with glee and started toward the carriage.

Isabella materialized by his side carrying a large box of tools. Briar realized with some surprise that she too was wearing coveralls. Somehow she'd missed that detail when coming down to the workshop. They were much cleaner than her father's. When Isabella bent over to deposit the toolbox on the floor, Briar had to look away. The pants left no part of her shapely posterior to the imagination.

"What do you think?" Briar asked while studying the lights above her.

"We haven't gotten very far." Isabella's voice became more muffled when she pulled herself under the carriage. "I need to access the engine compartment...there." Energetic clanking emanated from beneath the earl's prized vehicle. "Oh, this is fascinating. Father, you must see this."

Joseph joined his daughter, leaving Briar to her own devices. She tried to take stock of the work area once again but was overwhelmed by it all. The small explosion Isabella's father had caused was more than enough reason to keep her hands to herself. Part of her desperately wanted to track down the traces of infernal magic she detected in a dozen different places in the work space, but the rest of her was too on edge to contemplate poking around. She had to keep an eye on that carriage but not from too close. At this distance, she felt the barest bit of anxiety. Briar tapped her foot. The quicker this went, the quicker she could be home with her books and away from Isabella's provoking presence and the terror that awaited her in that carriage. She resigned herself to a long morning of watching other people work.

CHAPTER SEVEN

The carriage engine was unlike any other Isabella had seen. The designers weren't too keen on anyone else tinkering with the inner workings, for one thing. It had taken the two of them quite some time to even open the engine compartment. The manufacturer had used several non-standard fasteners. By the time they finally wrestled the hatch off the compartment, Isabella had worked up a full sweat. It rolled down her forehead and into her eyes. She had to blink constantly to keep the stinging drops from blurring her vision.

Once inside, Isabella wondered if they'd made a mistake by assuming the hatch led to the engine compartment at all. Inside was a container, some sort of squat cylinder with no visible closures, seams, or other marks. Its featureless brass exterior was marred only by the intersection of the front axle which was apparently also the drive shaft. There was no drive train and the engine, if that's what it was, wasn't separate from the shaft. The shaft ran straight through it.

"I think we'll need to take off the wheels and axle," Isabella said.

"Quite." Next to her, Joseph chewed on one end of his mustache while he considered the engine. Having full conversations while lying on their backs staring straight up was very natural for them. Isabella suspected she'd had more discussions with her father in the workshop than she had in every other room they'd ever occupied at the same time put together. Outside the workshop, Joseph Castel was withdrawn and introspective. Put a tool in his hand and point him toward a piece of machinery, and he could wax eloquent for hours.

Isabella pushed herself back, shooting out from under the carriage on the creeper she'd designed for this sort of work. It had been her first innovation, having found her father's version exceedingly uncomfortable and difficult to maneuver. It had three wheels instead of the four of his, allowing for greater maneuverability with only the slightest kick of one leg.

"We need to jack it up," Isabella said to Brionie.

Miss Riley had a vacant expression on her face which vanished when she heard Isabella's voice. Once again, Isabella found herself the recipient of Brionie's sharp gaze. *What was she thinking about?* It was too much to hope that it was her.

She noticed a large grease stain on the front of her coveralls as she stood up. A few half-hearted wipes told her it was a lost cause. That's what she got for wearing her good coveralls for a teardown. What had possessed her to even do so? Brionie hadn't noticed. It would take more than that to get her attention.

"Jack it up?"

"Yes. The engine is fascinating, but we can't get at it without removing the axle."

Brionie's brow creased slightly. Isabella couldn't tell if she was annoyed or confused. "I don't care about the axle. The engine is the problem."

Isabella nodded. "That's what's so interesting. They seem to be all one unit, which is really unusual." She rubbed her hands together. "I can't wait to crack it open."

"Isabella?" Her father's voice floated out from under the carriage. "Send for Jean-Pierre while we take it out."

"Jean-Pierre? Do you really think that's necessary?"

"I do. By the time he arrives, we should be ready for his opinion."

That was great. The last thing she wanted was that puffed-up bundle of pomposity around while she was trying to impress Brionie Riley. But if her father thought it was necessary, then it probably was. He had a nose for sniffing out demoniac involvement in machinery. While demoniac energy was certainly useful, Isabella was more of a purist. Her devices included as little magical enhancement as possible. She liked to see how far she could get without it. Jean-Pierre, on the other hand, had never met a problem that couldn't be solved with the judicious application of demoniac magic.

She stalked over to the messenger tube, coming down on her heels with a little more force than was absolutely necessary. It was a good thing her shoes were rubber-soled. No one would realize her irritation as she stomped about like a cranky three-year-old. She cranked on the lever to the side of the machine and waited. Finally, a voice issued tinnily from the cone-shaped speaker above the messenger junction.

"Send for Jean-Pierre LaFarge, if you please."

"Yes, Isabella." It was impossible to tell for certain who spoke on the other end. This was an early design of her brother's, one he'd lost interest in after developing it. Sound waves and related devices were of no interest to Isabella. She preferred devices that interacted directly with the world, not ones that passively recorded it. Still, it would have been nice if he'd tinkered further with the messenger tube, if for no other reason than to eliminate the hissing and popping that accompanied the sounds it transmitted.

She turned around and almost ran right into Brionie. Had her reflexes been slightly less sharp, she would have. As it was, they stood almost nose to nose. Brionie's eyes were brown, she noted. They looked like warm hot chocolate, and this close they didn't look nearly as hard as they did when she glared at Isabella from across a room.

"Miss Castel."

Apparently surprise was what had softened Brionie's eyes. She was no longer startled, and now they looked ready to bore straight through her.

"Sorry." Isabella backed up a half pace.

"Who is Jean-Pierre LaFarge? And why do you dislike him so much?"

"Jean-Pierre is my father's partner." Isabella moved to walk past Brionie. The blasted woman moved with her, refusing to allow her to pass. "They went to school together. Apparently he was some sort of prodigy. He's our expert with demoniac energy."

Brionie's lips pursed at the word "demoniac" and Isabella had to wonder if she was one of those with moral objections to the use of the energy. Given the methods she'd used to trap Isabella, that seemed unlikely. So why the disparagement? Many churches sermonized at length about how the evils of demoniac workings corrupted the machines and souls of their users. As far as Isabella was concerned, it was a tool like electricity, if more flexible.

"You don't like him."

"I don't have to like someone to work with them." No, she didn't like Jean-Pierre. His good looks, smooth manner, and inability not to flirt with the fairer sex had nothing to do with it, she told herself. "He's pompous, overbearing and very…French."

"Ah." That seemed to satisfy Brionie. She stepped back and allowed Isabella to pass before accompanying her across the workshop floor. In contrast to Isabella's almost noiseless stride, Brionie's heels clicked neatly along beside her, each step matching Isabella's with unnerving precision. "Lord Sherard thinks the engine uses 'demoniac' energy."

"It must." Isabella heard the slight emphasis on demoniac. There was definitely something going on there. Maybe Isabella wouldn't show Brionie too many of her own inventions, only the purely electric ones. "I don't know how it could work without extensive enhancement. That's why we need to get it out of the carriage to get a closer look at it."

"Very well." Brionie returned to perch on the small stool where she'd been waiting. As Isabella made her way over to the far side of the workshop for more tools, she could barely make out Brionie's last words. "I shall endeavor not to be too impressed by Monsieur LaFarge."

That was encouraging. Isabella whistled as she pulled out everything they needed to hoist the carriage. By the time she and Joseph had freed the strange engine and axle from the carriage, her shoulders cried out for some relief. They placed the entire rig on a nearby workbench. Brionie came over to view the device. She donned white gloves before reaching out to touch it, not seeming to care when their fingertips came back black and sooty.

The lift cranked to life and made its laborious way up to the surface. When it returned, Jean-Pierre LaFarge stood in the middle. As usual, he was immaculate, from the ends of his heavily waxed mustaches to the gleaming tips of his shoes. Isabella suspected that he dealt with demon energy because most of the time he could do so without getting his hands dirty. The only time he deigned to cover up his perfect clothes were when he charged demoniac runes with animal blood.

"Bonjour, all." LaFarge swept down the stairs, hat and cane in one hand. "What do you 'ave for me?" He bent at the waist in a mocking bow toward Isabella. As usual, he gave no indication that he registered her antipathy toward him. While she made every attempt to be civil with him, there were times when his attitude was too much to bear. The sharper side of her tongue came out, usually before she could censor herself.

"Monsieur LaFarge." Isabella refused to give him the familiarity of his first name. They were not friends.

"And who do we 'ave 'ere?" LaFarge bowed low to Brionie. She reached out her hand toward him, which he put to his lips before realizing the filthy state of her gloves. He dropped her hand quickly. A small smile played around the corners of Brionie's mouth. "Mademoiselle, your presence in dis dreary work area brightens it more than a t'ousand gas lamps ever could." The longer he spoke to Brionie, the thicker his accent got until it glopped like cold motor oil from every word.

"Jean-Pierre." Joseph beckoned over him with one hand without looking up from his perusal of the strange engine.

"Mais oui." LaFarge winked at Brionie. "Duty calls." He shrugged the coat from his shoulders and placed it across a bench. His derby hat and mahogany cane joined it. After fishing a monocle out of the pocket of his brilliant green brocade waistcoat, he deigned to join Joseph.

"What do you think, old man?" Joseph drew him closer, one hand on his shoulder to direct LaFarge where he should look. The Frenchman twitched his shoulder away, but not before the damage had been done. A dark smear stood out clearly on the previously immaculate fabric.

Brionie crowded in to gaze over their shoulders as LaFarge donned the monocle. He held out his hand expectantly. When Isabella ignored him, he looked up at her.

"Isabella, a pencil if you please." His voice was reason personified.

She fished around in the pockets of her coveralls until she located a china marker and dropped it in his open hand. It was little more than a nub, but he was lucky to get as much from her. Her gesture was lost on LaFarge. He was already submerged in the work.

Despite herself, she couldn't help but be fascinated as he sketched out runes and lines. What took shape beneath his scribbling marker was complex beyond belief. There was little of the cylinder that wasn't marred by markings when he was done. A definite seam emerged from the marks, though it was written through with runes in multiple places. For once, Isabella wished she could see the demoniac designs. She'd always left that to LaFarge, content to work with pure mechanics. Now, it seemed, she was far out of the loop. Another lens, one that would allow her to see magic, was what she needed. Her brother had made one with LaFarge's help. Attaching it to her goggles would take no more than a few minutes. It was something to consider. But how to do it without asking for LaFarge's help? Maybe her father would be willing to ask him on her behalf.

Brionie had produced a notebook from somewhere and scribbled away busily in it. To Isabella's astonishment, she wrote with her left hand. She didn't notice when Isabella sneaked a peek at her writings. It seemed Miss Riley was transcribing the runes and markings exactly as they were on the cylinder. Or almost exactly. The changes were subtle, but Brionie had altered some of the characters.

"Very impressive," LaFarge said when he finished. "Whoever 'as done this is quite talented. I do not recognize a few of the runes."

It was unusual for LaFarge to admit ignorance of anything. Likely, he'd been stumped by more than a few of the runes. Judging by the ones Brionie had altered in her transcription, it seemed like it might be as high as a fifth. How strange it was, Isabella thought. She herself had problems with reading and writing normal English. The letters seemed to shiver and reshape themselves as she watched them. Her handwriting was serviceable enough to pass without notice, but she tried never to write in front of an audience lest they notice how long it took her to form the words. She never had that problem with numbers, nor it seemed with these runes.

"Can you make out how to open it?" Joseph asked.

"Of course." His brows lowered slightly in affront. "I shall need…" LaFarge stood and crossed to the corner of the workshop he claimed as his own. A high apron went over his shockingly green waistcoat. After a bit of rummaging, he returned with a glass jar of red liquid and a brush.

"Is that…?" Brionie's mouth twisted and she didn't finish the question.

"Blood?" LaFarge smiled broadly, showing more teeth than a shark. "But of course, mademoiselle. It is necessary to charge the runes with blood. Do not fear, this is rat blood. We only want to charge them partway, enough to open the cylinder, not enough to activate the other runes. Somet'ing this complex, it must 'ave a higher grade of blood to engage all of ze inscription."

Brionie seemed doubtful of his assertions. She shook her head once and returned to her notebook. Joseph and Isabella stood back while LaFarge painted over the marks running through the seam. He took his time, painstakingly reconstructing each rune. Finally, he stood back and stared expectantly at the cylinder.

Nothing happened.

"Zut alors." His brows knit together as he glared at the offending cylinder. "Something, she is amiss."

Brionie checked her notebook, then looked back at the painted device. She put the fingertips of her left glove between her teeth and pulled it off. Never letting go of the notebook, she licked one fingertip and sighed before leaning forward. She sketched a quick correction to two of the runes before looking back at her notes. Another lick of the finger, ignoring the specks of rat blood now upon it, and Brionie amended one more rune. Isabella could have sworn her hands were shaking. There was nothing upon Miss Riley's face to betray any discomfort, but the tremor, while barely perceptible, was still there.

The cylinder popped open with a clear clang, like someone had dropped a bell on a stone floor. Brionie snatched her hand back before it could get hit. Her face paled considerably and she backed away a half step before steeling herself. Isabella didn't think the men had noticed. They both leaned forward to get a better view of the device's inner workings.

"Ah!" Twin exclamations issued from each man's throat, Joseph's of disappointment and LaFarge's an excited yell.

"Are you all right?" Isabella kept her voice down, not wanting to draw the men's attention to Brionie's discomfort.

She got a stiff nod for her pains. Miss Riley's lips were clamped together and she breathed harshly through her nose.

"Suit yourself." Isabella shrugged and took a look inside the cylinder. Right away the reason for her father's lack of enthusiasm was obvious. Isabella shared his disappointment. The cylinder's interior was almost as featureless as its exterior. The drive shaft ran straight through it. A gear at either end of the cylinder would serve to turn the shaft, but that gear meshed with nothing.

"Out of the way." LaFarge bent over the interior with his grease pencil. It took him much longer to complete the markings this time. When he was finished, he sat back, mopping his brow on one sleeve. "I 'ave never seen anything comme ça, uh…like dis." He wasn't exaggerating either. When Isabella peered over his shoulder, the interior was covered with grease marks. Not an inch went uninscribed.

"Do you know what it means?"

"This one is beyond even me. Certainement, there are some parts I can make out." He pointed with the nub of a pencil. "For example, dis part drives the shaft. And over dere, it allows for changes in speed based upon the driver's input. Dis area draws power from ze charging cylinder. But the rest." LaFarge shook his head in wonder. "I would love to meet the inventor. 'E is nothing short of genius."

Isabella thought perhaps he was laying it on a little thick. This amounted to little more than magic; there were next to no mechanics here. As far as she was concerned, magic was cheating.

There was warmth at her back, Isabella realized. Brionie stood there, looking over her shoulder and taking more notes. She scribbled furiously, the scratching of her pen loud in Isabella's ear.

"Do you want me to move?"

Brionie shook her head, dividing her attention only between the notebook and the cylinder. Finally, she lowered the pen.

"Thank you, Isabella. Gentlemen. I believe I have what I need. Please reassemble the earl's carriage." She walked back over to her bench and sat, watching them expectantly.

"Can you close the device?" Isabella asked LaFarge.

"Of course I can. It is simply a matter of reversing the runes that opened it." He produced his jar of rat's blood and the paintbrush. Even to Isabella's untrained eyes, the runes he put down seemed slapdash and malformed compared to those he had so recently traced. When he finished, he sat back and waited. Once again, nothing happened.

LaFarge blew out his mustaches in irritation. If he was trying to impress Brionie, so far he wasn't doing a very good job. He muttered to himself in harsh consonants and guttural vowels as he traced a finger over the markings.

"There is the problem," he finally proclaimed. "There is a failsafe. Once ze cylinder is opened, it may not be closed again using a reversal charm." He stood and looked over at Brionie. "I am afraid it will take some time before I will be able to close the engine, if at all. I am désolé, mademoiselle."

A muscle jumped in Brionie's jaw. "That is quite impossible, monsieur. I require the use of the carriage to return to the earl. We have an afternoon appointment." She pulled a pocket watch out of her reticule, opened it, then closed it with a snap that cut through the air. "If I do not leave immediately, I shall be late, and that is unacceptable."

"You can use our carriage to get back," Isabella said. "I'm sure the earl has more than one vehicle."

Brionie ignored her and leaned forward. She snatched the paintbrush from LaFarge's hand and glanced over his runes. What she saw did not please her. She hesitated a moment, then clenched her jaw and moved right up to the engine. With a hand that trembled slightly at first, she applied the brush to the brass cylinder. "You will want to make sure your hands are well removed from the engine," she said.

Isabella yanked her hands out of the way, as did LaFarge and her father.

"...and there." Brionie made one last swipe of the brush, completely obliterating a section of LaFarge's symbols. He opened his mouth to protest. The engine snapped shut with a hollow clang. LaFarge closed his mouth.

"I shall be over here while you reassemble the device." Brionie turned on her heel and marched over to the far side of the shop from where she'd been watching most of the afternoon. Isabella didn't think the others would notice, but the further Brionie got from them and the engine, the less tense she became. By the time she reached the stool, she looked quite at ease. Or as much as she ever did. Her back was still ramrod straight, but that was normal. If the woman ever unbent completely, Isabella would probably go into shock. Millie would have the vapors.

Isabella followed along behind her. "I'd like to take a look at the rest of it. There's some sophisticated work that's been done here."

"I need to leave as soon as possible. I have an appointment."

"Of course you do. And this has nothing to do with the fact that you're terrified by your employer's new toy."

"I am not frightened." Brionie drew herself up to her full height. "I am merely concerned. And I need to be on my way. I shall wait above. Please send Johnson around to wait with me. I expect the horseless will be reassembled with all due haste." She swept over to the lift and waited impatiently, her fingers tapping a rapid tattoo on the top of her thigh.

There was no more to do except let Brionie have her way. Isabella should have been happy to have Brionie's imperious presence out of her shop, and she was. At the same time, disappointment lurked that she hadn't gotten to show Miss Riley any of her own devices. Hopefully there would be more time for that later. So far, this was much more exciting than dancing lessons or picking out silks for a new ball gown. She turned back to where Joseph wrestled with the axle. The real fun hadn't even begun yet.

CHAPTER EIGHT

Two days later found Briar ensconced in a small cab with Isabella. Being in a horse-drawn conveyance after so long dealing with horselesses was no treat. She'd managed to forget the smells associated with the animals until she'd climbed inside. When Isabella had sent round a note saying she'd be by to pick Briar up before lunch the next day, Briar had been less than amused. One of the earl's new collections had arrived and she had been happily sorting and arranging the various papers and books when the poor footman had appeared at her elbow. To her embarrassment, she'd been less than cordial to him.

There she'd been, gloves off and handling a stack of correspondence, tracking the connections she felt through the papers. Typically during this part of the process, she insisted on being undisturbed, but she had informed the staff that she wanted to receive notes from Isabella Castel immediately. The chagrin she felt now was as much because of her ill temper as a result of her own instructions as it was the unwanted thrill she had received handling Isabella's note with unprotected hands.

And now the object of her distraction was crammed right next to her on the small bench seat. One of the earl's carriages would have been much more comfortable, but Isabella had insisted on the cab. Apparently, they were supposed to avoid attracting notice.

Briar shifted on the bench, trying to open some space between them, but she only succeeded in digging her elbow into Isabella's side.

"Are you all right?" Isabella asked. "You've done nothing but fidget since you got in here."

"I am quite fine," Briar said. "There isn't as much space as I'm used to."

"We're going incognito."

"You said that already." Briar stared at Isabella's brilliant orange dress. "Though I fail to understand how you'll avoid notice wearing that."

Isabella chuckled low in her throat; the sound tugged gently at Briar's insides. "I said we're going incognito, not that we're avoiding notice. There's an exquisite amount of difference between the two ideas."

"Is there really?" Briar wondered if she could get Isabella to make that sound again. "Enlighten me, O wise one."

The laugh wasn't low and deep like the chuckle had been. This one was full-blown and surprised. Briar found herself smiling along in delight. When she caught herself, she schooled her features back into something more befitting a sober demeanor, though one corner of her lip refused to be completely tamed.

"They're going to remember someone. What we want to do is make sure their memory is impossible to tie back to us." She looked Briar up and down critically. "Would it have killed you to wear something colorful?"

"This is colorful." She'd carefully followed Isabella's instruction and had picked out a blue dress suitable for being out and about in town. It matched her grey gloves and parasol quite pleasingly. "It's the most colorful frock I own that isn't an evening gown, which would be wholly inappropriate for our excursion."

"There is that. But the dress in no way qualifies as colorful. Maybe if we…" Isabella reached past her and plucked Briar's parasol from where it was looped over the door handle. She replaced it with the orange one that had been lying across her knees. "Give me your gloves."

My gloves? Briar froze, panic racing through her body. *I need those. She can't have them!* "What do you mean?"

Isabella's brow furrowed slightly at her obtuseness. "Those things covering your hands. Take them off."

"I can't." There would be no protective layer between her and the world. Briar would be paralyzed, under constant assault from the traces of people's lives that saturated every inch around them.

"Of course you can." Isabella mimed peeling them off. When Briar mutely shook her head, understanding dawned in her eyes. "You don't want to have your hands exposed in the kind of neighborhood we're heading to, do you?"

Close enough. Briar nodded vigorously.

"Then take mine." Isabella stripped off her virulent orange gloves in two quick motions. She shoved them into Briar's cringing hands. "Go on. I haven't any diseases."

Briar took a deep breath and carefully pulled off her beautiful grey gloves. She passed them reluctantly on to Isabella and stared at the orange gloves she gripped in one trembling hand. Isabella seemed too engrossed in working Briar's gloves on over her hands. Briar's hands were slightly smaller than hers, so it took her a little bit of time.

There's nothing for it. Isabella's gloves slid easily over her hands. Briar closed her eyes, waiting for the inevitable visions. Faint impressions of Isabella donning the gloves on her way out the door skittered through her mind. Flashes of outdoor walks—some in London, others on an estate—came and went from her mind. Then she saw dusty roads and brilliant sun. Poorly constructed clapboard structures lined an unpaved street. Two rough men faced each other, pistols drawn while onlookers observed from areas of shelter.

"What?" Briar came back to herself with a start. The vision was the last thing she'd expected to see. It had looked like one of the more fanciful illustrations she might see in the *Times* about America's Wild West.

"Are you all right?" Isabella removed her hand from Briar's shoulder. Had she been trying to steady her or wake her up? And why did Briar's shoulder tingle so pleasantly?

"You said that already."

Isabella's laugh snorted from her nostrils in equal parts relief and amusement. "Well, are you? You came over all strange for a minute."

"My apologies." Briar smiled to appease Isabella's concern and prevent further questions. "This cab is quite uncomfortable."

"I suppose it is at that." Isabella might have been less than convinced, but she seemed willing to let it go. "I believe we're almost to our destination, so your discomfort will soon be alleviated."

True to her words, the cab stopped shaking and clattering over rough cobbles a few minutes later. The cabbie rapped on the roof and they alighted cautiously. Despite Isabella's words about the kind of neighborhood to which they were heading, they emerged into a pleasant middle class area. While not as splendid as the areas of town she usually frequented, it lacked the unpleasant smells of excrement and rot that overwhelmed the truly rum areas of London. The modest townhomes of red brick that lined each side of the street were packed cheek to jowl. An office building on the corner dwarfed the townhouses in the area, rising four stories to their two. The grey stone gave it an imposing look, as did the pseudo-crenellations that defined the roofline. It gave Briar the impression of an autocratic teacher overseeing rows of schoolchildren.

"Wait for us, my good man," Isabella said to the cabbie, a scrawny man who had developed a permanent hunch from years of driving the hack. He nodded without looking their way and settled the reins over the horse's back.

"Where are we going?" Briar hissed to Isabella as they mounted the office building's stone stairs. She had to admit her grey gloves and parasol looked quite fetching with Isabella's dress. She on the other hand looked like something out of a carnival and a cheap one at that.

"You're worried about Mirabilia, so I thought we should check them out."

"Of course, but this isn't their factory."

"I couldn't find their factory."

"You also had difficulty there?" Relief filled Briar. She had started questioning her research skills when she could unearth nothing about the manufactory's location.

"So I thought we'd ask."

"Have you lost your wits? We don't want anyone to know we're curious. They'll... ah!" She suddenly understood the wisdom of Isabella's plan of going incognito. No one would ever believe Briar would be out and about in such an outfit.

Isabella grinned and nodded once. She opened the door to the building's small foyer. A short register on the wall directed them to the third floor.

The third floor hallway was populated with doorways every ten feet. Etched glass windows in many of the doors announced this company or that corporation. They walked down to the end of the hall without seeing one for Mirabilia.

"Which office are we looking for?" Isabella asked.

"Three-naught-six is what the register said."

Armed with the information, they made their way back up the hall. Briar stopped in front of the only door between offices 304 and 308.

"This must be it." She stared dubiously at the blank door. There was nothing to indicate it was anything other than a janitor's closet.

"Must be." Isabella grabbed the handle, then paused. She looked over at Briar, smiled brightly, took a deep breath, then pulled the door open. She swept into the office beyond as if she owned it. Briar followed along in her wake, trying to match the confidence Isabella projected.

"Ladies!" A man behind a small desk tried to finish the bite of his sandwich, wipe his mouth, and leap up all at the same time. He looked like the personification of the concept of accountant. A receding hairline combined with thick glasses that reduced his eyes to the size of almonds gave him the unfortunate appearance of the naked mole rat Briar had once seen on display at the natural history museum in Suffolk. His jerky response to their intrusion resulted in his collapse back into the chair. He coughed out the mouthful he'd tried to inhale into a handkerchief which he then stowed in his waistcoat pocket. "May I help you? Whose office are you looking for?"

"Why yours, of course." Isabella laughed, a high brittle sound not at all like the warm chuckles she'd produced in the cab. "This is the main office of Mirabilia Carriageworks, is it not?"

"It's Mirabilia Manufacturing now."

"Of course it is." Isabella waved off the correction. "My ladies' garden club is *so* interested in your horseless carriages. We'd like to book a tour for your manufacturing facilities."

"I'm afraid that's impossible."

Isabella drew back, her hand pressed to her chest before stooping forward like a particularly garish hawk. She peered at the nameplate on his desk, then back at him. "Mr. Atwater, we simply must view your facilities. If it's a matter of cost, that won't be a problem, will it, Mildred?"

With a start, Briar realized Isabella was addressing her. She assumed a sour expression. "If we must."

"She's our treasurer. We can barely pry even a farthing from her grasp, unless it's for perennials. Still, it's why we voted her in. No one watches our money like Mildred does." Poor Mr. Atwater nodded, looking very confused. His gaze was pinned on Isabella, similar to the way a small rodent watched a raptor in full stoop. "So money is no issue. How much will it be for…" Isabella looked away from Mr. Atwater and he relaxed visibly. "How many of the ladies were interested?"

"Twenty-seven, I believe." Briar considered for a moment. "No, twenty-eight. Millicent had been on the fence, but she has decided she'd like to come. 'Twill be twenty-nine if her husband decides to join us."

"So we'll say twenty-nine, including us, of course. What do you say to that, Mr. Atwater?"

"St-still impossible, my lady." He swallowed hard, Adam's apple bobbing crazily among the folds of his neck. "No one is allowed to visit. Trade secrets, you know."

Isabella pinned him back to his seat with her glare, then seemed to relent and turned away. She wandered around the front of the office, peering at the sparse decor, lips pursed. Briar watched her, breath half-held wondering what she would try next. This side of Isabella was not exactly unexpected. It rather reminded Briar of the Isabella she saw at parties, though this one was much more forceful.

"I have it!" Isabella whirled around in a dramatic swirl of orange silk. "We'll simply have your founder visit our garden club! It's genius, isn't it, Mildred?"

Briar hoped her nod was convincing.

"I'm afraid Mr. Holcroft doesn't do appearances, madam." Mr. Atwater pushed himself to his feet. "He hasn't the time, too busy running the company and devising new inventions. Now, I must ask you to leave and not to return without an appointment. I must finish my lunch." As he said the last, he wilted back into his chair, his backbone having run its very short course.

"Very well, then." Isabella sniffed audibly. She swanned over to Briar and linked their arms together. "But do not think we shall forget your intransigence. Our husbands shall hear about it, shan't they, Mildred?"

"Oh, yes."

Propelled smartly along by Isabella's arm through hers, Briar hastened to keep pace with her. Their footsteps sounded almost as one across the bare floors of the office; they were muffled into next to nothingness when they hit the carpeted floor of the hallway. Briar tried to reclaim her arm, but Isabella was having none of it.

"Keep walking," she hissed. "Is he watching?"

The thought hadn't occurred to Briar. Now that they'd left the office, she'd assumed they could drop the charade. She sneaked a glance back over her shoulder. Mr. Atwater was indeed watching them. When he caught her eye, he disappeared back into the office, closing the door quietly behind him.

"Not anymore," Briar whispered back.

Even with the reassurance, Isabella refused to relinquish her hold upon Briar. She marched them down the stairs, out the front door and into the waiting hack, refusing to drop her facade of outraged haughtiness until they were well away from the office building.

"That was exciting!" Isabella said through delighted laughter. She squeezed Briar's arm one last time and finally let go. "Not as informative as I'd hoped, but better than nothing."

"I suppose." Briar was less amused. "Mildred?"

"What? It was perfect for you." Isabella's face split open in a wide grin that Briar had trouble not returning, irritated though she was. "When you make that one face, you're most assuredly a Mildred."

Briar wrinkled her brow and looked Isabella straight in the eye. "What face is that?"

"The one you're making now is pretty close. Tilt your chin up a bit and straighten your back, and you'll be right there."

She had to be teasing, thought Briar. This was what people did to each other when they got along, or so she'd observed. Her opportunities to be this close to anyone else were limited. The only one she ever teased was Imogene, though she feared that one day soon the girl would be too old for such a level of familiarity.

"You need to loosen up, Brionie," Isabella said. "You're wound tighter than the springs in my workshop. Too much more of that, and you'll snap."

"I am not wound too tightly, Miss Castel." The use of the given name she used in the mortal plane warmed her. Even Imogene called her Miss Riley.

"See, right there. You should really call me Isabella. We'll be spending a lot of time together, and I think we know too much to keep calling the other 'Miss.'"

She had a point. "Very well. Isabella." At Isabella's encouraging nod, Briar took a deep breath and continued: "I would like it very much if you would call me Briar, then."

"Briar?" Isabella cocked her head to one side, eyes twinkling. "As in a bramble? Something prickly?"

"Yes. It's what my mother calls me." Only because it was the name Carnélie had given her, but Briar was aware the name would be considered highly unusual here.

"Very well, Briar." Isabella gave the appearance of tasting the name as it passed over her lips. Distracted, Briar couldn't help but watch her mouth closely, thrilled at the hint of Isabella's tongue hiding behind white teeth. "I have to say, it fits."

"Of course you do. And I have to say, Isabella fits the girl I see at balls, not the one who crawls around in her father's workshop."

Isabella lifted her shoulders, then let them fall. "We can't all be what we're expected to be. The world would be a boring place indeed."

Briar didn't miss the implication. She knew she seemed boring, both by the standards of the Isabella she saw at parties and the Isabella who worked with machinery and broke into people's homes at night. That was fine. Boring was better an option by far than chaos.

They passed the rest of the ride in silence that no longer felt awkward or strained. Isabella was a reassuring presence at her side.

"You should come in," Briar said when they arrived back at the earl's townhome. "We still have much to discuss. I'll ask Johnson to take you home when we are done."

* * *

The suggestion seemed like a good idea to Isabella, and she counted it as a victory of sorts that it was a suggestion and not an order. She followed Briar through the house, taking it all in. She'd been here before, to be certain, but everything looked so much different in the light of day. Servants bustled here and there, never getting in their way, but always on the business of keeping a large household running. Her own home looked positively rundown in comparison to this gleaming, spotless jewel.

The library was a little different than the last time she'd been here. The table upon which Briar had placed the box to entice her was now covered with papers and books. A desk not far away was even more overfilled with paper. It felt dusty in here. She could see gleaming motes dancing in the sunlight coming through a crack in the room's heavy curtains, but not a piece of it marred any of the library's surfaces. It was as if the dust dared not settle in Briar's domain. Isabella couldn't blame it; she could barely conceive of settling here either. Of course, the last time she tried, she'd been held in a cage of magic.

"I know we didn't get all the information you wanted," Isabella said, taking a careful seat on an old chair that managed to look comfortable without being ragged. "I think we have a good start of it, however."

"We still have no idea where the factory is," Briar said, her voice sharp with frustration. "Whatever they're doing to create those damnable engines, it'll be happening there. The gloves, if you please?" She pointed to Isabella's hands. "We need the grimoire they're using. That will tell us what they're up to."

"Grimoire?" Isabella dropped the grey gloves in Briar's outstretched hand. "I haven't heard that word before."

"No? Surely your Monsieur LaFarge uses a grimoire."

Isabella shook her head to the contrary. "And he's not my Monsieur LaFarge."

"He must have something he uses to look up his...spells, for lack of a better term."

"He has an old notebook. Sometimes he uses it to copy out of, and sometimes he makes notes in it."

"That's his grimoire. Every practitioner of infernal magic has one."

"Do you?"

"Of course not." Briar seemed highly offended. She looked more like a Mildred than when she first joined Isabella in the cab. "I'm not a magician. I am an archivist."

The denial stopped Isabella cold. She stared at Briar. Was this an attempt at humor? If it was, there was no evidence of it on Briar's face or in her bearing, but then the woman was almost impossible to read. "Surely you jest," Isabella finally said slowly. She still watched Briar for any clue as to what she might be thinking. "I've seen you do magic. As far as I know, it was demoniac magic."

"Oh, that." Briar had the grace to look a little embarrassed. "I don't think you can really count that. It's merely something I picked up in my studies." She glared at Isabella when she opened her mouth. "As an archivist."

Whatever moment they had shared in the cab was over. Isabella had no idea what had changed, but the air between them was almost glacial now.

"At least we have a name," said Isabella, eager to leave the discussion of grimoires behind them. "Perhaps you could go from there?"

"Me?"

"I'm afraid so. I can break into whatever place you want me to, but I need to know where that is. You're the archivist. Presumably you know records. See what they say about Mr. Holcroft, head of Mirabilia Manufacturing."

There was no question that Briar Riley was a deeply intelligent woman, yet she had some odd blind spots. Clearly, she was much more comfortable around books and papers than she was about people; checking the records was an obvious next step. Even Isabella knew there were records. Her father had applied for more than one patent over the years, though he usually let LaFarge apply on his behalf. That would be one place to start, but she knew her own limitations. The records were there, but Briar was much better equipped to search through them than she was.

"Yes, the records." Briar thought about it for a moment. "The company is leasing that office. There will be records of that. I could talk to the landlord."

Isabella nodded encouragingly. "The office was awfully strange, was it not?"

"A little small, perhaps," Briar said, her tone vague. Her eyes still looked inward, mentally pressing forward with the question of records.

"Small. And Atwater was the only occupant. There were almost no personal effects aside from his, and those seemed to have been placed there to give the illusion of occupancy."

"Wasn't there another room?"

"An empty one. I could see through the crack of the door, when I was looking around. Atwater is supposed to be functioning as the clerk, but there's no one else in there. I don't doubt all he does all day is eat lunch and take the mail. Shouldn't an organization the size of Mirabilia have employees to pay? Where were the records? I saw no boxes or cabinets for files when we were there."

"No employees?" That had gotten Briar's attention. Her back was ramrod straight again. "That's impossible."

"Either they have no employees, or they have ones they aren't paying." Both ideas were beyond comprehension. "Perhaps there is a payroll office at the factory. And accountants and receivables." Having an office solely as a place to accept mail made no sense at all. Mirabilia was paying a man to do nothing or at least next to it from what Isabella could tell. "I need to take a closer look at the office. Tonight perhaps."

CHAPTER NINE

The large leather-bound volume already smelled musty. Briar supposed it was the fate of all government records locked away on a shelf and used by precious few. Not that their keepers made access easy. Only the Earl of Hardwicke's title had opened up the small room to her without an appointment weeks hence. She'd heard the London County Council was acquiring other buildings. Spring Gardens was much too small for their purposes, as evidenced by the cramped records office. The reading room consisted of two tables and a window where one might ask the clerks to procure relevant documents. She had the luxury of being the only one using the room, though minor functionaries had been in and out of the office all day on this errand or that task. They frequently left with arms full of ledgers and documents and only rarely seemed to return them. That did not bode well for her search. Neither did the impending move. In her experience, people used a change of quarters as an excuse to shed themselves of materials they no longer deemed useful. Briar hoped they had a trained archivist to assist them; otherwise important information might be lost for all time.

She leafed through page upon page of incorporation documents, trying to determine when Mirabilia had first come to life as a company. It was no easy task; London had hundreds, if not thousands of new businesses opening every year. Briar only had the barest idea when Mirabilia might have incorporated.

She sighed heavily and turned another page. Normally the task would have wholly occupied her as she bored in to discover a single nugget of information that few other people could locate. The chase thrilled her and made her feel alive. Today, she would have given her eyeteeth to be anywhere else. The room was too small and the walls too close. The gas lamp on the wall didn't give off nearly as much light as it should have.

How many more pages did she have left in the volume? Briar sneaked a look and sighed again. Too many. But there was only one way to go, and that was forward. She had her own part in the task at hand, as surely as Isabella did.

Isabella Castel. Now there was someone worth contemplating. It was funny. Two weeks ago, Briar would have politely told anyone who asked that Isabella was a simpering twit who had no more brains than a particularly dim chicken. And yet, there was far more to the woman than she could possibly have credited. Not only was she mechanically gifted, but she had the impertinence to bedevil the upper crust and avoid the authorities in a series of daring burglaries. Briar could have forgiven herself for missing all of that in view of Isabella's prodigious gifts for dissembling, but she prided herself on her ability to read others. It was how she made her own living, after all. She had powers granted to no one else, as far as she knew, to read objects and connect them with their owners.

Briar had been too willing to believe the worst in Isabella. It was the only explanation, and the faint burn of shame settled upon her cheeks as she contemplated it. It behooved her to do better.

The day passed by slowly as she checked record after record, but with no luck. Mirabilia Carriageworks was real; she'd seen the horseless they built. If not for that, she would doubt its very existence. They appeared nowhere, not in the tax records, nor in the incorporation records, nor even in the insurance atlases. Either the company was exceedingly new, or they were taking care to do business under a different name.

She was going through records of industrial building licenses for the previous year when the clerk from behind the window approached her.

"It is time to leave, Miss Riley. We're closing down for the evening."

There were no windows in the room and no way of telling the time since the only clock's hands had been showing 7:30 for the entire time she'd been there.

"Thank you for your assistance, sir." Regretfully, Briar closed the file of licenses. She was no closer to locating Mirabilia's manufactory. Perhaps Isabella would have better luck with an evening visit to their office. "At what time do you open tomorrow?"

"We shall be open at precisely nine o'clock."

"And will you hold this file for me?"

"Very well." He drew a watch from one pocket and flipped open the top.

Briar took the hint and gathered her materials. "Thank you again," she said on her way out the door. "I shall be back on the morrow."

"Very well, Miss Riley."

Though the morning had been sunny when Briar entered Spring Gardens, the day had taken a decided turn for the worse while she'd been indoors. Instead of spring sunshine, a cool drizzle greeted her on her way out of the building. It was barely more than a mist, but the rain coated her quickly, introducing a chill into her bones with stunning rapidity. The stone buildings around her were rendered even darker and more depressing by their coating of rain. The skies were almost black with the onset of evening; a faint light remained only in the western corner, and that too would disappear soon.

The night would be perfect for burgling, Briar thought. Isabella would be pleased. With the rain, no one would tarry outside or look up if they had the misfortune of needing to leave the warm confines of their homes. The wind came up, driving heavier drops of rain before it, and Briar ducked her head, trying to avoid a face full of cold wetness. She was only partially successful.

She stepped closer to the curb and raised her hand to hail a cab, keeping an eye out for carriages. It had been raining long enough for significant puddles to have accumulated. She tried not to look too closely at the trash and filth that created an unappetizing skim on top of the water. If a carriage went through that at speed, she would be covered in it. An umbrella would be very convenient, but there had been no sign of this weather when she'd left the earl's home. Nor had she planned on spending the entire day immersed in dusty records, and her stomach was rumbling its pique. Neither situation should have been overly vexing, but with nothing to show for the day's work, she could feel a dark mood descending upon her. She only hoped Isabella would have better luck.

* * *

It felt strange to be out without her rig, and the false mustache upon her upper lip itched abominably. The coarse horsehair had seemed like a good idea at the time, but Isabella had to force her hand down once again to keep from scratching at it and ripping away large chunks. It had made sense not to come out in her Spring-Heeled Jack gear when she'd first conceived her plan. The last thing she needed was the police investigating something here and tracking it back to her and Briar's visit. Not to mention, this was a completely different type of break-in. All she needed here was a convincing disguise and her lock-picking tools.

The street was dark enough, and the rain that had shrouded London since early afternoon continued to fall. She'd seen no one since she'd prudently parked the carriage two streets over. The heavy coat she wore over the suit of rumpled tweed kept the cold spring rain from chilling her too much. Her breath wreathed her head before being swept into nothingness by insistent drops. Her head was more or less protected by her shabby bowler. It was a good thing there would be no one in the offices; if she took off her hat indoors as manners indicated she ought to, her hair would spill out for all to see. All the false mustaches in the world wouldn't save her disguise then.

At least the hat sheltered her glasses from being speckled with raindrops. She'd removed the lenses from the goggles she wore with her rig and transferred them to a pair of spectacle frames. One allowed her to see in the dark, the other would highlight where objects had been recently moved, bringing disturbances in dust or recent scratches on hard surfaces into bright contrast. It was unlikely she'd need any of the other lenses, and they looked odd on the glasses. The point was to blend in as much as possible and avoid detection.

The office building was ahead of her on the left. Fortunately, there were only two streetlamps on this block, and both were at opposite ends of the street. As she unhurriedly mounted the stairs in front, she was pleased to see an abundance of shadows in which to hide herself as she tinkered with the door's locking mechanism.

It was a good thing, too, as the lock, while exceedingly simple, proved stiff and unyielding. As Isabella tried to muscle the tumblers into place, she wondered if she'd have to go back home to get her jump rig after all and look for a way down from the roof. She should have brought it and left it in the carriage just in case.

Were those footsteps approaching? Isabella redoubled her efforts on the lock while straining her ears to listen over the ever-present sound of rain hitting cobblestones. Yes, those were definitely footfalls.

Should she melt back into the shadows of the small exterior entryway or continue fighting with the lock in hopes that it would open?

If you have time to wonder, then you have no time at all. Althea's words rang in her head. Decision made, Isabella heaved at the lock. The resulting click of tumblers finally giving way was the sweetest sound she'd heard since the last time she'd taken a woman in her arms and made her gasp aloud from their kisses. She opened the door barely wide enough to squeeze through and closed it softly behind her. The small foyer was even darker than the outer entry had been and she hid herself out of sight around the corner.

Footsteps mounted the stairs. Isabella's pulse hammered in her throat, threatening her ability to draw a full breath. Whoever was out there stopped under the overhang. She couldn't see much as she pressed herself deeper into the corner. All that was visible was a shoulder glistening dully in what little light there was outside.

The brim of a hat was suddenly lit from below by warm light and a small cloud of smoke drifted past the door's window. All was dark again for a moment, then that warm light glowed again as whoever was out there lit another match. The glow didn't go away completely this time, but dimmed almost into nothingness as small clouds periodically rolled past.

Isabella sagged back against the corner. It was just a bloke who'd found some shelter under which to smoke his pipe. She stayed put, waiting for him to leave before taking the risk of crossing the foyer. She certainly couldn't chance him glancing in at the wrong moment and seeing a shadowy figure disappearing up the stairs of a supposedly empty building.

Exactly how long does it take to smoke a pipe? Isabella wanted to get the night's activities underway, to get this over with. Her father smoked a pipe. If she recalled correctly, he could take quite some time with it, letting it go dark and relighting it again. If he was involved in something as he smoked, he might relight the pipe four or five times.

Fortunately, whoever the man was on the building's front stoop, he wasn't her father. There was no telltale light from another match, and eventually he wandered off.

Isabella didn't wait to see if he'd return. When he hit the bottom step, she was already halfway up the stairs to the second storey. A moment later she was on the third floor. The long hall with nothing but doors to relieve the empty walls was disconcerting at this time of night. It would have been nice if Briar had come along, for company against what might lurk in the shadows more than anything else. The shadows weren't impenetrable, not when she wore the glasses, but they were still there and she still felt vulnerable and exposed without her suit.

Her pace quiet but quick, Isabella was down the hall to 306 in very little time. The lock on this door was slightly trickier than the one to the building, but it was a good deal less tight. Of course, it hadn't been sitting in a rainy London evening. Still, it was nothing Isabella hadn't seen before and she was able to pop it open without too much thought or effort.

The deserted office beyond was as eerie as the hallway outside had been and felt even more desolate. The furniture, with its few personal items scattered about on the desk's top or on top of the sparsely filled bookshelves, couldn't disguise the layer of dust glowing softly through the lens of her spectacles.

The faster she did this, the sooner she would be gone. Making sure the door was locked behind her, Isabella swallowed, then crossed to the desk. As she'd suspected, there was very little inside it. Mr. Atwater had an interest in penny serials, it seemed. One drawer was stuffed full with them, a stack of the cheaply-made chapbooks crammed in along the edges. He worked very hard in his capacity for Mirabilia.

Isabella snorted softly at the unprepossessing Atwater, though she wasn't surprised in the least. Another drawer held little beyond a dozen or more carefully sharpened pencils. They were all the same length, and none looked to have been used. The contents of the remaining drawers were as useless in helping determine where the factory was located. Maybe there was a secret drawer or panel. Isabella had come across many of those in her exploits through the homes of the rich and well connected. She checked everywhere she could, knocking on paneling, checking the widths of all the drawers, and trusting her glasses to alert her of any scrapes in the wood where there shouldn't be any, all to no good effect. She sat back in the chair. Nothing.

The only other place to check was the other room, the one she suspected was empty. And she was right. The inner office held nothing, not even a decoy desk and chair like Atwater occupied in the outer office. Dust lay thick upon the floor and window sills, the only disturbances arising from her feet as she walked through. A small closet in the corner raised her anticipation until she opened the door and found it as empty as the rest of the place.

Back in the outer office, Isabella made one last sweep. In desperation, she checked behind the two framed pictures on the wall, one a cheap lithograph of a scene upon the Thames and the other an even cheaper engraved copy of Dante Gabriel Rossetti's *Ecce Ancilla Domini*. The cheap lithograph and insipid picture seemed out of place in the featureless office, and for a moment Isabella thought she was on to something. It proved for naught. The only secrets hidden behind the painting were chipped plaster and peeling paint. There was nothing to be found there.

Defeated, Isabella let herself out the door, taking care to lock it behind her. She hoped Briar had been luckier in her endeavors than she had been in hers. They were to meet for brunch the next day, and while she was looking forward to seeing the serious archivist, she was not looking forward to bearing bad news. Briar might be entertaining to irritate, but this affair was one she took seriously. Some harmless flirtation in the form of teasing and needling was far different from the very palpable fear Briar held for the so-called engine in the Mirabilia carriage.

As Isabella unlocked the building's front door, she happened to glance down at the floor. A small bundle had been placed in the corner. It was covered with brown paper and held together with twine. As she looked closer, Isabella realized there was an address on the top of the package.

Her breath quickened slightly with excitement. *Can it be? Surely not.* Despite her admonition, Isabella couldn't help but feel the uncoiling of butterflies within her belly. If it was, Briar would be very pleased, and there was nothing the matter with that. She picked up the package and explored its sides with sensitive fingertips. Isabella recognized the edges of envelopes or the like beneath the brown wrapper. She blinked at the writing until the words settled down. It wasn't an address she knew, but it was a London one. The return address, on the other hand, was to Room 306, though there was no indication of the company's name. Atwater did do at least one job. He was forwarding Mirabilia's mail somewhere.

This was it. This was what she'd been looking for. What Briar had been looking for. This was their next step to finding the elusive Mirabilia factory. If they were very lucky, the address might even be to the elusive manufactory. Isabella committed the address to memory, then put the package back down, taking great pains to leave it exactly as she'd found it. She let herself out into the cold London night.

CHAPTER TEN

The dining room certainly wasn't as large as the earl's, but it had a homey feeling Briar never experienced in her employer's house. The household's singular footman stood behind her chair. At least she suspected he was the only one. His hands trembled a bit with a palsy when he cleared away her dishes. Briar felt for him. He really should have been the one sitting down, not her. Behind Joseph Castel's chair was the house's butler. He wasn't as elderly as the footman and his back was so straight it was almost painful to look at, but he too could have been happily retired.

Still, brunch had been delightful. Viscount Sherard was a charming conversationalist, if slightly vague on occasion. It was as if he retreated into his head to retrieve a fact and became interested in something else he found there. Briar was the same way when she ventured into the stacks of any library, so she couldn't fault him. Althea Castel never failed to bring him back on task with good-natured prodding.

Through it all, Isabella was somewhat subdued. Oh, she was congenial enough when a question was directed at her, but she didn't volunteer much.

"How did you come to be in the Earl of Hardwicke's service?" Althea asked.

Briar dabbed at her lips with the serviette from her lap to buy some time. "I heard through a third party that he needed someone to arrange some papers." She shrugged. "I applied for the position. Based on my references and a demonstration of my capabilities, he saw fit to take me on."

"A third party, is it?" Althea leaned forward intently. "Doesn't one usually advertise for this sort of position in the paper? So you didn't find out from an advert?"

"I was out of the country when he was advertising, Lady Sherard. From what I heard he wasn't pleased with the quality of his applicants. I was lucky."

"Out of the country? I've done some traveling myself. Where were you?"

"In the Swiss Alps." Althea drew breath to ask another question and Briar kept going before she could ask it. The woman knew how to pull every drop of information from somebody. Isabella had the grace to look slightly embarrassed on her mother's behalf. "I was conducting research at a monastery. You'd be surprised what monks will hold onto."

She'd definitely been surprised. For a sect that railed against the evils of infernal magic from the pulpit almost every Sunday, the Catholics had an extensive trove of books and manuscripts on the subject squirreled away in dozens of abbeys and convents all over the Continent and beyond.

"Mother has done some traveling as well," Isabella said when Althea took a breath for another question. "She is American, you know."

"I did not." Briar turned to inspect Althea as if she could divine her American-ness from her looks alone. "You do not have any of it upon your speech." American English was clipped and nasal compared to what she heard here, though both were an improvement over the guttural harshness of the language of her mother's people.

"I've been here for many years now," Althea said. She smiled conspiratorially. Briar could see Isabella's grin in the curl at the corners of her mouth. "I've found the English take me a lot more seriously if I sound like them."

"It only really comes out when she's angry," Isabella said.

"And I'm sure you rarely hear it then," Briar said much too seriously. "I cannot envision you taxing your mother the least little bit."

A snort from the end of the table brought all eyes upon the viscount, who was staring studiously at his plate as though it were the most interesting thing in the world. He delicately speared a remaining portion of ham into his mouth and chewed busily.

"Hmm?" he said, as if only now realizing they were watching him.

"Izzy may have been an occasional handful when she was younger," Althea said after fixing her husband with a mock stare that he ignored. "These days, she's a credit to her mother."

"I'm certain she is," said Briar. It was her turn to ask questions. "Which part of America are you from?"

"Heavens, aren't you aware that the only part of America that exists is New York City?"

"I've done my research, madam."

"Of course you have. I'm from all over, I'm afraid. I grew up on the east coast, then spent some time in California. Eventually, I met Isabella's father and moved back here with him."

"Is that so?" Briar was skilled enough at evasion to recognize it in Althea. There was more to the viscountess than met the eye.

On that note, Althea wiped her mouth and gestured to the footman that he should take her plate away. "I'm sure you two have plans, so I shall take my leave of you. Dear?"

Joseph harrumphed and waited for the butler to pull out his chair. "Of course, my darling."

Arm in arm, they left the dining room.

"Your parents are very nice."

Isabella smiled a bit. "They're…unconventional."

"I suppose." Maybe on this plane. Briar thought it might have been nice to have parents like Isabella's; in that moment, she envied her fiercely. "Did you have a good night?"

It was Isabella's turn to wipe her mouth and wait for the butler to pull her chair away from the table. "Why don't we go for a walk?"

"Very well."

There was a park not far from Isabella's house. The day was yet cool, though with the sun shining and no clouds in the sky, it seemed likely that would change soon. The effects of the previous night's rain lingered as a slight heaviness to the air. The damp seemed to permeate everything, though the grass was greening up nicely. Early spring flowers dotted the precise beds at the edge of the park's patchy brown lawns. They had company, though not enough people were out for a stroll that they couldn't speak without being overheard.

Isabella nodded at an older couple strolling slowly along. When there was no one within earshot, she pulled a scrap of paper from her reticule.

"Is this…?" Briar couldn't finish the sentence for excitement. After the previous day's defeat of her research skills, she had despaired of finding that dratted factory.

"It is." Isabella beamed at her. "I almost missed it, but there was a package of mail to be forwarded in the foyer. This is the address the mail is being forwarded to."

"You are positively brilliant!" It was a near thing, but Briar almost grabbed Isabella to give her a most undignified kiss upon the cheek. She restrained herself in time and instead settled for gripping her shoulder and pulling her in for a half embrace. Almost as soon as she swept her up, Briar remembered where they were and let Isabella go. This was no place to be so unseemly.

"I could be brilliant more frequently if I were assured of that kind of response." Isabella's smile was as wide as Briar had ever seen, and her eyes fairly sparkled with excitement. The overall effect was enchanting. Briar's heart sped up a tick in response.

Is she flirting with me? That seemed unlikely. Isabella's status would not permit her to dally with other women. More likely she was teasing Briar again. Yes, that seemed much more reasonable. Even with the rationalization, Briar couldn't stop the color from rising in her cheeks. What was it about Isabella that had her blushing all over the place? No one outside her family was able to break her composure so easily or so frequently. Her mother and sisters did it with unspeakably crude statements, but Isabella did so simply with teasing and something that treaded dangerously close to familiarity.

"I shall keep that in mind for the next time." Briar meant it as a prim put-down, but even to her ears the response sounded flirtatious. "What I mean is that you need to be equally brilliant again to be assured of any reward." That was worse. Her face was completely red now and the tips of her ears felt like they must be glowing. Was she flirting back? Surely not! Not that Isabella wasn't attractive, she certainly was, but Briar had no time for that type of distraction.

"Then I shall make sure to impress you upon a regular basis."

"What is our next step?" If she didn't get the conversation back on track, Briar was either going to burst into mortified flames or lose her shroud. At this point, she thought the flames might be the preferable option.

"You're asking me?" Isabella sounded surprised. "You're the one holding all the cards. This is your crusade."

"And yet you have the expertise. If this address is for the manufactory, how do we break in and retrieve our mysterious inventor's grimoire?"

"Do you mean that?"

"I do. You are in charge of this stage of the operation."

"And afterward? What happens once we have the grimoire?"

Briar thought about it. Their original agreement had been Isabella's aid in finding out what the problem was with the Mirabilia horseless carriages. Once Briar had the grimoire in her hands, she would be able to ascertain what that was. They would have no further reason to work together, a prospect that did not please her nearly as much as it ought to have. "I suppose," she said slowly, "that our bargain will be concluded. I shall give you the photographs and the negative, and we shall trouble each other no more."

"Very well." Isabella's smile was gone. Briar couldn't recall the last time she'd seen the girl look so serious. "Then I'll look into the address and investigate the factory if that's where it is. Once I am assured of the comings and goings, I will break in and steal the book you need. If it's not at the factory, I'll see what more I can find there."

"And I shall accompany you."

Isabella's eyebrows climbed so high up her forehead that Briar wondered if they might keep going. "You'll do nothing of the sort!"

"Of course I shall. We don't know what you might come up against in that factory. You may require my assistance."

"And what sort of experience do you have with second-storey work?" Isabella's hissed question sounded like the start of a diatribe, but she cut it off when the crunch of shoes on gravel heralded a pair of women wandering toward them from the opposite direction. They smiled their way and Briar responded in kind. "This isn't the kind of thing you can research in a book," Isabella said when they were once again out of earshot. "You'll get in the way. I can't do what I need to if I also have to worry about you."

"I don't doubt that you have much more experience in burglary than I do, but you have no experience with infernal forces like I do. You will need me."

"If I truly am in charge, like you said I was, then you'll have to resign yourself to waiting for me to do my work."

An angry response on her tongue, Briar drew herself up to deliver it, then stopped. Isabella was right. Briar had told her she was in charge not even a moment earlier. She had to trust Isabella could handle it. So far, she'd been given no reason to assume Isabella wouldn't be able to. And yet…

"Very well, but I wish to be present for any of the preparatory work that you think would be appropriate."

Her capitulation deflated Isabella, who looked to have been preparing her own retort. "That sounds very reasonable," she said stiffly. "But no more than that."

"I believe I can live with that."

"Very well then. The next step is to find a location where we can watch the factory. Once I've found that, I'll let you know. You can come along while I engage in surveillance of the property. That will likely take a few days. Once I'm confident that I will be undisturbed when I go in, I'll retrieve that grimoire."

CHAPTER ELEVEN

The factory was in one of the many industrial areas that had sprung up on the southern side of the Thames. Isabella was glad she insisted Briar wear something more appropriate for the area. Tall stacks belched coal smoke all around them, and every surface was coated with a layer of dark grit. She had to grin at the way Briar tried in vain to keep from brushing against some of the more obviously blackened surfaces. Her fastidious ways did little to keep her tattered skirts clean.

They stopped in front of a ramshackle rooming house across from the factory's front entrance. It wasn't yet dinner time, but a stream of men and women passed to and fro through the house's doors. They were as shabby or worse than Briar and Isabella in their disguises as working women. Perhaps she'd miscalculated, Isabella thought. If anything, their clothing wasn't shabby enough, though both of her hems were dotted with thin spots where the dye was worn completely away. But if they'd looked much more penniless, she'd worried they might be turned away as unable to pay. Apparently, she needn't have been so concerned.

A round woman in her middle years pinned them with a stare so sharp it was nearly aggressive when they pushed their way past the heavy glass doors. She leaned on the massive desk that ran the length of the back wall.

"And what d'we have here, then?"

"We need to rent a room." Isabella slouched against the desk as if exhausted. "What do ya got?" She was proud of her American accent, having been able to practice it with her mother. She doubted she would have sounded out of place in America, though the woman behind the desk seemed less impressed.

"Rent is by the week and up front." Without breaking her gaze on them, she leaned back to retrieve a packet of mail from the long row of cubbies behind her and passed it to a man waiting at the end of the counter. "I won't have any of my tenants jumpin' out on their bill." She eyed Briar up and down. "I also don't rent by the hour, so none of that in my place. This is a proper establishment, d'ye understand me? Rate's five shillings a week."

"We get it." Isabella gestured to Briar, who matched the landlady's glare with one of her own. It was a close thing, but Briar might have met her match. Isabella didn't think she could match the older woman's hardness, though she gave it her best.

Briar took care not to open her purse too far as she counted coins out onto the desk's peeling surface. It was a prudent measure in a place like this, and Isabella approved, but she still wished Briar would be a little more casual.

"Plus two against damages."

A muscle jumped in the corner of Briar's jaw, but she counted out two more coins to match the five on the counter.

"Names." The woman opened the register and pulled out a battered fountain pen from somewhere beneath the counter.

"Madge Tillman," Isabella said. "And that's Connie Brewster."

"Connie can't speak for herself?"

"'Fraid not." Isabella leaned forward conspiratorially. "She's dumb. Can't speak a word."

The woman's face made a very strange contortion, part pity, another part contempt, and something else Isabella couldn't identify. "Welcome to the Padgett Arms," she said loudly.

Briar winced and rubbed her ear. She hadn't been happy when Isabella had decreed she wouldn't be able to talk, but her accent identified her as wellborn the second she opened her mouth. Her attempt at a Cockney accent had been terrible and her American impression worse. Besides, the facade of being mute made it less likely that she would treat someone to the rough side of her tongue and give them away.

"She's only mute," Isabella said. "She hears just fine."

The landlady grunted. "I'm puttin' you in two-twelve."

"Does that have a view of the street? Connie feels better when she can see the road."

With pursed lips, one eyebrow cocked sardonically, the woman looked up from where she laboriously filled out the register. Her letters were childlike, but legible. "And I suppose a view of the cobbles helps with her… affliction, then?" At Isabella's nod she made a show of shaking her head. "Room three-thirteen then. It only has one bed."

"That's fine. We made do with less on the way over."

The woman grunted in acknowledgment and looked back down at the book. She crossed out the first room number then slowly wrote out the other. Turning the register around, she gestured at the bottom of the entry. "Make your marks here." She waited until they each made an X on the page before pushing a key across the desk. "I'm Mrs. Tattersall. Mr. Tattersall does the fixin' up around here. If you need something, you come down here."

At their nod, she pointed to her right. "Stairs be there. Rent is due again in a week. Don't you be goin' anywhere, Mr. Hastie!"

Isabella couldn't help but jump when Mrs. Tattersall suddenly barked past them at a man who was halfway to the front doors. She felt less silly when she realized Briar had also started at the sudden noise.

"Ye're two weeks in arrears, you blighter." Despite some considerable girth around her belly, Mrs. Tattersall bustled out from behind the counter in a flash. The poor man had almost made it out the door when she grabbed him by the elbow and dragged him back inside. "Oh no you don't! I'll be getting' what's comin' to me, I will!"

It seemed like a prudent time to make their getaway. Isabella grabbed the key and hustled Briar up the stairs. A small crowd started to gather as Mrs. Tattersall laid into a red-faced Mr. Hastie.

Three stories was not so high up, but with the carpet bag, Isabella's arm started to ache long before they made it to their room. The lock was old and the door somewhat warped. The key resisted turning for a moment until she hauled back on the door, then it clicked sullenly and the door swung inward.

The promised bed was shoved against one wall. The metal frame was splotched with age, but seemed sturdy enough. There was no sign of sagging from the mattress. Isabella dropped her bag on the floor next to the door and turned about to take it all in. The room had been more than adequate at one time, but now the wallpaper was faded and torn in places. Water had peeled a long swath of it off and stained the plaster underneath it. There was no smell of mold in the room, so that had happened some time ago.

They were lucky. The room afforded them not one, but two windows with a view of the factory across the street. The light of the setting sun barely penetrated dual layers of grime on the inside and outside of the window.

"Don't," Isabella said when Briar moved to wipe the accumulated layers of dust and dirt. "It makes us harder to see from the outside. You'll get used to it."

"If you say so." Briar's voice was doubtful. It really was difficult to see through the window. "Did you really have to make me a mute?"

"I really did. It would be all over the hotel that a lady of quality had moved in if Tattersall had heard you. We're trying to avoid attention."

"At least it doesn't involve wearing orange gloves, this time." Briar shivered. "I think I could stand avoiding that woman's attention for all of eternity. She's very…impressive."

Isabella smiled at Briar's sally. "That she is." Come to think of it, she couldn't remember getting those gloves back from Briar. The parasol, yes, but not the gloves.

"So what happens now?"

"Now we watch."

"That's it?"

"That's it." Isabella pulled the room's only chair to the window and settled down.

After casting about for a moment, Briar pulled at the bed. It moved across the floor with a thunderous scraping that both impressed Isabella and put her teeth on edge. The bed had to be quite weighty with its metal frame, yet Briar managed it quite well. A thumping from below summoned their attention and Briar quickly settled the bed in front of the window.

At Isabella's inquiring look, Briar shrugged. "We aren't going to use it for sleeping, so it may as well be useful in other ways."

"Uh, yes." A burst of heat through the pit of her stomach kept Isabella from forming a more cogent response. The thought of other ways she and Briar could use the bed were all she could think of as Briar settled herself on the mattress. She primly tucked the edges of her skirts along her legs to keep them from poking out. If Isabella told Briar it was fine to leave her ankles out, would Briar realize how much Isabella wanted to see the shape of her calves? How long before Briar got bored and left? Hopefully not too long. She turned to look out the window, though she saw nothing except the phantom shape of Briar's leg. A troop of Her Majesty's soldiers could have filled the street below and burst into a burlesque routine and Isabella wouldn't have noticed.

She wrestled her rampaging libido into check, though it threatened to break free at any moment. There was little activity outside the factory now, but the smokestacks disgorged black smoke. Someone was at work in there.

On the bed, Briar glanced back and forth between the window and the notebook on her lap. She scratched down notes onto the pages, filling the paper quickly with her neat lettering. Eventually though, she noted only the occasional item.

"This is less exciting than I had imagined," Briar offered a couple of hours later. She leaned her head on one hand, pen held loosely in the other.

"Try doing this behind a bush in someone's garden."

"That does sound a lot worse, yes. At least here we don't have to worry if it rains."

"Rain is very inconvenient." Isabella stretched, trying to work the kinks out of muscles that had been still for far too long. She rolled her head and was pleased to feel a pop in her neck.

"Then why do it?" Briar asked.

"Do what?" Isabella wasn't following at all.

"Why do you steal from others? Is it because your family is having financial difficulties?"

"Financial difficulties." Isabella spat out a laugh. It was harsh and humorless even to her ears. "That's a gentle way of putting it. My family skirts the edge of financial ruin more often than not. It's been this way for the past two years."

"Your father made some poorly considered investments, I suppose."

"My father had nothing to do with it. It was my brother. He's in Germany now, studying to become an engineer or so he says. We paid off his debts once, but most letters he sends home contain requests for more money." Isabella couldn't stay still any longer. She paced the length of the small room and back. "He bankrupted the family once, and when my parents sent him to the Continent to keep him out of trouble, he's continued to pile on the debts. Father doesn't know. Wellington mails his requests straight to Mother."

"Your father doesn't know about his continual requests? How is that even possible?"

"Because Mother sends him money from what I can manage to purloin. Father doesn't know how dire our financial straits are. Mother deposits most of what I make into the family accounts, which is how we keep the household afloat."

A warm hand around her wrist stopped Isabella's pacing. She was almost running; only the fact that it was five paces from wall to wall kept her from breaking into a jog. Briar pulled her gently down to perch upon the edge of the mattress.

"I'm very sorry." Compassion warmed her voice and Isabella's eyes prickled with heat. "That's a lot to endure."

"Yes, well." Isabella gripped the bridge of her nose and squeezed. She would not burst into tears in front of Briar. "It's better than the alternative." The display of sympathy threatened to undo her completely. There had been little time to consider her actions or their consequences. Briar's quiet empathy had her thinking along lines that were easier to avoid.

"And your mother is the one who taught you."

It wasn't a question. Isabella couldn't stop from looking up at Briar, guilt painted across her face. "How did you know?"

Briar laughed, warm and genuine. The sound, coupled with the gloved fingers still around her arm, sent electricity coursing through Isabella's center. She'd felt less jolted after touching one of her father's ungrounded contraptions.

"I've met your parents," Briar said, seemingly unaware of the difficulties she was causing Isabella. "I have no problems envisioning your mother crawling through somebody's window, though I imagine her bad leg would cause some problems. Not your father, on the other hand. It seems likely he'd be distracted by some object in the house he was trying to burgle. He would have been picked up by the authorities years ago."

I should really get my hand back. "I suppose so." The words came out breathy and distracted. Briar looked down and realized she still held Isabella's hand and dropped it with alacrity. *Oh well.*

"Where did she get the experience?" Briar asked. The tips of her ears were bright red and she refused to meet Isabella's eyes. "Was it during her time on the frontier?"

How does she know about that? Isabella wondered. *Mother never said anything about that.* "She never really said."

"Is that so?" Briar examined the tips of her gloves. "It's the strangest thing. I did some research on your family. Everyone agrees that your mother is some variety of American heiress, but no one knows exactly what she inherited. All they know is your father showed up with an American fiancée, married her in almost unseemly haste, then his estate was awash in money. It has even been speculated that she was pregnant during their wedding, but your brother wasn't born until years later. Even then she walked with a cane."

Isabella stared at Briar with her mouth agape. Research? How had Briar discovered so much in such little time? She'd said nothing untoward, hadn't even hinted at it, really; she'd simply laid her results out for Isabella to see.

"You've been busy," Isabella finally said.

Briar smiled. "I find ways to pass the time."

"You certainly do." Isabella turned to face Briar, crossing her legs and not caring in the least if her legs were exposed. "What I'm about to share, you must never tell another soul."

"Why would I?" Briar cocked her head to one side. "It would only open inquiries into how I come to know such things, which would expose your activities. I have no wish for you to end up in a jail cell. Unless you fail to get that grimoire, that is." The last statement seemed tacked on, as if Briar had perhaps let on more than she'd meant to and was covering her tracks.

"Very well." Isabella took a deep breath. "My mother used to rob trains. She and her partner did quite well for themselves until the day they robbed a train with a couple of Pinkerton agents aboard. They shot her and my father concealed her. He pretended she was his wife. Her partner was also wounded but escaped. He was apprehended two days later. Mother and Father went straight to New York and took the first steamer back to London, but not without stopping first for the money she'd accumulated during her career." She'd said almost the entire story with one lungful of air and was quite out of breath when she reached the end.

Briar stared at her. Whatever she'd been expecting, this clearly wasn't it. Feeling slightly offended, Isabella crossed her arms.

"You asked. I answered."

"I did and you did." Briar blinked a couple times. "That's an amazing story. I would accuse you of making it up, but it's too outlandish not to be true."

"I thought it was so romantic when I was small. He fell in love with her on the train when she demanded he empty his pockets. When she came limping back through, he pulled her into his berth." They shared a smile, Isabella's rueful and Briar's amused. "So tell me about your mother. What is she like?"

The smile on Briar's faced drained away, leaving no traces of levity. "She's like many mothers, I presume. She wants me to give her grandchildren."

Isabella nodded in understanding. She'd heard similar things from many of her friends. Althea wanted to see her get married and save the family's fortunes. On the subject of children, she hadn't said anything.

Her mother's main focus was stabilizing the family finances before her father found out what they were up to.

"She doesn't want you to get married?" The question slipped out before Isabella could stop it. To even suggest such things before marriage was quite rude, never mind that she herself had engaged in activities that would be the source of much gossip if they were to be made public.

To her credit, Briar didn't seem offended. "She views such things as…negotiable. In her mind, the grandchildren are more important than a ceremony. Or my happiness."

Isabella didn't think she was meant to have heard the last. She put her hand on Briar's arm. The sleeve of Briar's dress had ridden up, exposing a small band of skin between her glove and the sleeve. When Isabella touched it, Briar stopped moving. With a small gasp, her breathing cut off. Her eyes stared through Isabella, who yanked back her hand.

Briar didn't move. She stayed as still as a statue, not breathing that Isabella could see.

"Briar?" There was no response. "Briar!" Isabella raised her voice to no avail. She reached out and grabbed Briar by the shoulder, tugging at her, trying to shake some sense back into her friend. Briar listed limply to one side and Isabella caught her before she could crack her head on the metal bedstead.

She looked down into brown eyes that held hers. Isabella felt like she was falling forward into those chestnut eyes, which were now flecked with deep red motes that seemed to glow. No, she wasn't falling forward. Briar was moving toward her.

Soft lips touched hers, tentatively at first, then with more confidence when Isabella didn't pull back. They moved over hers and warmth spilled through her, running from her mouth and pooling in her groin.

"My god," Isabella groaned. Briar took the opportunity to slide the tip of her tongue over Isabella's lips, to dip gently into her mouth. Isabella ran the tip of her tongue over Briar's, meeting her halfway and sending electricity tingling through her.

Arms crushed her to Briar's chest, and a hand tangled in her hair, pulling back her head and exposing her neck. Their lips no longer touched. Isabella moaned in protest, then gasped when Briar nipped her way from her jawline down the side of her neck. She fastened her lips at the base of her neck where her collarbones met. She sucked at the sensitive skin of Isabella's neck, setting her aflame.

"Briar," Isabella breathed. "Oh god, Briar!" Nothing could have prepared her to deal with the lust that raged through her. She was tossed on a torrent of passion, helpless before it. Her body burned to be touched, to be possessed by this woman who was wringing such ecstasy from her.

"Isabella." Briar looked up at her. Her eyes glowed brilliant scarlet in the dim room. "I'm so sorry."

"Sorry?" That made even less sense than the glowing red eyes. Isabella tried to force her passion-fogged mind back to some semblance of logic. "I don't—"

Thunderous crashing cut them off. For a moment, Isabella thought it came from within her. Her heart certainly was beating a nearly deafening rhythm on the inside of her eardrums. Briar looked away and Isabella realized someone was pounding on their door.

The door shook in its frame when their visitor pounded upon it again.

"Open up, for the love of god!" a man's voice cried out.

CHAPTER TWELVE

Isabella looked at her, then back at the door. The man was loud, but Briar heard no other disturbance. If there was a fire in the rooming house, surely there would be all sorts of accompanying commotion, and he wouldn't be taking the time to pound at their door, he would likely be running for the street.

"Should we let him in?" Isabella's voice was a tad breathless. Briar felt a pang for their missed opportunity. She still ached for the beautiful burglar. It seemed like she'd been aching for her for days, weeks even. When Isabella had touched her bare skin and Briar had felt her desire as keenly as she felt her own, there had been no choice. She'd needed to feel more. She still did.

The door shook in its frame again as Briar blinked stupidly at Isabella.

"He'll bring Tattersall up here to investigate," Isabella hissed. Her eyes were sharp now, her movements crisp. She crossed the room in two long strides and threw open the door.

Briar's mind cleared instantly when she saw what he held in his hand. It burned with a virulent green fire that reached toward her as if she were a draft pulling flames up the chimney.

"It's you!" the man cried.

"Get him in here," she said as she cast about for something—anything—she could use to bring him down.

Isabella gave her a shocked look, then grabbed the man about the lapels and yanked him into the room. His eyes bugged wide open and he couldn't contain a strangled yelp. Briar abandoned trying to find anything to hit the man, so she did the next best thing. She balled her fist, pulled it back, and let it fly with all of her strength. She connected cleanly with his chin and felt the power of the blow explode in her knuckles and shiver up her arm. He'd still been moving forward from Isabella's yank when his face met her fist. With a crack she felt more than she heard, he went reeling back and collapsed in the doorway. His arms flopped above his head and into the hall.

Briar grabbed him by both ankles and dragged him all the way into the room. "Don't just stand there. Close the door."

Isabella started, then quietly complied.

The man was heavy. A portly fellow not quite in his middle years, he had the look of a working man about him. His face was dark with dirt or maybe soot, but even so, Briar could see the bruise purpling rapidly on the point of his chin. She pried his fingers away from the object he held in his left hand. Calluses lay thick upon the skin, and he had the sunken knuckles of a boxer. It was a good thing they'd taken him by surprise.

Now that she had the thing out of his hand, it no longer burned chartreuse; it settled into a fitful glow. Briar leaned forward to look at it. It was a compass, cheap both in parts and workmanship, but the needle pointed steadfastly in her direction, no matter which way she turned it.

"We need to tie him up before he comes to," she said, still inspecting the compass. The runes graven upon it were in a dialect she wasn't as familiar with, and it took her a few moments to puzzle out what they were meant to do. The compass had been enchanted to bring its user to the closest source of "other" infernal energy.

The use of other was an odd one. Surely there weren't that many sources of energy. There was another rune that perplexed her until she realized it meant alive. This human had been sent out to find the nearest living source of infernal energy. The nearest demon. He'd been sent to find any of her half-brethren who might be sniffing around Mirabilia.

"Is he tied up?" She looked over at Isabella. Somehow, she'd gotten the man onto the bed, but he wasn't restrained. Were his eyelids fluttering? She flew to the bedside and snatched up the threadworn top sheet, tearing a long strip out of it. "Here," she said, handing the piece to Isabella. "As tight as you can."

Frantic to make sure he'd be immobilized by the time he woke, Briar tore strip after strip off the sheet until there was nothing left of it. Isabella followed her instructions in bemused silence, and when Briar looked up with the last two strips in her hands, the man looked quite like an Egyptian mummy she'd once seen on display at the British Museum.

"Perhaps he's restrained enough?" Isabella said.

"I expect so."

The man's eyelids continued to flutter, though he showed no more sign of awakening. Briar took the opportunity to rifle through his pockets. A growing disquiet welled within her. Touching him put her quite on edge, even through her gloves. The man wasn't alone. Something else lurked within him.

"What's going on," Isabella asked. "Why did you knock him out like that?"

"He isn't what he seems, and he came here looking for me. I suspect someone in the factory knows we are here, that or they've prepared for people poking around and he's the poor devil who was set to look into it." Briar tapped her fingertips together. "We won't know unless we ask them."

"Them?" Isabella looked about the room. "There's only us and him."

"He has a…passenger, I suppose you could say."

"I don't know what you mean."

"You're about to find out." Briar pushed up her sleeves and took off her gloves. "I need you to stay out of the way while I work."

"But—"

"Isabella, please." Briar held out her hand and braced herself. When Isabella took it, the inevitable welter of emotions and images tried to impose themselves upon her. Chief among them were the burgeoning fear Isabella held firmly in check and the arousal that still lingered from their kiss, even with her mounting anxiety. "When we're done and we have the grimoire, I'll explain everything, but for now I really need you to trust in me." She looked into Isabella's eyes, pleading with her to understand, to believe. "Please."

"Very well." Isabella let go and arranged herself in the chair by the window. "But it needs to be everything."

"Done."

Briar knew what she needed to do, but it was a spell she had never performed herself. She took her time, tracing runes and lines on the man's face and neck with one saliva-moistened finger. Dim magenta lines appeared as she traced them, pulsing in time with her heartbeat. She had to pause frequently. Saliva didn't last as long as blood did, and her mouth would be beyond parched by the time she completed the diagram. She had one rune left to place in the middle of his forehead, the key which would activate the entire spell, but she needed a little something else. Human magicians like Jean-Pierre LaFarge thought blood was the most important material for spell creation, but they were only half right. Any biological fluid could be used. Blood had the advantage that it was almost always created in conjunction with fear or anger, which was why the blood of slaughtered animals and especially humans was so much more potent than the blood of the magicians themselves. The fluid was one part of it, the emotion the other. Magicians might use their own blood under extreme duress, but the stresses upon them had to be enormous to impart the same emotion as was held in the fluids of others. Her mother's people, the succubi and incubi, were also known to use other fluids. Briar's mind shuddered away from the thought. There was certainly emotion involved in the release of those fluids, but they were so messy.

Add in the runes and the diagrams for ritual, and you had your spell. All Briar needed was a dash of emotion, and she knew right where to get it.

She crossed the floor to Isabella. "I need a favor from you," she said. "I need you to kiss me."

"You need me to what?" Isabella's eyes looked ready to drop from her head, but Briar thought she detected a hitch in her breathing before she'd answered.

"Kiss me." Briar raised one eyebrow. "Is that such a hardship for you?"

"Good god, of course not!" Isabella surged to her feet and across the room in one bound. With unmistakable hunger, she pressed her lips to Briar's.

Briar was battered by Isabella's arousal. She held on to enough of herself not to be dragged back into the maelstrom of need and desire, but it was a close thing. She deepened the kiss, delving deep into Isabella's mouth with her tongue. The moan Isabella released almost undid her, but Briar pushed through the haze of emotion. Isabella's lips scorched hers, and her tongue branded itself upon the inside of her mouth time and again as Isabella explored her. How good would that tongue feel on other parts? Parts that even now cried out for completion, for the satisfaction she had long denied them.

With a gasp, Briar ripped her mouth away from that of Isabella, who whimpered at the loss of contact. Her eyes closed, she clutched Briar's upper arms with desperate hands. Briar looked down at her arms. Horror filled her when she saw grey opalescence shimmering back at her. She'd lost her shroud. She couldn't let Isabella see her like this, but if she raised the shroud before she completed the current spell, the emotion she'd harvested from Isabella would be redirected and she would have to start over.

"Keep your eyes closed," Briar croaked at Isabella. "Don't open them until I tell you to, no matter what you hear."

On legs that trembled, though whether from the shock of losing her shroud without knowing it or from the intensity of her kiss with Isabella, she didn't know, Briar made her way back over to the bed. She put her index finger in her mouth, though her lips still yearned for Isabella's. The saliva that coated her finger should be more than potent enough to do the trick. She traced the key rune and sat back. One at a time, the glowing letters flared to brilliant red life. Blood would have been quicker, but with the man restrained, they had time.

The man's eyes popped open immediately. They burned from within, a vile green that made Briar's stomach churn.

"Half-breed bitch, let free!"

Ignoring the thing's demands, Briar closed her eyes. It started to scream, a high wailing cry that set her teeth on edge. Whoever was living downstairs thumped again on their floor. Briar thought she heard a muffled curse. She forced herself to tune out all distractions, even Isabella, who she could feel as a point of lust on her internal horizon. A kind of peace settled over her as the shroud covered her once again.

"You can open your eyes," Briar called to Isabella. She got up and looked into the thing's face. "You should be quiet now, or things will not go well for you." She licked her finger and added a bump to the diagram, despite its thrashing to avoid her. Green eyes followed her, and the screaming died in its throat. "That's right. You know what I can do to you."

"Your kind only want one thing. Saw what you and girl were doing." It fluttered its tongue, sucking obscenely. "Know what you want to do. Won't say no if wish to go now."

Isabella shuddered next to her. Briar stopped herself just in time. She wanted to comfort Isabella, to let her know she had everything in hand, but she was afraid if she touched her, she would lose control and they would end up doing exactly what the repulsive thing wanted of them.

Its eyes burned as it watched her struggle for self-possession.

"Pass me my gloves, would you please?" That would give her another layer of control. She pulled on one while watching the man's passenger. "Isabella, what you see here is a man possessed by a demon."

"Hellfire and damnation." Isabella whispered the words as if she couldn't believe what she saw. Even she should be able to see that the man's eyes glowed green, though she might not have been able to see the crimson web Briar had woven around his head. "Demons are real?"

"Of course they are. Why do you think you call it demoniac magic?"

"I never thought about it that much," Isabella said faintly. "It's just a word, like electricity."

"This is the root of that energy." More or less. It was an oversimplification, but now was not the time for a lesson in magical theory, no matter how badly Briar wanted to impart that important tidbit of information. "What we need now is to find out what it is and how it came to be in this poor man."

The thing hissed at them through its teeth. "Won't tell."

Briar smiled and it shrank back against the mattress. "You don't need to, it's true. There's enough I can tell from your signature to guess you're an imp. Am I right?" She licked her finger and reached out toward the addition she'd made to the inscription.

It hissed again, its mouth open. "Yes! What's to you?"

"Now I know how to hurt you properly." She knew her smile was ugly, but her experience with imps had never been pleasant. The smallest of demons had delighted in tormenting her when she was a girl. As she was one of the few beings on the infernal plane who was smaller and weaker than they, the imps had never shied away from making her life miserable, sometimes at the behest of her sisters, but often of their own volition. The first research she'd done had been to the end of protecting herself from the cockroaches of the infernal world.

"No hurt! No!" It smiled at her, lips spreading wider than a human's face should have allowed. Isabella choked next to her. Briar placed her gloved hand on Isabella's arm. She hoped it was comforting.

"Why are you here?"

"Master sent. Said if compass glows, follow needle, report back. Found you and girl. Must return."

"You're not going anywhere."

"Master will know if don't return."

"Perhaps eventually." Briar looked at Isabella. "We need to go after the grimoire now. If we don't, at some point the magician who summoned this one will wonder where it's gone. They'll move again, and we'll lose our chance."

Isabella chewed at her lower lip. "I don't like it. I'll be going in blind. I've never been inside a factory, let alone this one. I haven't had time even to walk the outside of it."

"We can dress you up in his clothes." Briar sympathized with Isabella's look of disgust. She wouldn't want to touch anything the imp touched, whether directly or through its human host, but it was a good idea. "You'll blend in, I know you will. I can make you look just like him with magic." If she could have, Briar would have imparted her shroud upon Isabella. Sadly, that ability was personal, a gift from her mother's side of the family. Succubi could take the shape that most attracted their prey, allowing them to shift their appearance to almost anything. But it only worked on them.

"I thought you said you're not a magician."

She was stalling, Briar knew it. "I said I'd tell you everything once we're done, and I will. This is important. The imp's presence here makes it even more so."

"Then I go in tonight." Isabella straightened to her full height. "I brought my suit. If we're doing this, we do it my way. It's what I know and so has the best chance of succeeding. If you're right and we won't get another chance, it's the only way. There are some things I need you to get done while I'm in there."

"Whatever you need."

"Need girls kiss again," the imp muttered. "Then more."

"That's enough of you," Briar said. Licking her finger, she drew a line through the key-rune, obliterating their conduit to the imp.

The light snuffed out of the man's eyes and his lids drifted closed. Once again, he was only human, though Briar could feel the imp still in him like a layer of pond scum coating her skin after dipping her hand into fetid water.

"I know you can do this, Isabella," she said. "You must succeed."

"Not a problem." Isabella grinned cockily.

"I know." Briar didn't know, of course, but she wasn't going to say so to Isabella. If anyone could do it and get out again, it was Isabella. If only she could go along.

CHAPTER THIRTEEN

The factory loomed in the night, a brick cathedral to the industrial, its smokestacks rising like spires. If not for the coating of grime and lack of windows, it could have been a shrine. It was certainly imposing enough. Unless Isabella missed her guess, the Mirabilia factory had started out life as two or three smaller buildings. The builders had built up and up until it blotted out the sky. The haphazard expansions had run the buildings together to become something that was not only enormous but gave her no idea what the interior layout might be like.

How did I let Briar talk me into this? Mother would have my head if she knew I was heading in there without proper preparation. And all for a kiss or two? Her groin tingled, reminding her that those had been more than simple kisses. She'd never connected with anybody like that. Even her first experience with another woman couldn't hold a candle to what she'd felt while kissing Briar.

Briar. Whose eyes glowed red sometimes. Who did magic, but refused to be called a magician. Who knew more than she had any right to and yet whose blind spots were numerous and adorable. Well, mostly adorable. Isabella had the suspicion that no one else could have talked her into taking this risk. Briar was terrified by those engines and whatever evil she thought they represented. How could Isabella not do everything in her power to assuage that fear?

Isabella trudged along the roofline, looking for the best spot to make her jump. The rooming house had been too close to the front gate to be a good location to get in undetected. Fortunately, the apartments and hotels that lined the streets around the factory gave her plenty of choices. This one afforded her the best chance. The building was a little taller than the others, and the architect had built it out over the street a ways. It gave her a few extra feet; she would need all the help she could get.

She wrapped her hands around the controls of her jump rig. The helmet was seated firmly on her head. For a change, she'd actually done up the strap under her chin. It was a long way down if she missed this jump. It was at the edge of her range and if she didn't make it, she wasn't completely sure if the rig would have time to recharge and kick in again before she hit the ground. It probably would. But if she did make it, she knew she'd be able to get back. Her getaway route went over the rooftops, and if she couldn't make this jump, she wouldn't be in any shape to consider an alternate exit from the factory.

Here we go! Isabella backed up as far as she could on the flat rooftop. She set herself against the brick lip on the far side and pushed off, running for all she was worth. She launched herself off the edge and opened up the throttle on her rig as far as it would go. The shock of being thrust forward so suddenly almost snapped her head back; only the fact that she'd been expecting the kick and had braced herself against it kept her from serious pain. There was no time to dwell on that. She hurtled toward the side of the factory, off course from the small roof she'd been aiming for. Without much thought, she stuck out her left elbow and activated the thruster, aiming toward her small landing spot. A larger roof would have been ideal, but those were all higher than she could reach given the space she needed to cross. Besides, that one had windows, which afforded her a way in. If she was lucky, those windows went to an office, one where a mad magician might keep his book of magic.

The extra thrust did the trick to get her back on track, but she'd hit the apex of her arc too soon. She wasn't going to make it; being off on her initial jump had cost her dearly.

Isabella drew her grapple-pistol and fired it at the line of small windows right above the roof. Without waiting to see if it made contact, she ejected the line spool and popped open the winch at her belt. Wind whistled past her as she gathered speed on the downward slope of her arc. She tried not to think of the cobbles getting ever closer. If she didn't get this right, she would have no other chances.

Lightweight line whistled out of the spool, humming as it played out toward the window. Isabella snagged the end and engaged the winch, jamming the line in and hoping it didn't foul. The winch caught almost immediately; now all she had to do was hope the harpoon had engaged somewhere and that it wasn't flying back toward her.

Isabella was falling even as the winch spun. Those cobbles were damn close; she wasn't going to make it. Desperately, she tried to engage some thrust from her jump pack, but all she received for her efforts was a low hiss. It needed more time, time she didn't have. She was going to die of a broken neck.

The line caught, jerking her forward and away from the rapidly approaching ground. The winch groaned, overtaxed by the sudden addition of her full weight. It hadn't been built to pull her unassisted by the thrust of the pack. It wouldn't be able to absorb her weight for much longer, but if she was lucky it wouldn't have to. Isabella engaged the throttle again, cautiously at first. There was no response, and the winch labored against her weight.

Isabella tucked in her elbows, keeping any thrust from being wasted on steering and tried the throttle again.

It engaged with a thunderous whoosh, sending her soaring through the air once again. At her waist, the winch thrummed happily, doing what it had been built to do. It kept her on track on the way up to her entry point. Isabella cut thrust shy of the roof's edge and alighted easily. She didn't even have to roll to absorb the speed of her landing. Oil paper ripped under her feet as the winch pulled her toward the wall at the far edge of the roof. Isabella disengaged it and stopped sliding almost immediately.

Her aim had been off with the harpoon, but close enough considering her circumstances at the time. Instead of going through the window, it had embedded itself between two bricks below it. That was probably just as well. If anybody had been on the other side of the window, the harpoon and line would have betrayed her intentions immediately. As it was, her landing had been the opposite of stealthy. She crouched under the window to retrieve the harpoon and kept her ears open for any sound of disturbance from within. To her relief, there was nothing except the sounds of machinery and rhythmic thumping.

The window was a good enough place to start. Isabella peered through it, making sure to keep as low as possible. The glass was filthy. She spat on the smooth surface and rubbed it with her cuff, clearing a small space that was marginally cleaner than that around it.

I must have used up all my luck getting over here. The windows did not look into an office as she'd hoped. Instead, they looked over a cavernous room filled with equipment and men. In a veritable hive of activity, groups of workers gathered around the partially assembled carcasses of dozens of horseless carriages. A series of catwalks traversed the top of the room. They would have been an ideal way to get across; one of them passed not far from the window where Isabella was. The men who were wandering to and fro up there made it a very bad idea. They looked down and occasionally shouted at the workers below, then made marks upon clipboards. The yelling was likely futile, as the din in the factory was significant. Isabella doubted the workers could hear anything other than the clang of metal upon metal. She ducked down but not before noting the series of low rooms on the far side of the factory floor. Those looked like they might be the offices she was looking for. It was somewhere to start, in any case.

Isabella looked up. Making her way across the factory floor or the catwalks was out of the question. The man who was still tied up in the room they'd rented would have fit in well enough. His clothes looked similar to what the men on the catwalks wore. Maybe he was some kind of foreman. It was pointless to speculate. There was no way she would have worn his clothes, even as a disguise over her jumping rig, not after what she'd seen and heard. Up and over was the best option.

It was a simple matter to jump to the next roof, as it was well within the optimal range for her rig. A large open space greeted her, broken only by the smokestack at one end and a tall spire. She ghosted her way across as quickly as possible. Habit kept her footfalls light, though she likely needn't have bothered.

The spire reminded her of something, and she glanced at it continually as she crossed the roof. She was almost to the other side when it hit her. It was a mooring mast, though a small one. It certainly wasn't the size of the one at Hanworth Park, but that one was for large passenger air ships. Someone at Mirabilia had a personal zeppelin. Those were still relatively uncommon, though they were becoming less rare for civilians. A handful among the nobility had them. If she wasn't mistaken, Briar's employer was among that number. Mostly they were used as spotting stations for the British Army's artillery, or so she'd been told by a tiresome lieutenant at a ball. Doubtless, it was supposed to impress her that he'd been up in one. Perhaps if he hadn't been boasting to someone who arced her way through the London skies at night he might have had better results. Still, his efforts hadn't been completely wasted. He was now affianced to Millie, having resigned his commission in favor of the profit of a mercantile lifestyle.

That Mirabilia had its own zeppelin or was able to accommodate one was more impressive. *Are they building those also?* Isabella decided not to mention the possibility to Briar unless she knew for certain. There was no point in worrying her unnecessarily.

She peered over the edge of the roof. Below her was a side yard filled with dozens upon dozens of completed horselesses. Apparently all they required were owners. A small frisson of fear shivered its way delicately down her spine. If there was indeed some evil intent behind them, there were a lot of them—with countless more on the way. The manufacturing operation must have been running all day. It was almost midnight and yet the factory bustled as if it were high noon.

Directly below her, someone had built a long set of low outbuildings that now abutted the walls directly. They might have been separate from the factory at one time, but that hadn't been the case for a while. Unless she missed her guess, these were the offices. Hopefully she'd find what she needed there.

Isabella stepped off the edge and activated the thrusters halfway down. She didn't open the throttle more than halfway, trusting the thrust to cushion her landing and not to launch her through the air. She landed as softly as possible. The roof here was metal, probably tin. If there was nothing beneath it, her landing would echo through the space below.

A nearby skylight afforded her the chance to glance inside. The room below certainly had the look of an office. Desks sat in the middle of the room, while cabinets lined the walls. This was as good a place to start as any.

My luck must be recharging, Isabella thought. The room was empty. She tugged on the skylight gently, trying—and failing—to avoid the screech of metal upon metal that she feared might accompany its opening. Isabella winced and held still, but there was no indication anyone had heard it above the muffled sounds of pounding from the factory floor. The skylight stopped long before it was wide enough for her to squeeze in, unfortunately. She would have to break the hinges. She braced herself under it as well as she could and heaved. The hinges cracked and the window gave enough that she'd be able to slide in easily. Eventually somebody would discover the broken window, but she would be long gone.

She looked about and located a length of metal bar left forgotten on the roof. It was the perfect length to keep the skylight from closing behind her. Isabella propped open the window and levered herself carefully over the edge. For a moment she stayed suspended over the office, then let go. She came down square on top of one of the desks and rolled off the top to absorb the shock of her landing. Thankfully the desk was of sturdy wood, and it withstood the sudden assault easily. Twin footprints marred the papers on top of the desk. Isabella quickly shuffled those to the bottom of a nearby stack.

Inside the factory office, the sound of machinery and metal was much louder, though not as deafening as it had been on the roof where she'd landed. She couldn't imagine what it must be like to work there, having to withstand the constant din. Perhaps the clerks who worked here became acclimated to the noise. Her own workshop was occasionally quite loud, but since it was only her and Father in there, there wasn't the same relentless pounding.

This room had nothing that looked like plans or grimoires. These seemed to be invoices and receipts. This was more along the lines of the papers she'd expected to find in the decoy Mirabilia office. Here were the ledgers of sales and payroll to workers. Those were extensive. Mirabilia was quite profitable from what she could tell.

Still, there was nothing with Thomas Holcroft's name on it. It was unlikely the owner of the company would work in a room with rank and file clerks, but surely there had to be some sign of him. Isabella shuffled through more papers, trying to find a memo or other communication from him, but to no avail. He had to have an office here somewhere.

Isabella slipped out the door and froze. A long row of windows there looked out onto the manufacturing area. The windows were almost as grimy as those outside had been to her relief. Between that and the light being reflected back from inside the factory, it was unlikely anyone out there would see her skulking through the offices. She would have to be quick about it. Her presence would be exceedingly difficult to explain if anyone found her, and escape from here would be tricky.

She had a job to do and Briar was waiting for her. Disappointing her wasn't an option, so Isabella opened the door to the next office and stepped inside.

CHAPTER FOURTEEN

The driver's seat of the earl's new carriage was comfortable enough, but Briar had wrapped a blanket around her legs to ward off the damp spring air as she waited. While the seat was comfortable, the horseless itself was not. Of course it had been the only one available in the carriage house when she'd arrived home. The skin on her back crawled, and she kept looking behind her though she knew no one was watching. If nothing else, she was unlikely to fall asleep while waiting for Isabella. There was no sign of her, so she must still be in the Mirabilia factory. The thought produced a shiver that had nothing to do with the cold and damp evening. How would Briar know if something had happened?

It had taken her well over an hour to flag down a cab, then return with a borrowed horseless carriage. Fortunately, she'd convinced Johnson to show her the rudiments of piloting one of the carriages a few years ago. She'd rushed back as quickly as possible. For all her exhortations on the ride home, the cabbie had taken his time. She'd made up for that on her way back, to the tune of shouted curses and shaken fists as she blew by the few slow-moving, mostly traditional carriages that were out at this time of night. It seemed her haste had been wasted.

Her mind drifted back to the poor man who was likely still trussed up in the room Isabella had rented for them. They'd left the door to the room ajar, and sooner or later someone would wonder about that and discover him. If he was lucky, the imp would have gotten bored and left him. They weren't known for their attention to detail nor their attention spans. With some effort, she put him from her mind.

Briar rubbed her hands together. Gloved though they were, they still ached slightly from the cold. Blowing on them did nothing through the thin leather, but tucking them under her thighs helped immensely. She looked up, trying to will Isabella into appearing, but the line of rooftops above her stayed disappointingly empty.

* * *

The side of the building was rough stone, for which Isabella was eternally grateful. It made climbing up the side so much easier. She walked up, aided by the winch and line at her belt. After checking the gauge on the tank of her jumping rig, she had decided not to use any more of it. She had barely more than half a tank left. If she used too much more, she wouldn't have enough left for her getaway across the rooftops.

So far, the only sign of life in the building had been the hive of activity on the factory floor. She'd long since allowed the din of their work to recede from her ears; now it was simply more background noise.

As she climbed, it occurred to her to wonder what the large building to her left was. The building housing the chassis factory with all of its noise was on the other side of the wall she was on. She was doing her best to ascend to the small windows high up, almost to the roof. But there was another building, still large enough at half the size of the one she ascended. It was silent, however, and without the lights that streamed out of the chassis factory.

As she got closer to the roof, Isabella took note of the covered walkway connecting the two buildings. Unless she missed her guess, it went from the rooms that were her target to the mysterious second building. Maybe it was a storage area of some sort and the carriages she'd seen in the courtyard had been the overflow.

The row of windows that were her destination were right above her. Isabella reached out and tugged experimentally at the edge of one. To her relief, it swung out easily. She slithered over the windowsill and down to the floor. It absorbed her weight without even a thump. When

Isabella looked down, she saw why. The room's floor was covered in plush rugs.

She leaned back out the window and retrieved her harpoon, reloading it into the pistol before returning it to the holster in the back of her waistband. She turned and surveyed the room. It was so different from the offices on the floor that she wondered if she'd somehow ended up in someone's house. Beside the carpets that littered the floor, heavy drapery lined the walls. The room was large and ran the width of the factory. Unlike the main offices, it hadn't been walled off into different rooms, though someone had gone to the trouble to place screens at different points to create partitions.

This was obviously the office area. A heavy desk with lushly appointed furnishings took up much of the space. The leather chair looked as expensive as it looked comfortable. To the right of the desk was something Isabella recognized. She had one in what had been her dressing room. A drafting table and tall stool sat angled away from the windows, positioned to get the perfect amount of natural light during the day. It was where Isabella would have put it, taking advantage of the window's northern exposure. This was more like it!

The drawers on the desk weren't even locked, and, as she had expected, their contents were disappointing. The documents she found were copies of many of the reports she'd already seen down in the main office area. A few of them had notes scrawled in the margins. The handwriting was strong and slashed with messy vigor across the whiteness of the page.

The drafting table held a few half-finished diagrams. Some of the writing glowed green. Isabella closed one eye and the glowing runes disappeared; the new lens from LaFarge was working as advertised. The drawings were a cross between regular schematics and demoniac inscriptions. She carefully folded up two sheets and crammed them into one of her pouches. They would give Isabella as much insight as the grimoire should give Briar.

There was still no sign of the grimoire Briar was convinced would be here. *What if Holcroft took it him to wherever he lives?* The thought stopped Isabella cold. It had been hard enough to find the factory; finding his home would be even more difficult. With that in mind, Isabella kept her eye out for anything with an address on it. All she could do was search this place as thoroughly as possible. If there was no grimoire, she and Briar would figure out where else it might be. A few more pieces of paper went into other pockets, but Isabella did her best to leave the desk and table as undisturbed as possible. There was no point in advertising that she'd been in there.

Behind the first screens, the furniture had been arranged into a small sitting area, with a long table taking up much of the space in front of one wall. There was nothing of interest on the table. A large chair dominated one end, while a handful of mismatched, uncomfortable-looking chairs ringed around the far end. There were no chairs at all in the intervening space.

Someone has delusions of grandeur. This close to the drapery-swathed walls, Isabella could make out the faint sounds of machinery. She realized that almost none of the manufacturing noises penetrated into this room. The hangings and rugs muffled the noise, but they shouldn't have been able to reduce it so completely. She twitched a drape to one side and blinked at the sudden brightness as the light from the factory floor intruded into the dark space. The cacophony outside exploded in there along with the light. Isabella let the curtain fall, and both cut off again. She peered at the curtain, then noticed a faint green line along the drape's bottom. It met up with a similar line on the curtains to either side. Isabella turned in place. As much as she could see of the drapes around her, each one had that green line. She was in the middle of a circle the size of the room. Her skin prickled at the realization.

Keep moving, silly girl. There was little else of interest here. The chairs at the other side of the partitioned area were arranged as if in front of a fire, though no fireplace existed. A large crystal ashtray sat on a small table next to one of the chairs. A half-smoked cigar accompanied several cigar butts, but there was nothing else to betray that anyone had been there recently.

Another set of screens obscured the next area, as did a set of hangings that ran all the way up to the ceiling. Isabella was thankful for the goggle lenses that allowed her to see in the dark. This far from the windows, there was nothing to introduce light in that area. As she slid between the curtains at the gap between screens, Isabella remembered that the drapes around the main room hadn't allowed even the slightest hint of light from the work area to intrude. The small amount of light that had come in had been through the windows where she'd entered.

The little room beyond was dark, to her relief. If she'd thought the other areas had been lushly appointed, it was only because she hadn't been in here yet. A large daybed dominated the room. Unlike the heavy velvet drapes around the rooms, the four posts of the bed were shrouded in silk. Satin sheets clothed the bed and were in such a rumple that the bed's purpose was immediately clear. This was not a bed meant for sleeping. The same green line traced the circumference of this room as well. Isabella would have wagered that someone standing three feet away on the other side of the partition would have heard nothing, not even if an orgy was taking place in here.

A table next to the bed held implements Isabella couldn't name. Her mind shied away from considering their uses. There was little chance the grimoire would be secreted somewhere in here, but she rifled through the few pieces of furniture, giving the bed a wide berth the entire time. At least here she didn't have to worry about being neat. Everything was in such disarray that it was unlikely anybody would realize someone else had been there.

She found nothing. No grimoire, no drawings, no memos, only disturbing implements and an overwhelming sense of disgust. She was going to have to return to Briar with empty hands and nothing to show for the night's work. Briar would not be amused at all.

Unless... The walkway to the next building, the entrance to that was up here somewhere. But where? Though it was a reach to think it might lead to anything more than a storage area, she refused to admit defeat until she'd examined everything she could.

Isabella grasped the nearest curtain and pulled it back, revealing a brick wall. She worked her way around the room and finally found a door hidden right next to the bed. The handle turned easily under her hand. She pushed it open and ventured hesitantly into the darkened hall behind it. A low drone grew louder as she made her way to the door at the other end of the hall. Strange symbols and drawings lined the walls and floor. When she tried to look at them directly, they seemed to shift, giving her a sensation in the pit of her stomach like she was falling. She focused instead on the door opposite her, the door that it was taking too long to reach. The walkway hadn't seemed nearly this long from the outside.

By the time she reached the far end, Isabella was drenched in sweat. Her chest heaved as though she had completed a particularly grueling training session. The handle beneath her gloved hands felt slick and it resisted her grip. Finally, she took it in both hands and wrenched it open.

The door opened into Hell. The droning noise washed over her and green fire spread across half her vision. Isabella braced herself with both hands on the doorframe, trying to wrap her mind around what she saw. It seemed that green flames licked every surface of the huge room beyond. She blinked once, twice before realizing there were gaps in the flames.

Words written in inhuman characters lined every surface, their shape similar to those she'd seen LaFarge employ so many times. Dark shapes moved between her and the flaming letters, silhouettes of things that couldn't be. Above it all, a series of stacked tubes hummed and popped, dominating the back wall. They glowed from within, radiating that same sickly flickering green that filled the room.

This wasn't Hell, she decided, though it was certainly populated by its denizens. All of her wildest imaginings over what this building held could never have prepared her for the reality. In an eerie mirror image of the chassis factory floor, groups of beings surrounded featureless metal cylinders on the floor. The low drone that took the place of the banging and sounds of machinery turned out to be chanting voices overlapping into a disharmonious whole that made Isabella want to clap her hands over her ears.

Against her screaming instincts, she inched forward from her vantage point, a platform overlooking the demon-factory below her, to get a better look. She cast disbelieving eyes to one side and followed the line of a walkway around the wall and down to the factory floor. The metal railing beneath her fingers was cold. She clutched at it, trying to anchor herself. The heavy railing dwarfed the thin bars of metal holding it up. Someone had welded a lectern to the rail, she saw. A huge book sat on the lectern, chains crisscrossing it and holding down pages of curling vellum.

That's it! Isabella approached the book. The chains were a complication, but not a major one. She had her own answer to those. From a pocket high up on her arm, she pulled a metal-sheathed glass vial. She never carried more than one of these. Crushing it in a fall would put her in a world of hurt; the concentrated acid within ate through clothing and skin in seconds. Metal took longer. She upended the vial on a length of chain where it wrapped around the lectern's base.

Something flitted through the air between Isabella and the shining tower. At first she thought perhaps it was only a series of flickers from the unstable energy it housed, but it was too regular. There were no catwalks high up here, perhaps because whoever supervised these workers could fly. They crisscrossed back and forth, at least one flying close enough that Isabella should have been able to make out its features. All she saw was a silhouette against the green flames that still dazzled her. Whatever it was, the shadow had bat-like wings and horns. Was that a tail?

Isabella bent forward to check on the progress of the acid. She squinted and discovered that the link was no longer whole. With one eye on the flying creatures, she carefully unwrapped the grimoire. As soon as the chains were gone from the pages, they started slowly flipping back and forth as if an invisible hand perused the book.

Enough is enough. It's time to get out of here. Despite the brave words, Isabella had to force trembling hands out toward the malevolent book. It took both hands to wrestle shut the cover.

The sound of a gong rang out and the platform burst forth into brilliant light around her feet. The droning stopped and the fluttering figures froze in midair, then turned toward her. This was not good. Her worst nightmares should have taken notes. Isabella had an instant to realize she would be reliving this moment for years to come. If she survived it.

Fear lent her strength and speed. She snatched up the grimoire and turned to flee through the door. It took seconds to cross the walkway this time, and she burst out into the strangely silent rooms overseeing the chassis factory.

How far behind me are they? She couldn't stop to check. As she darted through the too-quiet rooms, Isabella struggled to wrestle the grimoire into a large satchel at her hip. Now she understood why Briar had insisted she bring such a large bag. She had to stop in front of the window that had been her entry point to get it settled.

The curtains to the far room parted and dread flooded her; a torrent of every fear she'd ever felt rooted her to the spot. Shadows poured into the room, boiling over each other as they came ever nearer. Isabella glanced up as shadows scudded across the ceiling, accompanied by scratching and screeching. Puffs of masonry rained down as furrows appeared in the plaster.

She needed to find Briar. Isabella threw herself out the window, shaking the throttle wands down into her hands as she fell. They landed in her hands with satisfying thumps. These she could be certain of.

You'd better be waiting, Briar, she thought.

CHAPTER FIFTEEN

Freefall had never felt so good. Anything that got her away from those shadows was a boon, even plummeting toward the ground. Isabella engaged the jump pack and careened toward the highest roof at the top of the factory. Her trajectory was off and she stuck out an elbow and thrust hard to the right. At the top of the arc, she glanced down at the window she'd just jumped out of.

It seethed with shadowy figures. They vomited forth in a never-ending stream. Some fell away toward the ground, others spread out on the wall like a churning ink blot, still others separated from the mass and hovered. One shadowy face looked up at her. All Isabella could see were green eyes, no other facial features, but they locked on her. Almost as one, the larger shadow shifted, moving toward her.

She hit the roof in an ungainly heap, shaken by what was after her. Getting her feet under her took much too long. Her break across the roof was unsteady and halting. The harder Isabella pushed herself, the slower she seemed to go, though her heart hammered in her ears like a piston. Finally, she was up to speed, the far edge of the factory roof approaching quickly.

Don't look back, she screamed inside her head. *Don't you look back, for god's sake.* She looked back. They were on her tail, some scampering with ease over the roof, the rest flying in a diabolical cloud of swirling shapes and chartreuse fire, all heading straight in her direction.

Isabella's toe dragged on something and she tipped forward, pulled by the weight of her gear and her momentum. She windmilled her arms and pulled up. If she went down, they would be on her and she was deathly certain she would never stand up again.

A thunderous susurrus of flapping wings filled the air around her. *How many of them are there?* A few stumbling steps forward was all she needed to get back up to speed. She would have to time the jump perfectly. If she took off too early, she'd likely be short of the rooftops across the way. If she was too late, there would be less surface area to thrust against, and she'd be even shorter.

One…two…and thrust. Isabella opened the throttle to its widest setting and rocketed off the ground in a cloud of vapor. The wind whistled past her exposed cheeks and howled through the ear holes in her helmet. She watched as the far-off roofline flew closer. Low buildings passed by far below her feet, then the street with its lonely streetlights that did much less to dispel the night than did the lenses in her goggles. She was going to make it. Unreasoning fear had apparently made her very precise in the timing of the jump. Taking off from a higher roof for the return trip had made all the difference.

The roof tiles loomed closer and Isabella tried to engage her thrusters to take a little something off the landing. She throttled open the controls and… nothing. Either the rig needed time to recharge or she'd used the last of the tank. There was no time to check; all she could do was tuck into a ball and hope the landing wasn't too hard.

Isabella hit the roof and bounced once, the air whooshing out of her lungs. She rolled forward and slapped the palms of her hand onto the tiles to try to bleed off some momentum. Something hit the roof next to her. A shadow figure somersaulted twice and landed in a heap, fetching up against the base of a chimney. Another impact followed the first one, and Isabella was suddenly surrounded by falling shadows. She skidded to an awkward stop, one leg striking the edge of a chimney pot and sending it clattering to the edge of the roof and over. Pain shot up her leg from the shin, but Isabella barely noticed it. There was no time for niceties such as injuries. There was only time for escape.

She shot to her feet and scrambled across the peak of the roof, then skidded down a short incline to the neighboring roofline.

An object hit her back, and Isabella staggered to one side. Sharp points of pain bloomed across her shoulders.

"Gotcha," a raspy voice crowed in her ear. A small hand wrapped itself around the front of her neck. "Give it back!"

One of the shadows was attached to her like a limpet. She grabbed the indistinct arm, and it dropped into focus. A little brick red figure clung to her. It bared sharp teeth at her in a closed-mouth hiss. A detached part of Isabella's mind noted its double row of teeth and the pointed ears. Scars roped their way around the thing's limbs. It flexed its fingers and black claws sprouted from the tips.

"Give it!" the thing screamed in her ear. "Give it give it give it."

"To Hell with you," Isabella shouted back. She yanked it off her, paying no heed when the points of pain became stripes of agony. She slammed it into the ground with strength she didn't know she had. Its head burst like a ripe melon when it hit the slate tiles. It lay there twitching, a widening pool of black blood and stench pouring from it. Wrenching her mind away from the nausea that flooded her belly, she pushed on and over the edge onto the roof.

Throttle at the ready, she jumped out over the street, hoping her rig had recharged enough to get her the short way to the line of roofs across the narrow side street. If it hadn't, this was going to get even more painful. The rig caught and pushed her over the gap. She sobbed with relief. She was almost to where she'd told Briar to meet her.

Isabella's landing was much more controlled this time. She kept her feet beneath her but gasped in pain when her injured leg took the brunt of the force. She limped forward between two chimneys and used them to propel herself onward, unable to put all her weight on the offending leg. The two-foot wall between the end of this roof and the next shouldn't have been much of an obstacle, but Isabella had to slow to navigate it.

Flapping wings were all the warning she had, and she pulled herself over the wall and rolled. A little red thing flew past her in the darkness, shrieking a shrill curse into the night. It banked and sped back toward her, but Isabella was faster. She ran toward it as fast as she could, her shin flaring pain up into her hip with each step. It screamed at her as it closed, eyes glowing bright with delight. Isabella threw herself to one side, turning with the thing as it flew past her. She was able to grab one scrawny leg and, using her momentum to pull them both around, launched it into the side of a chimney not five feet away from them.

This one's head didn't pop like the last one, but it slid down the chimney, its body blending in with the bricks, except for the trail of dark ichor it left behind.

Panting, both from exertion and terror, Isabella pushed herself on. A few more feet to the edge of the roof, that was it. She ran, stumbling, pulling herself forward with her arms to keep from slowing enough that the winged horrors could catch her. She skidded to a stop at the edge of the roof and looked down.

The street below was empty.

What? No! Briar has to be there. Isabella scanned first one way up the street, then the other. There, less than half a block away was a carriage at the side of the road, sitting next to the street's only lamp. *Bless her!*

She ran the edge of the roofs, pain shoved momentarily to one side by sublime relief. Flapping wings reached her ears once again, but Isabella didn't spare a look to see where the disgusting little things were. She hunched her head down, making it as small a target as possible. When she judged herself close enough, she jumped up on the roofline and dropped into empty space beneath her, her feet aimed right at the top of the carriage, and engaged the thrusters halfway down. They whooshed to life, then coughed and cut out. The canister was finally empty. Isabella dropped the last ten feet and careened into the carriage.

* * *

A thunderous crash shook the whole horseless. Briar grabbed the seat to keep from falling over. "What is going—?"

"Get moving!" Isabella's voice was like a whip. Briar had already thrown the lever that put the carriage in gear before she realized it.

High-pitched squeals and screeches filled the air. Briar was all too familiar with the sounds. Her blood ran cold with remembered pinches and scratches as leering faces tormented her younger self.

The carriage was moving, slowly at first, then faster as she pressed the accelerator. Small imp bodies landed on the carriage and on top of Isabella, tearing at her and trying to pull her free. If enough of them got their hooks in her, they'd be able to cart her away. Briar wasn't a little girl any more; she would not allow that to happen.

Briar steered the carriage back and forth, shedding imp bodies even as more rained down out of the sky. The carriage picked up still more speed as she pushed the accelerator all the way down to the floor. Johnson had cautioned her against going too fast—he'd said the vehicle was top-heavy—but she saw no other choice, not until they opened up some space between the carriage and the flock of imps.

They were almost at the next street. Briar pulled sharply at the wheel, sending them into a skid around the corner. The carriage groaned in protest, yawing over to roll on two wheels for an interminable moment before the suddenly airborne wheels crashed back to the street. Wood splintered where imps sank their claws into the wooden roof and sides to keep from being thrown free. Only a few were able to keep their grip. The rest tumbled from the vehicle to lie twitching on the stone cobbles. Some staggered to their feet, but most stayed down.

Briar knew that their only advantage right now was that the imps were much weaker here than in the infernal realm. They'd still be able to overwhelm Briar or Isabella if they mobbed together, but the longer they could stay out of their clutches, the weaker the little demons would become. The carriage was lighter now, and it leapt forward and out from under the cloud of imps, exactly as Briar had hoped.

"Can you drive?" she shouted over her shoulder at Isabella.

"Give me one more…" Isabella grunted with effort and another imp shot screeching from the top of the carriage. "Second." Another shriek was silenced by a loud thud. "Or two." She crawled forward until she was right behind Briar. "I'm ready."

Briar scooted to one side of the narrow seat so Isabella could join her. The seat hadn't been built to be shared. She pulled her skirts as far over as she could to make room for Isabella, while still steering as best she was able. Her foot slipped off the accelerator and the carriage slowed immediately. A communal squeal of triumph went up from the imps flocking after them. Isabella levered herself around and slid into the scant room Briar had made for her. She grabbed the wheel and the carriage shuddered to the left, heading toward a darkened storefront before Isabella yanked it to the other side and pointed them back down the street. At least they weren't on a major thoroughfare. There were no other carriages to bedevil them, and all any late-night pedestrians would see was an erratically driven carriage. It was unlikely they'd be able to perceive the imps, not unless they had demon blood of their own. They had to keep away from the pavement, though, or they'd chance striking someone out about their business, which would slow them down significantly. These areas of London never truly slept, not like those areas whose inhabitants were better off. Isabella would keep the carriage from running anyone over, Briar had to trust as much.

Her hands no longer occupied, Briar pressed the accelerator back down as far as she could. The carriage surged forward as if stung by a bee. The imps shrieked in disappointment.

"I've got it," Isabella said. She nudged Briar's foot off the pedal, freeing her up completely. "Now what?"

"Drive us somewhere safe! I'll take care of the imps." She turned around and levered open the window between the driver's seat and the cab. It was small, running along the base of the driver's narrow bench. It had been designed so the passengers could direct the driver. No one had made it to allow passage back into the cab, but she judged that she would fit, if barely.

"All right." Isabella's voice was steady, though Briar could see red stains on the undyed canvas of her jacket. There would be time enough to deal with wounds later. Right now Briar had to ensure they survived long enough to do so. The window opened and she squeezed her head into the cab, followed by her shoulders and arms. She pushed on either side of the window and muscled her ribs through the opening, though it was a near thing. She strained to get her hips past the window's threshold, but she was stuck, her legs kicking most indecorously through the window. *Damn these skirts!* The volume of material that made up her bustle would not pass through the small window. She struggled mightily to pass through, but didn't move so much as an inch.

Her dilemma was rudely solved when Isabella put her hand upon Briar's posterior and shoved her through the opening. Briar squeaked in outrage at the treatment of her bottom and again when she tumbled into the cab in a flurry of skirts and limbs.

There was no time to dwell upon the indignity. The clatter of carriage wheels over the uneven cobbles of London streets couldn't completely mask the thumps of imp bodies hitting the carriage, nor the scratching as they sank their claws into the top and sides and pulled themselves toward the unprotected driver at the front.

Briar ripped off one glove with her teeth, then sank her teeth into the tips of her ring and middle fingers. Blood welled up immediately, driven by the frenzied beating of her heart. She drew a rough circle on the ceiling of the carriage and started with the key-rune. The circle and character burst into crimson flame, as did each character she drew in rapid succession afterward. The fear and anger coursing through her lent extra potency to the runes. The inside of the cab was lit up by them.

When she finished, the cab's exterior lit up as well. A sphere of flame bloomed out from the drawing on the ceiling, pushing away the imps clinging to the carriage and flinging them into the dark. The cloud above them parted, its occupants shrieking in rage where the sphere burned them. A handful of imps burst into flames and plummeted to the ground like struggling meteorites.

The most pressing issue handled, Briar turned her attention to the floor. She knelt in the center of it and prepared a different circle. When she completed this one, they would be invisible to the demonic forces arrayed against them. These imps were too small and weak to be anything more than a front line response to Isabella's intrusion. Something else would come after them, something strong enough to survive the ravages of the human realm. That couldn't be allowed to happen.

She completed the inscription, but not without needing to reopen the small wounds on her fingertips. She worried at them again with her teeth, then activated the key-rune.

The gabble of imp voices above them grew confused, then less distinct. She risked sticking her head out the window and was relieved to see them dispersing. To them, the carriage and its occupants had simply disappeared between one breath and the next. They searched in a desultory manner before streaming back toward the factory, first one by one, then the remaining clump.

Briar leaned back against the seat and willed her racing heart to slow down. It would be a while before the recalcitrant organ would listen to her.

"Are we in the clear?" Isabella's voice floated through the open window.

"For the moment."

"What were those things? I've never seen their like before."

"Those were imps, the vermin of the infernal plane."

Isabella's head briefly appeared in the driver's window. Her eyes were wide with shock before she straightened up to watch the road. "Demons? I was attacked by demons?"

"I'm afraid so." Briar tried to put some apology into her tone, but she was unused to the sentiment. She should have known there was more going on in the factory when the imp-ridden man had appeared at their door. This was a bigger operation than she'd anticipated. When did she go to the earl or worse yet her mother? Best to wait until she had all the relevant information. "Were you able to get it?"

"Of course I was." Briar could hear Isabella's relief in her smile. "They didn't come after me because they disapproved of my outfit."

"Good." At least something had gone right that night. She relaxed against the leather seat. The grimoire was the answer to everything.

CHAPTER SIXTEEN

They were back on familiar ground, but that didn't stop Isabella from jumping at every noise. The only people out at this hour were delivery people. She looked steadfastly forward as they thundered over the cobbled streets. They must present quite the picture. If she stopped to acknowledge any of the onlookers, it would be only a matter of time before one of them sent for a constable. At least there shouldn't be any stories of Spring-Heeled Jack stealing a horseless and sending it careening through the streets. Once those things had cleared out, she'd removed her helmet and done her best to tuck her long hair into the collar of her coat. The blanket Briar had brought for warmth disguised her jump suit well enough once she was wrapped up in it.

It had been some time since the imps accosted them. The top of the carriage looked like it had been through a storm of knives; the sides hadn't fared much better. She'd heard little from Briar since Isabella had shoved her through the window. That push was likely going to come back to haunt her. Isabella couldn't imagine Briar would put up with such handling.

By the time her home came into view down the long street, Isabella was ready to sob with relief. The brick townhouse was the most beautiful thing she'd ever seen. Tension eased minutely from her shoulders. She was able to lower them from their hunched position up around her ears, though they still ached. She pulled around back and into the carriage house. Once the carriage was no longer in gear, she leaned back to speak through the window.

"Hold fast a little longer. I'm going to move us into the workshop." She didn't wait for Briar's response but jumped down from the driver's seat.

Her right leg gave out and she tumbled to the hard floor. With all the excitement, she had completely forgotten about her injuries. When she rediscovered the injury to her leg, the cuts and punctures along her back and sides decided to make themselves known as well. She gritted her teeth and pushed herself back to her feet, but a groan escaped her nonetheless.

Briar said nothing in response to her distress, and Isabella wasn't sure how she felt about that. Should she be relieved at not having to pretend the pain was nothing or annoyed that Briar couldn't be brought to show some concern about her condition? Her pain was certainly Briar's fault, at least partially. She never should have agreed to go into the factory, not with the complete lack of preparation she'd had.

Well, if Briar wasn't going to say anything, then neither was she. Isabella limped over to the wall and threw a large switch. Almost immediately, machinery spun to life under the floor. Cogs meshed together to bring the carriage down to the lower level. Isabella had to move quickly to get back to the carriage before the jump down was more than she could make on her bad leg. She undid the jump rig that suddenly weighed two hundred pounds and threatened to pull her over. She placed it carefully on the platform. Her gloves, helmet, and goggles joined it. Isabella leaned against the carriage door and watched as they made their slow way down to the workshop.

All was quiet and dark down there, for which Isabella was just as glad. Explaining to her father what they'd been up to wasn't something she wanted to contemplate. Mostly, she wanted to be out of the suit and into some clothes that had no extra perforations and that didn't smell of blood.

They came to a stop, but not before Isabella squeezed shut her eyes against her rising dizziness. After too much deliberation, she thought it best to sit on the ground before she toppled over.

"Is it safe to come out?" Briar asked.

Isabella nodded, then licked her lips before replying. "Yes." She shifted to one side.

The door opened and closed beside her, then Briar's cool hand rested on her cheek.

"You're hurt."

"Yes." *Thank you for noticing finally.*

"Where's the grimoire?"

That's what you're worried about? Isabella said nothing, but Briar pulled back her hand as if she'd been scalded.

"Right here," Isabella said. She opened the straps on the satchel attached to her front. It was one of the few places that had escaped the claws and teeth of the imps.

Briar reached in and drew it out. She looked about the darkened shop. "Over there," she said. She dashed across to one of the cleared benches and fairly threw down the huge tome. Bemused, Isabella watched as Briar drew with bloody fingertips on the top of the table. When she was done, she sagged, both hands pressed to the tabletop to stay upright. Exhaustion draped itself across her, then was gone as if it had never been. She pushed herself back up and dusted her hands together, then rejoined Isabella by the carriage.

"Now, let's get you cleaned up."

"Shouldn't that have been the first thing we did?" Her own exhaustion and pain combined in a peevish tone that made Isabella wince when she heard it come out of her mouth.

"If I hadn't taken care of the grimoire, it's likely we would have had company before too long. I expect there's a locator spell upon it. I've placed the book under a protective shield, essentially. I had a similar inscription over the carriage which served to confuse the imps. You left the protective sphere for a moment. I hope they weren't watching yet. If they were, we'll know soon enough, but imps aren't known for reporting their failures with alacrity." She touched Isabella's shoulder lightly. "I know you're in pain. Let me help you."

"Very well." Isabella stood with some difficulty. "Let's go over there." She pointed into the recesses of the workshop, to where her father sometimes stole a nap rather than taking the time needed to go into the house and bunk there. Althea usually scolded him for it. Apparently she missed his company when he was too deep in a project. Isabella shuddered. She did not want to think what her parents might do together.

"Are you feeling feverish?"

This was more like it, being fawned over by the woman she'd gone to such lengths to help. Isabella felt a bit like the conquering hero, returned triumphant from her quest. Pain lanced through her shoulder when she turned too quickly, and her feeling of accomplishment abated somewhat.

"Not at all." How to explain where her thoughts had wandered? Better not to even attempt it. Discretion was the better part of valor, or so they said. She giggled at the thought, then stopped, alarmed at the wandering direction her thoughts had taken.

"Oh dear. You are not doing very well, are you?"

"I'll be all right."

"Of course you will." Briar sat her down on the cot. "Do you have bandages?"

"In that chest. There is also alcohol and laudanum. But do not give that to me unless I ask for it. The pain isn't so unbearable right now."

"I have better ways of taking care of pain. You should disrobe."

Isabella blinked at Briar, confused at the suggestion. She'd come to hope Briar might say those words, but these were not the circumstances she'd envisioned. Unbidden, a slow curl of warmth moved through her center, pushing aside some of the discomfort as it worked its way to her groin.

"I will need to see your wounds to clean them," Briar said gently. "I can't treat them through heavy canvas."

"Oh." That made perfect sense. Isabella blushed, wondering what Briar must be thinking of her, so slow-witted as to need an explanation for taking off her clothes.

"I'll turn my back, if you'll be more comfortable."

"I'm all right." It didn't answer the question, but Isabella turned away and started carefully undoing the row of leather straps and buckles that marched down the front of the heavy jacket. She moved slowly, so as not to pull too much at the holes in her side. By the time she'd laboriously completed that simple task, Briar was setting all manner of medical supplies upon a low table next to the cot.

Without saying anything, she took over undressing Isabella. Carefully, she peeled the jacket away. Where fabric edges had adhered to wounds that were starting to clot, she soaked them carefully with alcohol until they separated more easily from Isabella's skin. She struggled to keep silent every time Briar started with another wound. The fire of alcohol in her cuts kept her from falling asleep where she sat. The silence between them stretched on and on as Briar worked and Isabella sat. Her eyelids would droop, then pop back open when Briar came to another tear in the coat.

"You said you would explain everything," Isabella said. Listening to Briar would keep her from drifting off only to be awoken by a spike of agony.

"I did, didn't I." Briar said nothing else for a long time, long enough for Isabella to start drifting off toward sleep again.

"So are you going to?"

"Yes." Briar hesitated, her voice uncharacteristically soft. "Yes, I will. But no matter what I tell you, you must promise be calm."

"Calm? About what?"

Briar took a deep breath, held it for a moment, then launched into what she had to say. Words tripped over her tongue, and Isabella had to listen closely to make sure she understood.

"I told you about my mother. She's not human. My father was, or so she says. I never met him. My mother is a demon and I was raised in the Infernal Realm, but I've been living on the Mortal Plane for years. I'm sensitive to what you call demoniac energy, and since I know the language of demons, I can manipulate that energy. It doesn't make me a magician, so much as…bilingual."

"That makes no sense." Isabella tried to crane her neck around to look at Briar and received a tap on the back of her head for her troubles. "I thought demons were an old myth spouted by preachers to convince people that working with demoniac energy is evil."

"Dearest Isabella, of course demons exist. They attacked you tonight."

Momentarily distracted by being called "dearest" by Briar, Isabella laughed nervously. "Then how can you be one of them? For one thing, if you're half one of those imp-things, then why do you look so human?"

"For the first part, thankfully my mother's people are not imps. Those are disgusting and vile little creatures. And for another, I don't look human, at least not completely. Now stick out your arms."

Isabella automatically complied with the instructions. Briar pulled the jacket off her outstretched arms and carefully laid it to one side. She moved around to the front of Isabella and took a seat on the edge of the cot before undoing the top button on her shirt. Isabella looked down and marveled at the sight of staid and proper Briar undoing one button after another. Another curl of arousal sifted through her belly.

"You look pretty normal to me." Isabella placed one hand over Briar's, pausing it in its task of undoing her shirt. "You look beautiful to me."

A visible shiver ran through Briar. "You don't see all of me." She closed her eyes. "Please remove your hand. I can't work when you're touching me."

"Oh." Isabella pulled her hand back. She must have misread Briar's intentions, though how she could have misunderstood the kisses they'd shared at the rooming house, she didn't know. "Sorry."

"It's not that." Briar opened her eyes. They glowed red for a moment, then she blinked and they were her normal brown. "I can feel what you're feeling when our skin touches. Your... excitement is quite distracting."

"Oh!" Isabella hadn't been expecting that. "I didn't mean to—"

"It is quite all right, Isabella." Briar looked down at the buttons. She seemed to be having some problems with them. "The attention is not unwelcome, but I fear what will happen if you see me as I truly am. And if I am to be with you the way you want me to be, the way I want to be, you will see all of me."

"Isn't that the point?"

The question startled a low chuckle out of Briar, a sound that wrapped around Isabella and did more to stoke the flames of her arousal than the touches to her back had done. It was nearly as arousing as the kisses they had shared.

The buttons conquered, Briar pulled the shirt down from Isabella's shoulders, moving carefully to avoid hurting her. She needn't have bothered being so cautious. Isabella burned for Briar's touch, and each unintentional caress of her fingers along Isabella's bare skin tested her control. The pain was as nothing to her now. It melted into the maelstrom of sensation building in her core.

"It may be the point, but if you see me as I truly am, without the shroud that makes me look human, you won't be able to control yourself. My mother is not an imp, she is a succubus. She is lust incarnate, and I share many of her traits."

"Briar." Isabella captured her hands and held them. "If you truly can feel what I feel, then you know I'm practically overcome by lust already. I haven't seen under your shroud, or whatever it is, but I want you." She squeezed Briar's hands hard. "I want you so badly I fear I may burst from it."

Briar's cheeks were flushed. Isabella might not have been able to feel what Briar was feeling, but the telltale signs of arousal were there. From her parted lips, to the way her chest heaved for breath against her corset, to the pulse at her neck, Briar looked as agitated as Isabella felt.

She drew back one hand and slapped Isabella smartly on the knuckles. "I must finish tending to your wounds."

Isabella relinquished her hold and caressed the back of her hand with the other. Heat from the smack joined the conflagration of her arousal. "I don't care."

"I do. I will not be the cause of further injury to you." Despite her words, she moved much more quickly now. When Isabella didn't complain at her rough treatment, Briar practically ripped the shirt from Isabella's body, then stopped. "I am so very sorry," she said when she could fully behold the wounds the imps had inflicted upon Isabella.

"They look worse than they feel." At the moment, they were little more than tender spots keeping her from what she needed.

"I certainly hope so. They look quite painful indeed. They will be even more painful while I clean them. Unless…"

"Unless what?"

"Unless you permit me to inscribe some runes upon you for the pain and to accelerate your healing. I won't do it without your permission."

"Will it hurt?"

"No. I'll use the blood from your wounds. All you should feel is my fingers moving over your skin."

"Very well." Isabella gripped the edges of the cot and closed her eyes. "I trust you."

"Clearly." Briar had noticed Isabella steeling herself and drawn back.

Briar had misinterpreted the reason for her actions, Isabella realized. She was not in fear of her; she was trying to keep from being swept away by the strength of her response to Briar's touch. "It's not that, Briar. Truly."

There was no response to her reassurance, but after a moment Briar's fingers moved over her back. True to her words, Isabella felt nothing more than fingertips tracing an incomprehensible design on her back. When Briar removed her fingers, Isabella experimentally flexed the muscles of her back. There wasn't even the slightest twinge of pain.

"Be careful," Briar said. "You may not be able to feel the pain, but you are still injured. Some of the punctures are deep enough to reach muscle, and if you move too sharply, you may damage them further. The rune of health accelerates your natural healing abilities, but you must be careful for a time yet." Her voice had lost some of its previous sharpness. If she really could read Isabella's emotions, then she would have felt no fear when she drew the runes on her back.

Briar returned to the task of cleaning the multiple punctures and cuts with brutal efficiency. It certainly would have been painful without the effects of the runes. Then again, the pain would have been a welcome distraction from her aching loins. Instead, she sat and endured her own excitement, until at last Briar no longer touched her.

She opened her eyes and beheld Briar gazing upon her body with open need on her face.

"Isabella," Briar murmured. "You are the beautiful one." She ran her eyes down Isabella's chest. Isabella looked down also. It was nothing special, as far as she could tell. Her proportions were not overly large, and her chest was sprinkled with freckles, no matter that she was almost never in the sun. Briar's skin was flawless, that she could tell, though she lacked Briar's current advantage.

"Hardly." Isabella gently stroked Briar's face, caressing her cheekbones and trailing her thumb along the bottom of her jawline.

Briar's lips fell apart and her eyes lightened, changing color as Isabella watched from the brown of tea with a hint of milk, to auburn, to a brick color, then shifting to brilliant red.

"Are you certain you want to proceed?" Briar whispered. There was fear in her eyes, fear and the desperate hope that Isabella would say yes.

"There is nothing I want more," Isabella croaked back, her throat dry. It was the truth. Isabella had never wanted anything as badly as she wanted to be with the woman in front of her. The infuriating, demanding, never-wrong woman who somehow managed to be more alluring than the most compliant of her bed partners. "Please, Briar. Show me."

CHAPTER SEVENTEEN

Isabella stared up at her and Briar tried to believe the entreaty she saw on her face. The problem was less that she worried Isabella would find her repulsive but that once she saw Briar's true form she wouldn't be able to resist her. Briar wasn't her mother; she had no wish for anyone to worship at her feet. Would she be able to trust Isabella's attraction to her once she was before her without the shroud?

There was only one way to find out.

Briar stood and moved away until she was out of Isabella's reach. She turned her back and let go of the shroud. Her hands bled pearlescent grey through the cream of her flesh. It was a color both darker and more luminescent than the human flesh she covered it with. It didn't glow from within, not like her eyes would, those seemed to collect the light and reflect it back at the viewer. She'd avoided the glowing gaze in the mirror often enough to know she shared her mother's eyes, no matter how much she might wish otherwise.

"Briar?" Isabella was at her shoulder, hands sliding around her waist.

"What do you think?"

Isabella pulled her back against her, molding their bodies together or trying to. The bustle somewhat ruined the attempt. She nuzzled Briar's neck, her lips shockingly warm in the cool air of the workshop. At the touch of Isabella's lips on her bare skin, Briar was swept away by the lust that poured from her. Was there more than there had been before? Briar couldn't tell, and at that moment she found she didn't much care.

She turned in Isabella's arms and pulled her in for the embrace she'd craved since their time together in the hotel. Their lips fit together perfectly, as they had before. Briar kissed Isabella with everything she had, with the passion she felt now and the terror she'd felt when the imps had pursued her back to where she waited. Desperation edged into her and she bit down on Isabella's lower lip. She had to be certain the other woman was really there, that this wasn't simply a dream and she'd soon awaken in her own bed, bereft and wanting.

Isabella moaned into her mouth at the nip and Briar smiled against her lips. She ran her hands over bare shoulders and down to where a brassiere covered Isabella's assets. She needed to feel as much of Isabella's skin against hers as possible.

"Help me," she whispered raggedly.

"With pleasure." Passion stained Isabella's pale cheeks soft red. She leaned forward for another kiss while her hands sought out the long row of buttons down the back of Briar's dress. They kissed again, tongues dueling around each other as Isabella fumbled with the buttons.

Finally, Isabella drew back. "To hell with it." She turned Briar around, much to her disappointment. Isabella grumbled to herself as she tried to shed Briar's dress. The faster she tried to undo the fasteners, the longer it seemed to take her. When she could take it no longer, Isabella grabbed either side of the dress and pulled. Buttons flew every which way, bouncing off the floor in a short-lived ivory hailstorm. The dress sagged immediately, and Isabella drew it down and held it there while Briar stepped out of it.

Briar stepped back when Isabella reached for the laces of her corset. "I think I'd better attend to that," she said, smiling to take the sting out of her refusal.

Isabella's lower lip protruded slightly in an adorable little pout that Briar doubted she even knew she was doing. She said nothing but pulled on one lace where it was tied at the top. The knot came open in her hand, the corset loosening noticeably already. With practiced fingers, she unlaced it, then stood before Isabella in her petticoats, chemise, and knickers, the corset gaping open.

"Oh, Briar," Isabella whispered. She pulled the corset from Briar's nerveless fingers. She shivered as cool air touched her skin. With Isabella's help, she stepped out of the petticoats, leaving them in a large heap on the floor. With gentle fingers, Isabella lifted the edge of the chemise, exposing Briar's body to her gaze. The touch of her fingers injected a new cascade of lust into her. Heat filled her from Isabella's caresses until she wondered why smoke wasn't rising from where their skin made contact.

Briar couldn't tell where her arousal left off and Isabella's started. It didn't matter. All that mattered was getting Isabella naked and beneath her, with all possible haste. She skimmed her knickers off and kicked them away before turning her attention to Isabella.

At her sudden aggression, Isabella backed away toward the cot. She bit her lower lip so hard Briar was surprised when her teeth didn't break the skin.

"May I?" Briar asked, skimming her fingers under the edge of Isabella's waistband. She didn't wait for a response before popping open the top button of the fly.

Isabella gasped and shuddered. When her knees seemed ready to give out, she grabbed Briar's upper arms. The last thing they needed was Isabella falling over and injuring herself further. Briar firmed up her grip at the waist of Isabella's pants and steered her all the way back to the cot. She pushed Isabella down but stopped when she heard Isabella's hissing intake of breath. Briar had been the one with the lecture on Isabella being prudent, and here she was treating her with no care whatsoever.

Isabella shouldn't have been feeling any pain. If she was, it was doing little to slow her down. The rough handling had done nothing to lessen her ardor, it seemed. If anything, it had increased it.

Naughty girl, Briar thought. *Isabella likes an aggressive woman.* From the overtone of surprise to Isabella's lust, this was a new discovery. Clearly, Isabella was anything but a virgin. She betrayed no anxiety at their actions, nor at her own surprise. Briar looked forward to exploring those possibilities with her. She would be happy to provide Isabella with a firm hand, if that was what she wanted. But first, those pants had to go.

She lowered her head to Isabella's beautiful stomach. She wore no girdle, and Briar was grateful for the ease of access the discovery afforded her. Isabella's abdominal muscles contracted nicely when she nibbled her way down her belly to the top curve of her hip where it peeked out above the waistband of her trousers. Briar made short work of the buttons and pulled the pants down. Isabella's drawers were no match for her either; she was able to divest them while still kissing and sucking her way across the smooth expanse of skin.

The thatch of hair between Isabella's legs was bright red. It seemed designed to draw Briar's eye, and she decided to investigate more closely. Isabella's hips twitched and her thighs fell open as Briar ran her tongue down the sensitive strip of skin that separated her thigh from her torso. Briar bit down sharply at the twitch.

"Keep still," she ordered, then laved the chastised flesh with the flat of her tongue. Isabella's only response was another intake of breath, but Briar had felt the surge of pleasure, more at the order than the nip. Her own pleasure swirled within her in anticipation. Isabella was responsive, and Briar was swept along with her excitement.

The scent of Isabella's musk flooded her nose. She inhaled deeply, wanting to take in as much of her lover as possible. She spread her fingers across Isabella's thigh and dove in, coating the bottom half of her face with the copious wetness that trickled from Isabella's most private place.

Isabella grabbed her head and held her there, tangling her fingers in Briar's long hair. The encouragement was unnecessary, but certainly welcome. Briar dipped her tongue into Isabella's entrance and was rewarded with a deep moan, one she felt as much as heard. She swirled her tongue around the entrance and easily rode Isabella's hips as they bucked against her face. She drew her tongue up from the entrance to where Isabella's clitoris quivered proudly, begging for her attention. She circled the eager protuberance once, twice, and again. Isabella no longer moaned, but called aloud in a torrent of curses and gasping, all interspersed with Briar's name or entreaties to her god. Briar could feel the echoes of what she did to Isabella deep within herself. Liquid trickled from between her thighs as her arousal reached a fever pitch she'd rarely experienced.

Briar batted at the tip of Isabella's clitoris with her tongue, then took it into her mouth, suckling upon it. Isabella was beyond speech. She clamped her thighs around Briar so tightly that Briar wondered if she was going to be able to breathe. She grabbed Isabella by the rump and held on as she continued to suck on her. She dug her fingernails into the taut muscles and Isabella jerked against her, the additional stimulus more than she could bear. She threw her head back and screamed her release to the cold, uncaring workshop. Faint sounds of her passion echoed back to them. Isabella collapsed back onto the narrow cot, which creaked alarmingly at being treated so roughly. Her thighs stayed locked around Briar for a few moments longer before releasing her.

Briar stayed where she was, unwilling to lose contact.

"My god, Briar," Isabella finally said. Her voice cracked from overexertion. "That was amazing. I don't think I've ever felt anything like that before."

Suddenly alarmed, Briar sat straight up. "Surely that wasn't your first time?" How had she misinterpreted Isabella's emotions so drastically?

Isabella waved a limp hand reassuringly in her direction. "Of course not. But that was the first time someone tried to make the top of my head come off."

"Oh." Briar relaxed, feeling unaccountably smug. "That's all right then."

"That was more than all right. That was…" Isabella hummed to herself instead of choosing a word to describe the experience. "I'm going to need a moment."

"Take all the time you need." It was the least she could do, after all.

"Why don't you come up here?" Isabella patted the cot next to her.

"It's very narrow, don't you think?"

"I'll make room." She angled her body so there was possibly enough room for Briar.

The cot was exceedingly narrow and had not been built with the idea of accommodating more than one, but Briar couldn't resist Isabella. She climbed up and slid onto the cot in front of her. Isabella had to wrap her arms around her to keep them both from rolling out of the narrow bed. The warmth of Isabella's embrace felt like coming home, as did the contentedness that radiated from her skin and into Briar. She relaxed for the first time, possibly in forever. Isabella's breath caressed the back of her neck, each exhalation sending shivers all the way down her spine to the tips of her toes.

How long they lay together, wrapped up in each other, Briar had no idea. It wasn't as long as she wanted, that was for certain, but when she felt Isabella's satisfaction recede and her arousal come to the fore once more, she was beyond ready.

Isabella's lips at her neck came as no surprise. Briar closed her eyes and enjoyed the shivers the contact awoke in her. Goosebumps pebbled her skin of her legs. She moaned aloud when Isabella reached around and cupped her breast. Her clever fingers plucked at Briar's nipple and the moan disintegrated into a gasp. Tension built within her, coiling tighter and tighter and centering on her groin.

Briar was unable to stop her hips from lifting in mute appeal. It felt like her entire life had aimed her at this moment, this perfect slice of time with Isabella. Isabella bit down hard on Briar's shoulder, wringing a high cry from her. Isabella knew exactly what she wanted, what she craved with every fiber of her being. Her fingers trailed from Briar's breast down over the curve of her hip. They tangled through Briar's bush. Wetness flowed from her in anticipation, but Isabella allowed her fingers to roam around her outer petals, refusing to give her what she ached for.

"Isabella, please." Her voice broke. Another time she would have been humiliated to sound so needy, but she didn't care, not when Isabella withheld the completion she so required from her. "Please!"

Those clever fingers dipped between her lips, into the wet, aching focus of Briar's need. Nothing else mattered now. If she didn't feel Isabella within her, the universe might as well stop spinning for all she cared.

Then her demands were answered. Isabella slid a finger within her, stroking that spot inside, the one her entire being was focused upon. Isabella pulled out and Briar growled in frustration, then cried out as one finger was replaced by two that reached deep inside, stroking her, knowing her. Briar barely noticed when Isabella shifted away from her, pushing her back against the cot. She withdrew again and Briar opened her eyes and glared at Isabella, who simply grinned back. When she came back, it was with three fingers, stretching Briar deliciously around fingers that thrust in and out, skating over spots guaranteed to bring her release.

The more Isabella moved inside her, the tighter pressure coiled around Briar's center. She was one with the pleasure that drove her, screaming before it. When Isabella leaned forward and took one of her nipples between her teeth and bit down, Briar could restrain herself no more. She exploded outward, everything she knew going with it. She was everywhere, she was nowhere. Briar was no longer; all that existed was pleasure. She reached the edge of her being and paused, floating in nothingness, before receding slowly back into herself. Everything tingled and her eyes tried to focus but couldn't. Eventually, Isabella's smiling face coalesced in front of her eyes.

"Welcome back," Isabella said. "That was quite a journey, wasn't it?"

"Very much so." Briar stretched luxuriously, willing life back into limbs still heavy with sensation. Her knuckles brushed something cold and hard. "What?" The ground was much too close, but that made no sense since they were on a bed.

"Oh that." Isabella shrugged. "We broke the cot."

"I have no regrets."

"Neither do I." Isabella gathered Briar back into her arms and held her close.

The shroud. She should have pulled it back on, but that seemed like so much effort. Isabella was there; it didn't matter. There would be time enough for hiding later. For now, she was happy to be able to drop the facade.

CHAPTER EIGHTEEN

It should have been uncomfortable, but when Isabella opened her eyes, she was anything but. Briar's arm lay heavy around her waist, snugging her buttocks into the curve of her pelvis. If she moved, either she would end up on the cold stones of the floor or Briar would, but she thought perhaps she could have stayed that way forever. Briar was a comforting warmth against her back. The thigh tangled between her legs was more distracting than comforting. The previous night's activities weren't far from her mind—or from her groin, judging by the heat that settled there when she thought of Briar beneath her, black hair spread across the cot, skin so luminescent it almost glowed.

Isabella shifted when her lust roared back to life. She had to have Briar again. She rocked her hips back against Briar, seeking the friction her nether region demanded. Briar's arm tightened around her waist.

"So soon?" Briar asked huskily. She chuckled low in her throat and Isabella thought perhaps she would come again simply from the sound.

"Oh yes," Isabella said, her voice rusty. "I can't get enough of you."

Briar stiffened against her and would have pulled away if Isabella hadn't held her arm against her. She looked down and watched as the pearlescence of Briar's skin dimmed then was swallowed by the appearance of her human skin. The arm felt no different.

"What's wrong?" Isabella didn't understand the shift in Briar's demeanor, but she was no longer trying to leave.

"You only want me because of my succubus blood. What you're feeling isn't real."

Isabella opened her mouth to rebut the statement, then closed it when nothing came to mind. The idea was so ridiculous, she didn't wish to countenance it, not even to speak against it. Briar was certainly extremely attractive, in her real form or wearing her disguise. But could it be true? There was no denying her attraction, and it certainly went beyond what she'd felt for the girls she'd dallied with on her father's estates. No, that had been fun. What she had with Briar felt like it went beyond mutual amusement.

"If that's true," Isabella finally said, "then why do I want you as badly now as I did a few seconds ago. You do yourself a disservice, Briar." It took some doing and no small amount of support from Briar, but Isabella was able to maneuver herself around to look her lover in the face. She ignored how fantastic their breasts felt mashed together and looked Briar in the eye. "You are beautiful, there is no denying that, but I care not one fig about that. Human or demon, I want to be with you. Your body is one thing, but your mind is truly stupendous. I love the way you view things and file them away for later. I love—"

At the far end of the shop, the lights came on. Cogs and gears groaned to life above their heads.

"The lift," Isabella hissed. "Someone's coming!" The blanket over them was nowhere near enough to preserve their modesty. No matter who was coming down the lift, disaster awaited them if they were caught together.

Briar leaped from the bed, pulling the cover with her. "Where are all my clothes?"

"You'll never get back into that dress in time." That and Isabella had completely destroyed the buttons. They had only one hope now. Isabella threw open a small footlocker against the near wall and pulled out her coveralls. "Put this on."

From the look on her face when Briar held up the coveralls, she would rather have eaten earthworms raw. "My corset," she said instead. "You must help me."

"For the love of…" Isabella bustled over to Briar. She'd already managed to do up half the ties. "Hold still," she ordered crisply when

Briar tried to pull on her bloomers while Isabella was attending to the remaining corset strings. It was fortunate the lift took as long as it did to descend, but with Briar's insistence on the corset, this was going to be close. She pulled halfheartedly on the strings before tying them. "There." It would have to do.

Briar said nothing and pulled on her underwear, then the coveralls, grimacing as she did so. While Isabella had none of the same compunctions about her work clothes, it felt strange to pull them on over bare skin. Her endowments weren't nearly so impressive as Briar's, but the canvas chafed at her sensitive nipples. She ignored the lustful surge in her belly. *Now is not the time for such distractions*, she told herself severely. Her body was deaf to her remonstrance and continued to yearn for Briar's touch.

The lift was almost all the way down. Isabella could see daylight at the top of the shaft. How long had they been down there?

"Get over to the work bench," she said. "We need to look busy."

Briar's nod was jerky, but she strode over to the bench where that damn book sat, surrounded by strange symbols in darkening blood. In Briar's blood.

Isabella didn't know if it was the loss of Briar's proximity or the relief now that they were no longer nude, but she bit her lower lip as the lacerations in her back and shoulders chose that moment to remind her of their existence. Her right leg throbbed, and when she pulled up her pants leg, she wasn't surprised to see a mottled bruise covering most of her shin. It felt considerably better than it had earlier, but the ache was constant.

There was nothing to do but look as if they'd been down there working all night. She handed Briar a hair tie on her way past and was rewarded with a brief smile at her thoughtfulness. Briar swept her hair back in one easy motion, and Isabella had to force herself to keep moving and not stand staring at the curve of her neck. Her suit was back in the small alcove with the destroyed cot, but her first priority was the jump rig. She was kneeling in front of it, inspecting it for damage when her father wandered into the area.

"Oh, hullo, Izzy," he said. If he noticed their somewhat bedraggled condition, he said nothing. His attention was riveted to the carriage still on the vehicle lift. "Blimey, what happened here?"

"Hail," Isabella answered promptly.

"Unkindness of ravens," Briar said at the same time. Of course she knew what a group of ravens was called.

"Yes." Isabella stared at Briar, her hands spread. *What was that?* she mouthed. "It was like a hail of ravens, the flock was so large. I told Briar—er—Brionie that I'd fix it for her."

"Ravens?" Both of Joseph's eyebrows were so high they practically disappeared into his hairline. "That's a devil of a thing." He ran his fingers over some of the worst of the rents in the wood. "They must have been quite sizable."

"Very." Isabella relaxed. Her father seemed prepared to accept the idea. Of course, what choice did he have, really? It wasn't like he'd think, or even believe it if he they tried to tell him, that they'd been attacked by a flock of demons.

It was hard enough for her to believe it, never mind that she'd seen and felt the imps herself. Briar's true form was further evidence, and she'd done more than touch that. Her demonic heritage should have been stranger, and perhaps had she not been pursued across London's rooftops by imps, she might have been more put off by her revelation. Instead, this new side to Briar fit her; more than that, it made a certain amount of sense. Beside all of that, Briar was still the same person, eyes glowing red or not.

Unaware of Isabella's internal deliberation, her father continued: "Still, Jean-Pierre will be pleased to have the chance to work with the carriage again. He was quite put out only to get a taste of the magic this conveyance uses to power itself."

"Of course." Isabella shut her mouth on the rest of her comment. Her father simply would not hear anything negative about his friend and partner. They'd been working together for years, and it was Isabella's opinion that LaFarge benefited far more from the arrangement than did Joseph. He never said anything when LaFarge applied for patents under his name alone, then sold them almost immediately. When Isabella had asked him about it, he'd shrugged and said that LaFarge had none of the advantages he did, so why not let him benefit? These days, their family would have been well-served by the remuneration from her father's inventions, but she couldn't tell him that either.

"I doubt it will do him much good," Briar said. Despite the cutting remark, she looked worried, though Isabella doubted Joseph would notice. To every external appearance, Briar seemed composed enough, but Isabella could read the tension in her shoulders as she turned back to the grimoire. She hadn't even opened it yet, but her notebook was already out, and her neat notations filled at least one page.

"What are you working on, Izzy?" Joseph leaned over her.

Isabella cringed at the use of the pet name in front of Briar. It made her sound about five years old, not an impression she wanted to leave with the other woman. "Simply inspecting my rig for damage," she said. "It was involved in a bit of a tumble." She held up her hand to forestall him. "I'm not injured, but the rig was banged up."

"Nothing major, it would appear."

"Thankfully not. I suspect the damage is mostly cosmetic, though I shall have to recalibrate it and run some tests."

"I see." His eyes turned vague as he straightened. "I will simply…" Joseph wandered off, his voice trailing away as he was subsumed by his plans for the day. Isabella was just as glad. Every time he was around the jump rig, the possibility existed, however remote, that he might wonder why on earth she needed such a thing. She didn't want to lie to him about it, but she simply could not permit him to find out what she was using it for.

She tinkered with the rig a little longer to make sure nothing was truly amiss. When she found a strap that had been almost severed, she shuddered. It hung on by a few threads. One of the imps had nearly managed to take her down. The accompanying laceration on her shoulder twinged when she realized how close she'd come to not making it to Briar and the carriage. That strap would need to be replaced, as would one of the valves that had been wrenched to one side, damaging the conduit there. That had likely happened after she'd used the last of the propellant in the tank. Otherwise, she would have gone winging off into the night at an odd angle and with little to no control. All things considered, she'd been very lucky.

The next order of business was to see if the suit or any of its pieces could be salvaged. She looked around to see what her father was working on. He was embroiled with some small components on a bench of the far side of the workshop. Good. When she brought out the suit, she didn't want to have to worry about him seeing the bloodstains.

As she passed Briar, Isabella stopped. Briar was bent over the grimoire, her neck arched delicately as she flipped slowly from one page to the next as if looking for something. Strands of hair had escaped her rough bun and curled alluringly at the base of her neck. She glanced Joseph's way again before dropping a quick kiss on the back of Briar's slender neck.

"Hmmm," Briar said. Isabella made out the corner of a smile, though Briar never looked up.

Cheered immensely, Isabella whistled as she retrieved her jump suit. While she was back in the cot area, she took a few moments to straighten up. There was no reason it had to look like they'd had a stupendous time enjoying each other's bodies. She folded Briar's clothes into a neat pile and did her best to corral as many of her dress's errant buttons as possible.

The first thing she did upon bringing the suit back to her bench was cut out the bloodstains before her father could see them. A nearby drawer of scraps was a good enough place to hide them. Once she finished the task, the suit bore more than a passing resemblance to Swiss cheese. There would be no salvaging it, so she bent to the task of extracting as many components as possible. She had a backup suit, but it had none of the tubing or thrust controls; she'd only made one set of those. As she worked, Isabella made a note to work up a set of backup controls as soon as possible. If she was going to continue spending so much time with Briar, it was likely she would need them.

One of the rubber tubes that snaked down the left sleeve was shredded. That would need to be replaced, and Isabella set it aside. Without it, she'd be able to make simple jumps only; there would be none of the fine-tuning she'd normally be able to manage.

That was it; she'd salvaged everything she could. All that remained was to transfer the working components to her backup suit and get to work on recreating what she hadn't been able to save. Deep in her work, Isabella hummed to herself.

CHAPTER NINETEEN

Caught in the same restless dreamscape that consumed most of his sleeping hours, he was nonetheless vaguely aware of his body. The irony of it all wasn't lost on him, even mostly asleep. The more success he had in the waking world, the worse his sleep became. There were nights when he thought he might gladly trade all the trappings his achievements had brought him for a decent night's slumber. Then he woke up and decided all over again that that would never happen.

The creeping realization that he was no longer alone brought him into full wakefulness in the blink of an eye.

"I told you never to come in here." God, he hated the stunted things. They watched him with glowing eyes, waiting for the slightest misstep before running to report to their mistress. Mistakes were impossible not to make, and each one was roundly punished by *her*.

"Sorry." It wasn't sorry, not with the wide smile cutting its brick-red face in half. It dry-washed clawed hands where it perched at the foot of his bed. The mahogany was already gouged and torn from the few seconds it had spent there. "Important."

"It had better be." He threw the heavy covers back and grabbed his spectacles from the bedside table. Runes and inscriptions snapped into focus around him. "If it's not, you'll be mine."

"Someone took it." It cringed, covering its head. "Someone took book."

"What?" This had better be some elaborate prank by the imps. Their sense of humor was crude at best. As a prank this was more than a little sophisticated for them, but the alternative was impossible to contemplate. "Do you mean to say my grimoire has been stolen? Which one of you miserable little pieces of excrement did it?"

"Not us!" it wailed. "Someone else. Someone from outside! Tried to get back, but too strong. Lost hands and hands of family." It spread both hands, fingers wide to demonstrate.

"Impossible." He bounded out of bed and grabbed the nearest pair of trousers from the floor. A shirt hung over the doorknob and he snagged that on his way out the door. He raced down the wide stairs, hollering for his driver to get the carriage ready. The imp flew after him, a dry fluttering of wings that rarely failed to send a chill down his spine.

If the grimoire was gone, they wouldn't be able to finish what they'd started. *That might not be such a bad thing*, part of him whispered. With the ease of long practice, he quashed the soft voice of his conscience. It rarely troubled him anymore, especially not when in his palatial home in London's most fashionable neighborhood. She would not be pleased, not in the least, and her displeasure had serious consequences.

The butler tried to stifle a yawn as he held the door open. It was hours before dawn, and yet the whole household was rousing in response to his shouted orders. The butler might be in his nightshirt and housecoat, but he still discharged his duty. He waited impatiently in front of the house, tapping one toe on the sidewalk until the driver brought around his horseless carriage.

"Out," he said. He scaled the side of the carriage, not waiting for his chauffeur, who had to jump down on the other side. There was a step on the driver's side to aid in mounting and dismounting the tall vehicle, and he thought nothing of forcing the help to go without it. His chauffeur said nothing as he scampered out of the way to stand in the street in a cloud of dust as the carriage peeled away.

No one knew these machines like he did. Even his own chauffeur didn't know the limits to which it could be pushed. He looked up and beckoned the imp to land next to him. When it came close, he seized it by the neck and bashed its head against the sharp edge of the carriage top. It had been too long in the human realm and burst easily. He dipped his fingers in its black blood and traced a small inscription on the driver's seat. The blood flared blue then disappeared, leaving crisp lines of pure demoniac energy behind him.

The carriage leaped forward as he magically reduced the friction of the vehicle to the air. It could be a dangerous maneuver, but one that wasn't so risky in the wee hours of the morning when the streets were practically deserted. The milk carts were about the only vehicles making their rounds. He cursed at one when it tried to pull out in front of him. He was upon it almost immediately but swerved in time to keep from clipping the side of the sturdy wagon.

Usually his address was a point of pride, but today it was too far from the factory. The closer he got, the more signs he saw that something was seriously amiss. Imp corpses littered the route, already rotting and stinking. All that made them recognizable was the dark ichor, the same shade that painted the top of his carriage. Most humans wouldn't even notice them until they were too far gone to be identifiable. Then they'd wonder how something could die and decompose to such a state without being remarked upon. Some of them might vaguely recall the terrible odor that had lingered for a few days, then shrug and go on with their day. Demons were inconceivable to much of humanity; their fragile little minds refused to recognize them. It didn't stop visceral reactions such as fear or disgust when in their presence, but to truly perceive them, they needed exposure.

His own exposure had been brief but intense. He saw all the things humans couldn't and knew he was the richer for it. Quite literally.

Finally the tall stacks of his factory came into view between canyons formed by tall buildings shoved together on narrow streets. To his frustration, he had to slow down. Work started much earlier in these parts of town, and the streets had already filled up. One shift of human workers was leaving the factory, and the next one was coming on. It wouldn't do for Thomas Holcroft to be seen charging in with his tail on fire. That would only lead to rumors, and they worked best by keeping a low profile. Or at least a normal profile. That meant no rumors.

He kept to as sedate a pace as he could manage without wanting to kill something else and pulled into the spot reserved for him only. The workers might be here, but the clerks wouldn't report for work for hours yet. He could still keep this under control.

He bypassed the chassis plant and made straight for the engine shop. The door was almost never used and then only by him. It opened easily under his hand, though anyone else—demon and human alike—would find the handle impossible to turn. The door to his office from the chassis building was the same way. It wouldn't do for the wrong human to interrupt him at an inopportune time. The only hand other than his that could open that door was *hers*.

The scent of demons assaulted the inside of his nostrils as he entered. He had a breathing apparatus to filter out the smell, but it was in his office. The stench wouldn't hurt him, but that didn't stop his gorge from rising. He pushed down the urge to vomit with the ease of long experience.

Groups of imps still gathered about the engines, with the larger eurynom keeping them on task. The infernal overseers were larger versions of imps with blue-black skin that appeared as a void in the darkened room; they lacked the wings of their smaller, more numerous brethren. They were still more than capable of snatching offending imps out of the air and twisting off a limb or two. Those imps would be out of commission for a short time as a new arm or leg grew back. From what he understood, the process of regrowth was as painful as the loss. It seemed an effective way of keeping the imps in line, and it provided a ready supply of blood for the polygnots who wandered among them, waiting to turn the engines from lifeless cylinders of metal to engines capable of powering a carriage.

Watching them for too long turned his stomach. The chaos and casual brutality churned before him while still managing to turn out a steady supply of engines for the chassis being built next door. He didn't need to know how their barbaric hierarchy worked, as long as it did.

If he was going to be honest with himself, he would admit that the upset of his bowels was as much at the scene in front of him as it was for the impending confrontation with her. He had no illusions that *she* would try to lay this at his door, along with every other hiccup that had happened along the way. This time, he knew he was in the right. Her imps were the ones that had turned this into a dog's mess.

He mounted the stairs along the outside wall. His presence was noted and the shrill screams and raucous laughter faded. Hundreds of glowing green eyes followed his slow progress up until he stopped at the platform where his grimoire typically resided. It was too heavy to carry with him everywhere. The platform had been a convenient enough place for it to be stored, as that was where he did most of his magic work, and the chain should have been enough to secure it against casual mischief. Someone had gone to great lengths to make their way here to abscond with the grimoire. The chain was in a careless heap on the metal floor; there was no sign of the book. The only way into this side of the factory, aside from the small portal to the netherworld he'd created with *her* help, was the door from his personal office.

The door to the bridge between buildings was ajar. There was no more time to waste. The longer that grimoire was gone, the more chance there was that whoever had it would turn what they found within its pages against them. His heart in his throat, he pushed the door open and made his reluctant way into his office. *She* would be waiting for him there. He bit the inside of his lip until it bled. The taste of iron on his tongue calmed him somewhat. It was a natural flavor, far removed from the demonic stink he'd just left.

She wasn't in the bed chamber, which was just as well. Maybe she wasn't there at all; that would be fine. He'd be able to get down to looking for the grimoire and perhaps getting it back before she was any the wiser.

His faint hope was dashed as soon as he left the partitioned-off area with the bed. *She* waited for him in the chair at the end of the conference table. Somehow, the leather chair looked like a throne when she sat on it. Imps draped themselves across the leather. Dimly, he knew they had to be tearing it up with their claws, but he only had eyes for her.

She wasn't tall. Even in the chair it was easy to tell that, but it was so easy to forget. Every time he stood next to her and loomed over her small frame, he was surprised. She occupied so much mental space that it was easy to forget her diminutive stature. Her glamour was on in full force today. She looked as human as he did. There was no evidence of the wings or tail he knew were part of her true form. Like her height, it was easy to forget about those. She smiled, razor sharp teeth in full view. The glamour could have hidden them as well, but she'd chosen to remind him how dangerous she could be.

"Dearest Holcroft," she said. She ran her fingers down the bare scalp of one of her attending imps. It shuddered at its Prince's touch and lost its grip, plummeting the short distance from the back of the chair to the floor. Another imp took its place, vying for the same attention.

"Prince Beruth." He gave his best bow. Flattery was one of the few things that worked with her.

"How could you allow this to happen?" She turned her head to look an imp in the eyes. It slumped forward, straining to touch her with one outstretched hand.

He laughed, and she turned to regard him levelly. The sound had surprised both of them, it seemed. "If you're referring to the loss of my grimoire, then you place the blame at the wrong set of feet. It was safe within the engine chamber. Your servants failed to keep it secure."

"And yet the intruder came in through your quarters."

"Impossible. No human can come through the front door."

"And the window?"

"The window?" The repetition sounded stupid, and he knew it. The window was more than twenty feet off the ground. There was no way someone could have gotten up there.

"Yes, dearest. The window." Beruth held up a newspaper open to an illustration he couldn't quite make out in the gloom. "My pets tell me this one stole our book."

"My book," he corrected absently. He'd inherited it from his old master and had added to it, just as his master had and his master before him. Beruth's contributions didn't make it hers. He got close enough to see the drawing but not close enough that she could touch him. "They saw Spring-Heeled Jack?" Imps weren't noted for their intelligence. As far as he could tell, they ranked somewhere above the most well-trained dogs, though with powers of speech and far less discipline. Likely they'd seen the picture and decided this mysterious figure would make a convenient scapegoat. "He's a myth, a fiction of the local rag. Something the lower classes made up to tell stories about on cold nights around the fire. The *Times* has let itself go if it's reporting such drivel."

"Is that so?" Beruth didn't seem convinced. "Then how else did someone jump twenty feet in the air to climb through your window?"

"There has to be a better explanation." He kept talking when she would have interrupted him. "Either way, the book was in the keeping of your imps and they let it be stolen." Her glare seemed designed to melt a hole straight through him. "Fortunately for both of us, I have the means of tracking it."

"That shows some forethought. More than I would have expected for you."

He ignored the gibe and instead went to his desk. He pulled a scrap of vellum from a drawer. It had been part of the grimoire before he'd removed it for exactly this purpose. He'd been more worried that one of the imps would make off with it at her orders than that a figure from local legend would break into his office, but in either case, it was what he needed. With a careless swipe of his arm, he cleared the top of his desk. His secretary could put it back in order when the man came in. He was useful for little else.

A map of London joined the vellum scrap on the table. From a different drawer, one he kept locked at all times, he produced a jar of pig's blood and a raven's flight feather. He pushed his glasses up the bridge of his nose then dipped the tip of the feather in the blood and started to inscribe his circle.

"The scrap will be attracted to the point on the map where the book is. Like attracts like, and the grimoire is enchanted to reveal itself to me wherever it is. Then we'll send in your imps to retrieve it."

Beruth stood at his elbow. She looked impressed despite herself. "I shall send a flood of imps to drown them in their own blood."

"Yes, yes." He kept drawing. The spell was complicated enough without her distractions. A final flourish and the basic inscription was complete. He looked over the runes to make sure he'd used the right ones. Without the grimoire to refer back to, this part could be risky and he'd already learned his lesson about sloppy rune formation. Everything seemed to be in order. He dipped the feather into the blood once more and painted in the key-rune.

The small circle flared to life. To his everlasting dismay, he still couldn't see demoniac energy with the specs. Without some trace of demon blood in his veins, he never would. The world was terribly unfair sometimes. Most times.

He painted a small circle on the scrap of vellum and sat back, waiting. The scrap rustled, then settled. It didn't move.

"What's the problem, dearest Holcroft?" Beruth sneered at him. "This is not working as advertised."

"The magic is sound," he said in protest. "I know it is! Someone must be shielding the grimoire." The vellum had shifted; the magic had worked. It was primed, but it couldn't latch on to its target.

"A convenient excuse."

"It is no excuse. As long as the grimoire is shielded, I won't be able to find it. They can't shield it forever." He bent back over the table, his chin on his hands. *As long as it takes*, he told himself.

"Bah, this is as useless as you are." Beruth swept away, the imps rising like a cloud around her. "My children shall track it down."

"Best of luck. If it's shielded from me, they won't find it either."

"If it is shielded by anything other than your incompetence, you mean." If Beruth could have slammed the door to the bed chamber, he was sure she would have.

He refused to be distracted by her harsh words. He knew this would work, eventually. And when the thief let down his guard, he would strike.

CHAPTER TWENTY

The grimoire was fascinating. From what Briar could read, it represented at least four generations of magicians, spanning twenty-five to thirty years. Each one picked up where the previous magician left off. Indeed, there were notations in many of the margins and notes in different hands adjusting the inscriptions of various spells. Some of the notes even made the spells more effective, though many did next to nothing.

Briar ran her fingers over each page as she read the inscriptions and accompanying annotations. She'd donned her gloves after about three pages. There were too many emotions involved in the creation of the book's contents. The lust, ugly and raw, was as difficult to deal with as the alternating pain and exultation. She might have learned more without the barrier between the grimoire and her skin, but she would have been in quite a state of discomfort.

It wasn't unusual to see so many magicians in one grimoire, nor was it unusual to see them over such a relatively short period of time. The lifespan for practitioners of the infernal arts tended to be brief. If their apprentices didn't turn on their masters, something would go wrong with an inscription. Perhaps they'd attempt to summon a demon; more alarmingly, they might succeed.

It was not always possible to tell which fate had befallen each magician, save the second to last one. The last spell in his—or possibly her—hand, was one of summoning. The magician in question had neglected to specify which order of demon they wanted to bring to this plane. Chances were good they'd bitten off more than they could chew and that a demon had come through that was stronger than the runes of protection included in this particular summoning inscription. His apprentice must not have been around or the next set of handwriting wouldn't have been there.

There was another set of handwriting, in addition to that of the apprentice. This one had excellent grasp of the infernal tongue. If Briar hadn't known better, she would have assumed the words belonged to a demon. It was too glib, too facile with the language, and the annotations demonstrated a grasp of grammar not usually seen in someone who hadn't been raised in the tongue. However, demons didn't stick around to help magicians, not unless compelled. Few magicians realized how poor their grasp of the language was. Arrogance was a prevailing quality among them, and she didn't envision a demon being summoned for the purpose of teaching its language. Summoned to pay back slights—whether real or imagined—or to deliver power and riches, yes. Summoned for tutoring, most unlikely.

As she delved deeper into the most recent additions to the grimoire, she became more and more alarmed. There were some rather unorthodox ideas here. The apprentice had some mechanical aptitude, that was clear. Holcroft, at least she assumed it was him, had taken the spells he learned from his master in a much different direction than she had seen before. He seemed to be attempting to apply properties from the human realm to infernal magic. She couldn't fault his reasoning, more often than not, nor his results. Most magicians, if they dealt with mechanical workings at all, did what LaFarge tried to. They applied infernal magic to human constructions. To do it the other way around was quite unheard of, and yet Holcroft's ideas were plausible, for the most part.

Briar turned to the last of the written pages. He'd included plans for something he called a demoniac battery. It might store energy, but to her eyes, it had more in common with alchemical treatises from decades previous. Was he deliberately including alchemy along with engineering into some unholy amalgam of technology-driven magic? Or was that mere coincidence? It was impossible to tell without talking to the inventor or at the very least reading more of his notebooks. There had to be something else. The grimoire contained ideas that were close to fully formed. Where was he working out the details of his contraptions?

Not far away, Isabella started humming a tuneless ditty. She had many good qualities, Briar granted, but musicianship did not seem to be one of them. Not only could Briar not identify the song, but she was reasonably certain most of the notes were flat. She cringed. Still, it was nice to work in proximity with her. She rarely worked where anyone could observe her. Usually it was to protect knowledge of her abilities from being revealed to the wrong person or indeed anyone. Isabella already knew the worst of her secrets and didn't seem to care.

It'll be fine, Briar told herself. *This is nice. We're working together on the same project.* Her jaw muscles flexed at a particularly flat note and she made herself stop grinding her teeth. *Normal people work together all the time.*

Isabella stopped humming and started ratcheting on something. Briar tried not to let it distract her. She forced herself to pay attention to the page in front of her.

This one wasn't a battery, as the previous pages had outlined. It was the engine that powered the Mirabilia carriages, its inscriptions laid out for her to read with ease. She read the description of the intended effects with mounting horror. This didn't harness energy or store it as many of the other spells were designed to do. This inscription seemed designed to hold two different locations at the same place. She knew of no way to do such a thing in the mortal realm, nor in the infernal realm. This plan borrowed from both places. It created a pocket of overlap between the planes. The next page described a transfer of energy spell. In itself, that was no big thing; it was the basis of much infernal magic, after all. What made this incantation so insidious was that it described not the transfer of energy from the infernal to the mortal plane, but from an infernal *being* to the mortal plane. Each version of the spell would have to be different and include the signature of that demon.

"Dear me," she said, staring at the inscription.

"What? What is it?" Isabella pivoted to look at her.

"He's done the impossible or next to." Briar looked over at the exposed engine they had removed from the earl's carriage days ago. "He's figured out how to power spells with demons themselves instead of the energy from their realm."

"Isn't that already being done?"

"Not at all. Magicians create small tears between this world and that of my mother's. Energy leaks through the tear. Its potency is in the transfer from one plane to the next. In turn, mortal energy leaks through to the demon world. It's a small, more or less stable tear that seals itself over time. Certain inscriptions can extend that time and make them near enough to permanent, but usually the effect fades after a while."

"Which is why I have to get LaFarge to redo the enchantments on my equipment from time to time."

"Exactly. He's made himself a shortcut by engraving the runes into your equipment, and all he has to do is fill them with the appropriate fluid and they'll be reactivated. That's what is in the supposed fuel cylinders. They're filled with blood that reactivates the inscription and keeps it active. They don't fuel the horseless so much as they fuel the spell. What our inventor has done by powering his inventions with demons instead of their energy is create a tear that grows over time. It's much more potent, and the fabric between our plane and that of the demons is worn thin. Eventually, the demon will be able to influence what is going on in our world. At some point, he will be able to enter our world."

"That doesn't sound good."

"You see my concern then? The atmosphere here is quite inimical to demon-kind. The opposite holds true as well. I dare say that if you were to spend time upon the plane of my birth, you would be very uncomfortable and would end up sickly and weak. You might even die, though you seem of sturdy enough health for that to be unlikely. Demons summoned here, especially those of the lower orders, have the same problem. They must be protected within the circle of summoning or banished soon after or they'll die. The imps who chased us last night were suffering from exposure to your world, which is why they were so easy to defeat. As a hybrid, I am able to survive on either plane, which isn't always the advantage you might think it is."

"That's not so bad." Isabella exhaled. "I thought we were in some real trouble."

"We still are. Imagine a demon that has been taking in energy from our realm. This is what is used to power magic on the infernal plane. He is full of as much energy as he can possibly hold, and then he comes over. It will be much longer before he starts to suffer the effects of this world, if at all. Mortal energy may well inure him completely to the deleterious effects of the human world."

"Why would somebody do such a thing? It makes no sense."

"Who knows. Our mysterious inventor could be insane. It certainly isn't unheard of among practitioners of the dark arts. Or he could be working with a demon who is trying to gain an advantage in the infernal realm. This has the potential to transfer a great deal of mortal energy to the other world. I'd have a better idea of which of the realm's princes would stand to benefit if I knew which demons the spell targeted. The imps by themselves aren't a good indicator. They are used as fodder by many of the rest of the infernal races."

The lift at the other end of the workshop groaned to life again. Isabella's head snapped up. "We need to hide the grimoire."

"Very well." A large piece of canvas drop cloth seemed like it would do the job. Briar folded it in half and settled it carefully over the book, careful not to disturb any of the runes.

"That won't work." Isabella whisked the cloth back off it. "That can only be LaFarge. If he gets hold of this book, nothing good will come of it."

With an irritated twitch of her wrist, Briar settled the canvas back over the tome. "It will have to work. If we move the book out of the circle, it will be exposed."

Isabella glanced over her shoulder. The lift was far enough down to see a pair of shoes, but it still had a long way to go. "The man is an odious plodder with no real power. This could give him what he's always wanted. Do you really want it falling into his hands?"

"Of course I don't!" At Isabella's shushing motion, Briar lowered her voice to an insistent hiss. "Of course I don't, but there is a very real possibility that somebody is waiting for the grimoire to be revealed. If that happens…I don't know what will happen."

The finish was somewhat less convincing than she'd hoping for. She sighed. Not knowing was the worst of it. How could she plan if she didn't know what would transpire? She didn't even know who the players were, beyond some hazy suppositions.

Isabella threw off the canvas shroud and closed the book. She flung out her hand toward a large cabinet on the far side of the workshop. "Open that up and clear off a shelf. Don't worry about breaking anything. You can make a new spell in there. I'll bring the book over when you're done. If we're lucky, Holcroft won't be watching."

Briar hesitated and looked back at the slowly descending elevator. It was almost halfway down. If she hurried, she might have the time.

The cabinet was quite deep, and Briar thought it might be possible to make a circle big enough for the grimoire. She seized the doors and heaved back on them. They didn't move. Desperately, she jiggled the handles and they opened quite easily, throwing her off balance. Inside, all manner of tools littered the shelves. A portion of her mind tutted disapprovingly at the disarray before she reached out and cleared the middle shelf with one swipe of her arm.

She tugged the glove off her left hand and looked around. A small knife sat among the tools now on the floor. Briar snatched it up and ruthlessly dragged it across the tips of her index and middle fingers. Blood flowed freely and she bent feverishly to the task of scribbling down runes in the proper order and arrangement to create another barrier against the locator spell in the grimoire.

A loud clang rang out through the workshop. The gears overhead ceased their turning, and silence fell only to be broken moments later by a male voice's "Bonjour!"

Isabella snatched the grimoire off the bench and dashed over to where Briar still inscribed her spell.

"I'm not ready yet," she called. There was still a third of the inscription left to complete.

"Finish it up!" was Isabella's unhelpful response. "Hurry, hurry." She managed to keep her voice down, but while still having it reach Briar's ears without losing any intensity, a feat Briar would have found quite impressive had she not been standing with her head in a cabinet, trying to draw out a spell in a hurry with fingers that dripped blood a little too freely.

"I. Am. Trying." Briar forced the words out between gritted teeth. She had less than a quarter of the way to go.

Isabella reached out and tried to deposit the book before Briar had checked her work. She held out her arm to slow Isabella down.

"What are you doing?"

"I need to make sure it's right."

"Of course it's right; you did it." Isabella brushed her arm aside and dropped the book on the shelf, one corner a little too close to the edge of the circle for Briar's liking. It wasn't touching, so it would have to do.

Briar drew in the key-rune and sagged a bit with relief when the runes ceased their fitful glowing and kindled into flame. She'd completed the spell. She closed the doors. How long had the grimoire been unprotected? Surely not long enough for someone to notice.

They turned around and Briar suddenly found herself almost nose-to-nose with Jean-Pierre LaFarge. He smiled hugely, revealing large white teeth

"Bonjour, petites. What 'ave we 'ere?"

CHAPTER TWENTY-ONE

"Monsieur LaFarge," Isabella said, taking him by the arm and drawing him away. He resisted at first, then allowed her to lead him to a nearby workbench, not the one where they'd recently been working. Leaving Briar's vicinity was to his advantage. Isabella hadn't missed the way she'd subtly recoiled when she turned around to find him right there.

"Beautiful Isabella." He grinned widely, mischief crinkling the corners of his eyes. "What are you two up to? There are signs of magic here."

"A simple experiment, that's all."

"Ridicule. You do not do ze magic, so it must have been the wonderful Mademoiselle Riley, non?"

Isabella glanced back at Briar, who had casually wandered over to the bench where they'd been at work. She pulled the canvas cover back over the blood-sketched runes.

"Zis is zo exciting! A woman 'oo does magic? It is like a trained dog." The idiot made no attempt to keep his voice down.

Briar's back stiffened and she turned on her heel, then stalked across the floor toward them. The effect should have been ruined somewhat by her lack of shoes, but somehow the sound of her bare feet slapping on stone was as intimidating as the clack of heels would have been.

"You dare to call me a trained dog?" She stuck her finger straight against LaFarge's breastbone with enough force to make him grunt. A smear of blood marred his pristine white shirt. "You, who know nothing of the grammar of the language? Who barely knows the most basic words?" LaFarge backed away, trying to put some room between them, but Briar followed him step for step. "It's a wonder you haven't pulled yourself straight into hell as you seem determined to do. Your runes are so deformed half of them are nonsense and the other half mean the opposite of what you think."

By the end of her diatribe, Briar's face was so close to LaFarge's that they must have been breathing the same air. Isabella did not envy the man at all, but she would have been lying had she said she wasn't also somewhat aroused. This side of Briar was one that never ceased to excite her, the side she'd been coaxing forward ever since she'd started tormenting her at balls. Briar's eyes snapped with righteous fury. Though Isabella had already seen her lose control of herself in passion, Briar's rage was equally as exhilarating. She was glad someone else was on the receiving end.

"M-m-my apologies, mademoiselle." The words dropped from quivering lips. LaFarge had backed into a thick support pillar. His eyes shifted as he looked for an easy escape. The piled equipment and components around him made that impossible.

"Not good enough, monsieur." Briar stared down her nose at him. "You will stay out of my way from here on out, or I shall be much more unpleasant to you." She leaned forward, touching her nose almost to the tip of his. "Do we understand each other?"

"Yes, ma'am." He swallowed hard, sending his Adam's apple to bobbing in his throat.

"Maybe you should let him past," Isabella said. While it was exhilarating to see LaFarge put in his place and so forcefully, they still had work to do. She started at the glare Briar shot her way.

"Very well." Briar stepped back giving LaFarge barely enough room to squeeze past her.

A sharp ping resounded from the other side of the workshop. Briar turned and craned her neck to see what was going on. The earl's horseless was back there.

"Briar?" Isabella said. "Was that you?" She turned and looked also. There was no one with the carriage, nothing should have made that noise, as far as she knew. Concern crawled prickling up her spine.

"It was not." Briar took a few steps toward the far end of the shop before stopping. She didn't move; her body swayed slightly. She looked terrified.

The horseless shook. It was subtle at first, a vibration she felt through the soles of her feet more than saw. Before long, however, it was rocking from one side to the other, its wheels lifting off the floor, before coming down to the opposite side.

"What is going on down there?" Joseph came over to join them.

Before Isabella could answer, the horseless tipped all the way over and hit the ground with a thunderous crash. The engine popped open along the seam, brilliant light bursting forth from it, searing into her vision. Eyes suddenly streaming, Isabella jumped back. It was less a graceful leap and more the panicked scrabbling of a terrified cat, not something she would normally have permitted herself to do around LaFarge, but his response was as skittish. She reached out toward the nearest tool shelf and picked up the first thing that came to her hand.

Briar dropped to her knees. Isabella squinted around the afterimage still plaguing her sight. She firmed her grip upon her...screwdriver? She looked down at the tool in her hand. It certainly seemed a weak defense against whatever was about to happen.

"Father," Isabella cried. "Defend yourself."

Joseph disappeared into one of the workshop's storage areas. Isabella looked around, blinking furiously, trying to get an eye on everyone. LaFarge cowered behind her workbench, Briar was drawing a circle on the floor. A flicker of movement caught her attention, and she looked forward. Something was coming at her. She ducked back and felt the rush of air against her face as something passed right in front of it. Slowly her vision came back. Blurry forms flitted around them.

Something clamped on to her upper arm with a grip that would not be denied. Isabella choked as she was pulled hard to one side. She looked down and saw runes in Briar's blood around her feet. She was inside Briar's circle. There was only room for one. Her head whipped up at the realization, seeking out Briar.

One imp accosted her as another harried LaFarge away from the bench and into a corner. Briar dodged the imp, but it still caught a hank of her hair and tugged hard at it, pulling her to one side. Isabella threw the useless screwdriver at it. Her aim was true and the imp squawked, letting go of Briar's locks. It turned its head slowly to find the source of its pain and its slitted green eyes landed upon her. An impressive hiss revealed double rows of black teeth as sharp as needles. With stunning speed, it pivoted in the air, its body catching up to its head in a split second. Isabella flinched back at the impossible maneuver. It flew at her so fast it was a blur. This imp was nothing like those that had chased her from the Mirabilia manufactory.

It came at her, teeth snapping. She leaped back out of the circle before she could stop herself. The imp shrieked in pain and bounced off something she couldn't see. It careened, smoking, into tall shelves along the wall, striking them in a cacophony of screams and tumbling metal.

Isabella whirled when a weight hit her solidly between the shoulder blades. The smell of sulfur and iron threatened to overwhelm her. She gagged once, twice, then stopped when a hand reached around and dug clawed fingers into the soft parts of her neck.

"Where's the book, pet?" the imp asked in sibilant tones. "Give it."

"Go back to Hell," Isabella said. She whirled around, trying to dislodge the thing.

It tightened its grip around her neck, the claws drawing blood so cleanly she didn't feel any pain at first. "More come. Give it now, or face worse."

Isabella backed up. She hoped the invisible wall was still there. Maybe she could scrape the imp off on it. She leaned back as hard as she could. The imp howled and let go of her or tried to. Isabella grabbed its spindly arm and held it firmly in place on her back. Its flesh smoked and blackened while it thrashed against her, tearing at the thick canvas of her coveralls with increasingly desperate claws before finally going limp. To be certain it was dead, she held the small demon against Briar's barrier. Finally, the wall gave way and she stumbled back into the circle, clutching the imp's corpse to her back. She coughed at the smell of burning flesh and dashed the charred thing to the ground.

When she looked out again, Briar was trying to drag an imp off of LaFarge's head, but with little success. Why she would even bother with the Frenchman after he'd been so rude to her, Isabella couldn't understand. For her part, she would have been happy to let the man rot, but if Briar had to cover both herself and him, she was going to be in trouble. Another imp circled overhead, looking for an opening.

Their attention wasn't on her for now. Isabella left the safety of the circle and pulled the largest wrench she could find off a nearby shelf. Its weight was reassuring in her hand. She hefted it experimentally, then strode into the open.

"Oy, you stupid little thing," she yelled. The wrench was out of view, held alongside her body.

The flapping imp turned in midair. Its eyes lit up at the sight of a new victim. Heavy wingbeats accompanied it as it made its way higher then stooped on her like a hawk. It screamed at her, front claws extended for maximum damage. Isabella stood her ground and waited. The imp drew closer, and she checked her urge to move. This had to be timed exactly right; she wouldn't get the opportunity again. Finally, when she could almost see the scales around its nostrils, Isabella stepped to one side and assumed a pose any bowler would have recognized. It had been years since she last played cricket, but she'd been considered a fair batsman before the boys had discovered she was a girl dressed as one of them and had run her off. She pulled back the wrench and put all her weight into the drive, hitting the imp square in the body and sending it arcing across the room. It disappeared into a dark corner. Something shattered as the imp hit it, and the sound of objects hitting the ground accompanied its fall. Faint rustles came back to her from the corner. The imp might not be dead, but it was definitely down.

With that one out of the way, Isabella advanced on Briar and LaFarge. The final imp was still hooked into LaFarge, though it was no longer wrapped across his face. It had a grip on his shoulders and wouldn't let go.

"Drag him into the circle." Isabella had to yell to be heard over the cries of both man and demon.

"You're supposed to be in there!" Briar turned her head to shout back at her. The imp took the opportunity to pull one of its legs from her grasp and dig clawed toes into LaFarge's lower back. The Frenchman howled anew.

"I don't need it." Isabella grabbed one of his legs and hauled back on it. "But he does!"

He would be safe within the circle and she and Briar could take care of the last imp without having to put themselves in jeopardy to help him. The man weighed more than she did and would have been hard to move on her own even without his wild thrashing. Add in the weight of the imp and Briar impeding her path and Isabella pulled him maybe three inches. Either Briar saw the wisdom of her counsel or she didn't have the energy to argue, but she abandoned her attempt to dislodge the imp and grabbed LaFarge's other leg. Together, they hauled him kicking and screaming to the circle.

The imp launched itself off his back when it realized it was no longer being accosted by Briar. It circled overhead for a moment, then flew directly at them. Isabella dropped LaFarge's leg and took a hasty swing at the imp. It evaded her easily, but it also missed Briar, who continued shifting LaFarge. The Frenchman hadn't realized the imp was gone and he continued to fight, swatting violently at nothing. It took Isabella two tries to regain her hold on his leg. They were over halfway to the circle and the imp was coming back in for another pass.

Isabella dropped the man's leg again and swung again at the little demon. Her swipe was early and it evaded her easily, but it managed to score a hit along one cheek. It felt like her face had been brushed by fire, and she clapped one hand to it. Slick, warm blood smeared across her fingers.

"For the love of god!" Isabella screamed at LaFarge. "You're not being attacked. Get up, you utter ass, and get in that circle."

He paused in his thrashing and dared a look around. Seeing no imps in his vicinity, he leaped to his feet and sprinted to cower in the circle. Blood flowed freely from multiple rents on his face and ran down his scalp to dye the collar of his white shirt scarlet.

The imp flew at LaFarge but managed to twist away when he reached the inscription.

Isabella tightened her grip on the wrench, both hands wrapped so tightly her knuckles ached. Her blood practically boiled with the desire to beat the demon's head to a pulp. It had come into her workshop and injured Briar. Twin wounds showed through tears in the back of Briar's jumpsuit as she turned in place to keep an eye on the imp.

A nearby thunderclap stunned her into immobility. Something shot through the air and missed the imp by less than a foot. Whatever it was clanged against the stone wall in a shower of sparks before clattering to the floor.

"Blast," came Joseph's voice from behind her. She chanced a quick look at him. A large contraption of brass and knobs rested on his shoulder. Even now, as he lowered it, his eyes were still on the imp. He fumbled at a large quiver at his waist, trying to pull out another harpoon without looking.

Though even the imp had been stunned at the turn of events, Briar was completely undeterred by the noise. She'd managed to grab the length of canvas she'd first tried to use to hide the grimoire. The imp came for her but Briar simply threw the cloth at it.

The length of fabric unfurled in the imp's path. Fouled up, it tumbled to the ground. In less than a second, Briar pounced upon it and wrapped the thing up. Isabella waited until Briar had wrestled it into submission, then she came in like an avenging angel. She raised the wrench high over her head and brought it down on the squirming canvas package. Again and again she beat the wriggling bulge until it ceased all movement and black blood saturated the rough fabric. She looked around, but there were no signs of other imps. Suddenly exhausted, Isabella dropped the wrench that dragged at her weary arms. It clanged to the ground and she flinched at the noise.

"Are you all right?" The question came from each of them at the same time.

Isabella croaked a little laugh. "A little bloody, but alive."

"You're more than a little bloody, darling."

The smile that spread across her face hurt where it pulled against the slice on her cheek, but she couldn't help it. Briar had called her darling. She threw her arms around Briar, pulling her close, assuring herself that she was indeed all right. At Briar's intake of breath, Isabella remembered the wounds she'd seen on her back.

"Let's see you." She spun Briar around. The cuts were deep and looked to require medical intervention. "You need a doctor."

"As do you."

Isabella flapped a hand at her. "They're only shallow cuts. Yours are much deeper."

"The grimoire!" Briar struggled to get out of Isabella's grasp. "Did they get it?"

Isabella let go and raced with Briar to the cabinet. The doors stood ajar. Briar pulled it open, but the book was gone. All that remained were the smeared runes of her protective circle.

"No! Not after all that." Briar slammed a hand against the cabinet's side.

"That's not all," Isabella said. "One of the imps said there were more coming. We can't stay here. My parents!"

The sound of a throat clearing behind them brought Isabella up short. Her father carefully set aside his harpoon cannon and surveyed the damage to the corner of the workshop. His brows were drawn together so they almost met over the bridge of his nose and he puffed at his pipe with the ferocity of a steam engine at full steam.

"Isabella Langston Castel, I don't suppose you'd like to tell me what the meaning is of all this." He crossed his arms and glared at her.

"I will, but for now, we need to leave," Isabella said.

"Viscount Sherard, you're not safe here," Briar said on the heels of Isabella's words. She gestured at the misshaped lump of canvas where black blood was starting to bleed through.

"We shall see about that," Joseph said. "Upstairs, both of you. Your mother will want to hear all about this."

Isabella cringed. Involving Althea was the last thing she wanted to do. Her mother was not going to be happy to hear she'd been out with Briar instead of using the time to acquire something of actual monetary value.

"Yes, there's no point in explaining this more than once," Briar said. She started toward the lift, compelling Isabella's father to keep pace.

With one final look around, Isabella realized something was missing.

"Where's LaFarge?" she asked.

CHAPTER TWENTY-TWO

Lady Sherard had been much more receptive than her husband to Briar and Isabella's insistence they leave the city right now. Briar wasn't sure whether Isabella's mother had responded to Briar's vague reasons, the increasing concern in Isabella's voice, or their strange and blood-spattered appearance, but whatever the case, they were on the road. She did wish that Althea hadn't chosen to ride along in the carriage with her.

The driver sat above, studiously following her directions. It had been impossible to send the servants ahead, as normally would have been the case. They would be following with those essentials that hadn't been packed in their frantic departure. Briar wished she could have convinced the Sherards to forego packing up even those things, but Joseph had insisted upon having his books along. Althea had been ready to go, a trunk already packed. While Briar approved of her preparations, she wondered where the woman had gotten the habit. She supposed life as an outlaw would ensure one got into the habit of being ready to move in an instant's notice.

Joseph's need to gather his books had allowed Briar to write a quick note explaining to the earl that they would be heading out of town to his Yorkshire estate. She mentioned that his horseless had been damaged and that she would send a letter explaining everything in more detail. She'd pressed it upon the Sherards' elderly footman, asking him to find someone to deliver it as soon as possible. There was no point in going into everything in the note; she would have to have a long discussion with Hardwicke when they returned. Hopefully he wouldn't be too cross about the loss of his newest toy.

"What did you say was the reason we should leave so hastily?" Althea asked.

"An imminent attack, Lady Sherard."

The viscountess waved away her formality. "Under the circumstances, you may call me Althea. Now what is your source of information?"

This was not the first time Briar had been the focus of Althea's probing questions. If she wasn't careful, she would end up revealing too much. "When we have arrived at the earl's hunting lodge, I shall tell you and Viscount Sherard everything I can." She held up her hand when Althea opened her mouth to press the matter. "I'm afraid I must insist. There is no call to tell the story twice."

"Very well." Althea smiled, her lips pressed tightly together. "Then perhaps you'd like to enlighten me as to the nature of your relationship with my daughter."

Her mouth was gaping open; Briar closed it with a snap. "Your daughter and I are friends, and we've been working together on a project."

"Is that so?" Althea raked Briar's body with a look such that she felt her clothes might catch fire. "Then how do you come to be wearing Isabella's coveralls while being naked underneath?"

"I am by no means naked. I am wearing my corset and bloomers, thank you quite kindly." Her face burned with the shame of discussing her intimate apparel with somebody else. "This conversation is not seemly, madam."

"What is unseemly is your lack of discretion, Miss Riley. I will not have you dragging Isabella's name through the mud. She needs to marry well and soon, and you will not ruin her chances of a good match."

"I can assure you I have nothing more than Isabella's best interests at heart," Briar said. She stiffened her spine and schooled her face to blankness at the thought of Isabella married to some man. She doubted Isabella would be happy with the situation, unless perhaps she found someone like her father, someone who would allow Isabella the leeway to tinker with her machines. Even then… Did Isabella take a fancy to men at all? She certainly fancied Briar, though they hadn't discussed how much further her sapphic feelings went.

Briar herself would be as happy with a man as a woman, which was to say not very much in either case. Emotional entanglements were messy and largely unnecessary. She had her work; she needed little else. Why then did it feel like her heart was drying up in her ribcage? Why did each heartbeat feel heavier and more ponderous than the last at this talk of Isabella and marriage?

Althea was content to allow their strained conversation to lapse into silence, completely unaware of the emotional maelstrom into which she'd plunged Briar. Briar gave the driver directions as he asked for them, but gazed sightlessly out the window as they traveled out of London and through the countryside. Her thoughts strayed to LaFarge more than once when given free rein. His disappearance was concerning. Was it coincidence, or was there something more malevolent behind it? That he might have been the owner of the grimoire was laughable in the extreme. No, the grimoire's owner was a much more adept magician than the Frenchman. He struck her as an opportunist, however. Had he decided to take advantage of the situation to curry favor with the mysterious inventor? That idea was at least within the realm of possibility.

Eventually Briar refused to let her mind indulge in obsessing over the man. She had bigger problems to worry about, and there was nothing she could do about him, in any case—not without some evidence of his malfeasance. For now, she had to survive this trip with only Althea for company. It would take them the better part of the day to travel to the small hunting lodge the Earl of Hardwicke kept in Yorkshire. He hadn't yet sold the estate, but it had been years since he'd been out to it. The earl didn't think much of hunting, preferring to spend his time with the strategy and intricacies of British politics. There would be no one there; Isabella and her parents would be safe while Briar determined what she would do next to stop the inventor.

Though fatigue did its level best to drag down her eyelids, Briar was too stubborn to give in to her exhaustion. She resorted to pinching herself sharply on the arm to keep from falling asleep. As the only practitioner of the infernal arts in the group, Briar knew she was their best line of defense; sleep was a luxury she couldn't yet afford. She'd felt some relief when they left the suffocating confines of London. In the countryside, she would see a swarm of imps long before they could attack. It did her more good than she'd realized it might to see the sky again, unbounded by rooftops on all sides. The air was cleaner, the birds sang, but Briar still couldn't relax, not until everyone was there and safe.

By the time they rolled into Grimsby Lodge's carriage yard, night was almost upon them. The sky was still light enough to see by, though darkening swiftly in the east. A few stars were already visible in the darkest part of the evening sky. Briar alighted from the carriage, ignoring the driver's hand as was her wont. Althea accepted the aid gratefully and made her slow way down to solid ground. Pain creased her face and her movements were labored. They'd stopped for meals and provisions, but it had been nine hours in a carriage. The lack of movement had not been good for her leg.

The lodge was dark, exactly as Briar had hoped. The building's stone wings and walls would not have looked out of place centuries before. Spring had a bite to it this far north, which Briar hadn't considered. Althea wasn't likely to be very comfortable here, though she had yet to complain.

Briar made her way up to the main doors, towering things through which someone could have comfortably driven a small herd of cattle. The door was locked, which was unsurprising. As Althea made her labored way over to her, Briar licked her fingers and sketched a small circle around the handle. When she keyed the final rune, the lock clicked open and the door creaked a few inches inward. Briar pushed it open enough to allow Althea to make her way inside.

"I'll have to light the lamps and kindle a fire," Briar said.

"It appears no one has been here for decades," Althea said. "I imagine that will take some time. I shall assist you. There are matches in my trunk."

"If you prefer, you could be seated. I'll have everything lit presently."

"I'm not dead yet, girl. If I sit now I'll be so stiff that movement will swiftly become impossible."

"Very well."

The driver pushed open the door further and staggered in with Althea's trunk. It was much too large to be handled comfortably by one person. He put it down with a thud after Althea pointed him at the nearest wall.

"Patterson," Althea said, her voice brisk, "see what you can find in the way of wood. Let's do what we can to dull the edge of this chill."

"Yes, m'lady." The chauffeur left quickly.

Althea opened her trunk and dug around inside it while Briar looked around. The entry hall was large and echoing. Much of the decor consisted of hunting trophies that hadn't stood up well across the intervening years. A stuffed pheasant at one end of the large mantel had lost most of its feathers and looked quite diseased. It had been too much to hope that some wood would still be laid in the fireplace. Whoever had closed up the lodge had done an excellent job, much to their current inconvenience.

Candles still stood in their holders, at least those that had been left behind. Briar carved the rune for fire into the stiff wax, and the candle came to life with a small gasp. It burned red for a moment before the color receded to the warm yellow-orange of a normal flame. She touched the flame to the wick of a nearby candle and wordlessly handed one to Althea who was still looking through her trunk. It contained an interesting assortment of objects. The top layer had been clothes, but Althea had pushed those aside in her search. No less than three pistols sat to one side of the trunk, complete with ammunition and a kit Briar assumed was for cleaning the weapons. Next to those was a closed doctor's bag. That would come in handy if it did indeed contain medical tools. Based on the gadgets and contraptions Briar couldn't put a name to, that was an even chance at best.

Joseph and Isabella showed up soon after they'd found and distributed candles throughout the ground floor hall and parlor. The driver was trying to coax a fire to life on the hearth, but with little success. Althea set him to checking the flue. Sure enough, it was clogged with years' worth of accumulated debris.

"It's quite chilly in here," Joseph said, rubbing his hands briskly. "Are you comfortable, my dear?"

Althea crossed over to him. After taking one look at her pronounced limp, Joseph hastened over to her and gathered her up in a large hug. He kissed the side of her cheek and Briar found herself looking away. Their affection was real, that couldn't be denied. She found herself staring at Isabella, who watched her parents, a small smile playing around the corners of her mouth. Somewhere along the way, she'd cleaned up the wounds on her face and neck. They looked much less angry now, though the scratches were unmistakable. It was Briar's fault Isabella had come to be wounded twice in less than twenty-four hours. Her own injuries had already started to itch. She healed more quickly than most humans did, at least she hoped it was that and not an infection. Imp claws were not known for being overly clean. She should have Isabella take a look at them to make sure they were all right when she changed out of the coveralls.

"Oh no," Briar muttered under her breath.

"What is it?" Isabella asked as quietly.

"I have no clothes to change into. Everything I own is at the earl's townhouse."

"Never fear. I have something you can borrow. Mother had a trunk standing by for me and one for Father."

"She's a well-prepared kind of person, isn't she?"

"That she is. Sometimes a little too much."

The driver leaped back from the fireplace as the materials clogging the chimney chose that moment to break free. A large cloud of soot and dust belched forth and settled on the floor, covering furniture like a smothering blanket. He stammered apologies, though everyone had been far enough away to avoid the mess.

"Never mind that, Patterson," Althea said. "Just get us a fire, if you please."

"Of course, ma'am." Now that there was some airflow over the hearth, the wood caught quickly. Before too long, a fire roared away cheerfully on the hearthstones.

Patterson removed the coverings from some nearby chairs and pulled them as close to the hearth as possible. Althea levered herself down into the nearest one. Her face smoothed as she allowed herself to let go of the pain of keeping herself together.

"Oh yes, Izzy and I stopped at the village pub to pick up some dinner," Joseph said. "We'll be right as rain in no time."

"That sounds lovely, Joseph." Althea smiled up at him. "The girls should get changed for dinner, however. They're in quite a state."

Briar stared longingly at the paper-wrapped packages he'd produced. At the mention of food, her stomach had tried to wrap itself around her spinal cord. It gurgled loudly in the stillness of the hall.

Althea ignored it. "Make yourselves presentable, then we'll discuss what happened today."

"Yes, Mother." Isabella grabbed Briar by the elbow and pulled her into the cold hall. "It's best to do as she says when she gets like this."

"I don't let my own mother order me around like this. I'm not going to let her do so."

"Then we'll find ourselves bundled up and back in London before you can say anything."

"She can't—"

"She will. I know it's difficult for you, but you need to let her be in charge of some of the small things right now."

It was hard enough having Althea arrayed against her, but with Isabella taking her mother's side, Briar felt like she might as well be pushing a boulder uphill. She was exhausted, she ached deep within her bones, and all she wanted was a few days' sleep. Using her own blood for magic had put quite the strain on her. She still had no idea how many hours she and Isabella had managed to sneak last night while curled around each other on the remains of the cot, but it hadn't been enough to recharge her. Their time together had provided some respite, but she refused to use Isabella in that way. She would have to allow her energy reserves to replenish naturally, which would take time and rest. Lots of rest.

"Very well." There would be time enough to fight about it after she'd gotten some sleep. Hopefully Althea wouldn't have gotten used to having her way by then.

She assisted Isabella in bringing in her trunk from the horseless they'd rented for the trip up. It looked quite different from the one owned by the Sherards. After spending hours on the road staring at the modifications Isabella's father had made to his carriage, the standard one seemed quite unremarkable, spare even.

They maneuvered the trunk upstairs. By the weight, it seemed likely that, like Althea's luggage, it was packed with more than clothes. They stuck their heads into a few of the upstairs rooms before deciding on one that looked like it might be an adequate sleeping chamber.

Briar took a moment to recover on the edge of the bed. Isabella pulled a white sheet off a heavy wooden dressing table that hadn't been fashionable for a century or more.

A large face dominated the mirror. It glared at them, eyes glowing red.

"You're not Briar," her mother boomed. "I demand to talk to my daughter!"

CHAPTER TWENTY-THREE

Isabella blinked at the face staring at her. The resemblance to Briar was unmistakable, especially through the cheekbones and the sensual lips. Briar didn't have the jet-black horns that curved back proudly from this woman's forehead, and Isabella thought perhaps she'd caught a glimpse of pointed ears.

"You're a pretty one, aren't you?" The demon wet her lips with the tip of her tongue. "Are you perhaps the one responsible for my daughter's current state? Come closer so I can get a better look at you." She leered deliciously, one eyebrow arched high on her forehead.

Isabella took a step forward without meaning to. When she realized she'd taken a step, she forced herself to stop, trembling as her body fought not to answer the demon's call.

"Mother!" Briar stepped up next to her, taking the full force of her mother's regard and shouldering Isabella away.

Glad though she was to no longer be the object of the demon's attention, Isabella still longed to gaze upon her. Sweat trickled cold down her back. She clenched her hands until the knuckles ached and her nails scored the tender flesh of her palms. The pain gave her something else to focus on and she bit her lip in an attempt to further clear her head. The sharpness of her teeth reminded her how Briar had bitten her on the thigh while they made love. Arousal built hot and demanding within her; she watched the side of Briar's face, the way her lips moved as she said something savage to her mother. Her eyebrows pulled together highlighting the fierceness of her eyes. This was the one Isabella needed, not the one in the mirror who tried to use her own body against her.

"What do you want?" Briar was saying. "I'm extremely busy."

"I'm quite aware of that. Too busy to take care of yourself, it would seem." The demon looked Briar up and down, critically this time, not the lascivious inspection Isabella had been subjected to. "Why have you been using so much magic?"

"How do you know that?"

"Briar, dearest, your flavor is all over the magic we've been receiving. You don't expect a mother to know her daughter's signature?"

"Do you mean to tell me you monitor the bore for the signature of each of your children?"

"Of course not." Briar's mother didn't even have the grace to appear embarrassed. "The others are all pure-blood. They haven't the same impediments you do."

"They don't have the same value, you mean."

"I don't understand why you refuse to have even one child. Think of the power a child of yours could bring to our family."

"My childhood was quite horrific enough. I won't subject another to it. If I ever have a child, you will have nothing to do with it."

The demon gestured irritably. Her fingers were tipped with immaculate black claws that made those on the imps look dull by comparison. Isabella watched them with sick fascination.

"I am quite well, Mother. Now if you would be so kind as to depart."

"Briar." Gone were the pouts and outrageous flirtation. What remained seemed close to genuine concern. "You aren't well, I can feel it. Drop your shroud so I can get a proper look at you."

Concerned, Isabella peered more closely at Briar's profile. She seemed well enough, or did before she dropped her disguise. The opalescent shimmer of her skin was muted. Instead of collecting light and reflecting it back, it was almost matte. Her eyes glowed faintly red; they no longer shone as they had the night before.

"As I thought." Briar's mother shook her head in reproof. "You haven't fed, have you?"

"I've been eating just fine."

Isabella doubted that very much. She and her father had stopped twice on the road to eat. If Briar and Althea had stopped once, it would have been a miracle, given how insistent Briar had been that they get to the lodge and as quickly as possible.

"You know that's not what I mean. You've depleted your magic past its ability to regenerate naturally. It needs to be restored more quickly, and there are two ways to do that if you don't plan to convalesce for a month." The demon's eyes flicked over at Isabella. "You have the means for one at hand, and it seems you've already sampled her… charms."

Isabella glared at the seductive face that still pulled at her from the mirror. Briar's mother grinned, exposing pointed teeth that Briar thankfully hadn't inherited.

"I am fine and I will thank you not to insert yourself into my life, Mother." Briar pulled herself up to her full height and glared at the face in the mirror. Isabella hadn't realized how sunken in on herself Briar had been until she did so. Her skin flared to something more akin to its previous pearlescence for a moment, then died back to flat grey.

"You are still my daughter, however much you might wish that weren't so." The demon's face darkened, and her hair took on a life of its own. The ends rose, sluggishly at first, like they were caught in a gentle breeze. Before long, they whipped about her head in a frenzy. "Take care of yourself, Briar. If you don't, I'll know and I *will* do something about it. You may be certain that I'll be keeping an eye on you. If you truly want me out of your life, then I suggest you do something to preserve it."

The mirror went completely black, then rippled and showed their shocked faces staring back from it. Briar slumped down onto the room's bed. "That was Carnélie. My mother."

"So I gathered. She's very impressive."

"Among other things. I couldn't let her get her hooks in you. I saw the way you reacted to her attention. You liked it."

The last was accusing. If Briar had slapped Isabella across the face with all her strength, the pain still would have been less. "She surprised me." The response was weak—Isabella knew it—but it was the best she could muster when she hurt so badly inside.

"It's not your fault. It's what she does. What we do. No one can help but be attracted to a succubus. We're poison."

"I couldn't stop the attraction, not until I looked at you."

Briar looked at her sideways, scoffing openly. "Impossible. She's much more powerful than I."

"Don't tell me what I felt." Isabella had to get through to Briar. She could feel her lover slipping away. "Touch me and find out for yourself." She pushed her sleeve up and stuck out her bare arm. "Feel me, damn you!"

Briar reached toward her, then pulled back as if afraid of what she might find. Isabella grabbed her hand and stripped off the ever-present glove. This had to work.

Briar's eyes flared bright red for a moment, then the light disappeared as they slid shut. Isabella frantically wracked her brain about every time they'd ever interacted and tried to remember how she'd felt. The first time she'd really noticed Briar had been at the ball when she'd picked up Isabella's lens. The fear and desperation she'd felt at possibly being discovered had been washed away by anger at Briar's insistence on learning more about it. The glee Briar's irritation had awakened in her hadn't been the most admirable emotion, but somewhere along the way, it had changed into excitement to see Briar. Whether that had happened before or after Briar trapped her, Isabella was no longer certain. Certainly, the admiration she'd felt for Briar had grown as they'd spent more time together. Somewhere along the way, admiration had morphed into attraction, then arousal, then something more. There was no denying the pleasure Briar's company brought her, but it was more than the intimate time they'd spent together. She'd spent the ride to this lodge wishing they'd ridden together. The journey had passed with excruciating slowness as a result. And now Briar thought she didn't like her enough or... Isabella wasn't rightly sure exactly what Briar was thinking, when it came down to it, but she knew that the idea of not being able to be around the overly proper, infuriating woman who had more courage than any dozen of the Queen's men left her empty inside.

Tears prickled at the back of Isabella's eyes. She blinked furiously; they wouldn't drop in front of Briar.

There was no response from Briar. The silence stretched between them, growing thinner and more brittle the longer it went on.

Finally, Isabella could stand it no longer. "Well?"

Briar lifted her eyes to meet Isabella's in the mirror. Like hers, they glittered with tears she was too stubborn to let fall. "That was a lot." She sniffled and let go of Isabella's hand to run a hand under her nose.

The action was completely undignified and Isabella couldn't help but smile for seeing it. "You've awakened a lot of emotions in me."

"I could feel that." Briar met Isabella's smile with one of her own. "It was rather chaotic, but I think I understand."

"So you don't think I'm under an enchantment?"

"I'm not sure why you feel so strongly about me, but it's too messy to be magic."

"It may not be magic, but it is magical." Isabella leaned forward and pressed her lips to the bone behind Briar's ear. She inhaled Briar's scent before pulling back. Could she smell any better?

Briar laughed. "You are ridiculous, Isabella Castel." She took Isabella's hands and brought her arms up. Isabella enfolded her in an embrace, marveling at how Briar relaxed against her. To think she'd wondered if this woman ever unbent. She'd never imagined that she would do so in her arms.

"Maybe I am, but it's the truth." Isabella squeezed Briar firmly for a moment. "But don't think you can distract me with compliments. What did your mother mean? And why do you look so...flat?"

When Briar's shoulders stiffened, Isabella tightened her grip and sent soothing thoughts her way. Briar could trust her.

"It's the magic I've been performing. It takes a lot of energy, energy that is difficult to replenish here. I had to use my own energy, instead of that of another. Translation of demonic energy in this world can be taxing, especially in large amounts." She shrugged against Isabella's hug. "All I need is time."

"A month's convalescence in bed doesn't sound very fun. I can think of better ways to spend that time in bed with you."

"She exaggerates. My mother is good at that."

"Maybe so, but you don't look like quite right. Not like your real self. What did she mean when she said you could replenish yourself."

"Absolutely not. I won't use you or anyone else that way." Briar shed Isabella's arms and started unbuttoning the front of her coveralls.

"Which way is that?"

"Pleasure or pain. My dearest mother sees nothing wrong with using another person for sex to feed her magic. The other option is to exploit someone else's pain. It doesn't matter if it's physical or emotional. It's one of the reasons she likes humans so well. She gains a lot of power from infatuating them, then breaking their hearts. She feeds very well on humanity."

"Oh." That hadn't been what Isabella had expected. She'd thought maybe a posset or a draught, possibly involving animal blood or some such. "I don't mind if you feed on my pleasure. There's a lot of it when I'm with you."

"There is nothing to discuss, Isabella." Briar got up and crossed the room to Isabella's trunk. She opened the lid and started pulling out gowns. "I won't feed from you. I am not my mother and I won't treat somebody else as a—a canapé. I shall be quite well, never fear. Do you mind if I wear this one?" She held up a teal gown with a high neckline. It was a recent acquisition, one purchased after Isabella had passed off Millie's necklace to be fenced.

"I don't mind." Isabella meant it as an answer to both of Briar's statements, but of course Briar took it only to mean about the dress. She stepped forward when Briar turned and did up the multitude of small buttons down her back. She would much rather have been pulling the dress off. The memory of the sound of buttons hitting the stone floor left her fumble-fingered on the last of the ridiculously small fasteners.

The two deep scores on Briar's back had closed and seemed to be healing, though one was red and puffy. Isabella made a note to do something about that presently, but she was aware of her parents waiting for them. It wouldn't be long before someone came to fetch them. She started pulling underthings out of the trunk. When she had everything out, she turned away from Briar to get changed, not because she was embarrassed, but because she knew where her thoughts would go if she was naked and looking at Briar.

"I shall have to take another look at your wounds," Briar said, "especially the new ones. They should be cleaned and bandaged."

"I cleaned them out as best I could while we traveled. Your own wounds need tending."

"Those accursed imps. There is not much filthier in either of our realms than an imp."

Isabella pulled on a brassiere and girdle. There was no one from polite society there and she would be damned if she would wear a corset when there was no need. Those were followed by stockings and a chemise. She sneaked a glance back at Briar. Their eyes met. Briar had been staring. She blushed and looked away when Isabella caught her. A wide grin spread across Isabella's face. Maybe being stuck here wouldn't be so bad. They simply needed to make sure they weren't interrupted by her parents. With no other distractions, Isabella doubted it would be too difficult to get her parents distracted by each other. If they survived the explanations.

CHAPTER TWENTY-FOUR

Would she rather have had another discussion with her mother or be heading down the stairs to try to explain the past few days' events to Isabella's parents? Briar didn't have to contemplate that question for more than a few seconds. As painful as this promised to be, it was nothing compared to being spoken to by Carnélie.

Without talking about it, they paused in the hall. Isabella transferred the candle to her other hand, then reached out and took Briar's hand for a quick moment. She had her gloves on again, but Briar found she rather missed the flood of emotions she felt when Isabella touched her bare skin. They shared a quick smile. Briar tugged at her waist, trying to smooth out some of the wrinkles the dress had acquired while stored in the trunk.

"There you are," Althea said when they entered the parlor. She was still in the chair, but Joseph sat on the floor in front of her, leaning back against her legs. "I thought perhaps you'd gotten lost."

"Sorry, Mother." An embarrassed flush tinged Isabella's cheekbones. Althea shot Briar a sharp look.

"We came as quickly as was possible under the circumstances." Briar wasn't about to enlighten them about her mother's visit. It must have taken a serious amount of power to track her to an unmarked mirror. Carnélie had been concerned, which was odd since her mother had not one maternal bone in her body. She did care greatly, however, about bettering the family's assets. As a succubus, she could and did read the body language of others with an ease that bordered upon telepathy, but she didn't have Briar's unique ability to read inanimate objects. Likely Carnélie was only worried about losing Briar before this trait could be bred into the bloodline.

"I see." When Briar didn't elaborate, Althea focused her oppressive stare back on her daughter. "Then perhaps you'd like to explain why we were forced to leave our perfectly comfortable home in London for this drafty monstrosity?"

"It's a bit of a story," Isabella said. "Perhaps Father would like to go to bed? You can appraise him of our discussion tomorrow."

Joseph's chuckle was dry and devoid of humor. "Thank you for the concern, Izzy. I'm sure you have nothing else but my continued good health at heart with that suggestion."

"You have been up all day, my dear," Althea said, placing her hands on his shoulders and rubbing gently. "You rose much earlier than I."

His face grew thoughtful and he stood up. The fireplace was the length of three of Joseph Castel's strides. He paced those steps off twice, hands clasped behind his back. "When my wife and my daughter both request my presence elsewhere, I find that my curiosity is piqued all the more. I shall remain." He stopped at one end of the mantel and captured some flame on a piece of kindling, then held it to his pipe. The smell of sweet tobacco filled the room.

This was it. Briar arranged herself on one of the couches Patterson had uncovered for their use. He must have swept in here while she and Isabella had been upstairs. The soot was gone from the floor along with the thick layer of dust. The couch was a strategic decision. Despite her words to Isabella, she was feeling the effects of her magical over-exertion. The couch would support her without betraying her weakness.

Isabella perched herself on the arm next to Briar. She took a deep breath and looked from her mother to her father, then exhaled. Briar jumped into the breach left by her hesitation.

"It all started with my first ride in the Earl of Hardwicke's new Mirabilia horseless carriage. I found I couldn't abide to be in it and wondered why. I engaged Isabella's help to determine what was awry with the carriage."

"We know that much already," Joseph said. He puffed busily at his pipe. "Isabella and I helped you with the engine removal. It's a fascinating piece of machinery. Or more accurately non-machinery. J.P. says it contains some alchemical components, which is unusual."

"That's what I thought, too," Briar said. "While it isn't unusual to find machinery augmented by infernal magic or locations amplified by aethereal magic, I thought alchemy was dismissed by modern magicians."

"As did I. I know of only a few alchemical texts still in existence. Once they realized the quest to turn lead into gold wasn't only impossible, but ill-advised, alchemy fell out of favor. That was almost two hundred years ago."

"About the same time infernal magic went on the rise."

"And about the time aethereal magic began to decline."

"That can be argued. Aethereal magic has been in much more widespread use for millennia, but most people these days simply call it religion."

Joseph withdrew the pipe from his mouth and used it to point at Briar. "I don't think you can make that argument. There's no real evidence that aethereal magic and religion have much in common."

Briar couldn't believe her ears. Here she was being lectured on the magic of the planes by a human, one who—as far as she could tell—could perceive neither infernal nor aethereal energy. "The forms are all there," she said. "Consider the words and the ritual of worship. The architecture of the great cathedrals are all designed for the transfer of aethereal energy."

"Dearest," Althea said. "We are perhaps straying from the discussion at hand?"

"Quite." He nodded at Briar. "We'll continue the other topic later. Please continue."

"Very well." She balled her hands into fists on her lap. This was the difficult part. Joseph knew about infernal magic—his partner practiced it extensively in the course of their inventions—so Althea likely did also. How much did he know, and how much could she avoid giving away while still satisfying their curiosity?

"After seeing that the engine was designed to use almost exclusively what you'd term 'demoniac' energy, I knew I had to read the grimoire of the person who invented the engine. We tracked down the Mirabilia factory and Isabella broke in to purloin the book." Was purloin the right term? It sounded more criminal than it had felt before she said the word out loud.

Isabella now found herself the target of her parents' combined attention.

"Isabella, we talked about this," Althea said furiously.

"Why would Izzy be sneaking into someone's factory to steal something?" Joseph wanted to know. It took him a moment to register his wife's words. "Thea, you didn't!"

"Joseph, darling, you will cause yourself apoplexy if you don't calm yourself."

Althea might be right, Briar thought. Lord Sherard puffed at his pipe with such intensity that smoke wreathed his head in a small cloud. His face grew redder at his wife's words.

"Isabella, did your mother instruct you in the skills of a thief?" he asked around the stem of his pipe. His teeth were clenched around it. It would be a wonder if the pipe didn't crack. Briar hoped he'd brought a spare.

Caught between her parents, Isabella said nothing. Her gaze flicked back and forth from her mother to her father and back.

"Althea?" Joseph stared accusingly at her.

"Joseph, I did what had to be done after Wellington went to the Continent. Our household is still intact, thanks to my efforts with Isabella."

"Whatever do you mean? We have enough funds, even allowing for our difficulties with the boy."

"He decimated our savings. The cost of his education in Germany has long-since used everything that was left once we paid off his debts."

"Impossible!" Joseph stumbled over to a nearby chair and dropped into it. He stared at Isabella's mother in disbelief. "I check our finances regularly, and there is always money. Our estates produce enough to provide for us."

"Dearest, the estates produce barely enough to cover their own expenses. Our household costs more to run, even in its much reduced capacity, than the estates can provide. That doesn't include the cost of Wellington's tuition and board, nor your supplies, nor what Isabella requires for her season."

"Then we should have sold one of the estates, and Isabella need not have come out this year. I can certainly reduce my work. And the boy…" Joseph's voice trailed off. "Why did you not tell me?" His voice was plaintive.

"I was trying to protect you. To protect the family. You haven't lived in poverty. I have. The inside of a debtor's prison has none of the romance of the stories. I don't know if I could have survived that again. Isabella would have been forever damaged, and you…"

Briar knew quite well what Althea meant. Privately, she agreed with her assessment of Joseph's ability to withstand prison. His head was far too much in the clouds to have the fortitude to handle such a place.

"Then what have you been doing to supplement the income of our estates?" Joseph closed his eyes as if he were afraid to hear the answer but knew he must. "What have you convinced our daughter she must do?"

Althea flipped her hand at Isabella, authorizing her to answer the question.

Isabella pretended not to have seen her mother's attempt at direction and focused on her father's face. It was time to lay everything out in the sunshine. "I have been using my jump suit to break into homes and steal valuables." When her father said nothing, Isabella continued. "I made sure to note who had impressive jewels when I was at a ball and to keep my ears open for those who had recent good fortune. I would watch their house for a few nights to determine the best time to break in."

"You stole from our peers? Our friends? This is unconscionable!"

"It is only meant to last until Wellington returns from university."

"Yes, the boy." Joseph shook his head. "His selfish actions started us down this road to ruin, and now I find out that my wife and daughter have finished the job. Without ever telling me." He buried his head in his hands. "Would you ever have told me, had it not come out this way?"

"Likely not," Althea said. "It would have no longer been necessary."

"You and I will talk more on this later," Joseph said. He turned his attention back to Briar. "Continue."

"There isn't much more to tell, truth be told. There was an alarm of some sort upon the book and when Isabella took it, a legion of imps tried to stop her."

"Imps?"

"Yes, small demons."

"Demons." Joseph wasn't the only one who looked skeptical. Althea had sat back and crossed her arms across her impressive bosom.

"Demons. What is it with you people who use demoniac energy, but don't believe in demons? The term is not coincidental, I assure you. Three imps came out of the engine in your workshop and retrieved the grimoire."

Joseph pursed his lips thoughtfully. "I thought perhaps it was birds. Or bats."

"What manner of bats, or birds for that matter, do you know who could do that much damage?" The capacity of humans to lie to themselves was remarkable and extremely inconvenient at this moment. Briar worked to keep her voice neutral and not to betray the impatience that burned within her. "They left six-inch-long gashes in my back. Surely you didn't miss that. You shot at one with a harpoon gun."

"When you say it that way…" Joseph struggled against the suggestion of his own traitorous mind. "Are you certain they weren't bats?"

"Father," Isabella said, "they were demons. And they could be after us. If they even suspect what we know, it's likely we should have seen another attack had we stayed home. Only this one would be much stronger than only three imps. What I saw in that factory is impossible to describe, but it was something straight out of Hell." She shuddered violently at the memory. Briar put her hand discreetly in the small of her back where neither her mother nor father would be able to see it. "Something is going to happen, something bad."

"The inventor of that engine has discovered a way of powering it using demons directly instead of the energy that comes from the infernal plane." The statement engendered no response from Joseph. He didn't understand the magnitude of the issue there, not surprising in someone who didn't yet believe in demons. "His grimoire also described a way to overlap an area of this world and that of the infernal. It would create a large portal for demons into the mortal plane, one this world is unlikely to survive unscathed."

"That does sound concerning," Joseph said. "I believe you should both retire for the night. My wife and I have much to discuss."

Isabella scooted out of the room in a flurry of skirts. She clearly had no desire to be around for that. Briar followed Isabella rather more decorously and found her waiting at the top of the stairs.

"I thought you could take the room next to mine," Isabella said quietly. She looked back down the stairs and seemed to be listening for what her parents might be saying. As far as Briar could tell, all was quiet down there.

"I have no objections," Briar said. If Isabella had been expecting a more enthusiastic response, she was doomed to disappointment. The only thing Briar wanted was bed and sleep. She followed Isabella down the hall and mumbled a quiet "good night" to her before continuing to the next door. The room was adequate enough. The bed was covered in a large dust cloth. Briar pulled it off as well as the one over the plain dresser, remembering at the last moment to keep the mirror covered. There were sheets and heavy blankets in the wardrobe; Patterson must have brought them up. She did the best she could to cover the bed, then bent down to undo the ties of her shoes. Those efforts sapped the remainder of her energy so she crawled under the blanket without removing her dress. She couldn't remove it without help, the rows of buttons went too far down to reach.

As exhausted as she was, her mind continued to churn and she found true sleep elusive. Briar couldn't keep her eyes open and at the same time couldn't drift off completely. When Isabella knocked at the door and whispered "Are you awake?" through the crack, she couldn't respond. Nor did she protest when Isabella crawled into bed next to her and took her in her arms.

CHAPTER TWENTY-FIVE

It hadn't been Isabella's intention to slide into bed with Briar, but once she'd changed into her nightgown, she'd been unable to stop herself from standing at the top of the stairs and listening for snippets of her parents' discussion. And after that she'd needed her comfort.

The light coming up the stairs had been faint, but there. Her parents were still discussing things in the parlor. Every now and then, Isabella heard the muted rumble of her father's voice. He hadn't sounded happy, not that she could blame him. She didn't blame her mother either. No, she knew exactly where the fault in this situation lay, and that was with Wellington in Heidelberg.

She'd slipped down the stairs, not even having to work at it to keep the old boards from creaking too loudly. There was a bench along the wall outside the parlor, and she'd settled there, pulling her legs up to her chest and wrapping her arms around them to ward off the chill of the room and to soothe the pain of listening to her parents argue.

"How could you have done that?" Joseph had asked in the tone of one who'd asked the same question before and received a rather dissatisfactory answer.

"How could I not?" Althea sounded almost as weary as he did. "We stood to lose everything. I did what I had to do. We are still afloat—"

"Barely, from what you've said."

Althea had ignored his interruption and continued. "Isabella's efforts have funded her season and our home in London. It won't be long before she charms a young man into making an offer for her. I'll make sure she marries well, and our money problems will be solved."

"This was your plan all along? Find Isabella someone to marry?"

"Do you have one that is better?"

Her father's shoes had sounded against the wooden floor as he'd paced up and down the room. She could only imagine how furiously he must have been puffing away at that pipe. "You expect her to get married when you've all but ruined her prospects."

"It would have been fine if not for her Miss Riley. As long as no one found out, the plan could progress."

"We should be glad it was only Miss Riley who found out. At least all she wanted was some help with a project. What if she'd been shot, Althea? What if someone had turned her over to the constables? How would her marriage prospects have fared if she were dead or imprisoned?"

"Joseph—"

Her father had continued, refusing to let Althea get a word in edgewise. Isabella had been quite shocked to hear her father speak to her mother in such a way. Her parents rarely disagreed, but when they did, Althea was usually the one to get her way. There was very little that Joseph got upset over.

"Does Isabella wish to get married? Have you thought of that? Did it ever occur to you that she would be ruined for marriage not through someone else's discovery, but through her own? Her world is too big for her to be satisfied being the wife of some puffed-up minor lord. How can she be content running a household when she's gallivanted across the rooftops of London? Can you ask her to make that sacrifice?"

"She's a good daughter. She will do what needs to be done for this family. It was the only reason she agreed to steal from our peers in the first place."

"It is one thing to ask her to go out on adventures every night and quite another for her to agree to be tied down for the rest of her life." Isabella no longer heard her father's feet on the floorboards, but his voice was quite loud now. She'd looked up to see his silhouette in the doorway. He was carefully avoiding looking at her.

"I did." Althea's voice had been quiet; Isabella had strained to hear it.

"Oh, darling." Joseph's voice had receded as he turned back into the room. "I know you did, but your circumstance was completely different."

"I'd been shot, for one." Althea's voice had been dry.

"For one. Surely you don't wish that upon Izzy?"

"Of course not."

"And you had me for another. You still have me. I wish you'd come to me, my love. I have other options, you know. We could have managed without turning to criminal acts." He'd tsked her quietly. "Why is your first course of action always the most illegal one?" The words had been blunt, but the way he'd said it had been so full of love that Isabella found herself smiling in the dark. Her parents knew each other and loved each other despite all that. They would be all right. She stole back up the stairs and up to Briar's room.

"Are you awake?" Isabella asked quietly. She held the door open a crack and listened carefully. There was no answer, no movement even.

She pushed open the door far enough to slip through. The hinges squealed in protest, much as those on her bedroom had. Someone must have oiled the hinges before the house was closed, but that had been a long time ago. She supposed she should be happy the doors weren't rusted shut.

The candle in her right hand cast a warm glow around the room. Shadows danced and swayed from a stray draft, but Isabella could still see well enough. Briar hadn't bothered with as much tidying up as she had. From the footsteps in the dust, she'd gone to the wardrobe for linens, but that was about it. She was ensconced under a blanket, her face in almost-complete repose, except for a tiny crinkle between her brows as though she still concentrated on something that vexed her. There were sheets upon the ancient mattress, but barely. She had spread them out, but made no effort to tuck them in. Isabella tugged gently at one edge in a vain attempt to smooth it down. It would be impossible to make the bed while Briar was in it.

She blew out the candle and placed it carefully on the dresser, then made her way through the pitch-dark room to the bed. Thankfully, the room was tiny, smaller even than her own. It was likely a servant's bedchamber, possibly for a ladies' maid, but more likely for someone's valet. She didn't imagine women had visited the lodge often. It was definitely decorated with a man's touch. Her own room had the head of a deer in it. Its glass eyes had stared down at her disapprovingly when she'd pulled the protective cloth off it in a prodigious cloud of dust. Isabella's hope had been that Briar might join her in her room, but even after the minutes spent stowing her clothing in the armoire and giving the room some lived-in touches, there had been no knock at her door. It wasn't surprising, not now that she'd seen Briar's room. Her friend had fallen into bed almost immediately. Perhaps there was something to her mother's admonishments after all. What had Briar called her? Carnélie, yes, that was it.

The bed creaked softly when Isabella slid under the covers next to Briar. When she snuggled up to Briar, though, her hands came in contact with heavy fabric not at all appropriate for bed. Was she still wearing her dress? Sure enough, when Isabella explored further, she encountered the line of buttons up the back. There had still been no acknowledgment of her presence by Briar. She was so dead to the world that even Isabella's careful explorations under the covers hadn't elicited any response whatsoever. This was not good.

Experimentally, Isabella gave Briar a tiny shove. Not enough to send her flying out of bed, but certainly enough to rouse a normally sleeping person to wakefulness. Briar had all the resilience of a corpse. She flopped forward a bit, a quiet sound of protest rising from the back of her throat.

"Oh, Briar. What am I going to do with you?"

There was no response, not that she'd expected one. She felt her way down the double row of buttons, undoing each one as she went. Briar would sleep much more comfortably if she wasn't wearing the dress. It was no easy task by feel alone, and for a moment Isabella wished she had her goggles. As she went, it got easier to undo the buttons. As long as she worked, she didn't have to think about the discussion she'd overheard. Her parents were so close. If anyone could weather these stresses, it was them. It was important that there be no more unpleasant surprises, however. Briar had kept back a lot of details and Isabella approved heartily of her discretion.

Now that she had the dress undone, Isabella did her best not to disturb Briar while she removed it. It was impossible to be unobtrusive about doing so. Briar slept through all of it regardless, though not without an occasional grumble of protest. Her eyes never opened, not even when Isabella had to raise both her arms and pull the dress over her head.

Then there was the corset. Of course there was the corset. Many women slept in them, which seemed like the height of insanity to her. She settled for loosening the ties. It might have been her imagination, but Briar seemed to be sleeping more comfortably. She was certainly going to be more comfortable for Isabella to cuddle up to.

Isabella burrowed under the covers, pulling the blanket up over both their shoulders. She slid her arm back around Briar's waist and nuzzled her face into the space where Briar's shoulder and her neck met. It smelled of her, comforting and dark. The tension drained slowly from Isabella's shoulders, leaving her truly relaxed for the first time since she'd woken up that morning. Had it really only been a day since she'd broken into the Mirabilia factory at Briar's behest? It felt like a lifetime ago. Her eyelids slipped down and she allowed herself to be drawn into sleep.

The layer of dust upon the lodge's windows only did so much to reflect the early morning sun. Isabella tried to burrow more deeply into the yielding surface beneath her cheek to get away from the relentless brilliance, but with little success. Instead, she got a low moan for her efforts. That wasn't a pillow beneath her head. Sometime in the night, she'd apparently decided Briar's bosom was a more comfortable resting place than the bed's ancient pillows. Isabella couldn't fault her sleeping self's logic. She opened her eyes and enjoyed the blurry view of cleavage not two inches past her nose.

Briar was on her back, that was good. She'd had enough energy to move during the night.

What time is it? Early enough that she could move back to her room without being caught. As progressive as her mother was in the more criminal areas of women's suffrage (women can be burglars too), Isabella had no idea how she would react to finding her daughter in bed with another of the fairer sex, one who was clad only in her bloomers and corset. It was a discussion she wished to avoid as long as possible. Never would be soon enough to tell her parents about her unusual tastes. If they were going to get grandchildren, those would have to come from Wellington.

She slipped out from under the covers, doing her best not to disturb Briar. She needed as much sleep as she could get. Perhaps later they could explore the effects of pleasure upon her recovery. Isabella smiled as she closed the door behind her. If they were going to be forced into this unexpected and awkward vacation, she might as well enjoy it.

The smell of frying bacon permeated the upstairs hallway. The servants must have arrived sometime in the night. If she'd slept through their arrival, she'd been very tired indeed. She counted herself as a light sleeper; it didn't take much to awaken her. A full night's uninterrupted sleep was generally a pleasant fiction for her, but last night had been one of those rare events. Had it been Briar's presence or her exhaustion? Perhaps a bit of both. There was only one way to find out, and she looked forward to it.

Are you getting ahead of yourself a little bit? The inconvenient voice from the back of her head likely had a point, but Isabella chose instead to dwell on the euphoria she felt at the idea of waking up next to Briar every morning. Her parents kept separate bedrooms, as was proper, but she happened to know they slept together almost every night. That was what she wanted, the companionship and affection Joseph and Althea displayed for each other whenever they were together. The idea of being married to a man whose attentions she'd be forced to endure until she'd delivered an heir was abhorrent. She certainly didn't want that, nor did she want her bed to be empty more often than not. Briar extended the promise of something more, if only she could reach out and take it.

Isabella held her breath when she pushed open the door to her bedroom, then released it when she realized it was still empty. She dressed for the day in trousers and a loose shirt. Another advantage to being on impromptu holiday, she supposed. The family servants were accustomed to her unconventional ways and rarely looked askance when she chose to dress after the masculine fashion. It was more comfortable than layers of crinoline that made fitting through doorways difficult and sitting without a ramrod stiff back almost impossible.

How did Briar feel about her? Isabella met her eyes in the mirror as she drew a brush through her hair. She was uncomfortably aware that her own feelings were rather too strong for the amount of time they'd known each other. She'd heard that intense experiences could make people feel closer than perhaps they actually were. Was that what was going on here? She continued to pull the brush through her locks. The tug at her scalp that lessened as she pulled the brush down to the tips of her tresses was usually comforting and brought back memories of her mother brushing her hair as a child. Now it brought ideas of Briar tugging on it, winding the locks around her hand, pulling her head back, and nibbling her way down Isabella's exposed neck to the supremely sensitive spot where her neck met her sternum.

Isabella gripped the brush harder and gasped aloud when the motion yanked at her scalp. She dug the fingers of her other hand into her thigh. She was almost overcome at that one. Briar couldn't wake up too soon for her.

She needs her rest. The reminder should have been unnecessary, but Isabella had to fight the urge to sneak back into Briar's chamber. She finished brushing her hair in record time and headed downstairs.

Not unsurprisingly, there was no sign of her mother. Althea was a notoriously late riser, probably due to the pain in her leg. Sleep was usually a fractured thing for her.

Joseph sat in a tall-backed armchair he'd moved to take advantage of the morning sun. The entry hall was possibly not the most comfortable spot for reading, but Isabella couldn't argue with the amount of light that streamed into it. Someone had cleaned the window he used to read by. He puffed absently on his pipe, though it was quite cold and likely had been for some time. The book in his hands captured his attention well enough that he failed to acknowledge her presence.

That was fine with Isabella. She followed her nose to the back of the lodge and found Mrs. Patterson frying up a prodigious amount of bacon in the kitchen.

"Miss Isabella," Mrs. Patterson said. "Would you like some breakfast, love?" Dark circles under her eyes were the only indication she'd been up much of the night. She bustled about the kitchen with the same energy she usually did, and her voice boomed out the same welcome it always had. If she harbored resentment over being pulled away from the townhouse with no warning, she didn't show it.

"Yes, please," Isabella said. She took a seat at one end of the long table in the middle of the kitchen. It was made to seat far more serving folk than would be occupying it. It had been scrubbed down until it almost gleamed. Isabella was suddenly aware of exactly how much she owed the people whose lives she'd put through so much upheaval.

"Head up to the dining room and I'll bring it up right soon."

"Oh." Mrs. Patterson had never objected to her presence in the kitchen before. "Very well."

"It's not my decision, love. Lady Sherard wants a word with you."

"Oh!" Isabella swallowed hard. When Althea was Lady Sherard to the staff, then her temper was up. "Oh dear."

Mrs. Patterson shared a commiserating smile with her before turning back to the stove.

"Send out two plates, would you, Mrs. Patterson? I'll take the second one up to Miss Riley."

"Will do, dear."

There was only one way to face the firing squad, which was with her head high and her shoulders square; Isabella's mother had taught her that. Dutifully, she made her way to the dining room, which took some doing. The lodge was laid out in the most unfamiliar fashion, but she finally found it.

Like the rest of the lodge, it was decorated with hunting trophies. Isabella goggled at the dozens of antlers that made up not one, but two massive chandeliers looming over the long table in a mass of yellowed bone. They were liberally coated with layers of candle wax, though the antlers' points still pushed through.

Althea had taken her place at the head of the table. Two revolvers and a newspaper lay on the table in front of her, and she devoted her attention to cleaning one of the pistols. Isabella cautiously took a place toward the center of the table. The table was too long to take the foot, though she'd considered it.

"Come closer, you silly girl," her mother said without looking up.

With great trepidation, Isabella got up and took a chair to her mother's left. If Althea was going to grab her by the ear as she had many times when Isabella was a girl, better that she have to reach for it. Isabella might well be able to avoid it then.

"What is it, Mother?"

Althea quirked an eyebrow, managing to look simultaneously irritated and amused by the question. "What do *you* think it is?"

"I'm not rightly certain. There are a few options to choose from."

"Then shall we start with the effects of your revelation to your father last night?"

"Oh. That."

"Yes. That." Althea put down the revolver and turned all her attention on Isabella. "You will be relieved to hear Joseph is somewhat less angry than he was yesterday evening, but this is a wound that will be long in the healing for him. He's quite honorable." The last was said wistfully.

For the first time Isabella realized her mother was less worried that Joseph had found out than she was concerned their plan had wounded his sense of honor. The anger he might feel toward her was less important than the knowledge that his family was involved in an extremely dishonorable pursuit, no matter how well-intentioned it had been.

"I'm very sorry about that. I didn't know how else to explain it, not when he asked."

"I suppose you can't be blamed for that, which brings me to my next point. Whatever possessed you to work with that Riley girl to rob Mirabilia? Really, Isabella! I thought I'd taught you better than that. You must never compromise your activities. Never!"

"I know! But Mother, she was so certain that something was wrong with those engines and she was right."

"Regardless. You've exposed this family to scrutiny in a way your second-storey work never did." Althea slid the newspaper over.

The front page was taken up by a large illustration of Spring-Heeled Jack. The silhouette of the factory was easily recognizable behind the devil-like character who bounded across the rooftops. A large headline took up the length of the paper.

"Spring-Heel'd Jack Is Real!!" it proclaimed in tall letters. Isabella winced and read on. "Witnesses Describe His Night-Time Exploits! Marvel At This Beast Who Traverses The Roof-Tops. Are Any Of Us Safe From His Predations?"

"Oh dear." She leaned forward to skim the article. It seemed that no fewer than a dozen people had seen her panicked flight over the rooftops, though interestingly there was no mention of the imps.

"'Oh dear' is quite right. We're going to need to do something about your rig. It is much too recognizable and I will not permit you to lead the authorities back to us. Your father would be destroyed by such attention, not to mention the damage it would do to your marriage prospects." Althea twitched the paper back and shook her head while reading it again. "The only reason I'm not applying a switch to your backside is that there is no mention of the burglaries in the article."

"I'm far too old to be switched like a child," Isabella said coolly. The threat rankled far more than anything else her mother had said. Althea didn't understand what had happened and instead seemed content to treat her as if this had all been her idea.

"If you insist upon acting like one, you'll be treated like one."

"You act as if I had no notion what I was doing."

"The only other option is that you knew and didn't care." Althea folded one hand over the other and stared at her, head cocked slightly to one side. "Is that what happened?"

"Of course not! You shouldn't make assumptions about things you know nothing about."

"Enlighten me then? How was this not the ill-advised plan of a child?"

"Briar caught me, all right? She captured me and held me until I agreed to assist her in her plan."

Althea's head snapped back as though she'd been slapped across the face. Her mouth gaped open. If Isabella hadn't been aware of the danger she'd just put Briar in, she would have laughed as her mother struggled for words.

"It's not as bad as it sounds," she hastened to say, wishing she could pull the words back into her mouth. Better that Althea think she was a silly girl up to mischief than to have the full force of her ire unleashed upon the unsuspecting woman upstairs. "By the time I robbed Mirabilia, I was doing this of my own free will."

"How dare she?" Althea fairly leaped to her feet, anger making the cane hooked to the arm of her chair completely unnecessary. "She dared to blackmail you?" Her mother snatched up the cane and strode toward the door.

"Mother," Isabella caught up to her in two paces and grabbed her elbow, pulling her to a stop. "Enough. She was right. We are all in terrible danger. If Briar hadn't done what she did, we'd have no chance to stop it. We would be defenseless. At least now we're safe."

"There had to be another way, one that didn't involve you." Althea allowed herself to be stopped.

"Maybe so, but that's not what happened. We have to deal with the situation we're in. Wishing won't change it."

"Damnation, Isabella, do not use my own words against me."

"Yes, Mother." Isabella had won, and she knew it. She released her mother's arm. "When did you come to believe her?"

"Not until the servants arrived." Althea sank down onto the nearest chair, her lips twisted in a pained grimace. Without rage on her daughter's behalf to sustain her, the pain in her leg had apparently returned with a vengeance.

"They saw the imps?"

"Not exactly, but the house was apparently set upon by a flock of ravens. They broke through the front windows and filled the place before leaving, all without dropping a single feather."

"Ravens don't act like that."

"Exactly." Althea nodded. "I've seen some strange things in my time. I'm much more prepared to accept the possibility of demonic forces than your father is. It's strange, isn't it? He's willing to use magical energy, but he expects it to have the same laws as other natural phenomena."

"He thinks it's akin to electricity but from a different source. Until recently, I was inclined to believe the same thing."

"Your new friend seems to have opened your eyes to all sorts of new possibilities, hasn't she? Is Briar her nickname?"

"Something like that." Isabella prudently left the rest of it alone. Her mother hadn't been dismissive, not exactly, but Isabella couldn't parse out the meaning behind her words. Better to leave it alone until she knew better.

Anything else Althea might have been about to say went left unsaid when Mrs. Patterson showed up with breakfast. Isabella fell upon the plate as though it were fresh meat to a starving beast. Her mother turned the conversation to other things and Isabella was content to let her. There would be other difficult discussions later, of that she was sure. Better to take the peace offered now.

CHAPTER TWENTY-SIX

The bed was nice and warm, and while it was not soft, Briar was so comfortable she thought perhaps she'd never move again. She burrowed deeper under the covers, then wondered at the lumpy mass that bunched up by her hip. It took too much effort to worry about it. She drifted further away from herself, back to the sleep that demanded her return. It was dangerous, she knew that, but caring was difficult. Her body barely registered in her senses any more, leaving her mind free to wander.

Isabella. The curve of her neck, the swell of her breasts, the way she bit her lip when her release was upon her. Of course that was the direction her mind would decide upon. It wasn't divorced enough from her body, apparently. Still, it wasn't unpleasant, though she briefly considered turning her attention to more pressing matters such as what they were going to do about the inventor. But why would she do that when she could turn her thoughts back to the dratted woman who refused to accept her rectitude about almost everything. That in itself should have disqualified Isabella as someone with whom she would enjoy spending time, but Briar found it had the opposite effect. Isabella's intransigence and her confidence in her own abilities made her more attractive, not less.

And she was going to get married.

Briar found herself in a dark place. She didn't mind the shadows. Her mother's home had many such areas of darkness and she'd spent much of her time in them as a child. Demons weren't evil, not exactly, but they had little concept of humanity and its fragility. Many of them couldn't wrap their heads around the idea that if you twisted off a human's arm, it would likely die. The lower order demons would writhe around in pain, then the limb would grow back and they'd be fine. As object lessons, dismemberment and impaling were routine. After a few days, maybe a week, the demon would be none the worse for wear. Of course it hurt, and most demons would avoid such punishment when at all possible, but it wouldn't kill them. The delicate half-human daughter of a Minister of Lust was a target too tempting for most demons to overlook. But she took longer to heal and most of the things the demons inflicted upon each other with appalling casualness would have resulted in her death.

Carnélie hadn't been a nurturing mother, but she'd done her best to make sure Briar reached adulthood. Somewhere or other, she'd procured a human nurse, a mountain of a woman with skin so dark it was almost black and decorated with swirls of white and cream. Yoweina had protected her charge with a cleaver in one hand and a bone saw in the other. She'd overseen little Briar for years until the day a group of imps had descended upon them. Briar had escaped by crawling through a hole in the rocks and into one of the dark spaces while Yoweina was ripped to pieces as she listened. The hole had been more than big enough for the imps to follow her, but there had been little enough left of them by the time Yoweina was dead. Briar had tiptoed past their mangled bodies as their eyes followed her.

After that, she'd had tutors. Briar learned how to protect herself. She would never again let anyone else take what was meant for her. The dark places remained places of refuge, but now for studying and for practicing the phrases taught to her, phrases she could manipulate and use to provoke reactions from the hellish place she endured. Calling it living was too generous. Briar survived her youth, and that was the best that could be said of it.

This dark place was not comforting like the ones of her childhood. This one was quiet and cold. She was all alone; there were no rustles around the edges to ground her to this place. There was nothing to see, not even her hand when she held it up in front of her nose. Briar touched the tip to be certain that she was really moving her hand and gasped a bit at the comfort her own touch brought. She could rely on herself and no one else. Would rely on no one else.

She turned to face the darkness and whimpered as it flowed into her, freezing her core. She would overcome this. She must.

The sun blinded her, painting the inside of her eyes with a shadowy tapestry of red roots. Briar blinked to clear the image, then sat up. She listed to one side when her body decided that staying upright was too much effort. Isabella reached over and caught her before she could slide out of bed.

"Easy," Isabella said, laughing. "Breakfast will be much easier to eat here than on the floor."

"Breakfast?" Briar sniffed the air hungrily. The scent of bacon permeated the room. Under that was eggs and butter. Usually she avoided meat, but today she couldn't remember smelling anything more delicious.

"Of course." Isabella deposited a tray beside her and whisked a towel off the top. "You won't recover if you sleep all day and eat nothing."

Actually, she would, though it would take longer. It would certainly be easier to sleep for weeks, then wake up ready to go, but the gesture was sweet and so like Isabella. Briar lifted her hand to reach the fork or tried to. Her arm lifted halfway off the covers, then flopped back down when her energy ran out. She stared angrily at her recalcitrant limb.

"I can help," Isabella said.

"I don't need help," Briar said, staring at her hand. The fingers twitched as she willed it to cooperate.

"Clearly." Isabella speared a slice of bacon on the fork and held it up. "Now open up."

"I will not be fed like a child."

"Briar, no one is calling you a child." The look on her face said clearly that she would have liked to but was resisting the impulse. "You're exhausted. You've been through a lot, and if it hadn't been for you, I wouldn't be here now."

"Without me you wouldn't have been in the situation at all." Briar's tendency toward brutal honesty spared no one, not even her own self. She would have preferred it to be otherwise, sometimes. The skill of self-deception was one she occasionally envied in others. But it wasn't her, and there was no point in hoping for things that couldn't be.

"Something is coming, isn't it?"

"Very likely. Almost certainly." She couldn't see the future to answer absolutely, but Briar knew what they'd discovered could mean very little else.

"And without you I'd have no idea it was coming. I'd be a damn sight less prepared, I know that much. And so do you." Isabella held the fork with its bacon out again. "Now open up."

Briar did as she was told, though it still rankled. Isabella's logic was impossible to argue against, not when her eyes wanted to slide closed again. Food would help her regain her strength more quickly, it was true. She concentrated on chewing, though that too was an effort. Isabella continued to feed her. The eggs were easier, since they were the perfect consistency and required little chewing. She turned up her nose completely at the toast.

"It's cold," Briar said.

"Of course it's cold." Isabella held up the little rack that held three pieces of room temperature bread. They had been warm once, and Briar mourned for that time. The British insisted on cooling their toast before eating it, which meant the butter didn't melt properly to coat every nook and cranny of the bread. Cold toast was like a clear day in winter. The sun promised warmth, but delivered instead bone-chilling cold.

Her eyes were drifting shut again. Isabella was there so Briar struggled to keep them open.

A cool hand upon her cheek soothed her, and her eyes closed of their own volition. The warmth of the emotions cascading through her from Isabella brought her down into sleep almost instantly. It was strange how those feelings no longer felt so foreign to her.

"I'll be back later," Isabella said dimly at the edge of Briar's hearing before it all went away.

This time the darkness wasn't so cold.

When she woke later, the sun was no longer streaming through the window. Isabella looked down at her, a smile crinkling the corner of her eyes. She stroked the hair back from Briar's forehead.

"How are you feeling?"

Briar smiled. "Breakfast helped." Truth be told, she felt about the same: exhausted. But Isabella's presence cheered her immensely and allowed her to forget her exhaustion for a few moments.

"I'm glad to hear it." The gleam in her eyes was no longer from happiness. Briar could feel the arousal rising inside Isabella and her own ardor built in response. "My parents have gone out to inspect the property. The servants are engaged in cleaning the main floor. I've wedged a chair under the door handle."

Her core clenched at the extremely unsubtle suggestion. Dampness gathered between her thighs and her exhaustion receded as her lust grew to match Isabella's.

"You heard what Carnélie said," Briar said. She tried to force down her arousal, to corral it into something more manageable. Isabella didn't know what she was offering.

"So what if I did? I want you. If it'll help you recover, how can that be a bad thing?"

"I won't feed off you. I don't use people that way." Briar ducked her head away from Isabella's hand, ignoring the flash of hurt on her face.

"Is it using me if I ask you to?"

"Do you know how this will help me recover?" At the shake of Isabella's head, Briar continued. "I'll be feeding off your life energy, off the stuff that keeps you alive. If I take too much, you could die. If I take only what I need, you'll still be tired and worn out."

"And if you don't take it? How long before you recover? Weeks? Months? Do we have that much time? The inventor knows we took his grimoire. He's on notice now. Maybe we have weeks to lie around and wait to recover, but I'd rather not wager on that."

"What if I can't control myself? What if I hurt you?"

Isabella shook her head. "I have never met anyone as in control of her faculties as you. I trust you. You've never broken a promise to me. I don't think you could if you tried. I trust you, Briar, with everything that I have."

"But you're going to get married." That hadn't been what she'd meant to say. There was nothing to do about it now. The words were out and they hung in the air between them.

"I have no fiancé, if that's what you're concerned about." Isabella spoke slowly as though trying to figure out what Briar had meant. "I don't know that I shall ever have one."

"Your mother said…" Briar whispered weakly around the lump in her throat that tried to choke her. "For the family…"

"Your mother wants you to have babies. Do you plan to accede to her whims?"

"Of course not!"

Isabella looked down and took Briar's hand between both of hers. "And neither do I. Briar, I've never wanted to be married. I go to the balls to have fun with my friends and determine who my next targets are. In a few years, I'll be on the shelf and will no longer have to bother with them. My friends will all be married. I'll go have tea at their homes, then come back to mine and continue to work on my machinery. Perhaps there will be a special woman in my life, and I shall spend my evenings with her. That has been my view of my future for quite some time. This flap with Wellington simply means it may take a little longer. There are patents I can sell. Maybe I'll get into manufacturing myself." She looked up at Briar through her eyelashes. "The only change I've seen in my plan is that, lately, I've begun to see myself spending my evenings with you."

"Oh."

"Oh? That's all you can say to that?"

"Well, it is rather unexpected, as these things go." Briar squeezed Isabella's hand. "Your vision of the future is rather unorthodox for a young lady of your breeding."

Isabella grinned evilly. "It's more than a little indecorous, also." She leaned forward and put her lips next to Briar's ear. "I want to do such things to you," she whispered. "I want you to do such things to me."

Briar growled deep in her throat. She inhaled Isabella's scent, a pleasant smell with hints of motor oil, then bit down on the delicate skin of her neck hard enough to make Isabella squeal. She gathered Isabella in her arms and rolled her onto the bed. That Isabella wanted this was impossible to deny, not in her emotions, nor in the excited anticipation painted across her face. Finally unleashed, Briar's lust spread like a rush of heat throughout her body, pushing her exhaustion and doubts ahead of it. Everything she needed was right here. Her shroud came down, but Briar didn't care; she had other things to concentrate on.

Isabella gasped as Briar nibbled her way up the column of her throat then nipped at the corner of her jaw. She strained against Briar, pushing into her. Briar tugged the hem of Isabella's shirt out of her trousers then skimmed her way over Isabella's abdomen. She loved to feel the play of the taut muscles beneath her hand. She loved even more the softness of Isabella's breast and its comforting weight in her palm. There was only one problem: there was fabric between her fingers and the nipple she could feel straining for her attention.

Briar pushed herself up, holding her weight on arms that trembled while she settled between Isabella's thighs. The pressure of her mound against Isabella's was almost more than she could handle. She closed her eyes to force herself to slow down. They should come together, a quiet corner of her mind said. That would have the best results.

Too much logic and not enough skin. Isabella seemed to be of the same mind. She bit down on her bottom lip as she worked on the ties of Briar's corset with single-minded concentration. Briar reached behind

Isabella and unfastened the brassiere. They exhaled in concert when Isabella's breasts were finally freed. It wasn't enough. Luckily, Isabella's shirt was loose and it was the work of mere moments to get it over her head and somewhere out of the way. Isabella's brassiere followed quickly behind. Her breasts were tipped with rosy nipples whose taste Briar remembered all too vividly. Unable to resist them, she bent her head to lavish first one nipple, then the other, with elaborate attention. Her tongue teased Isabella's nipples into peaks that rose proudly from the hills of her breasts. Beneath her, Isabella writhed and moaned, grinding their centers together and fanning the flames of Briar's lust to ever-increasing heights.

The pants had to go. Reluctantly, Briar left behind her assault of Isabella's breasts and turned her attention to the trousers that blocked access to her ultimate destination. She undid the top button and couldn't help but sample the delights that awaited her. She slid her hand down the front of the trousers. Her fingers tangled briefly in the thatch of hair that guarded Isabella's entrance, then she was sliding through slick folds. Isabella's gasp turned into a low keen and she thrust up to meet Briar's questing fingers. They slipped past her entrance and Briar felt walls of velvet grab hold of her fingertips and refuse to let go. She wiggled them experimentally and Isabella almost levitated off the bed. There was no question that Isabella was ready. Her arousal was at a fever pitch. It twined through Briar, brushing against parts of her core that tightened in response. The pressure was overwhelming. The pressure was intoxicating. The pants were still in the way.

With deep regret, Briar removed her hand and undid the remaining buttons. She rolled over, gripped the waist of the trousers and pulled them from Isabella's legs in one movement. Isabella didn't seem to notice the disappearance of her pants and drawers. She arched her back, thrusting her pelvis into the air, demanding a return of Briar's affections. It was a demand Briar was only too happy to accommodate. She pulled off her corset and made her way back between Isabella's thighs. There was nothing between them now but skin. Isabella's emotions consumed her. They wrapped around her both inside and out and with such vividness that Briar could almost feel on her own body where she touched Isabella's.

The void inside Isabella summoned Briar. It needed to be filled as much as Briar needed to be the one filling it. She straddled Isabella's thigh, painting the speckled skin with the juices that flowed copiously from her own entrance. She rocked back and forth, seeking the friction that would elevate her to Isabella's level of need. Isabella bent her leg slightly, moving her thigh against Briar. She threw her head back at the arousal that rocketed through her, seeking release, only to be turned back and come crashing back inside her. Briar reached down and grabbed Isabella's patch of red hair. She tugged slightly, getting a surprised rock of the hips in response. Pleasure chased the barest hint of pain far away. Isabella grunted and rocked her hips again, demanding mutely what Briar knew she wanted.

It wasn't long now. They were both at such fevered levels that the slightest thing might set one or the other off. They should come together, Briar briefly remembered, though not why. She shifted her hand, resting the tips of three fingers against Isabella's most intimate place. She left them there, teasing Isabella, enjoying the coil of their shared arousals within them as they tightened until any further ratcheting of tension was impossible.

Isabella shifted her hips forward, impaling herself on Briar's fingers. Briar felt them slide inside as if they had entered her own body, as if she were the one stretching to accept the digits. Bolts of sensation flashed through her groin, or maybe it was Isabella's. She couldn't tell anymore. She couldn't tell anything except that everything was about to give. The pressure built through them, past their skin and out, scattering Isabella's awareness until all that remained was sensation. Pleasure, pure and unadulterated by any other emotion, crested through Isabella and crashed into Briar. She gritted her teeth and threw back her head, staring unaware at the ceiling above. The pleasure kept coming and coming as their shared orgasm stretched on and on, rolling from one to the other and back again. Briar felt like she was drinking light, her body was weightless and hung suspended between this world and the next, Isabella poised there with her.

That wasn't supposed to be happening. Briar toppled to one side, breaking their connection before she drew Isabella all the way over. It was what she'd been worried about, that she wouldn't be able to stop herself and she'd drink up so much of Isabella's life energy that her heart would no longer have the power to beat. She felt great, reenergized and ready to take on the world, but what about Isabella?

Isabella was stretched out on the bed, thighs still spread, though she'd released her grip upon the blanket. Twin mounds remained where she had grabbed the covers and held on for dear life while consumed by the most powerful release she'd ever experienced. Briar could sympathize. She'd never felt one that strong either.

Isabella's naked chest rose and fell in the gentle rhythms of sleep. A smile haunted the corners of her lips. Briar leaned forward and kissed one curved edge. Isabella would be fine. She was fine too; Isabella had seen to that.

CHAPTER TWENTY-SEVEN

The air was foul, even through the mask. He'd thought the air in the engine crafting room had been rank, but when all those imps were crammed into tighter quarters, it was almost unbearable. Holcroft snarled at the nut he was trying to crank down, but it resisted his efforts. It was damp down there, and corrosion must have gotten into the bolt's threads. The need to hide was hard enough on him, but when his equipment started to suffer, it was difficult not to take it personally. If only his grimoire hadn't been taken. He'd managed to redeem himself by getting it back, but the Prince had still insisted they move their operation. Had she understood how much work it would take to do so? Of course not, nor had she cared.

He leaned back, stretching out his back where it ached from wrestling with machinery all day. Half the point of summoning a demon had been so he wouldn't have to work as hard. The other half had been riches and glory. That meant he'd achieved a bare quarter of his goals. He was forced into hiding and was working harder than ever thanks to Beruth. If her plans didn't pan out, he was going to have to figure out how to send her back to her world.

It wasn't as simple as telling her to leave. The summoning spell crafted by Holcroft's idiot master had been much too open. Not only had he not specified which order of demon to bring before them, but he also hadn't set the circumstances to return it. That meant Holcroft would need to develop a spell of banishment. Those weren't nearly as plentiful as one might think. It had only recently occurred to him to wonder why it was so much easier to find a spell of summoning than it was to find one to undo the summons.

Since his current plans were on hold until he got some more bolts, Holcroft carelessly dropped his wrench to one side. He mounted a set of three shallow steps and grabbed two spokes of the large handle on the vault-like door. Laboriously, he cranked on the handle, transferring his grip to first one spoke, then the next, until the bolts released in a set of clanking thuds. He hauled back on the heavy door until it was wide enough that he could slip through, then pulled it to behind him. He repeated the process on the next door. It wasn't until he'd pulled that door shut behind him and shot the bolts back home that he removed the mask and breathed deeply of the unsullied, if slightly stale air.

The room was small, barely wider than he could reach with outstretched arms and scarcely longer. His desk, piled high with books and strewn with plans, was crammed in here along with the grimoire that he rarely let out of arm's reach since the incident. A bedroll was snugly rolled up in a far corner. There was not nearly enough room to put it down in the space between the desk and the opposite wall, not that he'd had much time to sleep. Once the outer room was ready, he'd sleep on the bed in there, but until then, this was the better option than trying to get some rest in the ever-present demon miasma.

The bricks that lined the wall down here had already started to crumble in the damp underground air. It was a good thing they didn't plan on staying long.

This was the one place he could breathe for any length of time without the intrusion of the imps' reek. His books were safe from the curiosity of the imps, but there wasn't nearly enough room to work in here. This had probably been meant as a broom closet, and the room outside some sort of office or perhaps a lounge for the foremen. Beyond that, past a warren of cramped hallways and storage rooms, the imps still worked on finishing up as many more engines as they could.

Today's work was supposed to allow him to separate the old lounge from the rest of the sub-basement so he could get back to his work. Being able to stretch his legs without worrying about interruptions from Beruth or her minions would have been nice as well. Since he apparently needed to replace the bolts on the door frame he'd constructed only the previous day, today wasn't the day the project would be completed. Perhaps he could put the time to better use, like coming up with a spell of banishment.

Holcroft pulled out a sheet of vellum and dipped his pen into the inkwell. There was no way he could put this in the grimoire. Beruth had access to it, used it to refine his inscriptions and to make rude comments upon the work of the magicians who'd come before him.

Opening a door between this world and hers wasn't the problem. He'd done that before, many times now, but the trip through the rift was a one-way affair. He needed one that would go the other way, which should be easy enough to conceive of. All he needed was the proper words. Perhaps he could even reverse the runes of opening. No, that would create a spell of closing. That could be important, however. He didn't need her reversing the portal and coming back through. And there was the matter of keeping her in that world and making sure she couldn't come back to punish him. There was no doubt that she'd try something like that if he crossed her.

He scratched away, designing new circles and plotting out the runes, then drawing harsh lines through them and starting anew. He lost himself in the work. It was far better than creating a device. This was so much easier. All it required were words, blood, and ritual. It was elegant, without the sweat and strain actual construction required.

When the bolts in the door clanged open, Holcroft knew his free time was at an end. The other advantage to the heavy doors meant it was impossible for someone to sneak up on him. He folded over the vellum, hoping the damp ink wouldn't smear too much and pulled a set of schematics over the pages.

These were almost complete. They took the concept upon which he'd based his engines in a different direction. Instead of simply overlapping one point in his world and a demon in the other then allowing one to bleed into the other, this one opened a large rift on that point. Beruth hadn't been satisfied with the infernal battery. She claimed there was little point in saving up energy here if it couldn't be used on something. The portal was the answer, and he was so close to finishing it. All that remained was translating the power from the battery to the device, then running tests.

The inner door clanged open. Beruth strode through, clad in tails and top hat. She swaggered about with a cane only a little too tall for her. Holcroft had seen her use it to devastating effect among the imps. He was always surprised the cane wasn't lumpy black from the accumulated blood of her subjects.

"Are you working on it?" she asked. She placed one hand at the small of his back as she leaned around him to check out the schematics. "Good. It's almost time."

He sought out her eyes, but she was too busy looking over the drawing. "Time? I thought your plan was to wait until we were closer to some feast of your people."

Now she met his gaze. Her eyes gleamed ferally in the light of the gas lamp and she dug the tips of her claws into his back. "That had been the plan, but since you allowed your grimoire to be stolen, we need to move more quickly. I have enemies, it would seem."

Holcroft bridled at the injustice of the accusation. Not only had her imps been the ones to allow the book to be stolen in the first place, but they wouldn't have found it without his efforts. She wouldn't admit to the first and only grudgingly acknowledged the second when he insisted. It was a losing battle, one he was tired of fighting.

"It needs testing."

"There's no time. Who knows what forces are being arrayed against me while you tinker? If this is going to work, we need to move to the next phase soon. What do you need yet?"

"Supplies, as always." He still wasn't sure if the design would work. On paper it seemed feasible, but there was a big difference between the design and the application. He would have to test as it was built, which was less than ideal. "We'll need a lot of help to build it. This one is dangerous and there will likely be casualties."

Beruth waved her hand. "Your engines will provide strong workers. Bring some of them through."

"How many? I know you have plans for them."

"No more than one-fifth. The remainder should do for what I have planned."

"Very well. I should have the schematics completed to my liking in the next day or so."

"That's what I like to hear." Her hand rubbed small circles on his back, brushing up against the puncture wounds she'd just gouged in his skin. With every touch, pain jangled along his nerves. Beruth's smile widened as his discomfort grew. "And now you're in the mood for a little reward, yes?"

His own smile was more grimace than grin. He knew who was being rewarded here, and it wasn't him.

CHAPTER TWENTY-EIGHT

The weight of the covers seemed to drag at Isabella, enticing her back to somnolence. Nothing sounded better than burrowing into their yielding warmth and going back to sleep. Why was she even awake? Oh. That. A hand on her elbow shook her again. She moaned in protest, too tired to make the attempt to tell whoever it was to sod off.

"Isabella." The voice reached deep down inside her and woke a hunger at her core. "You need to get up, darling."

"Briar?" She cracked one eye open. A wide smile split Briar's face. That was enough to force her other eye open. She didn't think she'd ever seen Briar look so happy.

"Who else would be naked in bed with you? Don't answer that question." The corners of her eyes scrunched up even further to show she was teasing. This was definitely a different Briar than the one she'd known the past weeks.

"Right." No wonder the covers felt so good. Isabella loved to sleep in the nude, but rarely did so as it completely scandalized her mother's maid. How the woman could attend to Althea and still be put off by a little flesh was always a wonder to her. "How are you feeling?"

"As right as rain. My exhaustion is quite remedied, thanks to you." She tweaked the end of Isabella's nose. "But we should get you into your own bed before your parents return and have inconvenient questions for us."

"Very well." Isabella knew the importance of not being discovered in Briar's bed, yet the call of the covers was near-impossible to overcome. Her eyelids drifted shut again and she forced them open. It felt like someone was trying to drag them down with their fingertips, but she prevailed. The room swam out of focus, but after a few determined blinks she could see well enough.

"Come on." Briar pulled her unresisting form upright. She was much stronger than she looked. "You're going to have some fatigue for a few days, but it should pass quickly enough with rest."

"Good to know." Isabella leaned back against the headboard when Briar let her go. She had an excellent view of Briar's lovely backside while she pulled on her dress from the previous night. For a change, Briar forewent the corset, probably knowing Isabella was in no shape to assist her with the ties. In fact, she'd donned the barest minimum amount of underclothes for modesty before pulling on the dress.

"Let's go."

"I'm not wearing anything." Sleeping starkers was one thing, but parading around the upstairs hall without so much as a stitch was quite another.

"Don't worry. We're going to wrap you up in the sheet. Once in your room, I'll get you your nightgown."

Isabella frowned slightly. She didn't relish the idea of being hustled out of Briar's room and into her own wrapped in nothing but a thin cotton sheet. On the other hand, getting dressed for a ten-foot walk, only to disrobe and change into something else at the end of it sounded like far more work than she thought herself capable of at that moment. Briar waited patiently for her as she deliberated. "Very well." Isabella pushed herself up from the bed and managed to get halfway to a standing position before gravity reasserted its hold on her. She flopped back onto the bed.

"Oh dear." Briar looked vaguely ashamed. "I may have overdone things."

"It's fine. I didn't push hard enough." She gave herself a mighty heave and found herself flying out of bed when she realized she didn't have the energy to stop at the apex of her trajectory. Briar leaped to her side and steadied her, pulling her back from the fateful arc that threatened to leave her face-first on the floor. Isabella said nothing while Briar wrapped the sheet around her. She tried not to lean on her too heavily as they made their way over to the door. The more she moved around, the better her energy seemed to return. She was even able to remain upright, if slightly canted, when Briar let her go to glance out the door.

"We're clear," Briar said, her voice low. "Let's go." She took Isabella by the elbow and steered her around the door frame, down the hall, and back to her own room. Before Isabella knew it, she was ensconced in her own bed and in her nightclothes.

"Thank you, Isabella," Briar said. She dropped a light kiss on Isabella's forehead.

Isabella's eyes drifted shut again, lulled by the warmth of Briar's regard and the comfort of her own bed. "For what?"

"For giving yourself so freely to me. I could feel the strength of your affection."

Did she have the energy to blush? Apparently so, though she lacked the wherewithal to care about it. "That's good."

"It is." Briar's voice was receding down a long tunnel. "And I want you to know I share that affection."

That was good to know. If she'd been a little more cogent, Isabella would have chuckled at the very Briar way she'd put it. It was both formal and endearing. She smiled, but it felt like her lips belonged to someone else. Then she felt nothing.

When she woke, Isabella had no idea what time it was. The morning sunlight had already passed when she'd gone in to see Briar. It was still light outside her window, but impossible to tell how much time had gone by. She still felt a deep weariness, but not so much that she couldn't rouse herself out of bed. Hunger grumbled through her belly, reminding her that while she'd been indulging her weariness by lying abed, her stomach had been much neglected.

Isabella maneuvered herself carefully out from between the covers. Her thighs trembled, but at least her knees locked. Once she'd been on her feet a few moments, her legs ceased their complaints. She dressed herself, sitting down halfway through when her legs began to shake again and her stomach set to howling so loud that for a moment she thought perhaps the imps were back. Finally properly attired for leaving her room, Isabella headed down to the kitchen. There had to be some food available, even if she'd missed lunch as she suspected.

There was no sign of Mrs. Patterson in the kitchen. A plate of food wrapped in parchment paper sat upon the table. Her gut set to complaining again as soon as she saw it. Isabella hoped it had been left for her. If it hadn't been, she sent a silent provisional apology to the hypothetical person whose lunch she was stealing. The repast was good, but she ate it so quickly that she had no idea what it had been when she finished. Two apple cores sat on the plate and perhaps half a dozen crumbs. Isabella licked the tip of her finger to pick up the crumbs, then devoured those as well. No sense in letting even the smallest bit go to waste. It would allow her to make do for now.

She was fortified with enough energy to see what the others were up to. Her mother was ensconced back in the chair in front of the fireplace, though the lodge had warmed up considerably in the sun. She most assuredly noted Isabella's presence, but she did not look up from her book. Briar and Joseph were nowhere to be seen. They weren't in the trophy room with its dead animals staring down accusingly at her, for which Isabella was exceedingly grateful, nor were they in either parlor. She wandered for a good while until she heard Joseph's voice raised in question. Briar's voice answered his. Isabella turned the corner to find them sitting side by side at a dusty table in the brownest greenhouse she had ever seen. Nothing lived in there, though many pots contained the remnants of plants long since dead.

Briar was pointing to something on a piece of paper. Isabella drifted closer to get a better look. It was a diagram with three rectangles and arrows going from one block to the next.

"Izzy!" Joseph exclaimed upon seeing her. "You're about. Your friend assured us you were merely exhausted from yesterday's ordeal, but I was beginning to worry. You are well?"

"I am." Isabella gave him a quick peck upon the cheek and settled into the chair across from them. "What are you two up to?"

"Brionie is giving me a lesson on magical theory. She is quite learned in the matter."

"But don't call her a magician."

"Quite so," Briar said. "Nor sorceress, enchantress, or witch. Those terms are imprecise."

"Then what is the best term?" Joseph's eyes lit up at Briar's dignified refusal to be categorized.

"Linguist might perhaps be the closest term."

"Linguist? That's an odd preference."

"Not at all." Briar's voice grew lively with the passion of her defense. "What you call magic is no more than a set of instructions set out for infernal energy. I am intimately familiar with the language, having studied it most of my life. I know the structure, the grammar if you will, and the vagaries of the vocabulary. English is a complicated-enough language on its own, but the language of demons makes it look like one designed by toddlers."

"If that's the case, why then can we not simply use human languages to direct the magic from this realm?"

"The magic of the mortal realm is too inert when on its own plane. It permeates the world around you, but it is difficult to harness on its own. The alchemists did a passable job at it. Remember, the magic lies in the transition of the energy from one realm to another, not as much in the substance of the energy itself." Briar stopped, visibly frustrated at her inability to communicate the concept as clearly as she would have liked. "The transition of the energy from the infernal plane to this plane is what charges it. If I were on the infernal plane, I would have to use the mortal plane's energy and transfer it to that of the demonic plane. Here, one must draw energy from the infernal plane to the mortal plane or it would have no charge. Do you understand?"

"I think so," Joseph said. "It is like the steam that turns a turbine. It is the conversion of the water to steam that moves the turbine to produce energy."

"After a fashion. The comparison is rather a tortured one, I'm afraid."

"Then what about…" The two stuck their heads back together, Joseph continuing to ask more questions about magic and Briar answering them in her precise way, all while dancing around the reason she knew so much about it. She was quite slippery about it, and Isabella wondered if her father even noticed how skillfully she evaded his questions in that direction.

Isabella allowed her eyelids to droop again and was quite content to doze while they conversed. Eventually, Briar noticed her sleeping and sent her back to bed. She was happy enough to go. She undressed quickly and flopped into bed, her eyes shut before her head hit the pillow. She was asleep almost instantly.

The next few days followed the same pattern, with Isabella forcing herself to leave her bed to feed her hunger when it would no longer be denied. Briar would find her wherever she'd curled up to sleep, then send her back to her room. Sometimes she would accompany Isabella. They would steal kisses and cuddles until Isabella could no longer keep her eyes open. She would awake a few hours later, and they'd repeat the dance. With every day that passed, the time between Isabella's naps increased and they were able to spend more time canoodling before she fell asleep.

And so it was that Isabella was dozing in a comfortable chair in front of the fire in the parlor when the front doors were pushed wide open.

The congenial spring weather had taken rather a turn for the worse the previous day. Gone were the sun and fluffy clouds in bright blue skies. In their place had come dark and heavy clouds that threatened rain, and they'd made good on that threat more often than not. A chill wind howled through the door, pushing with it a well-dressed gentleman and two other men, servants by their livery. From her seat in front of the fire, Isabella felt the chill draft as it curled through the room, tugging at the blanket upon her lap. From her angle, she couldn't see much more of the men through the doorway.

There had been no knock; the gentleman had simply strode in as if he owned the place. One of his men was helping him with his coat, and Giguere, their elderly footman stood to one side. The gentleman leaned forward and spoke to Giguere, who nodded and made his laborious way to the parlor where Isabella and Althea waited. Isabella stayed put beneath a heavy blanket. Garbed as she was in trousers and a man's shirt, she was in no way dressed to receive company. She wasn't even wearing a jacket, let alone the appropriate apparel of a young lady of her station. Althea waited because with the damp turn of the weather, her leg had decided to give her more trouble than it had in years. They would have to return to London soon, if only so Althea could have some relief from the cold. But what awaited them in London? She'd tried to raise the question with Briar, who had refused to give anything resembling a concrete answer. Briar disliked prevarication, and Isabella suspected that until she'd made up her mind, Briar would prefer not to answer the question than to give an answer that might be wrong.

"Charles Yorke, Earl of Hardwicke, has arrived, ma'am," Giguere said to Althea. "He requests to speak with Miss Riley and Miss Isabella."

Isabella sat up straight in her chair. She had no idea the Earl of Hardwicke knew who she was. Surely Briar hadn't betrayed her secret life to him. She couldn't rightly imagine that she had, not when Briar had promised to keep it to herself until she'd retrieved the grimoire. So why did he want to talk to her now? Briar worked for him, so there was reason enough to want to talk to her. Isabella realized that she had no idea if Briar had informed the earl of their plan to stay at his hunting lodge. Had Briar told him? Was she about to be sacked?

"Lady Sherard," Yorke said upon entry to the room.

"My Lord Hardwicke." Althea smiled at him from her seat. "May I present my daughter, Miss Isabella Castel?"

"Miss Castel." The earl flicked an appraising glance over her inappropriate garb but held his tongue.

"My apologies, Lord Hardwicke. I've been unwell and we weren't expecting visitors."

"I'm hardly a visitor in my own home," Yorke said. He looked around the room, his eyebrows drawn down into a fierce scowl. "Though it's been thirty years or more since I last set foot in here. Still, it can't be helped. I shall be in the drawing room. When you are prepared, please meet me there with Miss Riley. We have much to discuss."

CHAPTER TWENTY-NINE

The earl didn't seem too put out. Surely his message to meet would have been different had his anger been known. And whether he be angry or not, Briar knew she had done what she could. The situation was a difficult one, but she did her best to ignore the butterflies that had cavorted in the pit of her stomach since the Sherard's elderly footman had passed on his lordship's summons. The butterflies declined to lessen at her refusal to acknowledge them, so she settled for acting as though they weren't there.

The drawing room door was closed, but she heard the murmur of voices behind it. Briar paused and smoothed out her skirts. They were actually Isabella's. It was a good thing Isabella had taken to dressing almost exclusively in men's garb, as that meant Briar was in little danger of running out of dresses. She had to admit the combination of a starched white shirt and collar with Isabella's long red hair made her heart beat a little faster as well. She looked so natural in trousers that it hadn't been until Briar saw her in them that she realized how uncomfortable Isabella looked in skirts. Her movements in a dress were small and necessarily demure, but in trousers Isabella moved with lithe confidence.

This was the moment of truth. There was no sense putting it off any longer. She pushed the door open and sailed through without hesitation.

The earl stood behind the large desk, glaring at the map spread out across the top. Isabella stood to one side, seemingly content to let her parents take the brunt of his attention. Althea studied the map with almost as much intensity as the earl. Joseph was in the middle of a question, Briar was sure. The man questioned more than anyone else she'd met. His thirst for knowledge was insatiable and matched her own curiosity in its intensity and quite outstripped it in its breadth. Briar was quite certain Lord Sherard would pepper Death with myriad questions upon his demise.

Hardwicke looked up at her entry and motioned her over.

"My lord." Briar dropped into a deep curtsey. "It is a surprise to see you."

"Miss Riley." Hardwicke inclined his head to her. "Perhaps not so surprising as being forced to do without my favorite horseless following your unenlightening note about a sudden retreat to my long-empty lodge. I never received the letter you promised would explain everything."

Briar felt her mouth fall open into a horrified O of surprise. She closed it with a snap. "My apologies, my lord. The letter seems to have slipped my mind completely." Between her mother, Isabella's mother, and Isabella, she'd forgotten to send it on. Such things never happened to her. One thing she prided herself on was her dependability, but with recent events she'd lost track of that promise. She willed her face to cease burning, but her mortification refused to recede and stayed on display for all to see.

"And you must forgive me for suspecting that you might somehow be involved in the troubles London is currently experiencing."

"Troubles?" Briar looked down at the map. The streets of London sprawled there like a particularly messy spider web, following little order that she'd ever been able to discern. A dozen or more points were inked onto the map, though for no reason that she could ascertain from their locations. They appeared purely random.

"Very much so. Over the past few days there have been reports of strange creatures in the city. The locations of the fourteen we have confirmed are on the map. I suspect there may be more that were given short shrift at the beginning of this plague, but now we know all too well the penalty for ignoring them."

Horror mounted in Briar's breast. Was he implying what she thought he was? Her palms were uncomfortably moist in her gloves and she had to lick her lips to work moisture back into them. "Creatures?"

"Imps."

"Oh dear." She thought they'd had more time. The inventor's plans hadn't seemed that close to fruition, not in his grimoire, nor in the drawings Isabella had purloined.

"Imps?" Althea looked up. "Weren't those what attacked my husband's workshop? What have you gotten my daughter into?"

"Mother," Isabella said. "This isn't the place."

"Isn't it?" She limped over to Briar, standing threateningly close to her. "I know what you did to her."

Briar's mind flashed quite inappropriately to their morning of passion those days ago, regrettably the last such they'd been able to steal between Isabella's subsequent incapacitation and the presence of her parents. How could Althea know about that? They'd been most discreet or as discreet as it was possible to be when having the most astounding sexual relations of her lifetime. A blush rode high upon her cheekbones as she stood, balanced between mortification at having been caught and anger at the woman for daring to bring it up at such an indelicate time.

"Without your little trap," Althea said, "we would be well out of this."

Is that all? Briar wanted to sag with relief but wasn't about to give Althea the satisfaction. "I did what I had to do."

"And my daughter is in danger because of your thoughtless actions."

"Is that so? It seems to me that your actions are the ones that made it possible for her to walk into my trap, not to mention where we'd be without it."

Briar watched Althea sputter with no small amount of satisfaction. The actions of Isabella's mother were well-justified in her mind, and she still couldn't see how anyone might call her upon them. Briar was more than willing to do so. Her satisfaction withered abruptly when she saw the look on Isabella's face. Helpless anger was writ large in the twist of her lips and the anguish in her eyes. She was doing to her beloved the same thing Isabella's mother had done to Isabella. She was using her to further her own cause against Althea. Now was not the time, nor would it ever be the time.

"I'm sorry, Isabella," Briar said. "You are more than capable of fighting your own battles."

Isabella smiled wanly in response. "We've had this discussion, Mother. I won't have it again and certainly not here. This is my decision. It may not have been at the beginning, but it is now."

"We shall discuss this later," Althea said, drawing herself up in cold fury. "You've been through enough already. You've barely been able to stay awake the past few days."

"No, we won't." Isabella responded to her mother's anger with calm resolve. "I've made my decision. I am an adult and this is my choice."

"While you live under your father's roof—"

"Your father will respect your decision," Joseph interrupted. He laid a hand on his wife's arm, attempting to calm her. "She's grown, my pet. You can't hold onto her forever."

"Until she's married…"

"Do you really think that's likely?" Joseph drew Althea into a comforting embrace. "There's far too much of both of us in her to be satisfied with the role she's been told she must play. I'm afraid she has the best of the worst of us."

Lord Hardwicke cleared his throat, an embarrassed sound that served better than his raised voice might have to refocus their attention. "Yes, well," he said. "Now that the family drama is out of the way, perhaps you'd like to bring me up to speed on your activities, Miss Riley. All of them."

"Of course, my lord. It all started with your Mirabilia carriage, actually." With short sentences, Briar filled the earl in on what had transpired over the past weeks. She'd purposely kept him in the dark, not wanting to concern him when her own worries had been so formless. Explaining herself now and in front of others was the price she had to pay for her omission. She glossed over her recruitment of Isabella, though it had been impossible to exclude her from the narrative altogether. Instead, she concentrated on what they'd found, both the presence of so many imps and the contents of the grimoire.

"I wish you still had that," Hardwicke said.

"As do I. However, from what you've reported, I believe our intervention has put some larger plan into motion."

"It certainly seems likely." The earl drummed his fingers on the table. "Why did you not report any of this to me?"

"At first I had little to go on. I certainly didn't wish to burden you with my imaginings. By the time I was certain there was some malevolence at play, we were being set upon by still more imps in the Sherards' home. I judged it more important to leave town before we were injured. I was going to let you know when we returned to London. I'm afraid I have misjudged the time frame under which the inventor is operating."

"I think you may be forgiven for that, though I wonder if your mysterious inventor is indeed the one who has his hands on the reins."

"There is some evidence that he has help, based on the notations in the grimoire. I thought perhaps a demon familiar or the like. But I've seen no evidence that he is being controlled. What about you, Isabella? You saw his offices."

"It's hard to say, Miss Riley." Briar wondered if Isabella's uncharacteristic refuge in formality was to avoid dropping into the familiarity of her real name. "I saw someone who runs an organization and who also draws up his own plans. He certainly had people who reported to him, based upon his papers. There were a lot of imps, and other demons too, in his engine-works."

"I find it difficult to believe that any magician, no matter how skilled could successfully control all those demons by himself," Hardwicke said.

"Perhaps he can't, and that's why you're seeing reports of imps and their mischief," Briar said. There was so much about the situation that didn't make sense. "It may be that this is the inventor's botched attempt at becoming a rich man. We've seen such attempts go awry in the past, though rarely on this scale."

The earl nodded thoughtfully. "That may be, and if it is, we shall be about putting an end to it quickly. We would be remiss not to consider the other possibility, especially in light of the fact that the imps aren't up to mere mischief. There have been deaths associated with their appearances."

"Deaths?" Briar's stomach roiled in rebellion against the idea. She didn't want to be responsible for anybody's demise, especially not through such a grievous miscalculation. Violence at that level put a different lens on the subject. "Then this is a coup."

"I believe so or at the very least we must take that into consideration. A large incursion of demons into our world generally means someone is trying to unseat the Duke in our area."

"The duke?" Joseph asked. "Which duke would that be?"

"The strongest demon in a geographic region in the mortal realm is called a Duke," Briar said. "It is a title that allows her or him to rule the multiple factions of demons who exist in this plane."

"How many would that be?"

"More than you'd think and enough to require someone at the helm."

"Who knows about this?" Althea asked. "Surely the government won't allow that many demons to set up shop in our city."

"You may be certain the government takes a serious interest in such things, madam," Hardwicke said. "The Committee on Demoniac Interference is tasked with keeping an eye on the magicians in all of England. Knowledge of demonic activity necessarily goes hand-in-hand with our activities."

"I've never heard of such a committee," Althea said.

"I should be quite surprised if you had. While the use of demoniac magic—or infernal magic as Miss Riley prefers the term—is necessary for the running of the Empire, the masses' knowledge that demons are real would come as quite a shock. It is in all our interests to keep it that way. In that light, it is doubly important that the issue with the imps be resolved as soon as possible. Whoever is behind this doesn't seem to understand the value of secrecy. Not to mention, the current Duke is amenable to working with us. There is no guarantee his successor might feel the same way."

"Then what do you want from us?" Isabella asked. "Surely all this exposition is leading up to a request."

Briar nodded approvingly. She could trust Isabella to see to the heart of the matter of what needed to be done. Briar's inclination was to find out as much as she could about the situation, but this was not one that could be solved through study.

"The Committee continues to monitor the situation," Hardwicke said. "We need to fill in the Duke, but even with what you've told me, our information will be less than helpful. I need you to see what remains to discover. I shall have someone investigate the Mirabilia factory. I suspect the inventor has moved along since you located him. If that's the case, you should see if you can discern anything further about his plans. If he's been rash enough to stay, our people will take care of him."

Isabella moved as if to object, likely about the idea of the inventor being "taken care" of by the earl's mysterious people. For the other part, the plan was sound. She and Isabella were certainly the best equipped to survey the area and decipher the intentions behind the activity of the imps. She hoped it was simply the matter of a plan for riches being upset, but she had no illusions that her hopes were likely in vain.

"I won't permit my daughter to undertake something so dangerous," Althea said.

"I'm doing it, Mother. Unless you tie me up and lock me in a closet, you can't stop me."

"Don't think I won't, if that's what it will take to keep you safe." Althea shook her head. "Don't you see, Isabella? This isn't our fight. There are others out there who will take care of this."

"Maybe so. But I couldn't live with myself if it turned out there was something I could do but didn't. Besides, they've talked about two possible reasons for what's going on, but no one has mentioned the most worrisome implication."

"What are you thinking?" Briar asked.

"Maybe this isn't a coup of the demon world or an accident. Maybe someone is trying to establish their own rule in England, and they're using demons as their foot troops. Or maybe they just want to wipe us out. I assume there are enough demons to do that?"

"More than enough." The possibility was remote, as far as Briar could calculate the odds. But then, she'd also thought they had more time before things started to develop. Who was she to discount Isabella's fears?

"Then we need to do this and soon."

"It's decided then," the earl said. "We shall return to London tonight."

CHAPTER THIRTY

They did return to London that night, though not without further protest from Isabella's mother. Isabella had balked, unsuccessfully, at being forced into the clothing befitting a lady of her station. Briar could sympathize, even though she had no desire to wear what Isabella found comfortable. It was terrible to be forced to portray someone you weren't, but Althea hadn't been willing to overlook such niceties this time. The earl wouldn't have minded, even if he'd noticed. He had other things on his mind now.

"Make certain no harm comes to her," Althea had said to the earl as their few belongings were being loaded into the belly of the earl's zeppelin.

"Of course, Lady Sherard," had been Hardwicke's response.

"And you." Althea had rounded on Briar. "If one hair upon her head is out of place, I shall take it out of your hide." When Isabella's mother spoke, her accent flattened, betraying her American roots. This woman was nothing short of formidable, and Briar didn't doubt she would make good on her threat.

"Isabella is quite capable," Briar had said. "As capable if not more so than the rest of us, I'm sure. She is more than able to take care of herself. A trait which I have no doubt comes directly from you, my lady. Isabella is a credit to you, both in her breeding and her training."

Althea had stared at her, undoubtedly trying to decide if the last statement had been a compliment or a very pretty insult. Briar had simply smiled back blandly and allowed her to make of it what she would.

Now that they were in the dirigible, Briar looked forward to studying her notes. Surely something they'd been through could shed some light on their next steps. It wasn't as easy to read as she thought it would be. The problem wasn't the dirigible; in the passenger compartment, it was quite comfortable. The seats were exceedingly soft, allowing her to sink into the cushions as she liked when reading. Nor was it so loud in there. The engines were far enough away in the aft end of the ship that here they were little more than a humming noise that could be easily tuned out. No, the problem was Isabella. She seemed incapable of sitting still. If she wasn't sneaking looks over at her, she was leaning forward trying to see out the windows. That was a wasted effort, of course. It was as dark as her mother's soul out there. What little light there was came from the dirigible itself and that functioned to highlight wisps of mist, at the most.

The way back was long, though not as long as it would have been by carriage. The earl had made the trip in his personal dirigible. With the gravity of the situation in London, he'd had little other recourse. For the trip back, they were on their own in the small compartment, while he was elsewhere on the dirigible.

It seemed Isabella had recovered from her lack of energy. It was quicker than Briar would have believed, but a good thing given what they were heading into. She watched as Isabella stretched out her legs until they almost reached the far seat and flexed the muscles along the tops of her thighs. She then twisted her trunk. Briar couldn't help but cringe at the popping of her spine, but she clearly still felt the need to move about.

When she got up to examine the joins around the window, Briar had had enough. "What has you so twitchy?"

"I've been sitting too long," Isabella said, a sharp edge of complaint touching her voice. "I feel like a steam engine under too much pressure. I don't suppose you'd like to help me release some of that?" She looked over, her eyebrows raised in hopeful invitation.

The suggestion startled a deep laugh from Briar. "I'm sorry, darling. This isn't the best place for it."

"Isn't the place for it? This is the perfect place!"

"We shall have quite the spot of trouble explaining our behavior should someone come in and find us…occupied."

"You think…" Isabella bit down on her lower lip. "I was thinking of taking a tour of the zeppelin." The grin she'd been trying to hide peeked through.

"Oh. Of course." Two spots of color bloomed high on Briar's cheeks. She'd been certain Isabella had been making a much more lascivious request. If she was going to be honest with herself, as she must, she had to admit she was disappointed. "I have made prior acquaintance with the captain. Shall I request a tour?"

"That would be lovely." Isabella settled in more closely to Briar, snugging her arm around Briar's corseted ribcage and pulling her firmly against her. "The trip is likely to be long. I'm certain we can find other ways to distract ourselves once the tour is over."

Briar's cheeks fairly blazed at the brazenness of her words, but she said nothing to dissuade her lover.

"Then it's decided," Isabella said, patting Briar on the cheek. "Tour first, other pursuits afterward." She hopped up and extended a hand to Briar, who took it without hesitation. The door from the passenger compartment to the hallway running through the center of the gondola was quite narrow, as was the hallway itself. Briar twitched her skirts through to keep them from getting hung up on anything, and Isabella followed her lead. She hiked them further than necessary, and Briar caught a glimpse of a shapely stocking-clad ankle. Her gaze lingered until Isabella dropped the hem. When she looked up, Isabella was watching her, one eyebrow cocked and an inviting look in her eyes.

The throbbing of the airship's engines echoed down the hall. Isabella's head turned this way and that to follow the conduits and hoses that ran from one end to the other. The harsh electric lights here were quite bright, reflecting off metallic surfaces of brass and steel.

Briar grasped the six-spoked wheel at the end of the hall and turned it. The compartment beyond was small. Equipment of every possible size and description was crammed into every spare inch of space. Four men were bent over the various collections of levers and screws. A fifth stood at the very front of the ship. From the peaked cap on his head, this was the captain. He held a spyglass to one eye and peered through the glass windows lining the front of the bridge.

"Can I help ye, m'ladies?" One of the men looked up from his post at their entrance. He didn't get up, nor did he doff his soft cap as he ought to have. Before Briar could say anything, he jotted down a notation in a log book next to his device.

"Yes," Briar said. She waited patiently until he was finished with his notes and looked back up at them. "My friend would like a tour of the zeppelin."

Captain Giasson gave no indication that he knew they were there. The intense man put all his focus into running his ship, an attitude of which Briar quite approved. His tan skin and hooked nose leant him an air of hawkish ferocity. Two of the other men shared his general look, though neither seemed as severe. He closed the spyglass with a snap and bent over to have a quiet word with the man nearest to him. His aide nodded, then got up and made his way over to them. There was a narrow aisle between the machinery and diagnostic equipment.

"Captain Giasson has authorized me to give you a quick tour," the man said, his voice pitched to carry to their ears and no further. He didn't quite come to attention, but there was much about his bearing that said he was a military man or had been at one time. He did doff his cap, exposing a mass of light brown curls threatening to escape layers of shiny pomade. "I'm Lieutenant Hale. If you'll follow me."

The emphasis the lieutenant had put on "quick" should have been disappointing to Isabella, but she wasn't letting it get to her. Instead, to Briar's amusement, she bounced on her toes and settled down before anyone else could notice her unladylike anticipation.

Hale preceded them through the vault-like door and closed it behind him after they passed through. "That was the bridge."

When he prepared to move on without any further elaboration, Isabella raised her hand. Hale sighed and nodded to her.

"How thick are the windows at the front of the zeppelin, and how are they manufactured so free of imperfections?"

Hale opened his mouth to answer, but Isabella kept going.

"I noted at least two different anemometers and a barometer. What's the purpose of having two? And what purpose does the barometer serve?"

"The anemometers measure wind speed both fore and aft. The barometer—"

"Of course." Isabella nodded vigorously. "You'd need to adjust for that to keep the airship from yawing."

"That's exactly so." His face had warmed somewhat, so Isabella continued with her questioning. Before long, they chatted like school chums while Briar followed along bemusedly in their wake. She stopped at the door to the passenger compartment. Isabella looked back, both eyebrows raised in question.

"You go ahead," Briar said. "I've had the tour already. I'll look over my notes while you're gone." That way, when Isabella came back, they could engage in other activities. Discreetly, though. That would be the difficult part.

Isabella nodded and trotted up abreast of Lieutenant Hale. Briar could hear her peppering him with more questions as she let herself back into the passenger area.

They were gone for much longer than Briar had expected. Unless she missed her guess, it was longer than the lieutenant had anticipated when he'd mentioned a quick tour. Isabella had likely kept him talking as she tried to winkle out every bit of information on the vessel that she could. Briar was going back through her notes a second time when she heard the door open behind her.

"Was the tour enjoyable?" Briar asked, looking up.

"Of course it was!" Isabella replied. She bounced across the room and took a seat on a settee that afforded her a view from a large porthole. "This airship is fantastic! Do you think the earl will let me take a real look around, one day?"

"I would be surprised if he didn't insist on taking you on his own tour." Briar put down her notebook, then settled herself next to Isabella. She watched with interest as Isabella's interest changed from the mechanical to matters of a more physical nature.

"I believe I'd promised some alternative activities for the rest of our trip." Isabella waggled her eyebrows in a clear invitation.

"I think not. Too much opportunity for interruption. We've already discussed this."

"Why not?" Isabella voice was eminently reasonable, and Briar felt her reserve start to melt. "There is no one about. The door can be barricaded. No one will ever know."

"Oh, Isabella." Briar shook her head. "I am so very fond of you." The words were out of her mouth before she could stop them. To cover her slip, she patted the seat next to her.

Isabella scooted closer to her friend. Her face lit up at Briar's declaration of affection, and the last of her restraint crumbled. She placed her lips against Isabella's ear, knowing full well what it would do to her. "The problem is not what someone might see," she said, "but rather what they shall hear. I'm afraid I'm completely incapable of discretion when you touch me in certain ways. We do not need someone breaking down the door and checking on us because they think something is amiss."

"Oh." Briar could feel Isabella's disappointment. She shared the goosebumps that flared at the touch of her lips to Isabella's earlobe. They left behind a feeling of anticipation that coiled, prickly and warm, around the base of her spine.

"That is not to say there aren't some things we can do to while away the time." Briar caught the shell of Isabella's ear between her teeth and bit down lightly.

Isabella couldn't stop the quiet moan that rose up in her throat. Briar wasn't the only one who experienced a lack of control. She turned her head, pulling her ear free from Briar's mouth and captured Briar's mouth with her own.

CHAPTER THIRTY-ONE

They spent much of the remainder of the trip back to London amusing themselves. By the time the twinkling lights of London's streetlights and windows appeared below them, they were both quite mussed. Strands of hair hung down from Briar's head, her chignon quite in disarray. Spots of color bloomed high on her cheekbones, and Isabella had no illusions that she looked any more put together. What they'd been up to would be obvious to even the most casual observer. With much reluctance Isabella pulled herself away from Briar.

"I'll need to stop at my workshop," Isabella said after returning her hair to some semblance of normal and straightening the collar of her gown. For all of Briar's insistence that they do no more than kiss, somewhere along the way, the neck of her dress had been unbuttoned.

"Very well. I shall pass that on to the earl." Briar was already put together, looking as if nothing untoward had just happened. It must have been nice to wear a shroud for such occasions, though Isabella really had no idea if it worked that way. Still, if she'd had one, she would have abused it greatly if it meant she could dally with Briar with no one being the wiser.

Briar pulled open the window, letting in the chill air of the spring evening and the foul stench of London's streets. Even as high above the city as they were, there was still an unpleasant aroma that was all London. It was something Isabella had to get used to every time she left the city and returned. The country had much more pleasant air. It was no wonder people had to leave London for their health.

The city passed by beneath them, streetlights poorly outlining roads and thoroughfares in the darkness. Isabella knew when they were over areas of quality, as the streets widened so too did the spaces between them. There were also more streetlamps.

Ahead of them now was a veritable beacon in the darkness, a spear of light that reached up toward the heavens and beckoned them closer.

"Do you suppose the light will attract the imps?" Isabella asked.

"Maybe so, but I suspect the demons have been given specific instructions. Unless one of those directives is to check on the light, they should ignore it. And besides, without it, the dirigible will never be able to land in the dark."

The explanation made sense and was somewhat comforting, but Isabella still felt the need to keep an eye out. She couldn't help but watch closely, though, as they docked on the roof of the earl's home. How she'd missed the zeppelin's docking mast when she'd cased the house those weeks ago was beyond her. Certainly, the dirigible hadn't been docked when she was watching the townhouse. Or had it? Isabella had a moment of doubt, then shook her head. No, she was good at what she did. The zeppelin hadn't been there.

A group of men waited below them on the roof. As one, they reached for the lines one of the air-sailors threw from the nose cone. One man grabbed a line and held it long enough for others to take hold as well. The second line was corralled almost as quickly. Oh, how she wished she was on the bridge, but she suspected the captain and his men wouldn't have appreciated an audience. Certainly, she'd received a tour, but the feeling she'd gotten from her guide had been mostly of amused indulgence, as if she were some rare specimen to be tolerated.

The airship floated in place as the ground crew wrestled the mooring lines into submission. Before long, they were tugged through the sky, then the lines were lashed securely to the roof. She couldn't see around the front of the large inflated gas-bag, but she knew the spindle at the front was likely being affixed to the mast. The ground crew was well-trained. As soon as the lines were secured, they split into smaller groups, each after a particular task. Isabella couldn't watch them all at once, but she wished she could.

One group wheeled a platform with steps up to the gondola. She heard a series of clunks.

"That is our cue to disembark," Briar said. She'd mostly ignored the excitement of the landing, barely looking up from her ever-present notebook. She leaned forward and pressed her lips to Isabella's cheek in a soft kiss which even in its chasteness sent Isabella's heart pounding. "We don't have time for that," she said, when Isabella turned her head, seeking a more thorough kiss in return.

She was right, much though Isabella hated to admit it. Briar led the way through the narrow corridor at the center of the gondola, then to the exit door. A steward offered her a hand which she ignored. Isabella followed in her wake, also spurning the steward's assistance. The metal stairs were narrow, and it took her a moment to negotiate her skirts through them. Briar had no such issues and floated down the steps with the airy confidence of experience. She was deep in conversation with the earl when Isabella caught up to her.

"The earl is notified of our need for a side trip and the chauffeur is being awakened," Briar said.

He nodded to them with great respect, but the earl's eyes were elsewhere. Clearly the cares of their situation weighed heavily on him. With no more than a bow and a murmur of excuse, he left. Two men, both in military garb, awaited his pleasure, and they were deep in conversation before they even left the rooftop.

Barely five minutes later, Briar and Isabella were ensconced in a carriage. Johnson, though bleary-eyed from being woken at such a rude hour, took them quickly enough to her home on Cavendish Square. Isabella was content to sit quietly next to Briar. Since her exploration of Hardwicke's blimp, her legs and arms no longer vibrated with the need to move. However, with her and Briar's explorations of each other, it felt like that impetus had been drawn from her limbs and concentrated in her nether regions. She fairly dripped from need and Briar's pressing up against her in the confines of the horseless didn't help. Moving away would have been a different torture, so she was content to stay in her place.

An eternity of lustful thoughts later, though it was a bare twenty-minute ride between their houses, the driver stopped in front of the stately townhouse. Isabella alighted first and held out her arm for Briar. To her delight, Briar deigned to take the arm and tucked her hand in the crook of Isabella's elbow, allowing Isabella to escort her to the front of the house. What Isabella needed was in the workshop, but she had a couple of odds and ends she wanted to retrieve from home first.

A small stack of letters sat in the small entry hall. Isabella picked those up before proceeding into the foyer. She turned up the gas on the hall lights enough to see by, then stopped dead in her tracks. The house's facade had been completely undisturbed, with nothing to indicate the chaos they would find within. The servants had carefully covered the furniture in dust cloths before they left, but those had been torn to shreds by thousand of claws, the scraps left to gather wherever they might. Not content to destroy fabric shrouds, the imps had also shredded the furniture. If it had been upholstered, raw wood now gaped through dozens of rends. Slivers of wood littered the floor near tables and cabinets, their formerly gleaming surfaces now marred with dozens of scratches and gouges.

"It's a good thing we removed your family," Briar said quietly. She squeezed Isabella's arm in a wordless show of support.

"Yes, it is," Isabella replied. She supposed it would have looked much worse in here if one of the servants had been caught up by a swarm of imps. It would probably smell worse too, though she did detect a note of decay in the air. Something was rotting in the house, probably in the kitchen if she had to hazard a guess. "Will they be back?"

"Possibly." Briar looked around critically. "It seems they've been here a few times, probably trying to find you. The inventor isn't happy we took his grimoire, even after getting it back. I wonder what else I missed in there."

"We'll figure it out." Isabella put down the stack of mail on the deeply scored surface of the table in the hall. She stopped, then picked up the letter on top. "Wellington."

"What was that?"

Isabella held up the envelope. "It's a letter from Wellington in Heidelberg." She tore open the envelope and squinted at the contents. It was too dark to read, so she lit the lamp on the table. Her fingers trembled enough that it took her a couple tries. Able to see, she bent her attention to the letter and took her time reading words that shuddered and rearranged themselves on the page. Wellington thanked their mother for the money she'd sent but asked if they couldn't send a little bit more. He needed to purchase some books for his research. Aside from that, his studies progressed apace and he was hale and fit.

The letter was so normal as to be banal. He hadn't mentioned being troubled by demons, but then why would he? Isabella checked the date on the letter. It was from two weeks earlier, long before her first tangle with the imps. As usual, he was completely insulated from the troubles of the rest of the family. At least he wasn't to blame this time.

"I need to go to my room."

Briar said nothing, but she accompanied Isabella upstairs. The damage was as severe on the upper floors as it had been below. Isabella concentrated on moving through the house without looking about too much. There were more important issues than the destruction of furnishings. Her room hadn't been spared. The drawers from her dressing table had been pulled out and tossed about the room. The contents were strewn about like so much trash among the accumulated detritus. She gave a half-hearted tug upon the drapes to close them before realizing they'd been shredded into uselessness. If someone was watching the house, they would be able to tell someone was in there. A prickle of sweat lifted the hair on the back of her neck. The longer they stayed here, the more chance there was that the imps would make another pass and catch them.

She couldn't leave without what she'd come for. Somewhere in this mess was the box with all her lenses. Isabella turned up the lights as far as they would go. More light meant an easier and faster time searching.

"What do you need?" Briar asked.

"A wooden box about this big." Isabella sketched the shape in the air with her hands. "It's of light wood and plain."

Briar nodded and leaned over, hunting through the trash that had been Isabella's room. After a moment spent surveying the corners from where she stood, Isabella rummaged through the piles of refuse. They found the box quickly enough. To Isabella's great relief, it was still intact and unopened. The simple clasp on the lid had done its job. She was lucky the imps had been after casual destruction and nothing more malevolent. Even so, she opened the box. The lenses appeared to be intact. The padding around them had kept them from breaking under their mistreatment.

"Is that all of it?" Briar looked up at the nearest light, her meaning obvious.

"Yes." Isabella extinguished the wall lamps and picked back up the lamp from the hall. "I need my rig from the workshop, then we can continue back to your earl's."

"He isn't my earl."

"He's more yours than mine."

Briar didn't argue the point as they made their way swiftly down the stairs and out the back of the house. Isabella had been right about the kitchen. What food had been left had been gleefully dashed against the walls and allowed to rot.

Outside the back of the house, there was no indication of imp activity. The back garden was as immaculate as could be expected after days of inattention. The foliage seemed fuller, though as yet there was little evidence of blooms. The light of the moon was dim enough so as to plunge much of the garden into deep shadows. Isabella wished for her goggles.

Soon enough. She led Briar to the gazebo and pressed the button hidden in the decorative metalwork that held up the roof. As always, there was an long pause before the machinery ground to life. As long as she'd used the gazebo entrance to the workshop, Isabella was always convinced this was the time the mechanism would fail.

Her heart pounded loud in her ears as the grind of gears ushered them into her sanctuary below-ground as they rode the lift down into the darkness. It hadn't occurred to Isabella to wonder what might be awaiting them down there, not until they descended. The workshop was inaccessible except by the gazebo lift or the screw lift in the carriage house. She doubted the imps would be able to make their way down unassisted. Doubts weren't assurances, however. She had no weapons. Her mother's revolvers were in her luggage back at the earl's. She would undoubtedly take them with her to the Mirabilia factory, but she hadn't counted on needing them here. Isabella reached out her hand and caught Briar's in the dark. She received a comforting squeeze for her efforts.

Light bloomed around them, illuminating the smooth grey walls around them. Isabella gasped.

"It's quite all right," Briar whispered. "The light is mine."

"Warn me next time. I almost had a fit."

"Sorry, darling. I thought it might put you at your ease."

To Isabella's relief, there was no evidence of further imp activity in the workshop. Everything was much as they'd left it, more or less. There were no signs of imp corpses. She should have been able to smell those.

The lift ground to a stop and Isabella stepped down. She reached over and threw the switches that powered the lights. The lights came on one by one, starting with those closest and marching to the far end of the space.

Briar stepped down next to her, squinting at a point some twenty feet away. "Is that—"

"LaFarge?" Isabella called.

He drew closer, his arm extended. When he got closer, he stared at them, seemingly unable to comprehend who stood before them.

"LaFarge," Isabella said. "Jean-Pierre, are you quite all right?"

"He has a weapon," Briar hissed in her ear.

"It's fine. He can't hurt us. Not with that." Isabella could see how Briar might be confused. The object in LaFarge's hand certainly looked like a pistol, but Isabella had spent enough time with it to know better. She'd created it after all. It was her line gun, but he hadn't even loaded it with a grapple.

LaFarge drew closer and stopped. He lowered his arm. "Thank god," he said with no trace of a French accent. "You're back."

CHAPTER THIRTY-TWO

"What happened to your accent?" Briar asked. The not-so-Frenchman blinked at her for a second as if wondering what she was on about.

"Where were you?" LaFarge asked. "I've been down here for days." He blinked again, this time at the ceiling. "It has been days, hasn't it? It's so hard to tell below ground."

"Yes, it's been days," Isabella said. "What happened to you? We couldn't find you after the imps were in here."

"I ran away, didn't I?" His lips twisted on the taste of his own cowardice. "Those horrible little demons were down here, so I headed for less demonic pastures. Only I think they had my scent or some such. They came after me again, only there were more of them, so I came back here. There are far fewer ways to get in here than in my apartment."

"You've never seen an imp before this, have you?" Briar said. "Have you seen any demons? Most magicians try to summon at least one demon."

"Not I. I've always been perfectly happy to harness the energy of their realm. Never have I had any desire to see an actual demon up close."

So he was ever the coward. Briar watched him closely, not sure what to make of him. Was the cowardice real or affected, just as his accent had been?

"You still haven't told us where your accent has gone," Briar said.

"Oh, that." He flipped a hand wearily. "It may come as a surprise, but I'm not French."

"No." Briar put a hand to her chest in mock shock. "I would never have guessed that." It was altogether too playful a reaction for their situation, but she couldn't seem to help herself. Isabella was rubbing off on her in more ways than one, it seemed. It was time to get hold of herself. They had an important task ahead of them, and this was no time for mucking about.

He favored her with a small smile at her feigned surprise. Without the facade of the Frenchman to play up to, he seemed smaller, less grandiose, and more likable. Briar had met her fair share of the French and found them quite an enjoyable people. It seemed he'd taken hold of all the worst stereotypes in creating his alter ego, then proceeded to try to live up to them.

"Do we have time for this?" Isabella's voice was sharp. "The earl is expecting us. Worse yet, if they tracked him by his scent, then they're likely able to do the same with us."

"We're safe enough down here, aren't we?" LaFarge asked. "Nothing has made its way in."

"Not yet, at any rate," Briar said. "But we will have to leave, something that will be much more difficult to do if they're waiting for us outside."

"Are they?" The whites showed bright around LaFarge's irises. She could practically smell his fear. No, the cowardice wasn't feigned.

"I need my rig." Isabella strode away from them, deeper into the workshop. Briar followed swiftly, and LaFarge kept pace with them, clearly not wanting to be left alone.

"So the accent?" Briar prodded as they followed Isabella.

"Yes. I'm not French, like I said. I did spend some time there as a boy." LaFarge shrugged. "I needed to get away from my old life when I was a youngster. The debts were piling up, so I changed my identity and moved to Cambridge for university. Without the creditors pounding at my door, I was able to make my way through the Classics program. I became friendly with Joseph after we collaborated on an invention, and we stayed partners afterward. It's not an impressive tale."

Isabella moved to and fro at the bench where the remains of her jump rig were still laid out. "LaFarge," she said without looking up, "I require your assistance." She was curt with him. Briar understood her irritation; it must have been difficult to reconcile the new identity of someone she'd known all her life with the information that he'd been lying to them the entire time.

To his credit, LaFarge jumped in to help without hesitation. "I'm not mechanically gifted, Isabella."

"It's Miss Castel. Believe me, I'm quite aware of your limitations, but you've been around long enough to know one end of a wrench from the other. So either aid me or crawl back into the hole where you were hiding."

He sighed. "Very well, Miss Castel."

Isabella grunted in acknowledgment. "Hold that."

Briar watched with admiration as Isabella deftly reassembled her suit. The various pieces made little sense to her on their own, but as Isabella worked, Briar began to see how the whole unit worked together. It was a little like how she arranged manuscripts, except Isabella didn't have the vibrations of the pieces to help her along. All she had to rely upon was her knowledge, and she did so without hesitation. The most amazing part of the entire rig, now that Briar could see the whole of it, was how little it relied upon infernal magic. There were pieces here and there that did, but by and large the suit and pack worked as a result of Isabella's mechanical aptitude. Though Briar had little to compare it to, she suspected that Isabella's abilities were close to genius.

"Is this all your design?" she asked quietly, so as not to break Isabella's concentration. If Isabella needed to focus, she would be able to tune out Briar's discreet question.

A smile curved Isabella's cheek. "Almost completely. I had to ask for help from my father on a couple of parts. Regulating small changes of pressure through the elbows to steer was a bit of a challenge, but we managed well enough. And of course, I had to get LaFarge to enchant a few pieces when what I needed proved impossible to achieve through purely mechanical applications." Her smile disappeared at the last and she shot him a dark look. Either LaFarge missed it, or he pretended not to see it.

They worked in silence a little longer, Isabella directing him to hold this or to hand her that. She showed no signs of wavering in her irritation with him. When they finished with the suit, Isabella turned her focus to the jump pack. She waved LaFarge away without looking at him.

It was hard not to sympathize with the man. As odious as he'd been while pretending to be someone else, he was much more subdued now.

She thought she read remorse in the lines of his body, in the hang of his head. She knew what it was like to pretend to be somebody she wasn't, and while for her the pretense was very much an improvement over the original, Briar suspected that it had been quite the opposite for LaFarge.

"What is your real name?" she asked him while Isabella switched out canisters in her pack.

"You may as well stick with LaFarge," he said. "It's been my name for longer now than the original. I don't know that I'd recognize it if someone used it on me today." He cocked his head to one side. "But you could call me Jean-Pierre, if you felt so inclined. Or J.P., as Joseph does on occasion."

"I shall keep that under advisement." The way Isabella's shoulders had tightened, bringing them up almost to her ears told Briar exactly what she thought of the suggestion. She didn't wish to anger Isabella, not while she was working. Or ever really. What she wanted from Isabella was the brilliant smile, the dimple in her right cheek, the sparkle in her eyes. Right now the only light in her eyes was a dangerous one.

The jump pack had apparently not been in too bad a shape, and Isabella was finished with it quickly enough. "A few more things," she said as she disappeared into the far recesses of the shop.

"Will you take me with you when you leave?" The speed with which LaFarge asked the question as soon as Isabella was out of earshot told Briar he'd been stewing on it for some time.

"You're quite safe here," Briar said. "Why would you risk yourself outside? You don't even know where we're going."

"There's an even chance that wherever you're going has a bed. The cot here is broken quite beyond my capacity to repair it. I've been sleeping on little better than the stone floor. I would kill for a chance to sleep on something more comfortable, even a Chesterfield. Besides I don't know if I can stand much more time alone and hiding. Every little sound I hear has my heart leaping into my throat."

"I don't see why we couldn't bring you along. The earl's house is quite spacious. There will be room for you there, and it is well protected against hostile magic."

The sound of objects hitting the ground behind them had Briar both leaping into the air and turning to face the noise. Isabella glared at the two of them, a hard-sided case and several curved pieces of metal next to her feet.

"If he's coming, he'll have to be useful," she said, biting the tail of each word as she said it, looking like she wanted to sink her teeth into

LaFarge. "He's wasted enough of our time already. I won't allow that to continue."

"Of course, Isabella. Miss Castel." LaFarge nodded hastily, his head bobbing up and down like a duck on a rough pond. "Anything you want, simply—"

"Pick up the case and grapples and take them to the lift." Isabella stalked over to the workbench and retrieved her jump rig. She shrugged the straps of the pack over her shoulders, which looked more than a little out of place with her dress. With the suit folded up and tucked under her arm, she looked expectantly at Briar. "Are you ready?"

"Of course." Briar refused to be ruffled in the face of Isabella's discontent. It obviously centered around LaFarge and she would get over it, though Briar wouldn't be surprised if she decided to make his life miserable in the meantime. She tucked her hand into the crook of Isabella's arm and was rewarded with the relaxation of her arms. The muscles jumped once, then ceased to quiver under her fingertips.

* * *

Is Briar actually accepting what he's saying? Isabella couldn't tell, but it certainly seemed likely. They occupied the seat in the carriage across from LaFarge, who jumped and twitched at every noise. She had to admit that his discomfiture, while not exactly welcome, certainly didn't displease her. He deserved to be uncomfortable. When she thought of all the times her father had allowed him to register for a patent under his name only, rather than sharing the credit and with it the financial rewards, Isabella wanted to strike him. It wouldn't be an open-handed slap upon the cheek either. If she hit him, it was going to be a great deal more painful. At the moment she was torn between kneeing him in the groin or driving a fist into his belly. Her mother had taught her that the best way to bring down a man was by damaging his most prized parts, but Isabella wasn't certain that she could call the person who cowered in front of her a man. If she attempted the groin shot, she might find her knee whistling through empty air. No, better the gut shot, then when he bent over in agony, she could "accidentally" strike him in the nose with her elbow.

Briar's hand rested for a moment on her thigh. She patted Isabella in what she supposed was meant to be a soothing manner. Isabella was in no mood to be mollified. LaFarge had lied to her, but worst of all, he'd lied to her father and for decades. It had been no surprise to hear that he'd needed to avoid his creditors. The way he spent money now, he hadn't learned that lesson. If they'd had the money from her father's patents to rely upon, she and her mother might not have needed to resort to thievery when Wellington's disaster had broken upon them. She wouldn't have stolen from her friends.

She also wouldn't have been in the Earl of Hardwicke's library in the wee hours of the morning. Briar would never have trapped her. Though their paths had already crossed, Isabella doubted she would have gotten to know her. Instead, she would still be carrying that torch for Millie and growing more depressed the closer they got to the day of her friend's wedding.

Would she have spent as much time in the workshop with her father? Certainly Althea wouldn't have taught her about the art of moving unseen, of making her way past locked doors and windows.

Isabella sighed and allowed some of the anger to drain from her. It wasn't helpful, no matter how good it felt. They were stuck with LaFarge for now. As long as he contributed to what they were about, or at the very least kept out of the way, she could tolerate his presence.

Tolerance was all well and good, but she was happy that the remainder of the drive was quite short. The earl's residence directly overlooking Hyde Park was not so far from her home. They stopped out front and a footman appeared at the door of the carriage. Isabella looked up, trying to see through the night's gloom, but she could make out nothing untoward.

"We're quite safe," Briar said. "There's a circle of protection around the house. It extends a little past the front door."

"Oh." That was a good thing. At least they didn't have to worry about imps here. "I didn't know the earl was a magician."

"He's not, but he is probably one of the foremost human scholars of infernal magic."

"Did you make the circle?"

"No. I try to keep my practical knowledge of magic as discreet as possible."

"Is that so?" Isabella had trouble seeing that. From what she'd seen, Briar was quite free with her use of magic.

Briar smiled at Isabella's raised eyebrows. "Quite so. Believe it or not, I almost never use magic. The events of the past few weeks have been quite exceptional."

"I'll say." Exceptional might not have been the word Isabella would have chosen, but then she wasn't sure how she would describe what they'd been through. There had been moments of terror, certainly, and also moments of sheerest bliss. Magical was a little too on the nose. Exceptional would have to do.

Briar slid her hand into the crook of Isabella's arm. The contact was more than welcome. Little seemed to center her as well as Briar's touch did. Nothing sent her to the same heights as Briar's touch either. There she went again with thoughts of a lascivious nature completely out of keeping with the situation. Hopefully others would mistake the color on her cheeks for the change in temperature from outside to inside. She knew Briar wouldn't.

Arm in arm, they mounted the steps and entered the earl's home. Behind them, carriage wheels rang against the cobbles as the horseless rattled off. They preceded LaFarge and the footman inside. The door opened under Isabella's hand before she could reach the handle and light spilled out to greet them. In welcome contrast to her own home, the interior was well lit and full of life. If she hadn't known better, Isabella would have thought it was mid-day from the amount of activity.

Footmen hustled past them up the stairs, bearing themselves away on unknown tasks. Surely one of them had her trunk. There was little to worry about; clearly the Earl of Hardwicke's home was run like a tight ship. The butler spied them standing in the hall and bustled forward.

"Miss Riley, Miss Castel, the earl awaits your pleasure in his study." He raised an eyebrow at LaFarge, who had managed to retain but a shred of his previous dandified glory. Stubble obscured the line of his jaw, and while his hair had been pomaded into place at some point, it mostly looked greasy now. The cut of his clothes were fine, but the wrinkles made it obvious he'd been sleeping in them for quite some time.

"If you could have Mr. LaFarge put in one of the guest rooms, Abbott," Briar said.

"If you say so, Miss Riley." The butler's studied lack of expression could have hidden just about any sentiment, though Isabella suspected it camouflaged contempt. Perhaps that was only wishful thinking on her part.

"This way, Mr. LaFarge," Abbott said, leading him up the magnificent stairway.

LaFarge favored them with a jerky bow before heeling after the butler.

Everything gleamed under the gas lights. Isabella looked about with more than a little envy. She'd grown used to the bare spots on the banister and the wear on the carpets at home. She didn't see them anymore, but now that she saw what a well-kept house truly looked like, she couldn't help but feel some embarrassment for the condition of her home.

Briar led her up the stairs and down a wide hall. Their steps were muffled by plush rugs. The door at the end of the hall was ajar, and Briar tapped lightly on it.

"Come," said the earl from inside.

The study was somewhat darker than downstairs had been. A large table dominated the space. To one side were the desk and chairs that had been pushed aside to make room for it. They crossed the room and joined the earl, who leaned over the table, his arms braced. The table was taken up by the most detailed map of London Isabella had ever seen. It had such detail as to almost render the buildings on each block. Round dots in various colors had been affixed to spots all across the map.

"Each color represents a different day, does it not?" she asked.

Hardwicke nodded in approval. "Exactly so. As you can see, the incidents have been on the increase."

"There are many more dots than were on the map you showed us this afternoon," Briar said.

"Those occurred while I was gone to fetch you."

"Can you tell which incidents are targeted, and which are simply the result of the imps crossing over into our world?" Isabella asked.

The earl shook his head. "Regrettably, no. We are reliant upon the descriptions of people who don't know what they're seeing. It limits us somewhat."

Briar pursed her lips in thought. "And what steps are being taken?"

"The army is on standby, though the disturbance isn't yet enough for them to move in any numbers. No one wants to start a premature panic. Some of our magicians have been visiting the areas on the map in the hopes of finding the imps and returning them to their plane."

"Best of luck to them," Briar said. "Banishment spells are far more difficult than spells of summoning."

"Then we must hope our magicians have practiced them assiduously. Sadly, they haven't had much occasion to use the spells. By the time they turn up, the imps have mostly moved on."

"You've known something like this would happen." The accusation burst out of Isabella before she could reframe it into something more neutral.

"We would be quite remiss not to have considered the potential for a demonic incursion," Hardwicke said. "Since the promulgation of demoniac magic with our increased industrialization, we had to consider that something like this might happen at some point."

"Then why do you need us at all?"

"Because while those of us in some quarters have been concerned about such an event, it has mostly been dismissed as fear-mongering to impede progress. Our preparations have been hampered by a keen lack of support. If this incident continues on as it has, we shall be overrun. Now is not the time to convince Parliament that they need to fund a demonic suppression force. That will come later. Right now we need all the aid we can get and that includes what the two of you can bring. If I am to be honest, we are in quite dire straits."

A quiet gasp pulled at Isabella's attention. She glanced quickly at Briar, but there was no indication it had come from her. Briar was well buttoned up at most times. Even if she had been concerned by the earl's words, she wouldn't have shown it. For her part, if she could avoid returning to the Mirabilia factory, she would happily do so. The idea of facing all those imps again made her stomach flip on itself. But it had to be done. And none of it had anything to do with the soft intake of breath she'd just heard.

"Someone else is in here," Isabella said. "Are they supposed to be?" Her skin prickled with the sudden need to search the place.

"Are you certain?" Briar asked.

"I heard a gasp."

The earl sighed and looked up at the ceiling. "Young lady, you will come out here right now." His voice held a whip-crack of parental authority. Isabella started a bit, certain for a moment that he was speaking to her. And yet, she was right there in front of him, so who was he referring to?

A soft rustle from the daybed in the corner was accompanied by a louder sigh. What Isabella had taken at first glance to be a pile of cushions and blankets was pushed aside. From under it emerged a girl not too many years younger than she was. Isabella hadn't seen her at the balls, so she was likely still a few years removed from her first season. She couldn't imagine that the earl would keep her from it.

"Imogene," the earl said, his face a thundercloud of disapproval. "You were to be in bed hours ago. And what have I told you about listening in on your betters?"

"Who can sleep with all the activity, Papa?" Far from being intimidated by her father's sour mood, Imogene seemed almost amused. "I wanted to know what was happening. You always say you can never learn too much."

"This is not one of your studies, my girl. This is quite serious."

Imogene nodded seriously, the ends of her dark braids swaying back and forth from the movement. "Are we going to be attacked?"

"They cannot reach us in here. We are too well shielded." The earl sighed. "Many others are not afforded the same luxury."

"I want to help," the girl said stoutly. "Don't hide me away."

"And how will you help us?" Briar's soft question startled both Hardwickes. Clearly they'd forgotten her existence.

"I don't know, but I can't sit around and hope that everything will be all right."

Isabella was struck by the girl's willingness. Without any idea of the horrors that existed in wait for them, she was still willing to do what she could. It was a direct contradiction to LaFarge's attitude. He wanted to bury his head in the sand and hope everything would be all right. At the first hint of safety, he'd jumped. And yet… It was Isabella's turn to sigh. LaFarge was objectionable, that was true. He was smug and overly confident where he had no reason to be. He might even be an abject coward, but he knew what was out there.

Perhaps she was being too hard on him. It was easier to have such charitable thoughts when he wasn't around, and she had no doubt that as soon as she saw him again he would say or do something to cause her to be ill-disposed against him. He couldn't help what he was, and though it seemed he didn't want to, he wasn't the source of her problems. If she had to be honest with herself, Isabella had the sneaking suspicion that she was so angry at him because she could be. The man was a ridiculous caricature of his own self, and he'd treated her poorly. It was much more comfortable to be angry at him than it was her mother or even Wellington. It was difficult to blame her family, to be angry at them while she loved them. A vague sense of shame filled her at her uncharitable behavior toward her father's business partner.

"Have her help you with your notes," Briar was saying to the earl. "Her handwriting is quite legible and she has an eye for detail. She has assisted me on more than one occasion, and I have no complaints over the quality of her work."

Hardwicke nodded thoughtfully, his lips pursed. "If I agree to let you do that, will you go to bed? You will be of no use if you are cross-eyed with fatigue."

"Yes, Father." Imogene gave him a quick hug. He harrumphed and patted her shoulder awkwardly. It seemed the earl was not given to displays of affection when he had an audience.

He turned her toward the door. "Off you go, now."

Imogene crossed the hall and looked back. She gave Briar a small wave. Isabella received a stiff nod, then she slipped out the door.

Hardwicke turned back to them, rubbing his hands briskly together. "I have already dispatched some men to investigate the manufactory. If they find it empty, you should go immediately. Until then, I suggest you get some sleep."

The energy that had burned through her on the ride back to London still smoldered deep within Isabella's muscles. She doubted she'd get much in the way of sleep, but Briar could likely use the rest.

They mounted the stairs to their respective rooms behind a bleary-eyed footman. Isabella proceeded into her room, then stood next to the closed door, listening for the footman's receding footsteps.

"Can I help you, ma'am?"

The woman's voice from behind her was the last thing Isabella expected to hear. She tried to recover some dignity after jumping a foot and a half in the air, but from the studiedly bland expression on the maid's face, that zeppelin had long since been unmoored.

"I don't require anything, thank you," Isabella said. She brushed the front of her dress and stood back to let the maid pass. If Briar was preparing for bed, she would be a while, giving Isabella the chance to take a look at the schematics she'd found in the pocket of her jump suit. They were the drawings she'd purloined from the manufactory; she must have transferred them from the old suit and forgotten all about them. They'd had more than enough to distract them, that was for certain.

She opened the small trunk containing her jump suit and the other assorted supplies she expected they might need. It was quite full, and it took some rummaging to put her hands on the drawings. The room had no proper desk, but the dressing table was large enough. Isabella paused to turn up the gas lamps and bent forward to get her first good look at the drawings.

It looked like Holcroft had been working on some sort of voltaic pile, not that different from what Joseph was currently tinkering with. The battery didn't use zinc and copper like any other pile she'd seen, and its proportions were massive. What did Holcroft expect to accomplish by creating a battery using gold and beryl? It looked like the whole thing had to be enclosed in a glass chamber, but the size of it made such a feat quite impracticable.

Visions of glowing green coils in the hellscape of Holcroft's second factory room leaped into her mind. Perhaps he'd already succeeded. But then why were these drawings unfinished? The notes he'd jotted in one corner made it seem like perhaps he hadn't put this one to the test. Below the notes were some hastily scrawled equations. Isabella scanned over them, then took a closer look. The number four had a curious construction she'd only seen from two other people, one her father, the other…

No, it was too insane to even contemplate. Isabella looked more closely. The eight was drawn as two balls atop each other, instead of in one piece. This couldn't be.

She pushed away from the bench and bent back over the trunk. Wellington's last letter home was tucked in with some other papers. Worried at what she might find and not quite believing it might be true, Isabella lay the letter on the schematics. Back and forth she looked, until she had to stop.

She sat back heavily in her chair. There was no way to dispute it. Holcroft had her brother. He had Wellington.

Isabella laughed out loud. The sound was bitter, even to her ears. It took her four long strides to get across the hall to Briar's room, and she didn't slow down to open the door.

"Miss!" The maid's outraged squawk didn't stop her.

"Isabella." Briar's gentler reproof brought her up short. She looked over her bare shoulder at Isabella as the maid resumed unlacing the corset.

"Ahem." Isabella looked away, her cheeks heating quickly. "I'll come back."

"Don't be silly." Briar pointed behind her at a comfortable chair by the window. "But perhaps you should knock next time?"

Isabella confined herself to a nod and took the indicated seat. It was funny. There was no reason to be embarrassed seeing Briar en deshabille. She'd seen her in less. She'd been present while other women were getting dressed. But seeing Briar being less than put together seemed terribly intimate, somehow. It was made even more so by the presence of the maid. She tried not to watch as Briar was readied for bed, but she couldn't help sneaking the occasional glance. For one thing, it kept her mind removed from the papers back in her room. For another, Briar was gorgeous. In this or her true form, Isabella could barely keep her eyes averted.

After what seemed like an eternity, the maid left, curtseying deeply to Briar.

"Thank you, Suzie," she said. Briar waited until the door closed behind the maid, then turned to regard Isabella. "What has you so worked up?"

"You need to see this." Isabella grabbed Briar's hand without thinking. When Briar gasped, she relinquished her hold. Briar wasn't wearing gloves.

"You're upset."

Trust Briar to resort to understatement at a time like this. She left the room, knowing Briar would follow. The schematics and letter were still on her dressing table. The crumpled paper at either end of the drawings marred them deeply, and Isabella tried to smooth out the creases. She hadn't remembered crumpling them.

"This is one of the schematics I pulled from Holcroft's office." She pointed at the letter. "This is my brother's latest letter. The hand-writing matches."

Briar bent forward to compare the two documents. "I don't know about the letter. Certainly some of the letter formations are close, but the slant and spacing between words is different."

"His writing has always suffered when he's in a hurry. Many of his letters home look little like the writing upon his drawings." Surely Briar had to see they were written by the same person. "I think my brother has been captured by the inventor."

Briar laid one hand upon the letter and her other on the stack of drawings. She stared at them without saying anything for a long time. Isabella licked suddenly dry lips.

"It's possible," Briar said. When Isabella took a breath to ask what their next steps were, Briar held up her hand. "It is not, however, likely."

The words and tone were gentle, far removed from the usual brusquely efficient way Briar spoke. Somehow that scared Isabella more than if Briar had started shouting at her.

"What are you thinking?"

"I believe this is the same hand-writing as the grimoire, but that's impossible to confirm now that we no longer have it." Briar took a deep breath. "If your brother wrote this letter and these schematics, it is my belief that he hasn't been captured by the inventor. Isabella, I think your brother *is* Holcroft."

CHAPTER THIRTY-THREE

A knock on the door to the guest room roused Briar. Isabella tried to burrow into the crook of her shoulder at the intrusive sound, but Briar turned away from her. Try as she might, Isabella couldn't snuggle comfortably into her. Briar gently shook Isabella's shoulder.

"You need to answer the door," she whispered. "I can't be discovered in here with you."

Isabella favored her with a dark and bleary look, then sighed and got up. She snagged Briar's housecoat from the back of a chair, then opened the door. Briar bit the inside of her lip. If anyone recognized the robe, there wouldn't be much point in hiding her presence in Isabella's room. Part of her cursed the instinct to join Isabella instead of spending the rest of the night alone, but she couldn't leave her love after the revelation she'd dropped on her. Beyond a few kisses and some cuddles, they hadn't indulged in intimate relations. Isabella had been nearly falling asleep mid-kiss. For all that she'd fairly vibrated with energy when they got home, that energy had drained from her practically before Briar's eyes when she'd told her that Wellington was probably Holcroft.

"What is it?" Isabella asked of the maid at the door.

It was too early for breakfast. The sliver of light Briar could see through the drapes was the silver of predawn. Briar scooted down among the covers so she wouldn't be visible unless someone were at the side of the bed.

"The earl, ma'am. He'd like to see you. He's at breakfast." Apparently it wasn't too early for the meal after all.

"I'll be there as soon as I'm dressed," Isabella said.

"Begging your pardon, but if you see Miss Riley, would you let her know? I tried her room first, but she didn't answer."

"Of course. She's a heavy sleeper sometimes. I'm sure she just couldn't hear you."

"Thank you, ma'am."

"Did she believe you?" Briar asked after Isabella closed the door.

"She didn't laugh in my face and call me a liar, so that's something."

"Isabella!" This was no laughing matter. She didn't wish to jeopardize her spot in Hardwicke's household by being indiscreet. Maybe it was time to start thinking of finding her own place.

"Briar!" Isabella mimicked her tone perfectly. "Don't worry so much about it. As long as we *act* like we're respectable, the serving-folk will follow along."

"You've done this before, haven't you?" The idea shouldn't have shocked her, but it did.

"Not exactly, but this isn't my first dalliance with a woman." Isabella looked Briar in the eyes. "If you want details, I'll tell you."

"No, that is quite all right. Perhaps we should preserve some mystery in our relationship." Briar twisted the edge of the blanket between her hands. "But promise me your affairs are over."

Isabella perched on the edge of the bed. "Of course they are! And you make more of them than they were. There weren't more than a handful."

Briar held up her hand. "I thought we agreed to no details. Besides, it won't do to leave the earl waiting while we discuss the state of our relationship. Consider the message delivered. I'll dress and join him for the morning repast."

"I'll see you shortly then." Isabella leaned forward and captured Briar's lips for a hungry kiss.

As always whenever Isabella touched her, Briar felt like she might levitate from the bed. There was no mistaking the passion that fueled the embrace, passion that was aimed fully at one target: her. She returned the kiss with interest, stroking her tongue lightly over Isabella's lips and delving deep inside her mouth when it opened eagerly at her wordless request. She grabbed Isabella's upper arms to steady herself, then broke off the kiss when it threatened to overwhelm her. The earl would be waiting a long time indeed if Briar took the invitation Isabella proffered.

"We should get dressed."

"That we should." Isabella took off Briar's robe, then undid the tie at the neck of her nightgown and let it fall to the floor. She was gloriously nude beneath it. Briar couldn't help but check out the bounty on display before her, the long curve of her waist, the swell of her hips down to the rise of her mound and then to the patch of flame-red hair that seemed to call her name.

Briar grabbed her housecoat and fled Isabella's room. In another second she would have been all over Isabella, Earl of Hardwicke be damned. She rang for the maid and was dressed in what she considered record time.

"Does Miss Castel require any assistance, ma'am?" Suzie asked when the last button was fastened.

"I doubt that very much," Briar said. "I'm sure she'll send for you if she does."

"Very well, ma'am."

After Suzie left the room, Briar reached all the way to the back of her dressing table's bottom drawer. She felt around a while before her hand closed on a hard leather scabbard.

The dress she'd chosen had loose, blousy arms, quite out of keeping with current fashion, but sometimes trends didn't keep up with the need for self-protection. She strapped the small scabbard to her left forearm, then slid the silver athame home in it. The motion was a practiced one, though she hadn't worn the knife for years. There had been a time when she was never without it. If the factory was empty, they would be investigating it. Who knew what secrets might be cloaked behind glamours or shrouds? The knife could come in handy.

Hardwicke and Isabella awaited her at the breakfast table. It wasn't the long table the earl used for dinner; this one was much smaller, almost intimate. On clear mornings, this was the sunniest room in the house, and it was a pleasure to come to full wakefulness under the sun's rays. They would have been considerably more crowded had the earl's daughters been there to join them, but they were likely abed yet. Briar herself could have done with another three or four hours of sleep. From the way Isabella stared into her tea, she could have as well.

They'd both been there for a while. Half of Isabella's tea was already gone, as were the eggs on her plate. A piece of ham kept company with the crusts from her toast. At least no one dared comment upon the time it had taken her to get to the table. The earl was dressed in the same clothes he'd worn the previous evening. From the circles under his eyes, he hadn't yet been to bed. For her part, Isabella was in the strange get-up she'd worn with her jump rig. The pale canvas coveralls were quite out of place for breakfast with a peer, but the earl seemed not to notice. A heavier jacket, padded in the shoulders and around the waist, kept the coveralls from being completely scandalous. Even so, Briar could still see where Isabella's breasts strained against the fabric.

A footman placed a full plate in front of Briar and another filled up her teacup. The tea was dark, as she liked it. With tea this good, there was no need to dilute it with milk or sugar. Briar held it up to her face, inhaling the rich tones of dark tea with an undertone of bergamot and another spice she could never quite place. The smell alone was almost as invigorating as the first mouthful.

"I assume the Mirabilia manufactory is empty, yes?" Briar said.

"Quite so," Hardwicke said.

"Good." Isabella picked up a fork and speared a piece of ham.

The clearing of a throat by the door pulled Briar's attention away from her eggs. LaFarge hovered there, not quite inside the room.

"Monsieur LaFarge, is it?" the earl asked. "How may we help you?"

"My lord," LaFarge said. He smiled coyly, seemingly restored to his former self. "It's how I can help you." He hesitated. "All of you, really."

"I doubt that very much," Isabella said. She attacked the ham on her plate with more vigor than it strictly required, severing a sliver from the greater with one stroke. She glared at it, then transferred her irritated regard to the man in the doorway. "What could you possibly offer us at this point?"

"You're trying to stop the imps, aren't you?" At the earl's cautious nod of acknowledgment, LaFarge stepped fully into the room. "I know demoniac magic, I can help. Please allow me to be of service."

The offer was a generous one and quite out of character for what Briar knew of LaFarge. He'd never seemed more than a self-serving fellow, and she couldn't understand why he might volunteer to put himself in harm's way.

"Why on earth would you do that?" Briar asked.

Isabella nodded vigorously from across the table. "Why indeed? Aren't you the world's most consummate coward?"

Briar half-raised a hand to caution Isabella against such an outburst but lowered it at the hurt look she received in response.

"It's a fair statement," LaFarge said. He sat down lightly in one of the chairs, looking like he might spring up again if there was the slightest objection to his presence. At Hardwicke's nod, he relaxed into the chair. "The truth of it is, I'm tired of being frightened. Those demons are looking for me and I can't spend my time waiting for them to appear. Not anymore. If I'm working to defeat them, I won't be sitting petrified in my room."

"A noble sentiment, Mr. LaFarge," Hardwicke said. "But why should the demons be interested in you?"

"Because of them, Lord Hardwicke." He indicated Briar and Isabella with the thrust of his chin. The accusation of the motion wasn't lost on Briar, nor, she suspected, on Isabella. "I was present when the imps first attacked Isabella and Miss Riley in the workshop. I can only assume they got my scent there and marked me as a threat."

"Perhaps. Very well, Mr. LaFarge. You may accompany the two ladies to the manufactory. It is well they shall not be unescorted."

Unescorted? Briar hadn't required an escort since being a very small girl. Across the table, Isabella's face was carefully neutral, but Briar didn't doubt that she seethed inside as well. Another set of eyes that could view the glyphs and runes of her mother's people wouldn't be amiss, but she had serious reservations over LaFarge's capabilities. His confidence was puffed up out of all proportion to his actual ability. Many people dissembled until they achieved true mastery in a subject. LaFarge seemed never to have gotten beyond the dissembling phase. Then again, his whole life was built upon layers of lies. How could she expect any differently?

"That was not exactly what I was thinking, my lord." LaFarge dry-washed his hands together. "I can be more useful from here, perhaps in tracing imp activity?"

Isabella snorted inelegantly at LaFarge's about-face. When Briar cocked an inquiring eyebrow at her, Isabella turned studious attention back to her breakfast.

"I have more than enough men who are already doing that," the earl said. "What I need is an escort for the ladies."

"My lord." LaFarge stopped and swallowed hard, his face a trifle pale, his hands shaking. "I simply can not go out, not with those demons lurking. I can go over documents or look through manuscripts or grimoires, perhaps even try my hand at scrying, but I would be of no use outside these walls."

"Very well, Monsieur LaFarge. I shall find some way to make use of your talents." Hardwicke looked over at Briar. "In the meantime, we still need an escort for you and Miss Castel. Perhaps Johnson?"

That was an idea Briar could support. She trusted the chauffeur implicitly, and better yet, she knew he trusted her. She nodded vigorously.

The earl took her approval in stride, as if he had expected nothing different. "My reports say the factory is only half empty. Chassis production continues unabated, but there is no sign of anything non-human at the site. The team went inside the building where Miss Castel saw the engines being constructed, but there was nothing out of the ordinary, save a large piece of machinery of glass and brass. They speculate it was too large to move when the occupants left. It appears to be quite inactive."

"Were there any sensitives in your group?" Briar asked.

"Two. They both reported no infernal energy signatures on the site, except around that machinery. Even there, they report that energy levels are falling. The area appears to be well and truly abandoned, which is good. I met with the Duke of London and Environs last night, and he is not pleased to be the target of a coup. Were it not for my request, he and his minions would be tearing apart the Mirabilia manufactory right now. It was only my assurances that his enemies have moved on which is keeping him from it now. He seeks their new lair. I imagine they will not be long for this world once he finds them."

"Very good." Her voice might be all cool assurance, but inside Briar shuddered. She had no desire to meet the Duke face to face. She knew him by reputation only but had no doubt that he was well aware of her existence. Her mother would have taken care of that, would have dropped hints that Briar would love to get to know him. Not only was she not going to satisfy her mother's desire for a child from her line, but she was never going to do it with a demon of the Rage-Lands. Lust and rage fed each other too well. Briar kept herself under a tight leash at all times, but there were few who had as good a reason toward rage as she did. To lose herself to it was unthinkable. To give herself to it willingly was even worse.

Across the table, Isabella raised an eyebrow in inquiry. She must have picked up on Briar's body language or perhaps something in her voice. The Duke was of no concern to them. He was busy and wouldn't make an appearance, not while his rule was being threatened.

"I am fine," Briar said. She put down the last forkful of eggs. She felt overfull, and they had work to do. The last thing she needed was to feel sluggish because she'd had too much breakfast. "And I am ready to go."

"As am I," Isabella said. "I will need some assistance with my rig, but beyond that I am quite prepared."

"Excellent. Johnson will take you to the factory."

"Very good. Hopefully we'll find something to help put a stop to this incursion of imps."

"That would be none too soon, I'm afraid," Hardwicke said. "The number has doubled again. If we can't do something about it soon, the army will be called into the city and the citizens will be evacuated. With so many people out on the street, we expect massive casualties, especially if the Duke decides to fight back. You must move and quickly."

"Then we shall do so." Briar stood up, not waiting for one of the footmen to draw her chair away. They were past the time for niceties.

CHAPTER THIRTY-FOUR

The neighborhood looked different during the day. Certainly, it was no less grimy and the character of the people in the neighborhood hadn't changed, but the factory seemed less imposing. Maybe it was that she knew it was empty of the things that still interrupted her sleep or maybe it was Briar's solid presence at her elbow.

She craned her head to see out the small carriage window. The earl had insisted they use his remaining horseless. If he had to leave the house, he had other conveyances at his disposal or so he'd claimed. They'd already seen one, the zeppelin, but Isabella wondered what other vehicles he might own.

The twin smokestacks still rose from the factory, but now only one disgorged smoke above the neighborhood. The stacks extended far into the sky, even over the brick walls that ran around the manufactory compound. The walls were tall enough that naught but the tips of the factory buildings themselves were visible from the street. A small door, the same color as the bricks, was set into a wall. She supposed that was to be their point of ingress. Isabella scanned the rooflines for signs of imps, but there was nary a horn, wing, nor tail to be seen. The sun had risen during their ride across town, and it peeked between buildings, soaking the opposite of the road side in bright light. It seemed much too nice a day to be thinking about demons. And yet, zeppelins patrolled the skies, their long bodies floating into view above their heads long after she could hear the drone of their engines. The occasional booming crack of cannons had punctuated the morning stillness on their way over, driving into her the need for a swift resolution.

But there they were, two women and their chauffeur, with designs on breaking back into a factory that had been broken into two times already, but this time in broad daylight. The back of Isabella's neck itched. This wasn't the way it should be. They should have been holed up somewhere to make their move after dark, but circumstances drove them to incautious behavior.

The number of people on the street here was in direct contrast to the rest of the city. Some parts of London never slept, and this was one of those. Men and women made their way to and fro, heading out to work or returning, the men in their rough clothes, the women in cheap gowns hiked up to show too much leg or in shabby dresses that had seen too much wear at the sleeves and knees. In this neighborhood, if they weren't men or workwomen, they worked on their backs. Tension shivered through them even here. With each far off thud of guns, wary eyes were cast at the skies.

"Did you see the map?" Isabella asked Briar in low tones.

"I took a quick look at it while you were being outfitted," Briar replied. "Why?"

"How did it look?"

"Grim. The earl has his work cut out for him if he's to tackle the problem."

"But the spread was still much the same? The random reports, with no discernible pattern?"

"As well as I could tell."

"Then why are there so many people out here?"

Briar took a look out the window and Isabella pressed her point.

"Most of the neighborhoods we traversed to get here were almost completely deserted. The inhabitants here seem to think nothing at all is amiss, aside from the dirigibles."

"By and large, humans can't see demons. Not unless they have demon blood in them or some previous contact."

"But they still know when something's wrong, don't they." It wasn't a question, Isabella knew from her own experience. "They stay hidden, like any animal who knows there's a predator nearby."

"That's true." Briar sat back, staring into the distance. "As I recall, the pattern was quite distinctly random, though there were many fewer occurrences in this area. Since they're coming from the engines in the Mirabilia carriages, it only stands to reason. Few of these poor people could afford such an extravagance."

"Surely there are engines still at the factory. What about those?" The last time she'd been here, the side yard had been full of horseless carriages. Unless they'd taken those with them when they decamped, the lack of imps in the neighborhood was troubling.

"I don't know if it's anything of note," Briar said, much more cautiously. "What do you think?"

Isabella's heart warmed, some of the tension within her chest releasing. Briar trusted her opinion. "I think we should be careful, but it's going to make getting into the factory more difficult. There are too many witnesses, and if I go out dressed like their Spring-Heeled Jack, we could start a panic."

Johnson slid open the window that separated his seat from the cab. "I'm leavin' the horseless at this tavern. You ladies ready to go?"

Isabella hadn't noticed that the carriage had stopped, another indication of her anxiety. If she'd been able to do this alone, she wouldn't have been nearly as worried. She knew what she had to do, but she didn't know if she could trust Johnson. He seemed solid enough, and Briar had been pleased at his inclusion, but she hadn't enough time to get a measure of the man. But Briar trusted her judgment. The least she could do was to return the courtesy until she had proof otherwise.

"Is it a long walk to the factory?" Isabella asked.

"No more than a block or two," Johnson replied.

"I shall have to take the rooftops, then, and hope no one notices."

"Don't concern yourself with that," Briar said. "I can make you less remarkable."

"You'll make me invisible? That would have been useful the last time I broke in to Mirabilia."

"Not invisibility. Simply something that will make you blend in to the crowd more."

"Oh." Disappointment rose up in Isabella. It would have been nice to be completely undetectable. She'd asked LaFarge once if he could do that, and he'd said no, that it was impossible. If Briar couldn't do it, the spell definitely didn't exist. Still, it was good to know she hadn't been keeping it from Isabella.

"Put on your helmet."

They were almost ready. The carriage rocked slightly as Johnson alighted from his perch outside. It was almost time. Tension coiled once again in Isabella's belly, not unlike the first curls of arousal. Adventure was what Isabella lived for, regardless of the fact that beneath the excitement lurked very real anxiety. She donned her goggles, then pulled the helmet on over her head. The goggles were jogged somewhat askew and she fussed with them, trying to get them to sit just right. It wouldn't do to end up with a headache halfway through their investigation. Daylight streamed into the carriage's interior as Johnson opened the door and leaned inside.

"Hold still," Briar said. She took off one glove and licked the tips of two fingers. She traced a complicated shape on the front of the helmet, then licked her fingers again and made a circle around it. Finally, she pressed both fingers to the shape, then sat back, but not before trailing the tips of her fingers along the exposed edge of Isabella's chin.

"Blimey!" Johnson craned his neck forward to get a closer look at Isabella's helmet. "It's harder to see the 'elmet. What's that letter mean, anyway?"

"The rune means ordinary." Briar pulled her glove back on in a quick jerk. "I'm surprised you can see it at all. Most people can't."

Johnson squinted at Isabella. "She looks like the lady, still, but me eyes don't seem to want to look at her helmet." He looked down. "Or them clothes. I can still see 'er working clothes. That won't do neither. Those around 'ere'll take notice of that."

"It's quite subjective. You're already familiar with Isabella's workaday clothes, so that's what you see. Everyone will see a different version of what they consider regular apparel. It will differ from one person to the next, but to each she will be quite unremarkable."

Johnson shook his head, still staring closely at Isabella. He closed one eye, then the other.

"Are we going to sit around and talk all day?" Isabella asked. She knew she sounded waspish but was beyond caring. "The earl is counting on us to return in a reasonable amount of time, is he not?"

Briar put one hand on her knee and squeezed gently. "We're with you, Isabella."

"Then let's get this expedition underway." She stepped past Johnson, shaking her head slightly at his extended hand. The sidewalks were narrow in the shadows of the wall. A man in a soft cap and with what looked like half a pig across his shoulders almost ran into her. He rotated his upper body to avoid striking her in the head.

"'Scuse me," he grunted, not bothering with a second glance as soon as he was past. Briar's charm was working after all. Not that Isabella had doubted it, but she knew the folly of trusting something before testing was complete.

Isabella looked around and noted Mirabilia's smokestacks over the rooftops. True to Johnson's reassurances, it wasn't far. She moved down the sidewalk toward the factory, her heart beating in her ears, drowning out the sounds of the street around her. Briar alighted and Johnson closed up the carriage, then both joined her. They were silent on the walk. Isabella went over what she would do if set upon again by imps. Those repulsive things wouldn't surprise her twice. She glanced behind her at Briar and Johnson walking two abreast down the pavement. Briar looked inward, likely lost in her own plans, but Johnson's eyes were everywhere. They flicked from one person to the next, from one object to another. It seemed nothing could avoid his notice. He carried a sledgehammer casually over one shoulder. It should have looked odd, but the massive tool suited him. Isabella's anxiety about him eased a bit.

By the time they reached the wall around Mirabilia's side yard, Isabella had worked her way into a high state of tension. They were supposed to be avoiding attention, so she turned away, trying not to look too interested in the door. The bustle of morning continued unabated around them, no one seeming to remark upon the three of them by a door that went out of its way to be innocuous. No one looked up. To do so invited conversation, something these people seemed disinclined to do first thing in the morning.

Johnson pushed on the door, but it didn't budge.

"There might be a locking spell on it," Briar murmured to her, "but see what you can do."

Isabella fished her tools out of a pocket. Johnson and Briar stepped back to give her room and to shield her activities from those passing by. The lock was simple enough, and she barely had to look down to pick it. Before long, the tumblers gave with an audible snick.

"Neatly done," Johnson said.

Briar favored her with a smile. "Not a spell after all." She reached past Isabella and pushed on the door. It swung open easily under her hand. She ducked inside, followed closely by Johnson. Isabella took up the rear and closed the door behind them.

The interior of the courtyard looked little like she remembered. Gone were the carriages that had been stored here. Isabella looked around. The extensive side yard on this side of the factory had been packed full of Mirabilia horselesses. There was no cover, but more importantly, where had the carriages gone? If each engine represented three imps coming into London, then there was the potential for hundreds more imps than they'd considered. She hustled over to Briar, who made her way across the empty yard toward the smaller of the two manufacturing buildings.

"The carriages are gone," she said, pitching her voice low enough not to carry far. Just because they couldn't see anyone didn't mean someone wasn't lurking about.

"I noted as much." Briar's face was grim, her jaw clenched. "They've been gone long enough that I no longer feel any disturbance from them."

"What do you think it means?"

"I hesitate to speculate."

"Of course you do." Isabella gentled the statement with a smile. Speculation wasn't in Briar's nature. "But if you had to."

"If I had to, I might wonder why someone needs a large number of imps on mobile platforms. They could be placed anywhere and be quite innocuous in many cases. Perhaps they'll be involved in an ambush or in leading the Duke into one."

"But whatever the inventor has planned isn't for here, then."

"Likely not." Briar hesitated. "Though I could be wrong."

"It really must be the end of the world, if you're admitting to that." Isabella rested her hand on Briar's shoulder. She wished Johnson was somewhere else, anywhere else. Nothing would calm her nerves like a kiss from her beloved.

They neared another small door in the side of the engine manufacturing building. The din from the chassis plant next door filtered over to them even here. By contrast, the engine building sat dark and lifeless. But then, that had been the case when she'd visited the last time as well. The absence of smoke from the tall chimney above them was quite reassuring. From what little Isabella remembered of the layout of the building in front of them, this door would open to an area other than the manufacturing floor. She supposed there were offices or storage rooms off the floor, but she hadn't gotten the chance to explore them.

"Once we're inside, we'll have to split up," Briar said. Her voice was barely louder than a whisper. "I want you to go with Johnson."

"Why should we split up? And why on earth would you think I should go with Johnson. If either of us needs him, it's you."

"We need to cover as much ground as possible. Every second we waste means more imps. It only makes sense, Isabella." She leaned in, close enough that Isabella could smell the scent that was uniquely Briar's. "And you need someone with you who can perceive infernal inscriptions."

"I can see them well enough through this lens." Isabella tapped the left side of her goggles.

"And what if you lose that lens?" Briar sighed. "I'd feel better if he went with you."

"I still think splitting into two groups is a mistake. We'll see more if there are three of us."

"And we'll take longer." Briar stopped at the door and took Isabella by her shoulders and turned her around. Isabella looked Briar in the eyes, and Briar searched hers in return. It wasn't likely that she could see more than her reflection in Isabella's glasses, but it felt like Briar was looking down into her soul. "We're better together, there's no denying that. I don't want to leave you either, but there is no other solution." She tugged off her glove again, but instead of licking her fingers, Briar reached up one sleeve and pulled out a small silver dagger. She made a small cut on her fingertip then raised it to the center of Isabella's chest. She painted a glyph in her blood, then pressed her still-bleeding finger to the center of it.

The glyph flared to life through the lens over Isabella's left eye. It glowed bright red. Experimentally, Isabella closed her eye, and the light from the rune disappeared, leaving not even a smear of blood behind.

"Take off your glove," Briar said. She waited patiently as Isabella complied. Briar took her hand. "This will sting," she said, and she pressed the tip of her knife to Isabella's finger.

Isabella gasped at the pain, but Briar's touch soothed it away. Briar took her finger and placed it on her own chest. She drew a different glyph, then pressed Isabella's finger to the center of it. Just like the one Briar had drawn on her, it burst into flames that died down quickly, leaving a pulsing crimson inscription in the center of her dress.

"If something goes wrong, lick your fingers and draw them through my name. I will know that something is amiss and come for you." Briar patted Isabella on the cheek. "I will do the same if something happens to me. The flames will go dark if I destroy your name on my chest. That way we can be assured of each other's safety, even though we're apart."

"Good idea," Johnson said. If he thought it strange that they should not want to be parted, he said nothing. Again, his eyes skipped about, taking in everything and missing nothing. "Should we not get goin'?"

"Into the belly of the beast, then." Isabella's bravado rang hollow, even to her own ears. She was as ready as she could be. This time, at least, she was prepared for an attack, however unlikely it was. It was impossible to be too prepared.

"Quite so, my dearest," Briar said. Her bare hand lingered on Isabella's cheek a moment longer, then she turned toward the door, pulling on her glove. She didn't replace the knife up her sleeve. "Open the door, Johnson."

CHAPTER THIRTY-FIVE

Her head still swam from the heady mix of Isabella's emotions: fear and the determination not to show it were there, but all beneath a layer of what Briar could only describe as love. It was gratifying to know their feelings were so strong for each other. Of course, Isabella had no way of knowing how Briar felt, and she resolved to tell her as soon as they were done with this and alone together somewhere. Briar understood the fear; it bubbled up much the same in her own gut, though without as much excitement as Isabella also felt. She was used to such things, and Briar was not. She avoided unanticipated adventures. In her experience those rarely turned out well. This time, there was little to do about it except keep moving forward. At least this adventure promised to be quite tame.

The room beyond the door was dark, though she could see well enough. She knew Isabella could also, but Johnson put his hands out in front of him and stopped in his tracks.

"Keep moving," Isabella whispered to him.

"I can't see," he said.

"Of course you can't." Briar kicked herself for not thinking of him. "Wait but a moment." She pulled off a glove and licked the tip of her finger, then reached out toward him. She stopped. "I'd like to use magic to help you see in the dark. Do I have your permission?"

Johnson uttered a noise of wordless surprise, then nodded slowly. "Nice of you ter ask."

Touching him with her bare skin would open her up to his emotions. Briar steeled herself, then reached forward again. She sketched two runes on his forehead, one for shadows, the other for sight. They flared red in her vision. She tried not to feel the anxiety coiled tight along his spine.

"Better?" she asked.

It seemed to have done the trick. Johnson blinked twice, then looked around. "Ayup."

There wasn't much to see. A hallway stretched before them, doors going off to the left and a blank wall to the right. The air hung heavy around them, nothing to move it along now that the door was shut behind them. Briar had been in catacombs abandoned for centuries that seemed livelier than this place. There was no sign of life; they were well and truly alone. The fear simmering within her belly abated somewhat, leaving behind only the occasional roil of anxiety.

"I'll take this room," Briar said in her normal voice. It echoed queerly down the hall, bouncing from one bare wall to the other, too loud in this desolate place. "You two check the next," she said more quietly.

Isabella nodded and walked ahead, her eyes sweeping back and forth. Johnson flanked her to the left. Isabella didn't acknowledge his presence, and she seemed content to allow him to split the room with her. Briar knew very well that his presence made her nervous, but hopefully she would come to trust him as she did.

The door to Briar's left opened into a small storage room. It was as empty as the hall, save for the tall metal shelves that ran the circumference of the room. Dust lay thickly everywhere and puffed up with every step she took. It appeared the room hadn't been used in quite some time, long before Isabella had come into the factory looking for the grimoire. There was little to do but walk around the small room to make sure she wasn't missing anything. There were no hidden runes or inscriptions. This room was exactly as it appeared to be: a storage room long disused.

Briar went back into the hall and paused at the doorway to the room where Isabella and Johnson still prowled. Something had been stored in there at least. There was almost as much dust as in the previous room, but when Briar peered inside, the square voids on the floor were ample evidence that something had been moved. There was more storage, but without the shelves of the last room. Everything had been stacked in the middle, and moved out when the inventor and his imps decamped. The only footprints belonged to them, Briar noticed with a chill. How had they moved out whatever was in there without touching the ground? Imps could fly, true, but they weren't known for their strength.

Satisfied that Isabella was quite well, Briar made her way down to the next room. Its door was ajar and squeaked quietly when she pushed it the rest of the way open. It too was empty. An overturned bucket lay forgotten in one corner. It gleamed against its backdrop of dust. Briar made her way inside, trying not to disturb the dust too much. Her nose had started to itch and run. She sniffed lightly to clear it, but only succeeded in increasing the aggravation within her nasal passages. Her eyes watered as she tried to hold the sneeze inside, but it was having none of that. Briar tried to stifle the explosion from her sinuses, but she met with little success. The sound of her sneeze, high-pitched and loud, was much too noisy to her ears. Once it was released, she was helpless to hold back two more accompanying sneezes. She remembered the athame held in her hand a moment before she accidentally scratched her face and settled for rubbing her nose on the back of her hand instead.

"Are you all right?" Isabella's quiet voice drifted to her from the hall. "Tell me that was a sneeze."

"It was a sneeze," Briar said. There was nothing more to see here, so she joined the other two in the hall. "This place is incredibly dusty."

"That it is. I don't recall it being so when I was here a week ago, but then I never got down to this part of the building. I spent little more than a few minutes in here."

"You said you spent more of your time in the inventor's offices. I'll want to see those. There may be something you missed."

"That's very likely."

Through unspoken agreement, they worked their way quickly through the remaining rooms. Briar was unsurprised when the rooms were as empty as the first three had been. If no one had come running after Briar's fit of sneezing, then they were likely alone. They were all storage rooms, save one small room with two quite dilapidated desks inside. Even that contained nothing else of interest and was liberally coated in dust.

A pair of metal double doors waited for them at the far end of the hall. Isabella pulled a large pistol-like object from the waistband of her suit and gripped it tightly when they got to it. Johnson firmed his grip on the sledgehammer, waiting until she drew abreast with him. They both expected the worst, and Briar couldn't fault them. Her own knuckles ached from the strength of the grip she held on the dagger in her left hand.

Briar placed her fingertips on the metal door. It was cool under her hand, even through gloves. She wasn't sure what she was expecting to feel, whether it was heat or some vibration telling her it was unsafe to enter. Whatever her expectations, she felt nothing. She pushed down on the handle, wincing as the mechanism released with a loud clang that reverberated through the hallway.

Beyond was a large room, nearly the size of the entire factory. They'd found the manufacturing floor. Nothing remained that looked remotely like the hellish scene Isabella had described, except the cylinder looming over the far end of the room. Dust carpeted the floor, still strangely devoid of tracks. Briar inched her way into the room, her eyes darting here and there, alert for the slightest hint of danger. Johnson slipped in front of Isabella without any comment. Isabella emerged quickly from behind him, her pistol at the ready. A narrow metal staircase climbed the wall to their right, then ran around the room to a platform with a door high above their heads.

"Is that the way to the inventor's offices?" Briar asked Isabella.

She nodded once in reply, never stopping her perusal of the room. Her eyes flicked this way and that, pausing at one point of interest, then moving on to the next one, then back again.

"I don't think we're alone," Isabella said. "This doesn't feel right."

"I haven't felt anything. There is no sign of demon activity." They might as well have walked into a long-forgotten church, with its high ceiling and echoing halls, not to mention the complete lack of infernal energy. She'd seen no active inscriptions, nor had she smelled even the slightest whiff of brimstone.

"I don't know." Isabella licked her lips. "I've been in abandoned buildings. This one doesn't feel right. It feels like the factory is holding its breath."

"How can a building be holding its breath?"

Isabella shrugged, discomfort in every tight line of her body.

"Maybe we should come back with some help," Johnson said. "I don't feel anything either, but maybe Isabella is right." His eyes took in the room before touching on them briefly. "Can we afford her to be right?"

"It's fine." Briar pushed down her impatience. "The earl sent his men to look into it, and they found nothing. We've found nothing. Or did you see something I missed?"

Isabella shook her head, but it didn't take physical contact to perceive her disappointment with Briar.

"If we see anything, even the slightest thing, we'll turn back. Unless that happens, we can't afford not to keep looking." Briar pointed to the door off the platform. "I'm going up there to see if I can find anything. You two take a look at that over there, the...what did you call it?"

"The voltaic pile." Isabella's voice was flat, but she didn't argue. She moved slowly around the room, never turning her back to it, at times resorting to a peculiar crab-like shuffle.

Once we're out of here, she'll be all right, Briar told herself. *We all will be.* For her part, she climbed the metal stairs, taking care not to step too hard on each step. Even so, her footsteps sounded too loud in the space. If anything, they echoed more here than in the hallway, and she cursed the hard soles of her shoes. She was only being cautious, not allowing herself to descend to the fearful wallowing to which Isabella had apparently succumbed. It was unlike her, and Briar hoped she would be able to hold herself together. Johnson was there to back them up. Between her magic, his brawn, and Isabella's insights, they could handle almost anything. Of that she was certain.

Briar stopped to examine the dais on the platform. Isabella had reported that this was where the grimoire had been kept. She could see well enough where the book had lain but no sign remained of the chains that had held it in place. Here she found her first remnants of an inscription. It had been inactive for a while and was starting to fade, but it seemed simple enough. It combined an amplification spell with pain and was keyed to those with demonic blood. It was a good thing Isabella's blood lacked any trace of demonic parentage or she would have had quite a shock when she'd reached for it. Apparently the inventor had felt he had more to worry about from the demons under his control than from outside interference. He'd been wrong, as it turned out. Briar kept her hands clear of the writings. Faded as they were, they would still pack a punch and she had no desire to be incapacitated by pain. Instead, she turned and faced the door.

Inscriptions covered its surface, these more concerned with locking in sounds and smells. Those were layered over and over, with the oldest ones little more than glowing patches and the newest ones still shining brightly. The nature of the demons made them difficult to conceal, especially with a building full of humans not fifteen feet away. Humans were curious beasts, and seemingly without the instincts of self-preservation that served their animal cousins so well. Even cats with all their inquisitiveness had better sense than did most humans. There was nothing on the door to suggest a painful surprise for anyone exiting, so Briar pushed down on the bar and made her way into a cramped hall.

Her gorge rose at the back of her throat almost immediately as the floor seemed to shift beneath her feet. The walls curved to one side, making Briar feel as if she were half a second from tipping over. She closed her eyes to center herself, and the worst of the disorientation ceased immediately. So this was how the inventor kept his imps from leaving. It was ingenious in its own way. She opened her eyes to find the runes he'd used but had to close them again. If she was going to get through the hall, she would have to do so blind. The idea made her uneasy, but she needed to see the inventor's rooms for herself. She had the best handle on infernal magic, and his offices were the place most likely to have something that could help them.

Briar took a deep breath and opened her eyes. She oriented herself to the door at the far end of the hall, then closed them again. With her right hand held out to get a fix on that wall and the left stretched out in front of her, she moved forward. The hallway seemed to stretch on forever, and she fought the instinct to look around. Too much more disorientation and she would likely lose everything she'd had for breakfast. She had to rely on what her right hand told her. The wall was still there; she was still going toward the far end of the hall. When her left hand finally met something solid, Briar almost sobbed with relief. She pulled in a shuddering breath and felt around for the handle. She pushed down on it and pulled it open, then walked briskly over the threshold.

She looked down on the darkened manufactory floor. She was right back where she'd started.

"Hell and damnation," Briar whispered. She peered over the edge of the platform. There was no sign of Isabella or Johnson. She glanced down the front of her dress. Isabella's name still glowed strongly. "She's fine," Briar murmured, not trying to convince herself of the fact at all. "She's fine," she said louder, believing it this time.

She turned back toward the door to the inventor's offices and pushed the door open. There was no sense of twisting yet. *When did I get turned around? Impossible to tell.* It wasn't going to happen again. Briar raised her hand and pointed the palm at the door barely visible at the end of the short hall. She licked her fingertip and drew two runes on the back of her hand. These would keep her on her true path. When she moved her hand left or right, the color shaded to blue, but when it was straight on course, the runes flamed bright red.

She stepped back into the hall and the nausea returned immediately. If she focused on the back of her hand, it was manageable, so she kept going. The door clanged shut behind her, and she jumped, her hand wavering and the runes shading to blue then back to red then blue again. Briar glared at her hand and shifted it left until the rune was once again a brilliant crimson. She kept on, ignoring the instinct to keep going straight. Every time she surrendered to it, her hand darkened to blue. If she went the way that felt right, Briar had no doubt she would find herself back on the platform above the engine floor.

The door at this end had a push bar, not a handle. She'd made it, of that she had no doubt. Briar pushed down the bar and stepped through.

CHAPTER THIRTY-SIX

The voltaic pile looked like what it was: a gigantic battery. At least, Isabella didn't see anything amiss with it from her cursory examination. Turning her back to the room to inspect it more closely made her skin feel like it was going to crawl off her body. The manufactory didn't feel right. Briar and Johnson might be convinced it was empty simply because they'd seen no sign of demonic activity, but Isabella knew what it was like to sneak around in a building. The occupants had been home in most of the houses she'd burgled from. They'd been abed and unseen, but the potential of their movement imbued the house with a feeling of being on the edge of motion. Mirabilia felt the same way. Sure, there was all of this dust and the empty rooms. She'd seen neither hide nor hair of imps. Did imps have hair? She hadn't noticed in either encounter with them.

Isabella shook her head to focus back on the matter at hand. Briar didn't believe her, preferring to place her trust in what she saw. They would have to discuss that. But since Briar was set on completing their exploration of the factory building, Isabella couldn't leave, not without her.

"What's so interesting?" she whispered to Johnson. He'd been investigating the exterior of the battery for a little bit now. He knelt on the floor a ways off, tracing his finger over a glyph at its base. It was so covered in dust that Isabella could barely make it out.

"The pile is covered with them funny letters," he said, much more loudly that she would have preferred. "There's more of 'em on the floor."

"Is that important? The factory is covered in them." Runes glowed a sullen green almost everywhere she looked. They were fading, with none of the brilliance she'd come to associate with a new inscription.

"But there's none 'ere."

"That's odd. Maybe we should go get Briar."

"Wait a tick." Johnson got to his feet but didn't straighten. He ran his hand through the thick layer of dust on the floor. Free of the dusty blanket, the floor was indeed blank. "It makes a square," he said. He followed the edge of the runes, brushing at the floor with his hand until he was hard to see, obscured by clouds of dust and darkness.

Isabella looked about, trying to keep an eye on the catwalks above and peer into the pitch-black corners while making sure the doors were all still closed. She gripped the grapple gun in her hand. If an imp popped up, she would put a twelve-inch length of steel through it. Then she would stop being polite.

"It's 'iding something," Johnson called over to her. "Come see."

Isabella made her way over to him. She looked up to where the roof met the wall, convinced she'd seen something, but nothing was there. She hunched her shoulders defensively, then relaxed them when she realized what she was doing. Her shoulders were going to ache the next morning. Maybe she'd be able to convince Briar to rub some of the tension out when they got home.

Home. It seemed a while before Sherard House would be habitable again. Maybe she could stay in the earl's stately townhouse.

She joined Johnson and looked down where he indicated. There wasn't much to see except the dust-laden stone floor. He'd uncovered a square devoid of runes that was maybe ten feet on a side. Isabella wracked her memory for what had been there when she'd seen it last, but couldn't recall. Her memories revolved mostly around the imps and the book, then her panicked escape across the rooftops. Beyond knots of imps being driven to work on engines by larger demons, she had no clear idea of the floor's layout.

"I don't remember that," she said. "It could have been anything."

"What d'ye make of it?" Johnson walked out into the center of the blank square and turned to face her.

"I think we ask Briar."

"Who?" Johnson leaned forward to peer at something under the dust.

"Brionie. Miss Riley. What are you doing?" Her voice echoed through the room at the last, but Johnson didn't stop.

He brushed dust away to reveal a small inscription, then jerked his hand away from it. "Somethin' cut me," he said, shaking his hand. Drops of blood were flung free of his fingers, landing on the ground with barely audible splats. The inscription sprang to life in virulent green. The floor rippled once, twice, then they were standing on a metal grate.

"What the devil?" Johnson said. He took a step back, the soles of his boots clanging softly on the metal, then stopped.

Below them, first one pair, then another, then dozens of glowing green eyes turned their way. She aimed her grapple gun at them but didn't depress the trigger. The chances that it would make it through the grate were slim. She took a step to the side. Her foot came down on something soft and she was met with a shriek of pain. Whatever she was standing on wriggled beneath the sole of her boot. More shrieks, these of rage, took up the call. She looked down. Fingers tipped with sharp claws stuck through the gaps in the metal. They reached for her but of course could get nowhere near her.

"We have to go!" Isabella yelled to Johnson. He was a statue in the midst of chaos, frozen in place and staring at the fingers that grasped for him. The top of the grate writhed with them, like red maggots crawling in search for flesh.

He reached out for her, grabbing her forearm and shoulder, slinging her toward the edge of the grate. Isabella slid for a few feet, then the soles of her shoes caught on something and she pitched forward. In a flash, the fingers stopped their crawling motion. Isabella looked down. The imps had their fingers hooked through the grate. They stared up at her; their fetid breath burned her nasal passages as their beady eyes locked to hers.

This is not good. Metal groaned beneath them, sounding for all the world like a great beast in gastric distress. The grate flexed under her feet, shifted, then she was falling. Isabella aimed down and pulled the trigger. The flash of powder in the gun lit up a hellscape of claws, teeth, and eyes, all trained on her and Johnson. One imp fell back, as did the one behind it as the length of sharpened steel from her gun ripped through them. It was wrested from her hand and pulled away into the mass of imps.

Johnson howled and tried to swing the hammer as he attempted to dislodge the hands upon him, all to no avail. Claws ripped at her clothes, trying to gouge out the soft flesh beneath. So far the heavy canvas of her jump suit kept her from serious harm, but it was being rapidly shredded. Johnson wasn't so lucky. His uniform wasn't meant to stand up to demon claws and he already bled from half a dozen or more scratches.

A roar split the heaving mass of imps. They scattered to either side, dropping Isabella flat on her back in the darkness. Johnson moaned in the back of his throat beside her. The imps were bad enough, but what could scare them off? Isabella scrambled backward, trying to find a wall to put her back to. There was nothing.

The dark was quiet now, no roars or shrieks, but something was there. Was that? Yes, it was. Breathing, in and out from a dozen throats in unison, and coming ever closer. Isabella gripped the glove on her right hand between her teeth and yanked it off. She licked trembling fingers, then drew them through the rune that was somehow still intact in the middle of her chest. The crimson flame winked out immediately. For better or worse, Briar would know they were in trouble.

If this was how she was going to go, Isabella would be damned if she would meet her end scrabbling backward like a crab. She pushed herself to her feet and made herself face the direction of the breathing. Feeling a bit like a gunslinger in a Western novel, she pushed back the corner of her canvas coat and drew one of her mother's revolvers. Johnson looked over at her, then clambered slowly to his feet. He located the sledge a few paces away and picked it up. Her heart still raced, but her hand was as steady as the stones beneath her feet. She pointed the pistol into the darkness and waited.

The inventor's quarters looked as if someone had stepped out only moments earlier. There was not a mote of dust to be seen. Aside from the room with the bed, everything was neat and tidy. She'd spent little time in the curtained off bed-chamber. One glance at the bed and the runes carved into the wood had told her all she needed to know about it. Strong emotion imbued the body's fluids with a more potent capacity for infernal magic. Those fluids produced during sexual relations were known to her mother's people to be quite potent, though she'd had neither the opportunity nor the urge to experiment firsthand. The inventor used magic as easily and almost as often as breathing, it seemed.

The toys arrayed carelessly along the floor next to the bed had never had any capacity to shock her. She was impressed at the range of phalluses the inventor had at his disposal, but his predilections were his own.

She'd moved on to the next room, but there had been little to discover. He liked his power. She could tell as much from the inscriptions on almost every surface. Many of the chairs had been marked with runes to render the person sitting in it more docile and more suggestible. The long conference table was graven with inscriptions along the same lines, as well as one that made it impossible for ink to soak into the surface. That was a useful inscription, and Briar tucked it away for later. She wondered if she could somehow work it into the weave of her clothes. She was forever getting ink stains on the wrists of her dresses.

While the inscription was useful to her, she doubted the earl would be overly enthralled by her discovery. She moved on, scouring the rooms for hidden compartments or objects disguised by spells. The bricks around the fireplace seemed reasonable candidates for such trickery. Briar moved in, eying the hearth from all angles, trying to discern an inscription of deception among the other layers of charms. There was a square enchantment graven into the bricks. Briar squinted to make out the runes. She ran her hand across the bricks but felt nothing to indicate the hearth wasn't one piece. Finally, Briar winkled out the key-rune. She licked her fingertip and obliterated the glyph. The spell blinked out of existence, revealing a hole carved into the fireplace. It was the right size and shape for the grimoire, but of course it was now empty. With exaggerated care, Briar ran her hands around the interior of the small compartment. Beyond some grime on her fingertips, she had nothing to show for her efforts.

This was getting her nowhere. Her hopes that the inventor had cleared his belongings out in a hurry, leaving some damning piece of evidence behind were rapidly fading. Maybe Isabella was having a more successful time of it.

At the thought of her lover, Briar dropped her eyes to the front of her dress, hoping to take solace in the rune there. Her stomach plummeted, and she put her hands against the rough bricks of the fireplace to steady herself. The rune was dark. Something had happened.

She crossed the room in a hurry, cursing the skirts that bound at her legs and forced her into an inefficient shuffle. Finally, she took a second to reach down with her athame and slit the binding fabric. Able to move more freely, she barely noticed the depravity that saturated the bedroom before she was back in the hallway between buildings.

Again, the walls shifted in front of her eyes and the floor dipped beneath her feet.

"I do not have time for this," Briar said aloud. The runes didn't care and she forged on despite the acid that burned at the back of her throat. She swallowed to keep it down and ran, stumbling every few steps to the far end of the hall. She yanked it open and stepped through into satin drapes and the still-lingering smell of sex.

"No!" There was no time. Isabella was in danger, and this carnival fun house of a hallway wouldn't let her through. Briar clenched her fists, her fingernails dug into the soft flesh of her right palm. She'd lost her glove. It didn't matter.

She placed her palm up against the door to the hallway. With deliberate strokes and gritted teeth, Briar used the knife's tip to etch the rune of Isabella's name into the thin skin over the tendons, then added a glyph for location. She would follow Isabella right back to herself.

Briar shoved the door open, then stepped forward, her eyes on Isabella's name. The rune burned red and she didn't look away.

CHAPTER THIRTY-SEVEN

By all the gods, but the little hallway had been stifling. Briar breathed deeply of the slightly-less-fetid air in the engine room. The rune on her hand still glowed brightly. She wished it was a guarantee that Isabella was well, but the rune would only take her to Isabella's body. It gave no indication of her well-being. Briar turned, watching the rune glow brighter, then darker. According to her magic, Isabella was somewhere beneath her.

"Of course she is," Briar muttered. "I'm thirty feet in the air. Most of humanity is down there."

There was no sign of Isabella on the manufacturing floor. She peered into the shadows by the battery but could see nothing. There was no evidence that something had gone wrong, at least not that she could see from her current vantage. Briar fought the urge to run down to the floor below. She would help no one, least of all Isabella, if she got herself captured. Despite a thorough scan of the area, she saw nothing amiss. Forcing herself to move cautiously, she made her way down the stairs.

How could something have happened to Isabella? Johnson too, since there was as little sign of him as there was of Isabella. She'd felt nothing to indicate the presence of demons in the manufactory. She still felt nothing, though she opened herself up to the point of being dangerously exposed. As best she could tell, there were no demons here. It felt almost as if there had never been any demonic presence.

Briar mulled that over as she crossed the floor. They'd been investigating the battery, so that was where she would start. Dust rose in little puffs around her feet, threatening her with another upper respiratory spasm. She wished for something to cover her nose and mouth, but had nothing. If she'd known the factory would be so dashed dusty, she would have brought a handkerchief or asked Isabella for a mask.

Briar stopped dead in her tracks. She looked down at the sea of dust around her. The unbroken sea of dust, save for the tracks of her own footprints. That wasn't possible. She'd seen Johnson and Isabella take much this same path to investigate the voltaic pile, at her request no less. This dust wasn't natural. When she turned to track her footprints back, she noticed that even the tracks she'd made upon entering the cavernous room and making her way over to the stairs were gone.

What else beside footprints did the dust conceal? Briar licked her fingertips and knelt, not heeding the grime coating her knees. The inscription was simple enough; she'd used it on more than one occasion to dust the earl's archives. She finished drawing in the runes and keyed the inscription. The dust disappeared, drawn upward in a sheet to filter between cracks in the bricks and around the boarded-over windows. In the earl's library, it had been simple enough to send it out the chimney, but she couldn't see the like here.

The floor fairly gleamed, even in the dark. Without the dust to obscure them, dozens of inscriptions littered the floor. Many centered on invisible points throughout the area. They served to amplify power, possibly from the battery. This must have been where the engines were built, each with a group of imps or other demons to impress the magic upon them. That was all well and good, but it got her no closer to finding Isabella. She stood on the tip of her toes, trying to get a better view of the floor. There had to be a pattern to the inscriptions. If she could see that, Briar could discern the breaks in the patterns. The most interesting things seemed to occur in the gaps between order and chaos.

She held out her hand, scanning for Isabella. Still underneath. Now that was fascinating. The earl hadn't indicated that the factory had a basement. Now that she thought about it, it seemed likely. Most buildings in London did. When space was at a premium, as it always was, people built up or tunneled deeper. Sometimes both. Isabella and

Johnson must have stumbled upon an entry to the lower level. Perhaps they'd fallen in the dark.

Her laugh was low and derisive. They hadn't fallen. The dust hadn't covered everyone's tracks on its own. The earl's men had missed something, and now something terrible had befallen Isabella and Johnson. She should have listened to Isabella. They never should have split up.

Her eye caught a glimmer of green fire on a nearby wall. The inscriptions on the walls were mostly older, and this one stuck out. She made her way over to it and examined the runes closely. An inscription of disguise, like the one hiding the grimoire's previous resting place upstairs. It traced a rectangle into the wall, one easily big enough to be a door. The glyphs were perfect. That was cause for concern. The inventor had more than imps bound to his control. Imps didn't have the intelligence to work infernal magic; they certainly didn't have the vocabulary for it. He'd bound at least one higher order demon.

This changed everything. Briar took her notebook out of the pocket sewn into her skirts. Though her heart urged her to go through that door and rush to Isabella's aid as quickly as possible, her head reminded her that she would get nowhere if not properly prepared. She slit the top of her finger, ignoring the jolt of pain, and proceeded to inscribe a spell in her own blood. She stopped short of keying the spell. When she finished that one, she turned the page and inscribed another, and another, and still another. By the time she finished the last inscription, her heart was screaming at her to move and her head was no longer proof against its urging. But there was one thing left to do yet.

Briar took a deep breath and starting drawing out runes and a circle upon the front of her dress. She needed to change her appearance. The shroud could be shifted, but it couldn't deviate too far from her regular appearance. Taking on the appearance of an imp was more complicated. She hated the things, but to get close enough to Isabella—and Johnson—she would need to look like one or they'd turn on her. With the urgency impelling her to move, it was a relief when she completed the inscription and keyed it to life. She felt no different, but when she looked down at her arms, the brick red skin of an imp was unmistakable.

With that, Briar reached forward and drew her fingers through the key-rune on the wall. The section within the square shimmered, then cleared, revealing a steel door where before there had been only bricks. Was it too much to hope that the door was unlocked? Briar grasped the handle and it turned easily under her hand. Apparently not. They'd relied upon the spell, then. A short-sighted reliance, but one she wasn't going to argue with.

Stairs led down, curving into darkness so deep it was almost tactile. Her eyes could only penetrate a short way into the gloom, but she started down nonetheless. Isabella was waiting for her.

* * *

Isabella squeezed the trigger, firing again and again at the thing that lumbered toward them. She didn't know where to aim, so she took aim at the center of the chaotic mass. The beast was a jumble of arms and legs, of torsos and heads. It was as if someone had taken a dozen imps and rolled them into an abhorrent ball. A bullet obliterated an imp's forehead, and its head flopped forward against the torso that stuck from the mass Isabella might have considered a body, but its multitude of hands never stopped reaching for her.

A cacophony of screeches issued from its mouths, a disharmony so intense that Isabella dazedly wondered why her ears weren't bleeding. Johnson crouched beside her, his face twisted in pain. He lifted the hammer, readying himself for when the abomination got within his reach.

The hammer on her revolver clicked once, then again when she cocked it and pulled the trigger again. Six shots weren't enough; they weren't even in the remotest realm of enough. With a Gatling gun she might have had some success. Only sheer firepower could triumph here.

Johnson stepped forward, swinging the sledge in a long motion. It impacted with a wet thud, driving through the forehead of an imp, obliterating it beyond all recognition. The thing didn't slow. Arms reached up and fastened themselves around the hammer, wrenching it from his grasp. He let go rather than be pulled into the struggling mass of demons.

She grabbed Johnson's arm and tugged. "Run!" she yelled, pointing away from the abomination.

It was likely impossible to hear her, even as close as they were, but he understood well enough. He shoved her forward between the thick columns, racing hot on her heels, then passing her. Isabella did her best to keep up, terror putting wings on her feet and driving her forward. Ahead, Johnson ducked and weaved, then turned hard to the right. He almost went down, but saved himself with an outstretched arm. He disappeared from her sight around the corner.

Isabella pounded after him and almost ended up with a faceful of imp for her trouble. It flew at her, arms reaching toward her. Allowing reflex to take over, she snatched the little demon out of the air and tossed it behind her. Frantically flapping wings kept it from hitting the ground and it shrieked, cursing at her in English and a language she didn't know, before cutting off suddenly.

Despite herself, Isabella looked back in time to see some of the thing's arms pluck the imp out of the air and stop it in its tracks. The arms grappled with the imp for a second then slowly pulled it feet first into itself. The imp howled, a high thin cry that went on and on until its head disappeared into the mass. Even then, Isabella could hear the echoes of its screams. She gagged, harsh bile rising in her throat, threatening to choke her with its acridity. The thing kept pushing, the imp's arms flailing. Suddenly, the arms stiffened then stopped waving. Isabella couldn't help herself. She retched, vomit rising suddenly in her throat and out her mouth, running down her chin and onto her chest. The stench of acid turned her stomach even more, but she dared not look away, not even to clean herself. The thing looked at Isabella and a roar issued from a dozen or more mouths at once. The arms sticking out of its side reached toward her, as did those elsewhere in its bulk. The legs underneath got going, and again the beast came for her.

Isabella took off once more and almost ran into a wall covered with imps. They reached for her, trying to tangle claws in her hair, promising to rend the flesh from her bones if she gave them the chance. A tug on her arm saved her from careening into them.

"This way," Johnson yelled in her ear. With his help, she backed out of their reach; they didn't leave their perches to come after her.

She turned back to face the abomination, waiting as it closed the space between them in a few bounds. Isabella dove out of the way. As she'd hoped, the beast was large and fast, but not maneuverable. Getting a dozen legs going in the same direction at once took time. It careened into the wall while the imps there scrambled to avoid it. Those that weren't crushed outright did their best to avoid the grasping arms, but many weren't so lucky. Imps were plucked off the wall and from the air to suffer the same fate as the previous imp.

She'd seen this show once and had no desire to view it again. Johnson yanked at her arm until it almost hurt. She wrested her hand away from him and ran on into the shadows. Imps flew at her from the dark, singly or in groups, sending her to one side or another to avoid them. Before long, she could again hear the ponderous bulk of the thing behind her as a dozen feet hit the floor in a heavy but steady rhythm. She had no time to plan, only to react. Isabella dodged claws and teeth, fighting against the ungainly weight of the jump rig that threatened to pull her over on more than one occasion. She ignored the stitch in her side and how her breath rasped in the back of her throat. The only thing that mattered was keeping her legs moving, staying ahead of the thing behind her and away from the imps that accosted her from the shadows.

Green fire blinded her in one eye and she had no time to react to the figure huddled on the ground in front of her. She tried to jump over its hunched form but didn't have quite enough height. Her toes dragged along its back and caught on something. Suspenders, perhaps? She tilted forward and yanked her foot free, trying to tuck herself into a ball and control her tumble. Her success was partial. She avoided landing on her face and breaking her neck, but she came down hard on her side. All the air drove out of her lungs with an explosive "oof" when the rig failed to take the brunt of her tumble. She stared at the ceiling, wondering why it was so light in here.

A face swam into focus in front of her, gaunter than she remembered and with longer hair, but heartbreakingly familiar nonetheless. Even with the goggles, she knew this face better than she knew her own.

"Hello, Isabella," Wellington Castel said. He didn't seem glad to see her, nor did he seem angry. "What on earth are you wearing?"

Wearing? He's worried about my clothes? Isabella shook her head to make some sense of what was happening.

Another face joined his in front of her eyes. A beautiful woman with the cruelest eyes she'd ever seen smirked down at her. "Yes, Isabella. Hello."

CHAPTER THIRTY-EIGHT

Isabella sat up, rubbing the back of her neck. She'd bounced her head pretty hard off the stone floor. It was a good thing she was wearing her helmet. A blow to the head would explain some of what she was seeing. Even with her previous visit, the scene in the subterranean room beggared belief. A row of squat voltaic piles, each much smaller than the one above, took up one side of the room, casting their green glow against the wall. Someone had carved a circle into the floor. It had to be twenty paces across. At equally spaced points around its perimeter, braziers smoked and smoldered. To one side a raised platform with stone stairs running up it presided over the scene, and across the circle was what Isabella could only call an altar. It was a thing roughly hewn out of black stone that seemed to absorb what little light there was in this place.

"Are you going to introduce me to this fascinatingly garbed creature?" the cruel-faced woman asked.

Wellington's jaw tightened slightly, but he complied. "Beruth, this is my sister, Isabella Castel. I have no idea what she's wearing." He gestured from Isabella to the woman. "Isabella, this is Beruth, Prince of Pain, Head of the Council of Agony, Lord of Torment."

Isabella resolved not to give the woman the satisfaction of seeming impressed by her litany of titles. She ignored Beruth in favor of giving her brother a hard stare. "There's nothing wrong with my clothes. They're what I need to get the job done. Too bad that seems to be you. So you're Thomas Holcroft? I'd hoped it wasn't you, but I knew you had to be involved after I saw your schematics."

"You're the one who stole my drawings?" His eyebrows lifted in surprise. "Then you must have taken the grimoire as well. Why would you do such a thing?"

"We knew Holcroft was up to no good after we took apart one of your engines."

"You and Jean-Pierre pulled that off." She'd thought his eyebrows couldn't climb any higher, but they disappeared under his hair.

"Sure."

"Jean-Pierre LaFarge? Father's partner who can barely enchant his way out of a burlap sack?" He rolled his eyes. "I don't know that I believe you."

"Believe what you like," she said, making a show of her nonchalance.

"She lies," Beruth noted clinically.

"Of course she does," Wellington said. "It was obvious almost from the beginning that Jean-Pierre didn't have the power or the knowledge to help me. We know there's someone else, someone from her realm." He pointed to Beruth.

"There's only us," Isabella said, her voice insistent. "The Earl of Hardwicke sent us here to find out what you were up to."

"Us?" Beruth walked around behind her to stop at the lump that had tripped her up. To Isabella's horror, she realized that had been a person she'd tripped over. The demon lifted his head, and Isabella stared into Johnson's slack face. His eyes were open, but insensible. "I don't think this is the us you mean."

"That's it. We're it." Isabella pushed herself to her feet and stared down at the diminutive demon.

"Hardwicke knows we're here." Beruth dropped Johnson's head with a hollow thud and rounded on Wellington, her lips pulled back from her teeth, transforming her pretty face into a feral mask. She drove a finger hard against his chest, sending him back a step. "If he knows, then you can bet the Duke of London knows. I told you we should have left this place."

"And if he knows, then why did he send a girl and a servant to stop us?" He swept her finger away. "Think, for once."

"He expects us back shortly," Isabella said. "If we don't return, he'll know something is wrong here." If she could convince him to let them go, there was a chance she could find Briar and they could escape.

"Those who oppose us are already hard-pressed," Beruth said. She fixed her gaze back on Isabella, trying to pin her back with only the force of her stare. If she hadn't been on the receiving end of Briar's disapproval on more than one occasion, Isabella might have found herself intimidated. As it was, the attempt only added to her already prodigious anger. "If we add a little more, they won't miss these two for quite some time. Long enough for us to prevail."

Isabella stared calmly back, trying to keep all trace of her rage from her face. This Beruth might think herself an important personage, but Isabella wasn't her subject. There was only one woman she owed her fealty to, and she rather doubted the Queen was pleased with an incursion of demons into her realm.

"She has some backbone," Beruth said. She smiled, the corners of her eyes crinkling merrily. "I shall enjoy breaking her."

"You'll do nothing of the sort." Wellington moved to stand between them. "She may be aligned against us, but she is still my blood. Once you have your new day, I'm sure she'll see sense and join us."

That was exceedingly unlikely, but Isabella kept her mouth shut on the retort. She smiled blandly instead, neither agreeing with nor refuting Wellington's hope.

"And still she lies about who she's here with," Beruth said. "Did you think I would miss that, little human?"

Little human? Have you looked in a mirror? Beruth was four feet tall if she was an inch. Isabella wondered if she was wearing heels to reach even that slight height. "There's nothing to miss."

"Is that so?" Beruth took to the air suddenly, her nose no more than a few inches from Isabella's. Despite herself, Isabella couldn't help but flinch backward. She could see every eyelash on Beruth's face. When the woman's eyes shifted green from eyelid to eyelid, relieved only by the slit of a pupil, Isabella pulled back even further. Beruth grabbed her by the upper arms, holding her in place while the pale cream of her skin was overtaken by the same brick red of the imps. She smiled, her lips pulling much further back than a human could have managed, exposing teeth as sharp as needles. Scales erupted from the skin at her jaw, overlapping their way down her neck until they disappeared under her collar. "Do you really want to test me, little human?"

"Let go of me." Isabella brought her hands up on the insides of Beruth's arms, knocking her hands away. She scrambled to her feet to get away from the demon.

"Isabella," Wellington said, his voice sharp. "Stop fighting her. Tell us what we want to know."

"She won't talk to you." Beruth's voice was soft. It reached down inside Isabella and caressed her, drawing out a shudder of revulsion when Isabella realized what was going on. That spot was meant for Briar only. "You're her brother. She's not frightened of you." Her smile grew impossibly wider. "She's not really frightened of me. But she will be."

"We don't have time for your games, not if Hardwicke and the Duke are on to us."

Beruth hissed sharply, the tip of her pointed tongue protruding momentarily between her teeth. "I'll pull the truth of the other out of her."

"Fine then." He turned sharply away from her. "Waste your time on my sister and lose your chance to take down the Duke."

Sharp pain bloomed on Isabella's scalp when Beruth grabbed a handful of hair and dragged her head down to her level. The demon-woman rubbed her cheek along Isabella's, twisting her hand in Isabella's hair as she did so. Her skin was dry, like that of a snake, but the edges of her scales were sharp. They abraded Isabella's skin. Isabella couldn't help but cry out as her hair seemed moments away from being yanked out of her head.

"You'll sing your pain to me soon enough, girl." Beruth shook her hand free. "Take her away," she called over her shoulder.

A coterie of imps scuttled over to them. Small hands with palms as hard as beetle carapace grabbed her arms. Their claws pricked into her skin, scant hairs away from drawing blood. The warning was obvious. If she dared to struggle, her arms would drip with her blood.

"And him?" Wellington pointed at Johnson's limp form.

"He'll be more useful here. We'll be opening the gate soon. His blood contains more than a trace of demon essence. It will charge the inscription more quickly. Unless you'd rather use your sister? She won't be as potent, but there's a certain symmetry to it." At his reluctant head shake, Beruth shrugged. "I thought not."

Wellington strode toward Isabella. The imps parted before him like the pigeons in Trafalgar Square did before tourists. "I'll take her down." He grabbed her upper arm and hustled her away from the platform and circle. When she tried to get her arm back, he jerked it hard enough to rattle her teeth.

"Don't let her get away, and don't tarry," Beruth called after them. "We must move."

"We have time enough," Wellington said over his shoulder.

They passed the row of glowing batteries, the green light making her brother look sallow and painfully gaunt. The glass lenses in his goggles flashed the light back at her, making it impossible to see his eyes or to give her any idea of his feelings. Soon enough, they passed into a hallway with the ceiling so low it felt more like a tunnel. Isabella glanced back and caught the glimmer of a dozen eyes behind them.

"They're following us."

"Of course they are," her brother said. "She doesn't trust me, not even after all I've done."

"What have you done?"

He shook his head. His wordless answer spoke more of resignation than defiance, however.

"Why are you doing this? Whatever this is."

A grim smile split his face. "It was mostly to prove myself at first. The mechanicals were so limiting. You were already pushing them to their limits, which left no way for me to distinguish myself. When I thought of all we could do if we incorporated even more demoniac magic into our designs…"

His voice trailed off and his eyes turned inward. "But Father wouldn't go any further than what Jean-Pierre could offer. I saw the limitations of his pathetic talents soon enough. Truth be told, I think his fear is more of a limit than his poor grasp of the magic is." Wellington shrugged and Isabella jostled within his grip.

"Let me go. I'll behave."

"If you don't, I'll let them do what needs to be done." He jerked his head toward their not-so-distant escort. There was regret in his tone, regret at what they would do to her, she imagined, but not at having to do it.

"I'll be good," Isabella said.

"Very well." He dropped her arm and clasped his hands behind his back as he strode down the darkened corridor with its vaulted roof. His head almost touched the top. His hair, which had always been so carefully groomed, now stood up from his scalp at all angles. Some of the longer tufts bent where they brushed the ceiling.

"Was LaFarge your first teacher?"

"He was." A ghost of a smile touched Wellington's lips. "We had a good time for a while. He was so proud of his abilities as a teacher when I picked it up so easily." The smile dropped away as if it had never been. "He was less pleased when I struck out on my own. That's when he found me a more advanced teacher. You know what happened after that."

The last was practically spat at her. Of course Isabella knew about it. She'd been there when her parents found out from their solicitor that Wellington had forged their signatures to drain the family accounts of thousands of pounds. He'd practically put them in the poor house by spending more and more money on successively more expensive teachers. He hadn't confined himself to demoniac magic, either. Some of the areas into which he'd dabbled had verged on mysticism. Isabella thought their father might have been able to forgive him some of it, but when he'd been forced to pay off an alchemist for Wellington's lessons, that had been the last straw.

"You couldn't leave well enough alone, though." Isabella struggled to keep the accusation she felt from her voice. Angering him was a foolish proposition, and yet she wanted to box him about the ears. "You kept sneaking out, even after they'd paid off your debts. Mother hid that from Father, but she knew they had to get you away from London, to send you where your habit couldn't be supported any longer."

"Ah yes, Heidelberg. That was my opportunity."

"How did you do it? I got a letter from you only yesterday."

"I wrote up a number of them and sent them with a friend. He posted them to you regularly, and in exchange he got to keep the money sent back with them. I transferred my ticket to him. I never even left London."

Isabella clenched her teeth on what she wanted to say. What would he do if she called him a conniving blaggard? He was the reason she'd had to do such things to her friends. He was the reason for all of it. It had been easier to swallow when she'd thought he was out bettering himself and moving beyond the problems he'd accumulated in London. Instead, he'd sent their money to someone else and kept to his same destructive ways without any consideration for the depths to which they'd had to stoop as a result.

"I had to make do on my own, which was hard enough. You should have seen the flat I was reduced to renting on the money Mother sent me off with. Little more than a room under the eaves. There was only a tiny kitchen where I had to cook my own food, and I had to go outside to access the commode."

"So sorry to hear it." Isabella forced the platitude past her gritted teeth and hoped he mistook her grimace for a smile. She needn't have bothered. He didn't even glance toward her.

"Yes, yes. But my fortunes soon changed. I apprenticed myself to a magician who was more daring than Jean-Pierre and I was able to see a demon-conjuration for the first time."

Wellington frowned, furrows Isabella didn't remember carving themselves deep in his brow. "He didn't survive it, but Beruth thought I showed promise. She's been teaching me ever since. In that time, I've become wildly successful, marrying magic and industry in ways no one else has had the vision to do." He sighed.

"Yes, you seem thrilled beyond all measure, brother."

"It's true that not all is as well as it seems." He was unaffected by her sarcasm. The look he shot back over his shoulder spoke volumes. "But it is as it is. Beruth's new order will change many things." He lowered his voice. "But not as she thinks."

If his dark look was supposed to mean something to her, Isabella missed its significance. She stared at him blankly.

He stared at her, then shook his head. "All will become clear in time. Or not." The resignation was back.

They continued on in silence. The basement was labyrinthine, low corridors twisting and turning, then opening into rooms before continuing on. She'd been counting out each turn, but she wasn't completely certain she'd committed it all well enough to memory. His revelations had been distracting enough, and she hoped she could make her way back on her own. She'd seen bands of imps, but not many. The further they got from the ritual chamber, the fewer of them there were.

"Here we are," Wellington finally said. They stopped in front of a large metal door that would not have been out of place on a bank vault. It was quite out of place in the dingy tunnels, gleaming as it did, all brass and polish. He produced a key from one of his pockets and turned it slowly. Tumblers gave way before it with muted thunks. He grasped the large wheel and turned it ponderously forward. More tumblers clanked, these decidedly louder. The small hallway echoed with the sounds of metal upon metal. The door popped open, swinging toward them much more smoothly than its bulk suggested. "You'll be safe in here. The imps aren't permitted."

Isabella looked in, trying to see what awaited her. She loitered too long in the doorway. Wellington placed a hand in the middle of her rig and shoved her hard, propelling her into the room with such force that she was halfway across it before she realized what he'd done.

The door slammed behind her and the tumblers turned. She whirled on her heels and dashed to the door. The wheel on this side spun slowly. Isabella grabbed it and threw all her weight into resisting its closure, but it was no use. Inexorably, it spun closed, each tumbler falling into place, sealing her in. The lock engaged in a series of quieter clicks.

She cursed briefly, then considered her options. Wellington didn't know she was adept at picking locks, she recalled with some gratification. He hadn't been home when Althea had taught her that particular skill. Of course, he hadn't been as far away as she'd thought, either. Isabella growled deep in her throat, her rage at his selfish ways rising to the fore of her mind once again. The growl stopped when she took a closer look at her side of the brass door.

There was no keyhole.

CHAPTER THIRTY-NINE

The darkness seethed with imps. Some were being herded by one of the black-skinned euronym, towering over their recalcitrant charges, but most were on their own. The larger demons looked like bigger, dark-skinned versions of imps and existed mainly to keep their small cousins in line. Briar found the presence of euronym troubling. If she were to compare the host of the Children of Pain to a human army, then they were the sergeants of the pain demons. Imps were too flighty, too undisciplined to work together on their own. If they'd had that kind of wherewithal, they would have taken over the infernal realm eons ago. The euronym were much less plentiful, which was a relief.

Briar skirted a knot of imps being overseen by an euronym. She took care to avoid the demonic overseers. The last thing she needed was one of them to send her on an errand or worse to recruit her into its little band of imps that skittered to and fro before it. This one was enlarging its group by snatching imps out of the air as they flew past. The one in its grasp dared to protest, its wail like nails on glass. The euronym clearly thought so as well. With breath-taking casualness, it twisted off the imp's right leg at the knee.

The imp screeched louder, then bit off its yells when the euronym transferred its grip to the imp's arm. Its black skin stood out against the red of the imp's, looking more like malevolent shadows than flesh and blood, but Briar knew from too-close experience that the euronym were physical beings. The imp ceased its struggles and a pained grin crossed its sharp features. The euronym shook it once in warning, then let it go. A handful of the other imps had snatched up the leg and clustered around it, gnawing away, though the toes still twitched.

"Leave it!" the euronym boomed. "All parts are to be saved, upon orders of the Prince." This euronym was male, by its deep baritone. Unlike the imps, these demons were not sexless.

"Yes, boss," one imp squeaked. It let go with alacrity.

Two of the other imps dropped the leg, but a third held on long enough to try sneaking a couple more bites. It received a cuff to the back of the head that sent it airborne but which also had the desired effect of loosing its grasp on the wriggling leg. The euronym kicked the leg aside and directed the group onward. He showed no sign of having seen Briar, frozen in the deepest shadows a short way behind them.

The Prince? Her mind raced as she did her best to keep out of sight, while also scouring the area for the next corner she could duck into without the euronym noticing. *How did the inventor end up with a Prince of the infernal realm?* That in itself wasn't so surprising; they were occasionally summoned, though usually only by the exceedingly foolhardy or the very stupid. That the inventor had survived such a summoning was the amazing part. Princes weren't known for being understanding to those who tried to control them.

She'd never met the Prince of the pain demons, but she knew Beruth by reputation. The demons she knew looked down on imps in general and Beruth in particular. She wasn't known to be overly bright, but she commanded grudging respect for the mass of demons she had at her beck and call. No demons were as populous as the imps. Briar suspected their manner of reproduction gave them an edge in that regard. If Beruth was there, who knew what mischief she might be up to. The Prince was a loose cannon if ever there was one.

As soon as the euronym and his imps were out of sight, two imps swooped down and snatched the leg off the ground. They showed no sign of wanting to devour it. Instead they carried it between them as they flapped from the foyer. There was probably a propagation pit somewhere on the premises. Briar shuddered. She would stay as far from that as possible.

For the moment, she was alone at the junction of two hallways. There was nothing to indicate which way she should go. She'd given up trying to follow the glyph on the back of her hand. Every time she thought she was heading in Isabella's direction, she hit a wall and had to track around. All she was sure of was where she'd been.

Now she had three possibilities, none of which seemed more promising than the others. She was so turned around after making her way down the stairs and through the labyrinth of subterranean passageways to get this far. She couldn't have told someone where north was, even if they'd offered to pay her handsomely for it. The one thing she knew was that however much she wanted to rush, now was the time for deliberate action. She would approach this logically and methodically. There was no way she could miss something, not if it meant passing by Isabella.

She took the hallway that went off to her right. It ended in a small room. From the stench, the imps were keeping food in here. They had two preferred ways of eating their meat: still twitching or rotten to the point of putrescence. Opening the door quickly, Briar tried not to look too closely at the flesh decaying in heaps around the floor. She didn't want to recognize anything. From the state of decomposition, they'd been storing meat down here for a while.

What other horrors are down here? Briar wondered. This kind of scene was expected in imp enclaves in the infernal realm. She didn't expect to see it in the mortal realm. It seemed orders of magnitudes more disgusting here, where it was so unanticipated.

There were no other doors in the room. A drain in the middle of the floor had once allowed liquid to pass through but was now stopped up by bits of fat and gristle. Blood and worse floated in a thin pool above it. Briar was reasonably certain there was no trap door, not with the presence of the drain.

That left two more corridors. She made her way back to the junction and chose the next hall over. This one was more promising. Lacking the tortuous ways of the corridor from the stairs, this one went straight on, the brick walls interrupted now and again by doors, some ajar, some locked tight. She peeked through the open doors, finding little of note. One room was piled high with imps, sleeping draped across each other. Some of those would die soon, of that Briar had no doubt. The very air of this world was inimical to many demons, and those of the lower orders found it especially intolerable. The euronym would be able to withstand it to a bearable degree, but even they would be weakened by exposure. The imps would all die, sooner or later. The labored breathing of the dying was audible among the snores of those who simply slept.

The next door she came across was locked. Briar hesitated in front of it. Was it worth the time and aggravation to get beyond the door? What if Isabella had been captured and was being held somewhere? She could be behind this very door, and if Briar didn't try it, she'd never know. *You have to be methodical,* Briar told herself sternly. *Who knows what you'll miss if you dash blindly on?*

A small band of imps fluttered past her. One of them spared her a sideways glance. Imps rarely walked if they could fly. It slowed down and turned toward her, hovering in midair. Briar bared her teeth and flashed it the rudest hand gesture she knew. The imp sneered back at her, but turned and flapped its wings heavily to catch up with its companions. Briar heaved a small sigh. Imps fighting in the halls wouldn't be noted—she'd already passed more skirmishes than she could count—but it would slow her down.

She licked her finger and sketched a rune on the door, then drew a circle slowly from right to left, mimicking how the key would turn in the lock. Nothing happened, so she tried it the other way. The lock snicked open and Briar let herself gingerly into the room.

This room was different than the last. There were no imps in here, but neither was it empty. Slumbering figures lay on pallets piled high with fabric and fur. These had the brick-colored skin of imps but were much larger, though they were not as sizable as the euronym who were taller than even the rangiest humans. These were similar in height to humans, though no human ever had such wings. They could only be polygnots, the highest order of imps, below only the Prince's circle. This was much more troubling than the presence of the euronym. Polygnots rarely left the infernal plane. They specialized in the magic of pain and wielded it to the advantage of their Prince. Only rarely had Briar heard of a polygnot being summoned by a human magician. They weren't well-known enough to be summoned and were almost always brought over by accident.

These were here for a purpose. And there was no way she could take them on. There had to be four—no, five—of them bunked down in here. A couple of other pallets were made up, but empty. Polygnots were rare enough in the infernal realm. Hopefully no more had been brought through. At the very least, Briar could make it difficult for these demons to leave the room if they were summoned.

She drew the athame across her two fingers and started inscribing the wall to the left of the door. She would have to be careful and quick. As sensitive as polygnots were to magic, they would feel when the spell was kindled in their presence. That in itself wasn't too worrisome—

they would feel the workings of each other constantly—but her magic had a different flavor than theirs. If they remarked on that, they would know something was amiss, so she would have to inscribe the spells, then activate them, with little time to check for errors.

The wall was rough under her fingertips, the mortar between the bricks soaking up her blood. She worked quickly, constructing the spell, then moving over to the door. To fool workers of magic, she needed to be clever. Fortunately, it wasn't difficult to be smarter than even a higher-order pain demon. They were cunning, but hardly brilliant. The trick was to give them something to concentrate on and hide what she had done in plain sight.

She finished the second inscription, then pushed the door open the slightest bit. Once she keyed the spells, she would need to slip out as quickly as possible. Force of habit caused her to cast a quick eye over the spells, but she shook her head. It was time to trust in her abilities. She slit open the fingers of her right hand and reached up to key both inscriptions at once. A door, identical to the actual one, shimmered into existence on its right, and the original one disappeared. While upstairs, she'd observed the glyphs used to hide the inscriptions upon activation and had worked them into this spell. Fortunately, it seemed to be working as she'd hoped. The time for experimentation was not in the field, but sometimes it couldn't be avoided.

One of the polygnots turned over, muttering in its guttural voice. "What goes on?" it asked. Other stirrings joined it.

Briar didn't turn to see which one addressed her. All it would see was an imp doing magic far too advanced for its capabilities. The confusion would give her time, and she made use of it by slipping through the door even she could no longer see.

"What goes?" The voice thundered through the open door. It might not be visible, but it let sound through easily enough. Taking every pain she could to keep quiet, Briar pushed the door shut.

And now to vacate the area. When they figured out what had happened, the trapped polygnots would be quite perturbed. Fortunately, one imp looked much like all the others. She suspected that the closest imp would become the victim of their anger at being tricked, and she wasn't going to be within arm's reach when that happened.

Briar turned and collided with something in her path. A whoosh of air left her lungs in a loud gasp as she rebounded off it and went flying back. Thick legs the color of obsidian were all she could see. She looked up and up, then up some more, before finally locking eyes with an irritated-looking euronym.

"Why do you tarry here?" the euronym demanded in the language of the infernal realm, her nostrils flaring wide across her face. Horns curled tightly back from her forehead, and she lowered them in what Briar could only interpret as a threat. "The Prince requires us all."

"Uhhh…" Briar had no response prepared. She supposed Isabella would have said something clever to get herself off the hook she was now on, but dissembling wasn't her forte. She did remember to affect the characteristic servile whine of the imps to one more powerful. Fortunately for her, imps weren't smart. There was the chance the euronym would buy it.

The euronym leaned in, her nostrils still flared, but no longer in anger. She sniffed the air around the head of the imp she thought was Briar. Though she saw an imp, Briar occupied half again the space above it. From her perspective, the euronym was sniffing about her belly button.

This is not good! Briar's entire being shrieked at her to move. She scuttled back before quelling the urge. Then she was surrounded by imps, their little bodies bouncing off her as they streamed past. They were so thick in the air that some were forced to run along the ground. Seizing her opportunity, she scrambled to her feet and allowed herself to be swept away by the tide of small demons. The euronym was left behind, shaking her head, but not for long.

"Keep moving, grubs," she hollered. She reached back for a straggler and tossed it forward into the surging mass of demons, toward what she undoubtedly perceived as an open space. It wasn't one. Because of the size difference between Briar and her disguise, the space above her imp image looked empty when it was in fact still occupied by the upper half of her body. Briar ducked as the imp screeched past her ear.

It was a good thing imps weren't known for their social graces or the demons around her would have looked quite askance as Briar brushed away those who thought they could zoom through the opening left by the imperceptible top half of her body. She did her best to hunch over, trying to make herself a smaller target. At best, the imps bounced off the slope of her back; at worst, she had to swat them away. Imp dignity was an oxymoron, and Briar had never been so relieved that it was so. She was close to the center of the mass, which disguised her to some degree but was also making it impossible for her to leave.

The imps continued to jostle against Briar as they surged down the cramped hallway. She kept them at bay as best she could, then suddenly there was room all around her. The hall widened, but she could see no offshoots or doors to afford her the chance to slip away. The euronym was close again, urging the slower demons on with slaps, prods, even the occasional head butt from her impressive horns.

She peered ahead, trying to see through the shifting curtain of flying imps, which proved impossible. The only thing she could make out was a green glow that they were headed straight toward. The corridor met with something. Around her, the imps' shrieking rose to head-splitting levels. She couldn't risk putting her fingers in her ears, that could easily be remarked upon, but oh how she wanted to. If this went on much longer, Briar was certain her ears would start bleeding.

She was borne into the green room on the surge of imps. As the space opened up around them even more, she took her opportunity and scuttled to one side, pressing herself against the wall. The brick should have been cool against her skin, but the room was so warm that the bricks radiated heat as well. Her glance around told her everything she needed to know.

This was a ritual room, one set up for something monumental. She'd never seen one in person in the mortal world. Even in her mother's realm, she'd rarely seen one this size. Such workings weren't uncommon among her mother's people, but humans rarely cooperated in their magical workings and didn't require large spaces as a result. Such things were undertaken in secret. The room wasn't overly tall and most of the light was supplied by the wall of glowing machinery and the braziers around the large circle carved into the floor. Someone stood upon the raised dais. He was bent over to avoid hitting his head on the low ceiling. That couldn't be comfortable at all.

Even less comfortable was the poor soul who was laid out on the stone table at the center of the circle. He probably hadn't been there long. Blood seeped from a dozen shallow cuts on his arms, legs, and torso. It pooled in the channels in the side of the table, then ran out the groove at the end of the table, filling the grooved inscription of the ritual circle. Or, more accurately, circles. The blood had filled a third of the first inscription. When that one was full, it would pool over into the next inscription. Whatever they had planned would take multiple spells.

She squinted at the table. They wanted to keep the sacrifice alive as long as possible, or so she surmised from the inscription on the side. The poor sod was still breathing, his naked chest expanding slowly, but not by much. He turned his head as though looking directly at her, though she knew he wouldn't be able to recognize her.

The bottom dropped out of Briar's stomach. It was Johnson.

CHAPTER FORTY

No keyhole? There has to be a keyhole! Isabella ran her fingers over the door, searching for any indication that the keyhole was there somewhere. The face of the door was smooth and cold and with no hairline cracks that might be hiding the damn thing. *Who builds a door that locks only from one side?* Maybe part of the problem was that she couldn't see so well. It was so dark in the room that even with her goggles on, she could barely see.

Not far from the door was a switch. Isabella turned it. Light bloomed from three gas fixtures where the back wall met the ceiling. She turned the light up as far as it would go. Shadows still clung to the corners, but she could see well enough now. There was so much light it hurt her eyes, and she popped up the night vision lenses from her goggles for the time being. It would have been safer to remove them completely, but she didn't plan on staying too long in this room, so instead she left them attached at the hinges.

But extra light on the situation hadn't changed anything about the missing keyhole. No matter where Isabella looked or how much she prodded, she couldn't find anywhere to stick a damned key! She tugged experimentally on the large handle that operated the door. Nothing. She grasped it between both hands and threw all her weight behind it. Still nothing. She put every ounce of muscle into trying to get the wheel to move until she was practically doing a handstand on it, but to no avail. Her brow dripped sweat and she took a deep breath and held it for a moment to calm her breathing and heart rate. She would get out of there.

Maybe something else in the room would help. Isabella turned to take in what she could. It was a converted storage room, most likely. It wasn't huge, maybe fifteen feet on a side, and close enough to square as to make no difference. The lights above danced a bit in a draft, even underground. There was nothing like good English construction, her mother always said. Drafts were a constant thing, but no one had taken care to mitigate them down here. The crumbling brick walls would have looked quite silly covered with draperies, though the tapestries of a medieval castle wouldn't have been too out of place given what was happening outside the room.

Beyond that, it looked strikingly like Wellington's room had back home. He'd never been the tidy sort. Isabella was aware she was casting stones, but his level of disarray made hers seem quite neat by comparison. Clothing draped every available surface in the corner where he'd set up a cot. Without a valet to pick up after him, Wellington seemed content to leave things where they fell. A stack of books teetered on a crate he was apparently using as a bedside table.

Building materials were stacked in another corner, which was much neater than where Wellington was living. Isabella recognized the same impulse in herself, most likely a result of their father's constant chiding to keep their workspaces neat. It was true that it was easier to work in a clean space, and Isabella's workbench was always neater than her dressing table, especially at the beginning and end of a project. There was no actual workspace here, not that Isabella could see, but he clearly was using them for something. She cast a quick eye over the stack of tubing, glass, and rubber. That might come in handy.

Large sheets of steel and bronze took up the far wall. The bronze was new and still gleamed in the light with not a trace of green verdigris upon its surface, but the steel was another matter. Dust and cobwebs hung from it. Steel resisted rust much better than iron, but after a while even it succumbed. These had been stacked in the damp long enough to have acquired a patina of rust across much of their surfaces, at least those Isabella could see. So Wellington had need for brass, but not for steel.

What was that past the sheets of metal? Isabella moved forward for a better look. There was another vault door, identical to that which she'd entered through. And this one had a keyhole!

She hummed to herself as she pulled out her lock picks. Things were looking up. If she was lucky, this door would lead to another hall and she could make her way back to the room where Wellington and his demon prince were up to no good. The lock was unusual, a lever tumbler lock not of the type she usually saw in the London homes of her peers. A skeleton key allowed her to bypass most of those. Althea had insisted she practice on all types of locks, of course, but she hadn't had much opportunity to encounter these in the wild. She'd have to use picks in conjunction with the skeleton key.

The lock stymied her, forcing her to keep picking at it, working her way around the problem as she'd been taught. No matter what she tried, it refused to give. Isabella pulled out the picks and tapped down over her right eye one of the lenses she used to see in the dark. She peered into the lock, trying to divine its secrets. If only she'd thought of a lens that would allow her to see through solid objects. She'd have to ask Briar about such a thing after this was all over.

What was Briar up to now? Hopefully, she'd noticed when Isabella had rubbed out the rune on her chest, but what came next? She had no doubt that Briar was smart enough to find her way down here. Her hands shook a bit when she reached out for the lock again. The idea of Briar down here alone with all those imps and the repulsive imp-conglomeration monster was enough to drive all thoughts of moderation from her head. Their best bet was to be at each other's backs, but she couldn't do anything like that while trapped in here.

In addition to the levers she needed to bypass, the lock looked like it had more than one set of tumblers. That was going to be awkward. A third hand would certainly have been useful right then. She stashed the skeleton key and pulled out two curtain picks. She held one in her mouth while she felt around with a tension wrench and the other pick. One by one, she felt the levers lift as she probed at them delicately. She took her time, regardless of the pressure she felt within to rush the process. One thing that couldn't be rushed was lockpicking.

All the levers were taken care of on the first half of the lock. The pick had no more give to it, so she had to assume it was at the end of the lock, though she wouldn't know until she triumphed over the other half. Would the pick hold when she let it go? Isabella held her breath and removed her hand. The levers snapped back down.

"Damnation!" she whispered around the pick between her teeth and bent back to the task of lifting the levers and allowing the wrench to pass. The process wasn't so tortuous the second time around, and quickly she was back where she'd been. *Now what?* How on earth was she going to keep the pick in place while working on the other side of the lock?

She worked at the lock until sweat dripped down her face, the little beads unnecessary distractions, but she couldn't reach up to wipe them away. Her hands were slick enough already, but she couldn't wipe those either. Her jaw cramped as she held the pick steady with her mouth. Her eyes burned from the effort of trying to see into the lock, and she could barely see for blinking furiously to clear them. Her labored breathing left an expanding cloud of condensation on the cool metal surface of the door, but she was finally making some headway.

Isabella let out a long slow breath, still taking care not to jostle the wrench. She held her breath and started turning all three wrenches at once, moving her head at the same rate as her right hand. A fraction of an inch at a time, the wrenches turned, then the tumblers inside the heavy door let free in a series of muted clunks. Isabella didn't think she'd ever heard a sound so beautiful in all her days. This was the chirping of birds at the earliest dawn after a long night, the Messiah chorus on Christmas Eve. She relaxed, slumping where she knelt. Her back ached, her jaw was on fire, and she wondered if she'd ever be able to see properly again. Rubbing at her eyes only made the fire worse. She blinked rapidly, until at last she could see again, though the objects around her seemed fuzzy and diffuse.

Isabella seized the great wheel between her hands and turned. It opened easily, the door swinging silently toward her.

There was no corridor beyond the giant door, simply another room, this one tiny in comparison to the one she was in.

"Blast!" Isabella gave the door a swift kick and regretted it immediately. There was no give to the brass at all; the only thing that gave was the toe of her boot. She bit back a series of curses, then thought better of it. Her mother wasn't there to chastise her for using unladylike language. She cursed until it was a wonder the air didn't turn blue around her. She grabbed her foot and hopped up and down. Tears of frustration welled up in her eyes and overflowed down her cheeks.

Eventually the rage ran out and Isabella was left staring into the tiny little room. Someone, probably Wellington, had seen fit to cram a desk and a drafting table in there. An abundance of papers covered a small table to the right of the desk, with still more papers nailed to the wall behind it. Something about the design was familiar.

Isabella moved in for a closer look. She lit the oil lamp on the table, then turned up the flame as high as possible. It seemed that almost every piece of machinery Wellington had built for the Mirabilia horseless manufactory was represented along the walls. The huge voltaic pile was missing, however. She rustled through the papers piled on the table, but those didn't include finished schematics. Formulae covered those papers, along with the mysterious runes Briar manipulated so well. She found the schematics for the massive battery on the drafting table, along with the drawings for the series of smaller ones located in that terrible chamber.

He'd made changes in pencil over top the ink to both sets of schematics. He'd crossed numbers and runes out, then rewritten them, sometimes multiple times. One page of the schematics looked like his plans for hooking the two sets of batteries together. Those had seen the most attention. What was he up to?

Isabella hooked the stool out of the corner with one foot and scooted it under her, then leaned forward for a better look.

CHAPTER FORTY-ONE

The longer Isabella stared at the schematics, the more convinced she was that she'd been wrong. The thing on the manufacturing floor above her wasn't a battery, at least not exactly. If anything, it was a collection device, not a storage device. She glanced at the other set of schematics. Those were batteries, that was certain. They'd been hooked together to create a set of energy storage devices, though not for electricity. From the drawings, Isabella recognized them as the glowing green machines Wellington had in the large basement room where he and that demon had captured her.

So what was the other device? She could be forgiven for mistaking it for a battery, certainly. It had some similar characteristics, but what battery needed to be opened up? Was that how the energy was accessed? No, that was impossible. The energy would simply dissipate back into the air. Or would it?

She flipped a page and ran her finger over the notations there. She'd been right: the device was meant to generate energy. From the sketches, the big device collected it and the batteries in the basement captured the excess energy not necessary to keep the machine running. Even an energy-collection device required energy to run it. It was like an electro-magnet, the largest she'd ever seen, and instead of attracting metal, it attracted something else.

The next page held more drawings, these of smaller internal components. Isabella flipped quickly through these. The last two pages were new, the paper of different stock and Wellington had shifted from black ink to blue. An interesting choice. Isabella wondered if the change of ink color had bothered him as much as it would her.

The ink and paper weren't the only things different about the newer pages. The drawings and figures were interspersed with scribblings in what she could only assume were magical characters. He'd switched around the components and added a new set of switches along one side of the machine. Isabella stared at it. Why? The changes were unnecessary, as far as she could tell. If he wanted the device to collect energy, then why create a shunt that reversed the direction of the flow?

Her eyes widened when she understood.

"Oh!" Her heart thundered in her ears and she jumped up from the stool, sending it flying behind her. "He's changing the polarity!" Unable to help herself, she snagged a pencil from the cup on the table and added her own calculations to the margins. The collection matrix had been set up to acquire energy at a steady rate, but the polarity reverse had none of that sophistication. Had he been in a hurry, or had he not cared that when the energy was reversed it would come out in a massive wave? Isabella jotted down a few more calculations. The duration of the wave would depend on the amount of energy accumulated, but it would be violent and focused in one direction.

That couldn't be right, could it? She ran the numbers again, then flipped back a page, then forward again. If Wellington's measurements were to be believed, and Isabella saw no reason not to believe them, the wave would let loose toward the middle of the room. It would have made more sense to disperse it out in a number of directions to lessen its deleterious effects. Hell, it would have been simpler to do so, but Wellington had chosen to do the opposite.

A muffled thud shook the room. Isabella looked up as mortar cracked and sifted down onto her. What was going on? Again she heard it, but this time it didn't stop. Rather, the thud continued, turning into a moan two hairs shy of a roar. The room shook steadily around her. She watched as a container of pencils and pens vibrated its way off the table and fell to the floor with a clatter that was barely audible over the din.

"What the—" Isabella braced her hands on the drafting table. Dust filled the room like smoke. There was no fire, at least none that she could smell.

Briar. Her head jerked up at the thought. *Did she do this?* Regardless, she was out there, and Isabella had no idea what she was doing. Knowing Briar, she was in the center of whatever was going on.

Enough of this. Keyhole or no, I need to get out of here. There was more than one way to get out of a room.

* * *

Johnson's blood continued to drip steadily from the table to the inscription waiting on the floor. Briar watched, mesmerized, as each drop filled the first inscription further. His blood traced an intricate pattern, its redness shocking and stark against the dingy grey floor. A few areas were empty, but those were small and filling up rapidly. The imps jostled into each other and her as more packed their way in to the area. She could see a Behemoth, thankfully far enough away that the multitude of arms grasping blindly from its bulk had no chance of reaching her. The imps in that area gave the thing a wide berth. She shuddered at the idea of being pulled into its mass. If there was one Behemoth, there were likely others, a side effect of packed propagation pits.

The voices of the gathered imps swelled with anticipation. They didn't know what was happening any more than she did, of that Briar was certain. But imps being imps, they thrilled to any possibility of chaos and pain.

She pulled the small stack of spells she'd prepared and shuffled through them. Whatever happened, she would be prepared.

An unexpected elbow to her leg made her look down. One of her neighbors had noticed the papers and snatched at them. "Give!"

"Get off," Briar snarled. She shoved it away hard. It went careening into the imps next to it, pushing them over. They were packed in so tightly that they in turn took out their neighbors. Like dominoes placed on end then pushed over, they fell, each taking one or more imps down with them. The havoc spread, and imps took to the air to avoid the disturbance.

On the platform, the human looked up and glared at the turbulent mass of imps. He shouted behind him, but Briar couldn't hear his words over the shrill voices raised in protest. Another figure joined the human. Even from a distance, she was obviously female and other than human. This must be Beruth, Prince of Pain. She didn't look all that impressive.

"Silence!" The order thundered from every corner of the hall. The brawling imps froze where they were; those on the wing hovered tensely in place before drifting slowly downward to settle back into the throng of imps. "You will remain where you are until the working is complete!"

A collective sigh of acquiescence rose from the throng. Briar looked out across the crowd, noting the imp faces raised as one toward the Prince, like sunflowers following the celestial orb across the sky. She would have stood out among them, like a mountain among hills, had it not been for her disguise. A chill settled into her bones when Briar realized the only non-imps in the room aside from her were the Prince and her inventor. The euronym had disappeared. If there had been any polygnots in the mix, they were gone as well. All that remained were imps.

Imps were expendable.

And at that moment, so was she. She swiveled back, in time to see the first circle start to glow as the last drops needed to fill it dripped from the platform.

She slit her thumb and pressed it to the paper, keying the final rune. A circle of protection sprang into life with her as the epicenter, sweeping imps before it as it expanded.

In almost the same moment, a much stronger bubble burst into existence around the dais and those standing there. A mere breath later, the first circle burst into green flames so high they licked the ceiling, bending this way and that, but unable to burn any higher only because of the stones in their way.

Snaps filled the room, silencing the shrieks of the imps. For a moment all Briar could hear was the roar of the fire that scorched the ceiling. Then more snaps split the silence. Long cracks filled with green fire formed on the ceiling, right at the edge of the flames and radiating outward, reaching toward the far wall. Briar shifted back, using her circle as a ram to move imps out of her way when she realized there were cracks opening over her head. More cracks were opening on the floor, visible only because of the space that had cleared around her. She moved swiftly, but carefully to avoid stepping on any of them. She was back almost to the wall before the fissures stopped moving in her direction. Above her head, a lattice of virulent green flame covered the ceiling. Chartreuse light spilled up from between the imps, rendering them into featureless shadows that flickered and shifted before the brightness.

With a roar, the glowing crevices opened up. Chunks of stone and masonry rained from the ceiling while the floor gave way. The imps rose into the air like a murmuration of starlings at sunset. Some were immediately borne down by chunks of rock into the chasm that suddenly yawned below them. Debris continued to rain down for long moments. Those imps under the safety of the overhang moved back and ducked as those in danger flew toward them. Briar threw herself to the floor, flattening herself against the cold cobbles as imps flooded the space above her. Those who ran across the floor in her direction found themselves shunted to each side by her circle. Unlike the protection around the dais, hers was only a circle, not a bubble. She had no protection from those who did not touch the ground.

Imps from the crush, caught on both sides by their fellows but unable to move forward because of her circle, found themselves flattened to death from behind. Soon, the front of her circle was bounded by the piled corpses of imps.

Daylight filtered down through the dust and imps in the air. Briar squinted and looked up before realizing the spell had taken out not only the ceiling of the basement room, but also the factory ceiling high above. The cloud of imps wheeled and danced, but not as one. Collision after collision took place, and before long imps rained from the sky, some as limp bodies, others locked together in desperate tangles of fighting demons.

Briar stood up slowly. The imps in flight had abandoned their attempt to fly deeper into the factory. Instead, they clawed it out above them, regardless of how the sunlight burned their skin. She turned her attention back to the raised platform. The human now stood straight without worry of hitting his head. There was no sign of debris in that area, but the ceiling above their heads was also gone. The circles were similarly unaffected. Johnson stared straight up at the sunlight that filtered through but stopped just short of him. The air seemed darker around the dais and the circle, a shadow that couldn't be dispelled by the sun's rays alone.

The inventor pointed toward her and Briar realized how visible she was. Beruth shook her head and grabbed the inventor, turning him around and pushing him toward the glowing green bottles that lined the back wall.

"Who are you?" The question boomed throughout the room. Briar knew it was meant for her. "Why are you here?"

Briar ignored Beruth's questions. She keyed another spell into life, then balled up the paper and threw it at the platform. The paper caught fire in a flash of brilliant crimson that grew into a huge fireball that arced toward the dais.

Imps shrieked and scattered, doing as much damage among themselves as would have occurred had they simply held still and surrendered to immolation. The fireball broke apart against the bubble of protection, drenching it in crimson flames for a moment before they were wiped out by answering green fire.

"It matters not," Beruth proclaimed. "Do it," she said, turning to gesture at the inventor.

He threw a switch on the wall and the tall piece of machinery above their heads whirred to life. Gears groaned and caught, sending up a racket as the top of the cylinder opened up. The liquid in the sides rushed to the bottom as the stacked pile rose, higher and higher until the exposed core stood proudly above the cylinder.

The inventor threw another switch and the groaning and crashing of gears stopped, only to be replaced by a deep hum that Briar felt in her bones as much as heard. A beam of brilliant white-blue light split the gloom, vaporizing any dust in its way as it reached into the heavens. It speared ever upward in a split-second and the hum became a throbbing roar.

The inventor threw one last switch. The stack started to spin, casting spears of white light against the walls and remaining ceiling as it opened up.

Briar felt a tug toward the stack, then a yank. She leaned over and dug her fingers into the cracks between the stones of the floor, holding herself in place in defiance of the inexorable pressure that dragged at her. Around her, imps were being pulled toward the cylinder of brass and light. They seemed powerless to resist the force. Briar stared at the pile through slitted eyes that were stabbed nonetheless by the brightening light. First one imp hit the pile and disappeared in an explosion of brilliance, then another, then half-a-dozen. Before long, so many imps disappeared into the machine that she could no longer observe it, even with her eyes next to closed. Tears streamed down her face and she turned away.

Beruth had left her place on the dais and had made her way across the circles to Johnson. She wielded a knife of obsidian that looked like a shard of shadow given form in her hands. It took no more than two swift strokes to open Johnson's veins. The blood that had been trickling into the circles became a stream. The second circle was much larger, but it was rapidly filling in.

Briar couldn't wait any longer, but if she let go, she risked being borne over to the stack with the imps. The only place that seemed immune to its effects was the area around the platform and the inside of the circle.

Briar let go with one hand. The pressure was there, but she didn't feel as if she were about to take flight. If she could stay down and keep as many imps as possible between her and the machine, maybe there was still hope for her. As much as it galled her to do, crawling was the only option left to her.

And so, on her belly, Briar made her way closer to the Prince of Pain.

CHAPTER FORTY-TWO

Isabella sized up the wall. Would it have killed Wellington to have left her a pickaxe or a shovel? At the very least a rock hammer would have been helpful. There was nothing you couldn't do with the right tools. When those weren't at hand, you had to improvise.

As it was, the crumbling mortar and bricks gave her some hope. All she had to do was pick the weakest point, though somewhere close to the ground would be best. The wall's thinnest part was high up where it met the ceiling. She made a note of it but kept looking. If nothing else panned out, that would have to do. She brushed at the loose mortar between two bricks close to the floor. A large chunk fell out.

"Oh ho," she said. "This looks promising." She dug harder and more mortar fell away. The brick wiggled like a tooth not quite loose enough to fall out, but Isabella knew, like any child of five, that nature could often be trumped by determined wiggling. Eventually, the remaining mortar gave up its grip and Isabella popped the brick out. One above it seemed as loose, and she was able to pry it free as well. She bent down to look through the hole. To her disappointment, all she saw was more brick. It had been too much to hope that the wall was only one layer thick. Well, all she needed was one more brick, and she'd have a hole large for her purposes.

Of course the final brick did all it could to resist her. The other two had been so easy. Isabella wondered if the masons who had built the wall had mixed up a different batch of mortar just to frustrate her. She took a break from the wall and ran her hand across her forehead while listening closely. The room still vibrated.

Her eye fell on the pile of building materials in the corner. A lever! Of course, with a long enough lever she'd be able to move pretty much anything.

She sorted quickly through the pile. The rubber tubing would come in handy, but not for getting that last brick out. Isabella took the length anyway, wrapping it in a coil around her forearm before shouldering it while she visually inventoried the materials. Sadly, her quest for a nice long lever seemed to be coming to naught. Rubber tube safely out of the way, Isabella leaned forward and dug through the pile, paying little attention to the bits of sharp metal that caught on her gloves and sleeve, tearing small rents in the fabric. Briar was out there while whatever it was went on. There was no time to waste.

Finally, at the bottom of the pile, Isabella found something useful. It was neither a hammer nor a lever, but she thought the drill might do the trick. Sure, its bit was worn down to next to nothing, probably why it had been discarded into the pile of odds and ends, but she didn't need it to last very long.

Isabella drilled into the mortar. Her forearms quickly ached from the strain of turning the tool, but the worn bit slowly ate into the stubborn substance. She ignored the pain in her arms and kept drilling, determined to get the last brick out of there. She threw her weight behind it, forcing the bit deeper into the mortar, and winding for all she was worth. It was almost there. She'd drilled four holes into the mortar of two sides and it was starting to crumble.

The bit snapped. Isabella stumbled into the wall, trying to save herself from bashing her face into the bricks by throwing up her hands. She was partially successful but still managed to scrape her nose and cheek against the rough masonry. Her helmet saved her from a blow to the forehead, but even so her ears rang for a moment from the impact.

She rubbed her cheek and stared at the brick. The end of the bit was barely visible in the hole she'd drilled.

Will nothing go right? Isabella's breathing picked up. She tried to slow it down, to force it out past the lump in her throat that threatened to cut off all air. She had to get out of there; crying wouldn't help anything. Hot tears collected in her goggles.

Isabella raised the drill over her head. She stared at the wall. Even though it wobbled in front of her, courtesy of her tears, she knew it was as solid as ever.

"Give it up!" she screamed and brought the drill down on the offending block. Nothing happened. The brick simply sat there, smug in its cocoon of mortar. "I. Will. Not. Be. Defied!" Isabella punctuated each word with another smash of the drill, pulling her hands back over her right shoulder and letting fly with everything she had in her. She battered at the wall until she could no longer see through the tears of rage that clouded her eyes, until her shoulders ached from the violence of her attack, until the knuckles on her gloves wore through and blood collected in her palms.

With heavy breaths, Isabella blinked to clear the last of the tears from her eyes. Somewhere during her tirade, the brick had snapped in half. Her airway was suddenly clear. She could breathe again. Would it be enough room? Isabella cleared as much detritus away from the opening as she could. It very well might be. She allowed herself some very cautious optimism. It wouldn't do to get too excited, only to have her hopes dashed again.

She shrugged the jump rig off her shoulders. One tank would probably do the trick, but she needed to shut them both off, or they'd both lose pressure. The small valve surrendered easily enough to her ministrations, then she unscrewed the left tank. They were both completely full, exactly as she needed. The remaining tank looked strange in the rig, but it might yet come in handy. She re-attached it to the tubing from the suit, then pulled it back over her shoulders. The weight was off, pulling on one side but not the other. She shrugged her shoulders in a vain attempt to settle it.

The rig tank barely fit in the hole she'd made. She forced it in and hoped that nothing in the wall pierced the metal sides in the process. The scrape of brick on metal put her teeth on edge, but she wedged it in as far as it would go. Now all she needed was a remote ignition source. She unwrapped the tubing from her forearm and carefully stretched one end over the nozzle that usually connected to the tubing in her suit. Hopefully the tubing would be long enough. She didn't really want to be in the room when she set off the tank. Isabella unrolled it carefully. It easily had enough length to make it to the little room with Wellington's drawings.

It was time to give it a go. Even with her in the next room, this could go catastrophically wrong and kill her a few times over. She didn't think it would, but if she'd miscalculated on any of it, she would be a bloody smear on the brick and Briar would be quite on her own. Of course, Briar was on her own already, so at least she wouldn't be any further behind, but if Isabella could lend her any advantage, she had to try.

Isabella opened the valve on the tank and ran to the little office. She closed the heavy vault door as far as she could, but kept it open a crack to allow the tubing to come through. There was no avoiding that. Hopefully she'd be safe.

She pulled a lighter out of one of her myriad pouches and struck it. She held it in front of the hose, waiting for the gas inside the tank to get to her. It wouldn't take long, pressurized as it was.

Seconds later a small whoosh was the only warning she had. The explosion that shook the room was easily as bad as any she'd been through in the workshop. The oil lamp toppled off Wellington's drafting table and shattered on the floor. Broken glass and flaming oil spread everywhere.

"Bollocks!" Isabella hissed. Now was not the time for a fire! Leastways, not in here. One leg of the drafting table, then another caught fire. The flames traveled straight up the varnished wood to the top. She lunged forward to save the drawings, but was too late. Greedy licks of flame devoured them and she had to retreat from the suddenly intense heat before it could blister her hands.

Coughing from the smoke that already filled the small room, Isabella pushed open the door and slammed it behind her. The fire would burn itself out in there; aside from the desk, table, and drawings, there was nothing else to fuel it.

She turned around and beheld chaos. She'd been hoping for a hole big enough to crawl through. What she had was one big enough for her and three of her friends to walk through with room left over. The wall had simply disintegrated where she'd planted the tank. Without the wall to support it on one side, the vault door listed out toward the hall. Wellington's bed and scattered clothes were aflame as well. At least with the explosion it was impossible to tell that the room had been a mess to begin with.

Smoke tickled her throat and burned her eyes, sending Isabella into another paroxysm of coughing. There was no point in sticking around. Hopefully the fire on Wellington's bed would be contained there.

She stumbled from the room into the empty hall. The smoke was being drawn quickly down the corridor. Isabella hunched down and ran in the same direction.

Briar, I'm coming!

* * *

Briar had made it almost to the edge of the largest circle before the Prince caught sight of her. She would rather have been closer and set before being noticed.

"Let go," Beruth shouted from inside the circle. "We need all of you, my children!"

At least the demon Prince thought she was no more than a stubborn imp. Some of those still clung to various surfaces, shrieking their terror and betrayal for all to hear. Between the noise of the imps, the deep hum of the device, and the hissing crackles emanating from the wall of green bottles at the back of the room, the racket made it next to impossible to think. The large bottles no longer glowed, but rather shone with a brilliance Briar thought might be visible all the way to Halifax.

The Prince was even worse to her "children" than Briar's mother was. Briar was reasonably certain that Carnélie wouldn't sacrifice all the lower order lust demons at her disposal into some great machine. Some of them certainly, if she could gain some advantage from it, but not all.

She forced herself forward against the pull of the machine. Her hand slipped and came back covered with blood, but not her own. She'd finally reached the edge of the circle. She tried to grab hold but struggled for purchase on the blood-slick stones. If only she didn't have those hard-soled boots on. They were quite fetching, but they allowed her to feel next to nothing with her feet. She scrabbled with her toes, lifting and searching for a crack to brace against. Yes! Her toe caught on something. She pushed back against it experimentally, and it went nowhere. Briar pushed harder against it, propelling herself into the circle.

Immediately, the force pulling against her top half fell away, though now her legs felt like they might be yanked off. She dragged her legs the rest of the way into the circle and stood up. There was blood on her skirts when she looked down. She was reaching down to brush them off when she realized she could see her skirts.

"Who in the seven hells are you?" Beruth asked from across the circle. "What are you doing here?" Her voice was less aggressive than curious.

Briar looked down at her hands. They were pearlescent grey under the blood that covered her fingers. She didn't doubt that her eyes glowed red also. She'd not only lost her disguise, but her shroud. She tried to pull the spells she'd written up out of her pocket, but all she came away with was a handful of ash.

"I am Briar, daughter of Carnélie, Fourth Minister of the Council of Lust." She bowed to Beruth. "My mother wishes to know if you require assistance."

"Is that so?" Beruth raised one eyebrow. "Now why do I find that so hard to believe?"

Briar shrugged, trying to look unconcerned. If only Isabella were here. She had no doubt her lover could have charmed the Prince into believing anything Isabella wanted. Briar's strengths didn't run this way. Her mind raced. How could she sell this to Beruth?

"Probably because I snuck in here pretending to be one of your imps, and now I'm covered in blood." When all invention failed, she might as well try honesty.

"Oh really?" Beruth stepped closer. "That's very true. It also occurs to me that you're wearing a lot of clothing for an Under-Minister of Lust."

"It's cold in England." Briar knew the response was weak. She turned to keep Beruth in front of her. "And I needed to blend in to the population. Something you might try, if you want to take over here."

"Is that so? Why should I care? Soon enough the populace will bow to me, and I will reign supreme." From up on the dais, the inventor coughed. "With Thomas Holcroft at my side, of course." Beruth rolled her eyes. Briar wondered how long Holcroft would survive Beruth's coup.

"It's time for the next phase," Holcroft said.

"Then do it," Beruth said irritably. "You don't need me to hold your hand, do you?"

The inventor said nothing but grasped the long lever on the side of the dais. With a grunt of effort, he threw it forward. Sparks flew from the contact point on the far side and he stepped back with alacrity.

The tower stopped spinning and the light from the top dimmed. The clear glass sides still shone too brightly to look at, as did the devices at the back of the room.

"The humans won't submit to one of our kind. Those who have been here a while know enough to work through proxies." Briar took a step toward Beruth. Showers of green sparks arced out of two conduits that snaked their way across the floor toward the circle. Briar took care not to step in the blood. Just as liquid conducted electricity, so too did blood conduct infernal energy. That much energy would hold quite the jolt, and she didn't know if she'd be able to keep her senses about her if she stepped in it.

"Humans." Beruth spat to one side. The glob of spittle sizzled where it hit the ground. "They are small and weak. Only those of demonic extraction can see our magic, and those who would call on the aethereals can't even do so without half a day of chanting and ceremony."

The demon Prince was one to talk about small creatures. Briar wondered if she was even four feet tall. She seemed to have more in common with her imps than she did with either her euronym or the polygnots.

"They have their advantages." Briar allowed a wicked smile to take over her features. It felt alien to be using it on this demon and not on Isabella. The smile made Isabella's insides quake with excitement every time. She hoped Beruth would feel the same.

"Trust one of your kind to make it about sex."

The infernal energy from the conduit poured into the circle just as the key-rune filled with blood. Green fire surrounded them, then licked its way around a larger circle Briar hadn't noticed before.

"And why should we not?" Briar took another step. Barely three paces separated them. She smiled at Beruth, licking her lips in provocation. She'd never tried to seduce anyone before, to use her sexual self as a weapon. It wasn't so hard. Part of her thrilled at the way Beruth's nostrils flared in response to her. "They have quite the capacity for pain, though they're much more breakable than your imps. On the other hand, their capacity for pleasure from pain could be quite an asset to your court."

Beruth laughed, exposing sharp teeth. "I know all about that." She cast a look over her shoulder at Holcroft. He was close enough to hear their entire exchange. From the ruddiness of his face, he was less than amused about the direction their discussion had taken.

"Then an alliance is certainly advantageous to us. We can provide you with what we know of this world, having existed among its people for millennia, and you allow us to feed unfettered. Imagine what we could do…together." Briar dredged up every last memory of lust, every passion she'd ever felt. She could feel its power hot in her belly, waiting to be unleashed.

"Your kind have never had anything but contempt for my children. Now that we're about to capture some real power, you're ready to curry favor. How appallingly typical. I think we'll keep the spoils to ourselves, but I think I'll keep you for me." She reached for Briar.

"My Prince," Holcroft called. "The polygnots are here."

Beruth pulled back her hand and looked about. Briar wanted to swear. The words were unformed on her lips before she snatched them back. So much for her plan to trap the demonic sorcerers in that room. Seven polygnots stood around them, one at each brazier. Behind each polygnot, with one hand on each shoulder, were a pair of euronym.

"Excellent. Start the chant, my children. Soon the rest of our brethren will join us."

Briar looked back at the new circle. It was a portal. How could she have been so blind as to miss that? Maybe it was because she'd never seen one so large before. The amount of infernal energy that would be needed to open one of that magnitude was more than her mind could comprehend. Beruth's enormous sacrifice of her imps made sense now.

The polygnots raised their voices in a rhythmic chant.

Briar reached out and placed her hand on Beruth's cheek.

"I'd like nothing better than to be yours," she murmured.

CHAPTER FORTY-THREE

The scene was one out of a nightmare. Isabella lurked inside the basement hallway, looking out into the room that she barely recognized. If it hadn't been for the platform and the row of batteries, she would have wondered if they'd been transported to another place. The ceiling was gone. That explained the shock she'd felt on her way here, the one that had thrown her to the ground of the tunnel and had added another ding to the collection on her helmet. One of her lenses had cracked, but it hadn't been one of those that allowed her to see in the dark, so for the moment she didn't worry about it.

There were no imps. Well, almost none. A few flapped around in the shadows, but they kept well away from the machines. The collection device on the manufactory floor shed enough light that it would have looked like high noon in there, except the shadows were all wrong. Between that and the loops and whorls of green fire that covered the stone floor, it was amazing there were any shadows left at all. The imps clung stubbornly to them. Isabella couldn't blame them. She didn't want to attract any undue attention either.

The larger demons she'd only caught glimpses of during her last visit stood around an expansive circle. Those in the center had their voices raised in a droning chant. The tall ones behind them had their attention on the pair standing among the flames, not far from where the stone table dripped blood onto the floor. It could only be Johnson on there. She didn't look closely to confirm it. He'd done his best for her; he certainly hadn't deserved this.

Briar was one half of the pair the demons watched so avidly. The realization sent a shock through the pit of Isabella's stomach. What was she doing with her hand on the cheek of that demon? And in her true form, at that. Briar never let anyone see her without her shroud. She also didn't allow people to see her if she was anything less than put together. Blood covered her skirts, a sleeve had been ripped away from her dress, and her hair had come half out of the bun she'd snugged it back into. Try as she might, Isabella couldn't look away from the tender gesture Briar offered to the demon Prince.

"Beruth," Wellington called from the platform. His voice treaded a fine line between respect and irritation. Isabella had been on the receiving end of the tone many times as a child. He'd been her best friend as long as none of his friends had been about, then he treated her like the annoying little sister she was supposed to be. "The next phase?"

The Prince shook her head as if trying to clear it. Briar had been clouding her thoughts, that must be it. Isabella's heart lifted a little closer to where it was supposed to reside in her chest. Briar hadn't gone over to the Prince's side; she was doing what she could to slow things down.

"Later you will be," Beruth said. She pushed Briar gently to one side and turned toward the dais. "Are we ready?"

"The dials were reading optimal power flow." Wellington looked down, then back up. "And they still do. Shall we proceed while conditions are right?"

Neither of them noticed Briar, but Isabella did. Briar sketched something in her own blood down her right arm. Her form shivered once, then seemed to shrink. Her hair raveled itself back into its usual flawless arrangement, only now it matched Beruth's style. She was shrinking also. It was impossible to see while Isabella was watching, but when she blinked, Briar's size diminished quite visibly. Her skin shaded from grey to red while the blood disappeared from her dress and it returned to pristine condition, though a completely different color.

She strode forward, taking steps much too long for her now-tiny frame.

"Cease!" Briar-as-Beruth bellowed.

The chanting faltered as the demons looked up and beheld two Princes.

"Do not!" Beruth tried to shove Briar out of the way, but she would not be moved.

"Remove this impostor!" Briar-as-Beruth ordered in imperious tones. Her voice wasn't a perfect match for the demon Prince, but it was far from her usual sweet tones.

This was Isabella's chance. She had to get to the collection device. The doors in the manufactory floor were long gone, along with most of the floor itself. There might be stairs down to the rooms and hallways of the basement, but there was no time to go looking for them. She still had one tank left on her rig. Surely that would provide enough lift to get herself up one story. There was only one way to find out.

Isabella slipped from the hall into the room. No one had eyes for her: they all watched the two demon Princes struggling with each other. She kept to the wall, making her way around in what shadows she could find. The unfinished canvas of her suit would stick out against the brick walls if anyone cared to glance her way. Isabella's skin prickled as she passed within ten feet of a trio of large demons.

A loud "oof" followed by a scream of rage stole her attention back to the circle. One of the Beruths had the upper hand, but only for a moment. She managed only a moment astride the other Prince before she was flipped back. Isabella had no idea which was which, not now. If she couldn't tell, she doubted the others could either.

The Beruth who had been pinned looked up at those watching. "The sacrifice!" she screamed. "Do it now!"

The shorter demons who had been chanting shifted in place, but the pairs of tall, ebony-skinned demons behind each of them tightened their grips. In perfect unison one of each pair grabbed the head of a chanting demon while its partner produced a knife blacker even than its skin. The knives reflected none of the light in this place. They existed as shards of darkness, shards the demons drew in terrible concert across the exposed throats of their now-struggling prisoners.

"My children," Beruth said. "Do not struggle. Your sacrifice leads to our glorious day!" She grunted when Briar kicked her solidly in the back. Briar danced back, away from the Prince of Imps who turned on her with murder in her eyes, murder even Isabella could see.

It was too late. The last of the demons bled out onto the floor.

Isabella quickened her pace. Ahead was an overhang where the floor above still seemed fairly stable. The ground jumped beneath her feet. Isabella broke into a run. The trembling increased, making it hard to keep her footing, but she prevailed, though with each step the floor threatened to turn her ankle beneath her.

Finally, she was within reach. As the tremble became a roar, then a deep-throated scream from a thousand voices, Isabella launched herself into the air. Her jump rig coughed once then caught, sending her into an arc that was barely high enough and definitely canted to one side. She careened toward the edge of the factory floor. She wasn't quite going to clear it.

Isabella crossed her arms in front of her face to shield it from the impact. She drew in her shoulders and barrel-rolled in the air. With a bone-rattling thud, she hit the edge of the floor and kept going, rolling up and over to fetch up against the base of Wellington's collector.

* * *

That had been Isabella flying up to the ground floor, of that Briar was almost certain. Her heart leapt. She was fairly certain she was the only one who'd seen the canvas-colored blur launch itself to the main floor of the factory. Whatever Isabella was up to, Briar needed to keep Beruth's attention on her for as long as Isabella needed. All she had to do was keep her feet long enough to come up with a plan. Posing as Beruth wasn't going to work any longer. She allowed the hastily constructed illusion to drop. Exposing herself to Beruth's essence enough to construct a convincing disguise had set her stomach to roiling and the relief that rolled through her upon dropping it was reward in itself.

The floor of the large circle disintegrated, stones flying outward to reveal nothingness beneath them. The screams of the infernal realm greeted her, some by name, though she tried to close her ears to their horrific voices. The green flames ringing the circle pulled in toward the center of it as though some being was taking a titanic breath. They flickered for a moment, shaking in time with the trembling that still rattled them around. Then they bowed the other way, the breath released in one long exhalation that brought along with it the sounds of wings.

Imps exploded from the dead space by the dozen, then by the hundreds. They streamed up as one, blocking out the sun completely. From one moment to the next, the light in the space went from that of day to night, so thick in the air were the demons. Groups of imps labored through with large cradles, each holding one or more euronym or polygnot. The cradles were quickly dropped by the side and their occupants debarked, turning their heads to look this way and that.

Beruth smiled at her. "You tarried too long, girl."

"We'll see about that." Her words were brave, but Briar quailed inside. Beruth with a hundred demons was powerful enough. With the thousands that had spilled through the portal already and who continued to spill through, she was well-nigh invincible.

The Prince stepped toward her, and Briar stepped back. The further she could stay from her, the better. Beruth didn't seem the type to excuse the hair-pulling or the indecorous way they'd rolled around on the floor. She was stopped by something cold and unmoving. The altar, it must be. Briar put her hands back to check. They came away bloody. She moved quickly to put the table between them.

"Miss Riley," Johnson whispered.

"Mister Johnson." Briar didn't look down. She reached out toward the knives that held him in place.

"I wouldn't move him," Beruth said, her voice matter-of-fact. She might as well have been discussing the price of eggs. "The only thing keeping him alive is that inscription."

"Do it," he said.

Briar had never seen such pallor on a living human. His dark skin, usually the color of fine mahogany, was ashen. He looked three days dead, but he blinked and talked and still the blood dripped from him. She dipped her fingers in his blood and sketched a rune of healing upon his chest. It flared crimson and some color bloomed in his cheeks. She sketched two more runes and keyed them. Johnson sighed as his agony receded. She pulled the knives from his wrists in two quick jerks, then those from his ankles. She had to glance away from Beruth to do so, and when she looked back up the demon Prince grinned at her from the other side of the table.

"Stay here," Briar murmured to Johnson. "Whatever you do, don't move." Until he regained some strength, if he left the table he would likely die from loss of blood between one breath and the next.

"You can't win, little one," Beruth said. "I will enjoy making you into my beloved pet."

Briar threw one of the knives at her hateful grin, but Beruth batted it out of the air. She sketched an inscription on the side of the altar while Beruth stalked around it toward her. The Prince was almost in arm's reach when a bubble of protection rose into place over Johnson and the stone table. Briar skittered backward, away from the Prince whose eyes glittered at the promise of the hunt.

Cut off from its supply of Johnson's blood, the flames of the first circle guttered, then died.

"That won't do anything, stupid girl." Beruth snorted her amusement. "That circle has served its purpose. The portal has the power it needs. Nothing can shut it down now."

Briar sketched the rune for fire into her palm using Johnson's blood. Intense heat radiated from her skin, so hot it was almost painful. She directed her hand at Beruth, who dodged out of the way of the cone of flame. Instead, a dozen of the imps who still spewed forth from the gate to the infernal plane were wiped out. They were reduced to ashes in seconds, their final remains swept along with their compatriots as they swirled into the sky.

Whatever you're up to, Isabella, you need to finish it soon! If this went on too much longer, the situation would be well beyond salvaging.

CHAPTER FORTY-FOUR

Isabella stared at the side of the collector, trying to remember what she'd seen on Wellington's plans. The thunder of imp wings and their attendant cacophony of shrieks made concentration a titanic effort. Add to that the way the Prince had been stalking Briar across the floor when Isabella had last peeked into the ruined basement, and Isabella's mind raced in multiple circles at once. She bit down on the inside of her lip hard enough to taste blood. The pain gave her something else to concentrate on, if only for a moment. Her disordered thoughts calmed and she stared at the wires in front of her.

This was where the batteries hooked up to the collector. He'd added hookups to reverse the connection. Isabella grasped one of the connectors and twisted. With a clunk that shuddered up her arms, it came away in her hand. The end glowed with blue-white light, energy arcing between the connector and its housing on the side of the collector. It resisted being moved too far away. Isabella gritted her teeth and hauled at it until the energy quit arcing. There was another socket around the side of the machine, and Isabella dragged the conduit toward it. Unlike the connectors from the collector to the batteries, this socket was on the side facing the basement. Why Wellington hadn't tried to make it a little more discreet, Isabella had no idea. Likely, it was something with the internal structure of the machine, but she wished he'd thought of that beforehand.

When she got close to the socket, the conduit in her hand stopped fighting her. It snapped into place almost without her doing anything, and she twisted it in to make sure it was well-housed. Knowing she was going to have to fight the conduits only halfway was a relief. As it was, sweat already dripped down the small of her back.

One down, twelve to go. Isabella got right back into it. She couldn't worry about being spotted now. There were thousands of potential eyes; it would happen sooner or later. The only thing to do about it was to move quickly. Now that she had her task in front of her, she was able to pick up her momentum. She dared not risk a glance at whatever was transpiring below. Briar's dire straits would only throw her off her pace. Methodically, and as quickly as she could manage, Isabella worked her way through almost all the connectors.

Her arms and back ached from wrestling them into place. The ninth connector had snapped into place when Isabella's concentration was rudely broken by her own name.

"Isabella," her brother called again. "What are you doing?"

What does he think I'm doing? Isabella ignored Wellington and unhitched the tenth connector. She threw her aching back into getting it away from its housing. Each one had resisted her more than the last, just as each one snapped into place more eagerly than the one before it. Her grunt of effort verged on a scream before she was able to drag it away. She took two steps sideways, then was being pulled toward the mess of connectors she'd already moved. Isabella snatched her hands away and let the connector crash into place. If her fingers had been in the way, she would have lost them.

"Isabella!" Wellington's scream was raw. She looked over at him in shock. He'd never used that tone with her before. Of course, she had also never foiled his plans for world domination before. His head appeared over the broken edge leading down to the basement. The reflection of green flames were caught in the glass of his goggles, then were gone as he faced her.

She stared at him as he pulled himself all the way up and stood.

He shook his head. "I can't let you do this. Stand back, or I'll be forced to…"

What did he think he was going to do? Even as kids, she'd been able to best him. They hadn't fought often, but when they had, she'd always beaten him physically. He held part of himself at a remove and was never willing to commit to their fights. She was only meaner now and she had better weapons.

She pulled out the next conduit. It was harder than the previous one had been. Dividing her attention between her brother and the device wasn't making this any easier.

"Go away, Wellington." She heaved the conduit away from its housing and dragged it over.

"Isabella." He grabbed her shoulder, squeezing hard enough to hurt.

She let go of the conduit and it shot home. When she turned around to face him she ducked, and his hand whistled past her face. The attack shocked her enough that she couldn't get out of the way of his backswing. The back of his hand caught her on the cheek, spinning her around and to the floor.

She landed on her hip and something hard dug into her flesh. *Mother's pistol.* "Never touch me again," Isabella said, drawing the revolver from her pocket.

"What did you expect? That you'd waltz in here and destroy years of work and I'd simply stand by and allow it? You've never known your place, dear sister. If you want any place at all, you'll put down the silly gun. If not…"

"You'll kill me?" She held the gun on him, her hand steady as bedrock. This wasn't going to go the way he expected. It never did, but only because Wellington's major failing had always been considering where others fit into his plans. Other people weren't extensions of him, and he was constantly surprised when they acted in their own interest instead of his.

"If I have to." He reached toward the gun.

Isabella hesitated only a moment before she squeezed the trigger. He was still her brother, even if he was part of an evil plan for the domination of London. But he couldn't stop her, and if she didn't stop him, what would happen to the others she loved? To Briar, to her parents, to Millie?

The slug tore through his outstretched hand, jerking it off to one side. Wellington stared at her, eyes wide and accusing.

"You shot me!" He couldn't believe she'd done it.

"I'll do it again if you don't get out of the way." Isabella stood up slowly, never taking her eyes from him.

"You can't do this. You don't know what she'll do to me if I don't stop you."

"And you know what I'll do if you try."

Wellington licked his lips, then dashed around her. He wrapped his good hand around the nearest conduit and heaved back on it. It shifted out of its housing before snapping back when he couldn't keep his grip on it. He tried again, this time hooking the elbow of his injured arm around the tubing.

Isabella lined up her next shot, waiting until the conduit returned again to its housing and he stopped in his tracks. She pulled the trigger, the shot to his shoulder spinning him around.

"The next one kills you," she said. "Don't make me do that."

He didn't answer but staggered away from her and the device. He collapsed to his knees at the edge of hole in the floor. Isabella went back for the next to last conduit as he howled in pain. She stuck the revolver through her belt and bent to the task at hand. The faster she got the polarity reversed on his collection device, the faster everyone would be safe. Then she and Briar could sneak out in the chaos. Maybe Briar's earl and the Duke of London could clean up the mess. It was going to take a lot of effort.

With the conduit safely in its new housing she spared a glance for her brother. He still knelt, but now he scribbled feverishly on the stone floor. Every now and again, he spared her a venomous glance. That couldn't be good.

"That's enough," Isabella said. "Whatever you're doing, you need to stop it now."

He laughed hoarsely. "Make me."

It was a common refrain from their childhood, and Isabella took a deep breath. She strode over to him, crouched among scrawlings in his own blood. She'd seen Briar do enough of these to know what she was looking for. The closer she got, the faster he scribbled. There it was, the little bump on the edge of the inscription that Briar always added last. There was no sign of glowing or colored fire through her lens, so she still had time.

With one decisive kick, she smeared the blood he'd used to draw out the runes. At the same time, she caught his hand and he jerked it back against his chest.

"You little—" Wellington surged up from the ground, slamming into her and sending her tumbling.

Her head impacted with enough force to stun her, even through the helmet. Everything around her went grey and Isabella struggled to keep the edges of her vision from collapsing on her. She forced herself to breathe steadily and not to give in to the heaving gasps of panic. *You've had the breath knocked out of you before. This is no different.* When her vision cleared, her eyes met Wellington's. They were screwed up in hopeless rage.

"Good, you're awake. I want you to know what's happening to you." He grabbed the lapel of her coat with one hand, twisting it around to get a good grip and hauled back on her. She slid across the stone floor. He heaved again, dragging her ever closer to the edge of the floor. "Do you know what happens when someone tries to go the wrong way through a portal?"

That didn't sound good. Isabella dug her heels in, looking for the gap between paving stones to use as an anchor.

Wellington laughed, the sound wild and pitched much too high for sanity. "Neither do I. You like to experiment. Let's find out!" He yanked on her again, but she went nowhere.

"You don't have to do this." Isabella strained against his hand, forcing him to shift his body around for better leverage. He stood between her and the terrible column of imps rising ever upward. Bits of blue sky were still visible around the corners of the shattered roof. It seemed impossible that it should be such a nice day out, not with everything that was going on. A large shape drifted through one of blue spaces. Isabella blinked at it while the muscles of her legs started to tremble. That looked like a zeppelin. It seemed the cavalry was arriving, but how much success could they have against this horde?

"I don't have to." Wellington grinned at her. "I want to."

It was past time to end this. Isabella stopped resisting his pull. She pushed off, using his own strength to go flying at him. He screamed and staggered back when her stiff arm hit the wound in his shoulder.

The scream hit a new pitch when his foot slipped over the edge into nothingness. He windmilled one arm to try to keep his balance, the other clutched across his chest, but to no avail. Wellington pitched backward. His scream cut off when he hit the ground some twelve feet below.

Isabella ran back to the device, scrambling to free the last conduit from its mooring. The flow of imps was showing no signs of abating. How many had come through the gate while she'd fought with her brother? She spared a glance at the floor. Briar had her back to the column of imps rising ever up. Beruth had backed her to the edge of the solid floor. If Briar took another step back, she would have nothing beneath her feet. The imps would claw her to shreds in a heartbeat. There was no sign of Wellington.

The final conduit came off with relative ease. Isabella suspected her agitation over what was going on below her was giving strength beyond her usual capacity. She stepped lightly and aimed the conduit at its new housing, then let go. It slithered out of her hands like a striking snake and met its housing with a click that was audible even in the din. Only then did Isabella dare step in. She turned the conduit in its housing. The side of the collector flared to life. It lit up, then went out, sitting there like a lump.

Isabella did the only thing she could think of. She reached out for the large switch on the side of the device and threw it.

* * *

Briar kept an eye on Beruth as she contemplated her next move. The demon Prince was enjoying toying with her, something that didn't alarm Briar too much as it gave her time to think. If Beruth thought she could intimidate Briar, she had another thought coming. Briar would never have survived her childhood had she intimidated easily.

The solid wall of imps rising ever higher at her back was a little disconcerting, as was the open portal behind her. Portals only went one way, so Briar couldn't see into the infernal realm. She could smell it, though. The scent of brimstone filled the air; its acridity bit into her nostrils, borne upon the wings of the hundreds of imps who rushed past her in every moment. Her eyes were starting to burn.

Beruth lunged at her, claws extended. Briar shifted to one side. There was no telling what might happen if she ended up falling back into the gate. Everything she'd heard about those who tried to enter a portal from the wrong side suggested the results were messy, excruciatingly so.

The device on the ground floor of the factory hummed back to life. Beruth stopped mid-lunge, a feat made impressive by the fact that she had only one foot on the ground, and looked back.

"Holcroft!" she bellowed. "What is going on?" There was no answer. "Holcroft!" Still no answer. A human form lay crumpled on the floor. Unless Briar missed her guess, the inventor wouldn't be answering her for a while.

Beruth turned, stalking Briar no longer of interest in the face of this new issue.

The top of the column opened and the core ascended once again. Infernal runes burned their way over the sides of the column, the glyphs coming to life one by one in a wave. At the top of the device, the core rotated, but not with the spin it had before. It rotated until it sat at an angle to the rest of the column, then started to turn, its white light growing in brilliance. The wave of magic crested across the device and it shimmered, like heat over London rooftops in deepest summer.

There was no nearly irresistible pull as there had been before. Instead, demons were being pushed away in all directions, with the core at the center. The demons emerging through the portal had the worst of it as they were shoved back against the matte black rift between worlds. A mounting chorus of shrieks reached Briar's ears as the pain demons emerged only to be wiped out almost immediately.

The black pillar of demon bodies dissipated in next to no time as their bodies were flung outward. Sunlight poured into the gutted factory, its rays blocked only by the dirigibles floating above them. Billows of smoke bloomed from the sides of the zeppelins, but the din of dying demons was such that Briar couldn't hear the firing of the cannons. Bright lights of all colors flashed above her head as the earl's magicians deployed their sorcery upon their imp foes. They made quick work of the demons coming their way. It wasn't as quick as what the collector was doing with the imps coming through the portal, but it was close.

On the floor, Beruth screamed at the senseless inventor, directing him to fix the problem. When he didn't move, she seized him by the scruff of the neck and shook him. If not for her desperate rage, it would have been amusing to see the tiny woman buffeting the much taller man. Her abuse did nothing to bring him out of his insensible state.

The euronym and polygnots still flew through the air into the portal, some as soon as they exited the other, but Beruth was showing no sign of feeling its effects, nor was Holcroft, though it was doubtful he felt much of anything. Apparently they were protected from the effects of the collector as well as she was. Briar watched as she dragged Holcroft with her to the dais where she pulled and pushed the various levers to no avail, then turned her attentions back to the portal.

Only the blood sacrifice of the polygnots kept the portal open. Briar knelt, ignoring the damage to her skirts. The dress was so far beyond saving that she would burn it if they made it out of this debacle in one piece. She drew the athame from the pocket of her skirts and sliced the tips of her fingers open. With any luck, this would be the last time. Her fingertips were going to be covered in a myriad of scars, even with her advanced powers of healing. She thought she knew what to do, but this was something she'd never attempted. She'd be making it up as she went along.

The glyph for water was a logical place to start. What else did she need for rain? Clouds. She sketched that one in as well, then quickly added the rune for the mortal plane. She didn't wish to conjure clouds from the infernal realm. What came from those clouds would melt the humans where they stood and leave the demons quite unharmed and probably rejuvenated.

As she continued to draw out the inscription, Briar moved more quickly. She thought less and relied more on instinct. She needed a deluge, so the water glyph appeared multiple times. Wind would be helpful, to buffet the imps out of the way and get the water more quickly to where she needed it to be.

She looked up when she was almost done, certain an hour had passed, and was surprised to realize that next to no time had gone by. Beruth was still screaming at the inventor. Across from them, Briar thought she saw Isabella's form above the batteries. Those had lost more than half their brilliance. The portal wouldn't stay open much longer.

Briar keyed the final rune and raised her head to the heavens. Even through the battling imps and zeppelins, she could see the clouds forming. They were dark, almost black and they billowed with implacable menace. Even with the light from the shining core on the device, the interior of the manufactory darkened perceptibly. A drop hit her face and splashed, huge and heavy. Briar closed her eyes against the shock of it. It was cold. Another raindrop splashed on her forehead, then one on her cheek. In the next moment, she was drenched by a wall of water. She opened her eyes and squinted around her. Puddles of water already stood on the floor, and the flames around the circle had waned considerably. The wind came up, whipping her hair about even in its soaked state. The imps were thrown into disarray, shrieking and crying out among the raindrops that thundered into the ground and into them.

Green fire guttered and went out. The imps dispersed, and no more came through after them.

"Yes!" Both arms raised above her head, Briar shouted her triumph to the skies. It was undignified, but she could think of no more appropriate a response. "Oh dear." The push of the device was in full force now. She flattened herself to the ground and tried to dig her fingers in to the cracks between the stones as she had before. The pavers were slick with water and her hands slid along them, finding next to no purchase.

"No!" Beruth's cry from the dais was animal-like, full of rage and disappointment. She grabbed Holcroft for support and hooked her claws into his waistcoat. The weight of his body kept her from going into the portal, but they were pushed off the dais. Still locked together with Holcroft, she rolled ever closer to the rift. Briar had successfully wiped out the circle of protection shielding the dais and the inscription circle, but the portal resisted the rain as it continued to be fed from the infernal batteries. Those had dimmed from their peak power, but they were by no means completely drained.

Beruth wrapped her legs around the inventor's torso, using him as an anchor. She dipped her fingers into a wound in his shoulder. She leaned over and drew a series of runes over those that still glowed green.

The portal shimmered, its edges coming undone. The shimmer increased, then the yawning blackness blinked out. In its place were dark skies split with yellow lightning. Clouds lined with silver and grey boiled in the distance, and below them rivers of fire split a landscape that itself seemed to breathe, contracting and expanding with destructive forces.

"Home." Briar whispered the word. She'd heard of a phenomenon called "home-sickness." When she'd first heard the term, she thought it must have meant when one was sick of one's home. She'd been shocked to find out that in humans the term meant a longing for home so strong it was almost physical. As she gazed upon her mother's world, she realized the mortal realm was her home now; she had no desire to go back.

"Briar!" Isabella called her name from above. A wave of acknowledgment was a bad idea. Briar could no more force an acknowledgment out past her gritted teeth than she could wave to let her know she'd heard. She scrabbled at the stones beneath her, slowing her progress toward the portal, but only incrementally. She was losing the battle, and she knew it.

Were those tears mixed in with the rain? That seemed likely. Briar knew what awaited her if she went home, and that was if she survived the tumble from the skies. Beruth looked to have opened her portal quite a way off the ground. She would be at the mercy of the imps and the others.

She grabbed the corner of a stone that stuck up higher than the others around it. The push still shoved against her, but she was no longer moving. Alone in the rain and the dark, Briar sobbed. She would not go back. She could not go back. She screwed her eyes closed and held on for everything she was worth. When would the batteries run down?

Something hit the ground next to her and rolled into her. She lost her grip and was sliding toward the portal again when arms wrapped around her and held her down. "I've got you," Isabella yelled in her ear. She tightened her grip, gathering Briar to her as securely as she could with one arm. They still moved but more slowly now.

Briar sobbed again, relief driving it from her in an undignified hiccup. Isabella drove something metal and pointed into the space between two stones and held on with all her might. They stopped. Briar drew a deep shuddering breath and opened her eyes.

Beruth looked up to where her children were being wiped out with the brutal efficiency only humans could manage. She directed a final look over at them and smiled slightly, then raised and lifted one shoulder. "Oh, well," her shrug seemed to say. She winked once and pursed her lips in a kissing motion. Beruth grabbed Holcroft under the arms and stood up, then they were airborne, flying backward into the portal.

"Wellington," Isabella whispered. She made no move to let go of Briar to to his aid, but the heartbreak in her voice was unmistakable. If she'd been able to touch Isabella's skin, Briar had no doubt she'd feel anguish.

They disappeared into the portal, the last to be pushed in. The batteries flared, then went completely dark. Isabella held her and cried, her shoulders heaving in wracking sobs while Briar held on and did her best to rub Isabella's back in soothing motions.

The most drawn-out minutes of Briar's life ticked away while they lay wrapped together. She'd been through similar moments of eternity on more than one occasion in the past, but these were by far the longest. The rain slowed and the wind ceased its howling before the portal winked out.

"Hold on to this," Isabella said. She guided Briar's hands to the metal spike in the ground. The portal was no longer active, but the collector continued to spin.

"Come back for me," Briar said. She hadn't meant to, but the words felt right.

"Of course." Isabella wiped tears from her face.

She wasn't gone long before the collection device's unearthly hum abated and the pushing ceased trying to drive Briar into the ground. She sat up and looked around cautiously. If a typhoon could form in an enclosed space, it would have done less damage. She was surprised the walls still stood. The dark clouds were dissipating above the factory and sun was filtering back through, though some rain continued to fall. The sun's light cast a spray of colors through the falling water.

"A rainbow," Briar said to Isabella as she picked her way over the rubble back to her.

"So it is." Isabella followed Briar's pointing finger and goggled for a moment at the cheerful arc. If anything had ever seemed more out of place, Briar couldn't remember it.

"I'm sorry about your brother."

"So am I." Isabella sat heavily next to her. Briar gathered Isabella into her arms and pressed a kiss to the side of her forehead. "It was his own fault, but still." The anguish was there, along with a healthy helping of guilt and worry. Was Isabella worried about telling her parents? Briar would certainly have been, if she'd had Isabella's parents and a brother of her own.

"Yes. Still." Wellington Castel's fate was not one Briar would have wished upon anybody. Far better for him if he died on his way through the portal. If he lived, his torment would be long and incredibly painful. *Should I tell Isabella her brother might still be alive?*

"Ho, down there!" A voice, much amplified, but still tinny, reached their ears.

Briar and Isabella looked up. A dirigible with the Earl of Hardwicke's crest upon it floated in the space where the factory ceiling used to be. Briar waved one hand over her head, Isabella took up the wave also.

"We're sending someone down. Is it safe?"

Is it safe? Briar looked around. There was no sign of demons. If the factory walls hadn't come down by now, they weren't going anywhere. She nodded, trusting they were being observed from above through a spyglass. There was no point in shouting. To do so would be useless and undignified. They'd defeated an incursion from the infernal realm, but that was no excuse for letting her standards slip.

A rope ladder unfurled toward them, tumbling through the air and coming to a stop.

Isabella turned Briar's head toward her with a finger on her chin. Her lips covered Briar's, hot and hungry, seeking solace and giving it. Briar closed her eyes and gave herself over to Isabella. Decorum be damned. They'd have time enough to be above reproach later.

Bella Books, Inc.

Women. Books. Even Better Together.

P.O. Box 10543
Tallahassee, FL 32302

Phone: 800-729-4992
www.bellabooks.com